GALAXY'S EDGE
CREATED BY MIKE RESNICK

Lezli Robyn, Editor
Lauren Rudin, Assistant Editor
Alicia Cay, Copyeditor
Shahid Mahmud, Publisher

Published by Arc Manor/Phoenix Pick
P.O. Box 10339
Rockville, MD 20849-0339

All material is either copyright © 2023 by Arc Manor LLC, Rockville, MD, or copyright © by the respective authors as indicated within the magazine. All rights reserved.

This magazine (or any portion of it) may not be copied or reproduced, in whole or in part, by any means, electronic, mechanical or otherwise, without written permission from the publisher, except by a reviewer who may quote brief passages in a review.

ISBN: 978-1-64973-137-1

FOREIGN LANGUAGE RIGHTS:
Please refer all inquiries pertaining to foreign language rights to Shahid Mahmud, Arc Manor, P.O. Box 10339, Rockville, MD 20849-0339. Tel: 1-240-645-2214. Fax 1-310-388-8440. Email admin@ArcManor.com.

ISSUE 62: May 2023

CONTENTS

EDITOR'S NOTE by Lezli Robyn	3
MOON AND SKY, FEATHER AND STONE by Rebecca E. Treasure	4
THAT SUNDAY ON THE TRAIL WITH THE MEREST BREATH OF SEA by Beth Cato	16
THE LAND OF PERMUTATIONS by Tatsiana Zamirovskaya, translated by Julia Meitov Hersey	24
THE INCONSISTENT HEART by Kary English	33
THE WEREWOLF by Jonathan Lenore Kastin	39
FRUITING BODIES by Xauri'EL Zwaan	40
XI BOX by T. R. Napper	46
KRISTIN, WITH CAPRICE by Alan Smale	58
THE DREADNOUGHT *AGAMEMNON*, ON COURSE TO CONQUER THE PEACEFUL MOON OF RE by Dafydd McKimm	59
PABLOVISION by Deborah L. Davitt	60
A FEAST OF MEMORIES by R.D. Harris	68
FIVE STAGES, OUT OF ORDER, OF WHEN THE STARS WENT OUT by Samantha Murray	70
PLANNED OBSOLESCENCE by Auston Habershaw	72
PROBABLY THE MOST AMAZING KISS EVER by Robert P. Switzer	80
MERCY by Stephen Lawson	86
THE BRIDE OF FRANKENSTEIN by Mike Resnick	88
THE BLEEDING MOON by Monte Lin	94
SLOW BLOW CIRCUIT by Lisa Short	99
SIX WAYS TO GET PAST THE SHADOW SHOGUN'S GOONS, AND ONE THING TO DO WHEN YOU GET THERE by Stewart C Baker	103
CARRION by Storm Humbert	107
THE WOMAN OF THE LAKE by Marissa Tian	112
YANG FENG PRESENTS: THE BLACK ZONE: MURDER IN THE LOCKED ROOM- by Fu Qiang, translation by Roy Gilham	122
GALAXY'S EDGE INTERVIEWS DANIEL ABRAHAM by Lezli Robyn	132
RECOMMENDED BOOKS by Richard Chwedyk	140
TURNING POINTS *(column)* by Alan Smale	146
LONGHAND *(column)* by L. Pendelope	149

A MEMBERSHIP BASED EBOOK ACQUISITION PROGRAM

GET ALL THE EBOOKS YOU LOVE AT A FRACTION OF THE COST

www.BookBale.com

EDITOR'S NOTE

by Lezli Robyn

We've reached the last publication of *Galaxy's Edge* in magazine format, and I have to share that it feels quite bittersweet. After ten years in print, 62 issues on our readers shelves, and a contract spreadsheet that boasts an incredible 692 drabble, flash fiction, short story, novelette, and novella entries, our bi-monthly magazine has published the breadth of science fiction and fantasy (with a generous pinch of horror!) by many of the newest and biggest names in the field.

As a gift for our readers, our last issue features double the fiction, with an impressive 22 stories—not unlike the number of stories an anthology would have! Since we're converting this magazine into a semi-annual anthology series, I feel that co-incidence is both an auspicious end *and* beginning!

While Jean Marie Ward usually does our interviews, for this last issue I had the pleasure of sitting down with Daniel Abraham in Santa Fe, New Mexico, and interviewing him about his solo writing career and how it diverges and intersects with his collaborative works as one half of James S A Corey, the author of *The Expanse* series. Our conversation evolved into the most interesting anatomy of a career, and I've no doubt that readers will be as drawn in as I was by how unique (and yet incredibly relatable) Daniel's path to publication and success has been.

Richard Chwedyk lowers the curtain on his Recommended Books column with his usual keen insight and conversational flare, and Alan Smale and L. Penelope return with one last entry to their own columns. The rest of the magazine is overflowing with fiction (including one by the aforementioned Alan Smale!), with stories covering the gamut of science fiction, fantasy, horror, and humor.

This issue opens with the empowering "Moon and Sky, Feather and Stone" novelette by Rebecca E. Treasure, about a young woman who wishes she could literally fly away from the oppressions in her life and join the Sky Maidens. Does she have what it takes to prove her worth—to the Sky Matrons *and* herself? In Marissa Tian's "The Woman at the Lake," Kang is put through the most profound trial of his life when he stops to help a woman trapped by vines. This breathtakingly haunting tale shines an eerie light on historic inequality of the sexes, and the promises that bind us.

Equally evocative is Deborah L. Davitt's "Pablovision," about the magical consequences one man's artistic vision has on the inhabitants of Santa Pau, Spain, and another's desire to reverse it. Auston Habershaw's "Planned Obsolescence" will also delight readers with its completely alien cast of characters. What is an assassin to do when his client refuses to pay for services rendered on a new frontier world where the native species are gigantic arachnids?

If a dash of humor with your dark fantasy is more your cup of (possibly poisoned) tea, then go no further than "Carrion" by Storm Humbert. To avoid spoilers, I can't say too much, but let's just say this story is a testament to perseverance. If you are wanting a splash of romance with your science fiction, you'll be thoroughly enchanted by Stewart C Baker's "Six Ways to Get Past the Shadow Shogun's Goons, and One Thing to Do When You Get There," which depicts the delightfully flirtatious conversation between two warriors *while* they're being repeatedly attacked by the Shogun's many goons.

While I would love to talk about the rest of the stories, this editorial can only be so long.

I can't help but feel that saying farewell to the magazine is to finally say goodbye to Mike Resnick, my mentor, my good friend. In a way, taking over editing *Galaxy's Edge* from him had kept a big part of him alive for me. (Apparently, the magazine is finding it equally difficult to part ways, because when I was finalizing this typeset it inexplicably glitched and deleted hours worth of work, clearly wanting us to spend more time together.)

Although I'm sad to see the magazine end, it's only happening because we're converting *Galaxy's Edge* into an anthology series that will enable us to reach even more readers in brick-and-mortar bookstores. I'm happy and excited to see where this change takes us, and while I invite you all on this new journey with us, I also want to acknowledge the two most important people to have worked on this magazine: Shahid Mahmud and Mike Resnick.

Without Shahid to fund and support this crazy venture, and Mike's passion for helping new writers, this wonderful, decade-long market for authors would have never existed.

And, because of them both, I know the Galaxy's Edge anthology series and The Mike Resnick Memorial Award will continue the legacy of "paying it forward" to the next generation of writers and readers.

Editor, signing off.

Rebecca E. Treasure grew up reading in the Rockies and has lived in many places, including Japan & Germany. Rebecca's short fiction has been published by or is forthcoming from Flame Tree, Zooscape Magazine, Galaxy's Edge, and others. Fueled by cheese-covered starch and corgi fur, Rebecca is an editor at Apex Magazine and a writing mentor.

MOON AND SKY, FEATHER AND STONE

by Rebecca E. Treasure

Lora never fit where she was. When the moon bells rang and everyone's eyes turned glassy, hers stayed dull and hollow. When Mother made blackberry tea, Lora snuck warm goat milk from the bucket. When Father sang the morning song and Ella cried with faith and passion, the music jangled in Lora's ears.

The closest she'd ever been to belonging was right here, mud squishing between her toes and her little brother's hand in hers as they prepared to jump.

Lora looked down into Oran's eyes. "Ready?"

He shared her grin, nodding. They scrambled up the steep granite over the swimming hole, a miniature mountain. Their breathing deepened, drawing in delicate perfume from lilacs surrounding the clearing. Three steps—Lora shortened hers so they leapt together—and they flew.

Lora knew where she'd fit, but it was in a place she'd never been, with people who were not hers.

Wind whistled in Lora's ears, pushing her cheeks up to a smile. She imagined rising, soaring above the valley floor to battle the sun and protect her people. Cool water cushioned her landing, swallowing Oran's giggles and her whoop of joy. They sloshed to the shore, mud coating the hem of her white shift, Oran's best pants and tunic dripping.

Lora wiped pond water from her face, the gritty swirl on her tongue. "We'd better get back. We're in enough trouble." She rinsed the worst of the muck from her feet.

Oran's face fell. "I'm in trouble. You're an adult now."

Lora grimaced, leading him through the woods toward the Temple of the Moon. "Worth it, though?"

He sparkled with pond water as they stepped into sunlight. "Yes. I'm going to miss you."

A chill ran up her spine, icy in her mind. No one was supposed to know. Even she couldn't be sure. "I'm not going far. Just another house in the village."

Oran threw her a skeptical look. "You'll join the Renaming?"

Lora shrugged, glancing at the sky, hoping for a flash of red wings. She would fit among the Sky People, who lived in the mountains and soared among the clouds. She longed to take flight, to leap from a snowy peak. Instead, she lived in the shadow of the mountains, always on the ground. *Would* she join the ceremony if they didn't come?

Oran sniffed. "You don't want to be here." He pulled on her arm, wide brown eyes staring into hers. "Take me with you? I'm smart and fast. I'll be good. Nobody else'll take me swimming."

Lora pulled him into a hug. "I can't do that. Besides, I'll probably get picked by the tanner and you won't want to be anywhere near me." She snorted in his ear. "Ewwwwwww."

He giggle-sniffed. Lora squeezed him once more, then stood, thoughts darting about like lightning in a storm. The closer they got to the temple, the more Lora slowed, her heart undecided as to whether it would race or thump. The villagers had gathered in their best clothes, white outfits standing out like snow drifts in a meadow of wildflowers. Lora's heart decided that thumping was the way. Oran squeezed her sweaty hand.

They joined the crowd outside the half-dome temple, familiar faces nodding their way. Mother's eyes flashed, taking in the muddy, soaked state of clothes that had been pristine that morning. Lora made an apologetic face, wishing Mother understood. She'd had to take Oran to the woods. He was right; no one else would.

Lora's fingers found the damp scarlet feather tucked against her skin. She wouldn't have to join the ceremony—they would come. Though Lora had been only ten the first time she saw one of the winged people up close, she could still remember seeing the sky maiden landing in the center of the village, wings unfurled and scorched by the fire of the sun. Lora had followed her through the village wide-eyed while the other children hid from the warrior. Lora's heart still sung every time she caught sight of a pair of wings in battle against the sun high above.

When the sky maiden had gone a day later, she left something behind—a single scarlet feather from her wingsuit slipped into Lora's hand. "For when you fly," she'd whispered. She'd *promised.*

The priest began the invocation, reminding the village of their duty to the moon that provided a respite from the vengeful flames, of the sun's envious claim on their worship. Granite and snow glistened in the distant sunshine, steep inclines of thin grasses giving way to scattered shrubs, hardly shadows in the distance. The further Lora's eyes fell from the sky, the closer the world grew, trees and hills pressing in the narrow valley. Her head spun. Surely the sky maidens would come, any moment, and take her away.

A shadow darted across the assembled villagers clustered on the grass in front of the temple. It could have been a bird or a passing cloud, but Lora's heart leapt. She craned her neck back, eyes squinted against the sun.

There! She's coming!

A sky maiden wheeled amongst the clouds. Her wings spread wide from her narrow body, casting flickering shadows along the valley floor. A flash—Lora's gasp escaped before she could stop it—and the maiden dodged a column of flames spun from nothingness into the clear air. A little gasp at Lora's side brushed against her and she squeezed Oran's hand, knowing his eyes, too, searched the sky.

Mother's hand gripped Lora's arm, but Lora could not look away. Oran's hand jerked guiltily. The wings curled and spread, the maiden diving and climbing amongst the clouds. Every few moments, a beam of flame nearly reached her, but she dodged it every time.

The maiden spun, disappeared into a cloud. Lora held her breath. Another plume of flame, more brilliant than the luminescent cloud or the blinding blue above, tore after her.

All fell still. The sky maiden did not reappear; there were no more flames. The priest finished his prayer, and the villagers moved toward the temple. Seconds turned to minutes, as empty as the sky. Lora's neck ached from the craning. Lora choked back a sob, longing torn from her throat.

"It's time, Lora," Mother said from far away and so near.

Lora blinked back her tears, staring into the sky—the empty, silent sky. They hadn't come for her. She briefly considered her other option—the easy way, the coward's way—to turn from the temple, refuse the Renaming, and abandon duty and family.

She took a shuddering breath, straightened her shoulders, and followed Mother into the temple.

☼

The priest, Mares, stood to one side of the assembled masters. His youthful face was handsome in a lofty way, with a strong jaw and thick eyebrows that enhanced his priestly glower. He pulled the long bell cord. The gongs within the cascading bronze bells dangling from the ceiling swung and clattered—the largest at the top the size of a stew pot, down to the tiniest thimble almost brushing the floor. Chimes rippled through the space, dozens of tones layered and building, echoing and refracting from the hard stone walls.

Four times he pulled them, and as always, Lora had to fight not to cover her ears. Her sister Ella's face turned up to the skylight, joy illuminating her soft smile. Even baby Tomas in Mother's arms clapped and cooed with the cacophony. Oran squirmed a little, eyes shut but a frown on his face.

As the masters made their selections, the priest's eyes rarely left her. She ignored him, the masters, the villagers, everything drowned out by a persistent thrumming in her ears. They'd left her. They didn't want her. Why would any of the masters want her? Tears seeped down her cheeks, dripping onto the white shift. Her feather's vibrant red pressed through the wet cloth.

Finally, only three masters remained, and two new adults to be chosen—Lora and Genn, a farmer's son she didn't know well.

Father stepped forward. His eyes fell on Lora and for a moment, one long terrifying breath, she felt sure he'd select her. The shame of such a decision flooded her cheeks, hot and heavy. He couldn't, he *wouldn't,* not just to keep her here.

Then his gaze drifted away. "I … will not select an apprentice this year."

The decision murmured through the villagers, glances darting at Lora's glaring eyes.

The village firstman stepped forward—only he and the priest remained. Lora could barely suppress her rising shame. There was no way the priest or the firstman would pick her. Wild, undisciplined Lora as a leader? Or, more laughable, as a priestess?

Next to her, Mother's chin thrust out in a stubborn dismissal of the clustered villagers' longer glances toward Lora. Lora flushed. Mother would be ashamed if Lora was left standing. Genn's family, too, received some odd looks, but Lora drew the most attention. Lora met each curious gaze with defiance.

The firstman stepped forward, sweeping his cloak back. "I select Genn Corngrower."

Genn's relief as he stumbled forward was so palpable the villagers chuckled. He knelt in front of his new master, declared himself "Genn Firstman", and all eyes turned to the priest.

He stepped forward and took a deep breath. "Lora Weaver."

☼

Lora Weaver no longer, but Lora Moon was no less unhappy. She wiped sweat out of her eyes with her forearm, a dripping rag in one hand. Her knees prickled where they pressed into the hard stones of the moon temple floor, and her acolyte's shift—heavy wool from Father's loom—clung to her in itchy patches. Muddy, soapy water added a tingle in her nose, and her damp hair tickled her neck.

Mares coughed. "Keep working, Lora. Humility is the first step—"

"—on the path of faith. You've said."

Mares scowled at her. "You should not interrupt."

She bent back to her scrubbing, wincing at her raw, reddened hands. Mares didn't want an apprentice. He wanted a servant. He stood up there, reading his texts and sipping his blackberry wine while she worked her fingers to the bone. True, he'd taught her to read the texts, and she'd had time to visit her family every few days, but the rest of the time, she worked.

And sometimes, late at night when the blackberry wine made his eyes shine brighter than the moon ever did, she feared he wanted something more. A month of sharing the priest's tiny hut, eating his simple meals of overcooked meat, undercooked vegetables, and stale bread, and she still didn't understand why he'd picked her, why he couldn't have just left her alone.

"Sometimes the most stubborn heart can harbor the greatest passion," was the most straightforward answer he'd given her.

Lora scrubbed the stone as though it had offended her. Sometimes stubborn hearts were just stubborn.

She sloshed water over the speckled gray and tried not to cry. A shadow passed over, but she didn't look up—trying to spot a sky maiden through the opaque moon window would bring the tears she fought.

Mother was so proud. Every visit, Mother would fuss over her acolyte gown, making Lora wear a shift and shiver while Mother washed it. Ella—who'd be sixteen in two years, but already knew the full course of her life—was weaving Lora a moonstone blanket and seemed to think that now Lora had a purpose, a duty, she would be content. Only Father and Oran seemed to understand. Father frowned at her, a sad grimace full of worry, and Oran clung to her hand when she visited as though afraid she'd suddenly take flight.

Mares crossed to her, a cup of wine in each hand. "Here," he offered her one. "You've worked hard. Take a moment."

She wrinkled her nose and sniffed at the blackberry wine before taking a sip. It coated her mouth, syrupy sweet, almost sticky with an aftertaste of sharpness.

Mares sighed. "What do you want, Lora?"

Lora looked down into the soapy bucket, suds swirling into milky clouds. "I wanted to fly."

"The People of the Moon do not fly. Our duty is here, on the ground."

"I know." She shrugged. "You asked what I wanted."

He tilted his head, considering her. "You would have left, then, if no one selected you? Your Father said you would."

She sipped again, her mind churning as well as her stomach. Father *had* asked the priest to select her, then. Her cheeks grew hot. "Maybe." Her chest ached anew. She couldn't have left—she'd had nowhere to go. They had not come.

"That's not why I called you, you know."

She looked up.

His eyes were hot as coals. He leaned forward. "I needed an apprentice, it's true, but … Did you know that temples are often run by couples? Husbands and wives."

Lora went cold, the wine in her stomach freezing to a block of ice.

He looked toward the moon window now, his voice trembling. "The moon changes, you see. Lightness and dark, shifting, sliding across the days, changing places. A married couple balances one another. They—"

"No."

She hadn't meant it to come out so sharp, but the word bounced around the temple. Mares' head came down, and he smiled, a little sad.

"You feel that way now, but in time—"

"No."

"You really shouldn't interrupt." He shook his head. "Finish the floor."

Lora stepped back, her cheeks hot against the ice climbing from her chest. In her fury she kicked over the bucket of grey water. It flooded over the stones, drowning out her efforts. Marriage? She'd never felt the stirrings of lust the other girls talked about, had no interest in children. Certainly not with Mares. She dropped the half-full wine cup, splashing dark purple into the water.

Mares opened his mouth again, startled, but Lora turned and ran from the temple. The light spring breeze was cold on her burning face, the fragile hint of peonies not quite soothing. She couldn't catch her breath.

If she stayed, that would be her fate. Just another wife, another life, another future as predictable as the phases of the moon.

Lora ducked into Mares' hut. The door closed behind her, leaving Lora in a dark oven baking her to a feverish shiver. Rounded walls leaned over her, pressing down. A thin beef and carrot stew simmered over coals in the hearth.

She couldn't stay, she didn't want to stay. She'd tried to do her duty, but this was more than she could give. Selfish, yes, childish even, but the thought of spending her life buried under stones, serving a faith she felt no part of, was worse. Dishonest.

She'd never felt a spark of faith for the flat silver moon hanging up there in the sky. If she had no passion, no zeal for anything, perhaps it wouldn't have mattered. But she did, every time she looked up to the craggy mountains and spotted a spread pair of wings.

She flipped aside the thin curtain Mares had hung to give her privacy. Her fingers slid under her pillow, pulling out her feather. Pressed into her face, the worn plume teased her nose with the memory of its spicy musk.

Lora ran it along her cheek, imagining what a wingsuit of feathers would feel like, draping her arms, weighing down her back until *whoosh* she rose into the sky, soaring and diving. Free.

Maybe they'd never planned to come to her.

Maybe she had to go to them.

Lora shoved her dresses into the canvas sack she'd used to move into the hut. She hesitated, but took the temple cloak, thick and fur-lined, because she'd need it in the mountains. The pillow from Mares she left, but Lora rolled up her blanket—made by Ella when she was scarcely ten years old. The wool was worn now, soft as moss. Lora's eyes stung.

Then she crossed the hut to shove a loaf of bread, some apples, and a half-moon of cheese into her sack. For a long moment, she thought of home, of the musk of wool dangling in the air, of Mother's cooking, Ella's high voice singing the morning songs, Tomas's cooing, and of Oran.

Of all her family, Oran understood her the best—and she him. How many times had they left their chores to run for the woods behind the village, jumping—flying—from a high rock into the swimming hole? They'd throw rocks at leaves, pretending they were sky warriors. He would understand this too, someday.

Heart pounding, she opened the door. Mares had just come out of the temple, his face falling, shoulders slumping, when he saw her. Lora ran up the hill into the woods, fear and something wild propelling her away from the village, away from the ground.

☼

Snow pelted Lora's face, fast and frozen. She could barely feel her toes or fingers, but for some moonsaken reason, she could feel every inch of her exposed cheeks and nose. Her leather shoes were soaked with melted snow, the cloak weighed down by damp and ice. Despite being freezing, hungry, and exhausted, a grin split her face—though only for a moment as the cold wind made her teeth ache.

She was almost there.

For six days, she'd worked her way up the hills, and then the slopes, and now the rocky peaks, winding through pines and aspens and creeks and brambles on her way to the Nest of the Sky People. She'd forgotten flint, unprepared as she'd been. The nights had been long and miserable. Now, the dark mouths of their caves flickered in and out of sight when the storm winds blew the snow clear. The bread had run out the day before. Once she'd cleared the treeline, there wasn't much to forage.

No matter. She would show the Sky People she belonged by reaching their home without wings.

She crested the peak she'd been struggling up for most of the morning. A weary cry fell from her lips. Instead of a low dip before the final ascent, she stood atop a short rise above a sheer cliff. A river cut deep and narrow into the rock. Lora sank to her knees in the ankle-deep snow. It would take her days to find another way, and she wasn't sure how long she could go on without food.

A low, resonant voice came from behind her. "Who are you?"

Lora started and fell forward, sliding down the hill, nearly off the edge of the cliff. Her sack swung out over the edge, but she managed to hang onto the thin neck. She spun on her back, heart pounding, and stared up at the speaker.

A tall sky maiden with a dark complexion and sharp green eyes stood on the rise above Lora. A thin metal weapon balanced along one hand, folded in half by a hinge. At its full length, it would be as long as her arm. Her other hand gripped her waist, which, like the rest of her armor, was layered with feathers. Lora forgot her cold and hunger at the sight of the ruby-red wings. The feathers were tightly packed, forming an arch on either side of the maiden's shoulders, falling down like waterfalls to wingtips of black. The maiden leaned forward to help Lora up and the wings unfurled with a snap.

Lora gasped, but took the woman's hand and clambered to her feet, clinging to her sack.

"I've been watching you for two days. Who are you?" The Maiden repeated.

"L-Lora."

"Lora what? Don't your people name yourselves after your work?"

Lora hesitated. She had no claim to either Weaver or Moon anymore. "Just Lora."

"What are you doing up here?"

Lora flushed. Now that she was here, speaking to a sky maiden, her request sounded ridiculous. A villager, joining the Sky People? Lora thought of what she'd told Mares, gulped, and raised her chin. "I want to fly."

The woman's other eyebrow shot up.

Lora shivered and pulled her cloak nearer to her skin. "I left my village. I can't go back. I want to …" She trailed off.

"You climbed up here on your own?"

Lora nodded.

"I see," said the sky maiden. She pursed her lips, taking in Lora's cloak and her worn clothes. "I will take you to the nest. The Matrons will decide."

Lora looked over her shoulder, down to the churning river below. "But … how?"

"I will carry you. You can't weigh much. I am Gian." Gian tucked her weapon into a sheath at her waist and pulled Lora toward her. Strong arms wrapped around Lora, squeezing her and the sack against the soft feathers, and Gian said, "*Gwynt*."

Before Lora could do more than open her mouth, a gust of wind erupted beneath their feet. The wings caught the rising air. Together, Lora and Gian shot into the sky, up and up, spiraling around the draft of air.

The world fell away from them. Lora's eyes watered from the cold, even colder than before, but she kept them open, craning her neck around Gian's firm grip.

The snow filtered her view like thick glass, but she could see through the whipping storm. The valley spread below, green at the bottom, dotted with villages and farms. Raging waters spilled into the wider, slower river running along the valley floor, now a tiny blue-green ribbon. Her face hurt from the wide smile creasing her cheeks, tears streaming from her eyes.

Then she gasped as Gian tilted suddenly, angling forward in a wide dive toward the Nest. Wind whistled past Lora's ears, the tears running back against her cheeks, and then they landed, light as a spring snow, before a cave mouth.

Gian released her. Lora wavered on her feet, her mind still soaring, flying above the clouds, trying to etch each detail of her flight into her memory.

"Are you alright?"

"Yes. That was … wonderful."

Gian chuckled. "It can be. Come. It is warmer inside."

The sky maiden led Lora through the cave entrance. A stone wall with a door—tall, wide, made of ebony wood—blocked their way. Gian opened the door, which had room for her wings to pass under the threshold without touching, and disappeared inside.

Lora stared at the door. The day Mares had chosen her echoed against her shaking breaths. Lora shook herself and followed.

Beyond the door was an open cave, but not dark or damp. Lora had imagined riches, ornate furniture, and a closeness, a nearness. Like a nest of birds, she realized. Instead, the welcoming space gleamed with polished stone and a smooth floor. Great bone chandeliers sparkling with candles hung from the ceiling; fire pits were scattered around the space. Freshness coated the air, thin and clean like bathwater or fresh linens. A crack in the rock above provided a natural chimney.

At least fifty people milled about, most dressed in feathered armor like Gian, but others wearing woolen dresses or tunics. Lora's chest tightened. Some of those could have been made by Father. Their voices were swallowed by the high ceiling, reducing many conversations to a happy murmuring.

Wingsuits hung in a row along the back wall, brilliant red feathers glistening. Lora stared at them, her eyes once again filling. A dozen, perhaps more, each hanging on a wooden frame with the wings spread wide. The dark stone wall behind them seemed black by comparison to their vibrant color.

Gian crossed to this wall. Another sky maiden helped her slip the wings from her back and hang them on a frame. Lora trailed after her, trying to smile at the curious glances from the Sky People.

While Gian brushed her wingsuit, Lora peered around the cave.

Nest, she corrected herself.

The simple furniture, the wide-open space, surprised her. Only the wingsuits fit her imagined images of the caves above her village. This vast cavern had no pressing weight, despite the stone walls and the mountain all around. It was as open as the air.

"Come along. We'll see what they want to do with you." Gian smiled at Lora. "Don't worry. The Matrons aren't so bad."

Lora nodded, but the fear she'd felt outside the cave entrance surged into her throat. Gian led her through a side door and down a long, dark corridor with a torch at the far end outside another door.

The corridor branched off in several places, lit by lone torches outside each door. Even so, Lora coughed in the thick, smoky air. They passed an open door into what looked like a sleeping cavern, lined with thick mattresses, where a group of giggling children tossed a leather ball in a circle. Lora winced, thinking of Oran left alone on the ground.

Gian took Lora to a room much closer to what she'd expected. Feathers lined the walls, layered shades of red and scarlet, some so light they were pink, others so dark they were almost black. The small, round room was lit by a few candles, but it was warm, hot even.

In the center of the room, three older women sat on a feather-lined platform. They'd been speaking when Gian led Lora in, but they fell silent, waiting. Headbands of tiny feathers swept back their short hair. Not crones—though their faces were lined, their jaws were still strong, strength apparent in their posture. They wore enormous capes of feathers, leather pants, and tunics.

On the left, a smiling woman with dark skin, in the center a woman with tones closer to reddish-brown who arched an eyebrow at them, and on the right a woman with lighter skin like Lora who pursed her lips, leaning forward.

Lora stared at her. Older, yes, but it was the sky maiden, the one who'd given a little girl a feather so many years before. Lora bit her lip, holding back her cries. *Why didn't you come? Why did you leave me when you promised I could fly?*

Gian stopped a few paces in front of them and inclined her head. "Matrons. May I speak?"

Their eyes darted from Lora's ruined shoes to her worn canvas sack, to her moon temple cloak, and then her face. She felt like a goat parted from the herd for slaughter.

The woman on the left nodded.

Gian beckoned Lora forward. "This is Lora. She climbed the mountains. She wants to fly." To Lora, she said quietly, "This is Awyra, Plunae, and Carrega."

The gaze of the Matrons grew more intense, boring into Lora from three angles. Lora kept darting glances at Carrega, torn between glaring and begging.

Plunae, in the center, spoke first. "Why?"

Lora took a breath, the dusty aroma of feathers giving her strength. She reached down into her sack and pulled out her own feather, worn and wrinkled from her journey, but still a brilliant red. "When I was a girl, a sky maiden gave me this." She looked at Carrega, who nodded once. "All my life, I've held this feather and watched them … you … fly above my head. It's all I've ever wanted."

Gian stared at the feather, a slight smile crossing her face.

From the left, Awyra spoke. "The People of the Moon do not belong here."

Carrega, opposite her, smiled faintly. "That's not entirely true. There have been some in the past." She looked at Lora, curious. "But not for many years. Were you treated badly in your village?"

Lora started to say yes, then stopped. Mares wanted a wife and a partner, her parents wanted a daughter that did what she was supposed to do, the village was content as it was. "No. But I was unhappy there."

"Do they know you've come?" Plunae tilted her head as she asked the question.

"Not exactly. I didn't tell anyone, but … well, I don't think it would be hard to guess."

"Hmm," all three said together.

Gian shifted her weight and Lora shivered. Had she done something wrong?

Awyra spoke again. "We have a long-standing agreement with the People of the Moon. In exchange for our protection, they provide us with food, supplies, clothing. We can hunt, of course, but nothing green grows up here in the sky. Part of that agreement is keeping our distance." She sniffed. "Your ancestors did not like our martial ways, though they needed our strength."

She turned her head to the other Matrons. After a moment, they looked back at Lora and Gian.

Lora wavered where she stood. If they did not let her stay, if they made her go back … it was too much to contemplate. The shame of it crawled along her skin, slimy and cold, leaving a trail in its wake she could almost see.

"Yes," said Plunae. "You can stay."

A shock thrummed through Lora. *She could stay.*

The woman raised a finger. "If."

Lora looked up, her brow furrowing.

"If you kill a phoenix."

Lora blinked. "A … what?"

Carrega gestured to Gian. "Explain."

Gian turned. "What the People of the Moon think of as the sun is a creature." Her face darkened. "An ancient enemy, a bird of fire called the phoenix. They live here in the mountains, but they hunt in the valleys. They made these caves," she gestured, "using their flames to melt the rock for their own nests."

"But …" Lora's mind buzzed. "I've seen flashes of flame. I was taught it was the sun's rays, falling to the ground from the Sun God's anger over our worship of the Moon."

Gian shrugged. "It is the phoenixes."

Awyra shifted. "For generations, our warriors have proven their mettle by going to the nests of the phoenixes and taking one as a trophy. Only those who can defeat a phoenix are allowed to wear the wings."

Gian frowned. "She is untrained. She's not of the Sky People. She—"

"She asked to join us," said Carrega. "This is the price. If she truly belongs here, she must prove it."

Carrega glanced at Lora, a look sharp as a feather's barb, and Lora understood. They had not come because she had to prove herself, earn her place. Lora straightened, meeting that glance with determination.

Plunae nodded. "You may train her for a few days. The next time the sky is clear, however, she must make her attempt."

"I can do it," Lora yelped, before Gian expressed more doubt or one of the Matrons changed their minds. "I'll do my best."

Carrega leaned forward, her gaze burning into Lora. "If you bring back a phoenix, its feathers will form the first layers of your own wingsuit. May the wind lift you."

It was a clear dismissal. Lora and Gian left the room.

In the corridor, Gian turned to Lora. "You don't have to do this." Her face was drawn, concerned. "I can take you home."

Lora shook her head. "It's not my home anymore. I can do it. I will."

Gian pressed her lips together. "Very well. In the morning we must get you some warmer clothes. I'll teach you what I can."

Lora followed her, mind reeling. A bird caused all those flashes of fire, the wildfires that roared through the high country in the dry season, the burnt-out homes that were testament to the need for the sky maidens? Lora tried to imagine a bird made out of fire, but all she came up with was a chicken with flaming wings, and *that* didn't seem terribly dangerous.

Lora lay awake, listening to the strangely silent cave, the way the air sprawled out in the cavern instead of pressing down against her face. The musk of feathers, torch smoke, and a light scent of sweat swirled through the air. The mattress beneath her was lumpy, but soft and warm.

A crack in the rock high above let in a sliver of moonlight, bright and clear, catching the smoke from the braziers in slices of glowing silver. Lora couldn't bring herself to regret her choice. She searched her heart, pressing against her memories and dreams for any spark of warmth for that glow. She found nothing, just the cold touch of moonlight on smoke.

Lora crouched behind a granite boulder, peering across a snowy meadow to a dark cave mouth, and wondered if she'd made a mistake after all.

Gian had done all she could to help Lora in the four days they'd had. Lora now wore borrowed tight-fitting feather armor with leather boots laced halfway up her shins. She'd tucked her feather underneath the vest, next to her skin. The armor felt amazing, as warm and snug as she'd always dreamed, and yet it sat uneasily on her shoulders. Unreal, temporary, a dream that would soon fade.

She carried a heavy pouch secured on a belt and resting on her left hip, full of shimmering, smooth stones the color of gold and flecked with black. Firestones. The firestones had an odd shape—all sharp angles and layered edges instead of round and smooth like the river rocks of the valley.

"Throw them when the phoenix catches fire," Gian had explained. "When it touches the flames, the rock will explode."

Lora had proven to be useless at the long weapon of the sky maidens, the atlatl, but thanks to hours in the woods with Oran, her aim with her hand was true. She'd spent two long days throwing regular rocks at flags on pulleys, hitting them more often than not. The problem with that method was she'd have to get quite a bit closer.

Gian had demonstrated the firestones once, on the cliff edge where she'd first found Lora. Lora's cheeks had been cold, her hair windswept from their flight, and though it still made her teeth ache, she'd grinned. They'd built a fire, tossed a firestone from a distance. The explosion had been sudden, sharp, like a thunderclap. Little shards of rock carved through the air—one flying back and cutting Lora's cheek.

She ran a finger along the scab, her jaw tight.

She stared at the cave, mouth sour with fear. She'd made her way around the mountain, much warmer than before in her new clothes, and down the steep peak Gian had indicated. Her toes were raw from rubbing against the unfamiliar boots, hot blisters painful as she crouched, but she'd made it. The pain proved she wasn't dreaming after all.

Now that she'd arrived, though, Lora didn't know how to begin. Charging into the cave where dozens of phoenixes roosted would be madness. She'd have to wait for one to appear. They only flew when they flamed, Gian said, and they only flamed when provoked, hunting, or mating. Otherwise, they stayed close to their nests.

The valley spread beyond, green and full of life. The phoenix nest was just above the treeline. Lora could almost make out her village, a smudge against the green in the distance. Did they miss her? Mother would have been so angry, Lora doubted she had any feelings beyond shame and rage. But Oran, Ella, Father, even Mares …. Yes, they missed her. Lora snorted. Even if only because Mares had to do his own washing now.

A keening cry echoed over the mountainside and Lora crouched, heart drumming in her ears. She peered over the top of the boulder and gasped.

An enormous bird, with a wingspan at least as wide as Father was tall, strutted in front of the cave. Even from where she hid, perhaps thirty paces off, the smoldering flames in its eyes outshone the sun. The females were their warriors, she'd learned, but Lora hadn't expected such size. The males were smaller and did not flame.

A brilliant yellow crest arched over the phoenix's featherless head, which ended in a sharp black beak. Scarlet feathers, of course, but with a golden shimmer not present in the sky maiden's wingsuits. The phoenix preened her body above strong legs of purple with claws as black as the beak and just as sharp. Keening again, her wings spread, and for a moment Lora forgot everything in the majesty of the phoenix.

Then Lora thrust her hand into the pouch. Her fingers closed on the cold firestone. In a swift motion, with her eyes locked on the phoenix, she stood and roared a challenge. Her voice broke, unused to the screaming wordless cry, but she poured her soul into it.

"The challenge is the most important part," Gian had said. "You must provoke the beast into flame, but not into flight."

Lora glanced up at the peak. Gian would be waiting, watching, in case the phoenix took flight. Lora had to keep it on the ground.

The bird's head snapped around, eyes narrowing. It flapped its wings, and Lora stepped from behind the rock. Her heart hammered, breath coming quick, but she did not tremble. She kept her eyes on the bird, as she'd been told, and waited. It screamed a challenge of its own, and those flaming eyes flickered.

Lora raised her hand, energy tingling through her. Flames darted down the neck of the phoenix. She threw the firestone as hard as she could, aiming for the body. The explosion cracked over the snowfield and the mountainside. The phoenix screamed again, staggering back, fully aflame now. Heat washed over Lora's face, reality resurging with a sharp plunge of her stomach. It was so big, so fiery. Had she missed?

Lora ran forward, reaching for a second firestone. The bird rose, obscured by blazing fire. No wonder her people thought them rays of the sun. She drew out the firestone, but as she raised her arm to throw the stone, her name echoed from behind her.

"Lora!"

Lora whirled and a shock as stunning as the crack of the firestones burst from her stomach, exploding through her body. Oran, filthy and hollow-cheeked, ran from the shelter of the trees toward her staring at the phoenix. His pants were torn, his tunic smeared with mud. A canvas sack flapped empty against his back.

The bird screeched behind her. A wave of heat passed overhead. The phoenix flew directly at Oran—who stood transfixed by the approaching danger with his mouth hanging open.

Lora threw the firestone. It fell short, the bird outpacing her desperate throw. Panic clawing her skin, she sprinted toward Oran, yelling for him to run, to hide, to get away. At the same time, part of her mind yanked toward the phoenix, determined to get her kill and her place in the sky.

The wounded phoenix, blood streaming from a gash in its breast, faltered as it neared Oran, wheeling to the side and falling to the ground in flame. Lora could stop, take aim, kill it—but more phoenix calls echoed from behind her. She glanced behind, still running. Others erupted from the cave mouth, their challenges rising with their flames, winging toward her.

Lora passed the wounded bird, glaring at it. Why hadn't it just died?

She scooped up her little brother without breaking pace, running into the shadow of the pines and aspens. Their sharp scent stung her throat as painful breaths jerked her chest in and out. After settling Oran behind a stout trunk, she peered back against the white-hot sky, looking for flashes of flame and the shadows of wings. She could see nothing, though, because tears ran down her cheeks and snot dripped from her nose.

Hiccuping through her sobs, Lora hid. Oran wept, too, hugging her legs and wailing. She shushed him, smoothing his rumpled, greasy hair. They had to get away unnoticed—the birds could be vengeful, following and stalking a sky maiden for hours if enraged.

A phoenix burst through the canopy above them, smoking branches hailing down, crackling into the dried undergrowth. Blood splattered ahead of the flaming dive. Lora leapt atop Oran, the heat unbearable, every breath burning in her throat. Oran moaned, and then Lora heard screaming, distantly aware it was her voice. Unbearable pain shot along her neck, leaving her dizzy and sick. She rolled away from Oran, trying to escape the horror searing her.

A crack punched through Lora. The phoenix fell into the bushes, dead at last, flames flickering into smoke and then nothingness. The small fires smoldering around them hissed and sparked. Lora jumped back to her feet, stomping them out with her borrowed boots.

She clenched her fists, her chest aching, her neck afire. She gingerly poked at the rising blisters on her neck, her ears, coming away with fragments of her singed hair. She would never get another chance—the matrons had been clear. Hugging Oran, she tried to release the pull of the sky from her breastbone. She'd had no choice, not really. She tried to stop the tears from flowing but grief and pain tore out of her in ragged choking gasps.

First one, and then more phoenixes flashed into the cave mouth, firestones raining down after them. Gian landed in the snowfield. She turned and walked toward Lora, her face solemn. When she reached them, she smeared a cooling oily gel over Lora's wound.

"Come," Gian said, nodding at Oran. "We'll take him home before returning to the nest."

Lora shook her head. "I failed."

Gian placed a hand on Lora's shoulder. She squeezed. "It was a valiant effort, Lora. The bird died easily with a second firestone."

A firestone that should have come from Lora's hand, but hadn't. She sniffed again.

"Your firestone killed it, after all. Our duty is to protect, which is what you did."

There was a hint there, a suggestion in Gian's voice. She would bend the truth, break it, to allow Lora to stay and become a sky maiden. It would be so easy, and Lora would have everything. Everything for a lie. Lora closed her eyes, pain clawing at her scalp along her neck. Shame so hot and heavy it made her nauseous churned through her.

Lora found Oran's hand and squeezed. "No."

"You threw the stone." Gian urged her now, trying to get Lora to meet her eyes.

"No," Lora said again, her mouth filling with acid bile. "I failed." She shook her head. "Take us home.

Just take me home." She would apologize, beg, grovel. Perhaps they would let her come back.

Gian's mouth opened. Closed. Then her shoulders slumped and she took Lora up in her arms. Another sky maiden landed and, trembling, Oran accepted her arms.

"*Gwynt.*"

The wind rose around them, and they were flying. Lora did not look down, did not even open her eyes. She simply stared into the blackness of her mind.

☼

Gian set them down outside the village, next to the Temple of the Moon. The softer breezes of the valley wafted familiar scents of wool and lilacs. Lora stepped back, looking down at the suit of feathers she did not deserve. Her neck hurt, but the medicine had soothed the pain to a distance.

"Lora? Oran!" Mares' voice called from the entrance to the temple. She looked into his face and gulped hard, shoving down her grief with a straightening of her back and a tightening of her jaw. She would not weep. Not here, not now.

She looked at Gian, running her fingers over the soft feathers of the armor. "Give me a few minutes, and I will change."

Gian smiled, sad. "I would let you keep it, but it's not mine to give."

Oran slammed into her side. "I'm sorry, I'm sorry," he kept saying. "Your neck, oh, Lora …"

Lora knelt. "What were you thinking?" The heat in her voice made her wince. She tried to soften her tone, edged with remembered fear. "You could have been killed."

"You left us," he gasped. "You didn't even say goodbye. I wanted to come, I want to be with you." His eyes widened. "That bird, Lora, is that the sun?" He cried anew.

Lora pulled him into her arms like she had when he was tiny, rocking on her knees. Mares had disappeared into the temple. Lora sighed. He would not be happy to have her back. She'd been a bad apprentice and had dismissed his marriage offer. She grit her teeth. She would serve in the temple, do her duty, but they could not make her marry him. She wasn't a length of wool to be spun into whatever pattern they demanded.

The moon bells rang out, three sharp pulls—the summoning bells. Everyone would run to the temple. Lora winced at more than the clanging tones. She'd wanted to speak to her family before everyone knew she'd returned. She closed her eyes and waited for the outcry.

"Lora!"
"Oran!"
"Lora!"

Their voices rose, carrying down the hillside from the village proper. Mares exited the temple and stared at her, his face a mystery. She knew she should step forward, speak to him, but she didn't leave Gian's side, not yet. For a few more moments, she would cling to the sky.

Ella, Mother, and Father were among the last to make their way down the hill. When they spotted Lora and Oran, Mother nearly fell, stumbling forward with baby Tomas in her arms and Father supporting them from behind.

Ella fell against Lora and Oran from the side, squeezing them and weeping, crying into Lora's unburned hair. Then Father came from behind, holding all three of them in his long, strong arms. Mother pulled Oran free, sobbing into his dirt-stained hair, but she watched Lora, eyes shining. She didn't look angry after all.

"Lora, look out!" Gian's cry broke through the babbling villagers like a crack of thunder. "*Gwynt!*"

The rushing wind cooled Lora's burn and she followed Gian's path up into the sky, up, up to where a phoenix dove toward Lora's family.

Lora looked at her family. She'd left them, rejected them, and in trying to come back had doomed them. Oran's eyes widened, reflecting the coming flame in two glittering orbs, panic rising fresh on his face. Lora shoved Ella back, whipped her hand into the pouch at her waist, and straightened. Her burns twinged in sympathy to the nearing fire.

"Run, Father, get them back!"

Father dragged Ella and Oran back. Heat scorched Lora's cheeks. The air around her wavered and sizzled. The glittering stone shot through the air, tumbling up into the sky.

Crack!

The phoenix swerved at the last moment, swinging over the temple with an ear-shattering shriek.

She'd wounded it, she was sure she'd hit it, but the fiery wings refused to fold. The glass of the roof shattered. The phoenix dove in. Though her neck burned fresh from the heat, eyes streaming from the smoke drawing hacking coughs from her chest, she ran into the temple.

The phoenix, flickering with orange flames, sat upon the dais, one wing hanging limp and bleeding. It spied Lora and keened, flames resurging along the feathers. Lora drew out a firestone, but clenched it in her fist. If she threw it now, inside the temple, the shards of rock could rip her to pieces as much as the phoenix.

The moonbells swung in the wavering heat of the spreading fire. Lora stumbled, coughing, across the temple and yanked on the cord once—twice—ringing the bells into a cacophony of tones.

The phoenix cringed back from the sound, spreading its wings, pulling the injured wing out with a screech of pain. It lifted up, up and away from the temple floor. As it rose through the shattered moon window, Lora threw her firestone.

Crack!

The bird fell out of sight. Lora ran from the temple, pulling up short at the headless, twitching body, the flames flickering, dying down, until they were gone.

Breathing hard, Lora stared at the phoenix. Long red feathers glistened in the sunlight, grass smoldering around the corpse. Then she turned, her eyes searching for her family. They crouched, flattened by the heat and the explosion, their eyes wide and their faces pale, staring back at her.

Oran jumped to his feet. "Woo-hoo! Lora!"

The cry echoed, rising over the terrified villagers.

Gian landed next to her, a wide smile on her face. Her wings shadowed Lora's family, backlit by the sun. "Well, that should be good enough, I'd say."

Lora blinked. Then she realized what Gian meant. She had killed the phoenix, saved her people. As a sky maiden should. Warmth surged in her chest, almost muting the pain from her neck. "Let me say goodbye."

Gian nodded.

Lora crossed to her family and took baby Tomas from Mother. She stroked his cheek, glancing at Mother. "I'm sorry I couldn't be what you wanted me to be."

Mother's eyes spilled over and she shook her head. "I can't believe … that giant bird … I'm so proud of you."

The words punched into Lora like a firestone. Her head fell against her Mother's shoulder, great sobs tearing from her throat. She hadn't realized she needed to hear those words so badly, but now that she had, they echoed in her mind, healing old wounds and filling her with joy and pain. "I'll miss you," she mumbled.

Tomas squirmed and Lora handed him back. Mother smiled through her tears.

Lora turned to Father. "Goodbye."

He sighed and stroked her uninjured cheek. She leaned into it like Tomas had. "Goodbye, little one. Come and see us."

"I will."

Ella cried so hard she couldn't get a word out, but Lora smoothed her hair and hugged her. "Thank you for always taking care of me. It's my turn to take care of you."

Ella clung to Lora, sobbing, but she nodded.

Finally, Lora turned to Oran. She knelt.

He tried not to cry, but his eyes were red and his little body trembled. "Someday, will you take me flying again?"

"Promise to stay home this time."

He made a wry face, but whispered, "I promise."

Lora hugged him. "Then I promise, too." She reached beneath her vest and pulled out her feather, tucking it into his clenched fist. "For when you fly."

Copyright © 2023 by Rebecca E. Treasure.

Nebula Award-nominated Beth Cato is the author of A Thousand Recipes for Revenge *from 47North plus two fantasy series from Harper Voyager. She's a Hanford, California native now residing in a far distant realm. Follow her at BethCato.com and on Twitter at @BethCato.*

THAT SUNDAY ON THE TRAIL WITH THE MEREST BREATH OF SEA

by Beth Cato

Rosamund had hopes that the family reunion wouldn't completely suck after her mom told her it'd take place in Cambria, right on the California coast, but as Mom drove up a narrow winding road flanked by squished-tight houses, Rosamund's enthusiasm withered up like a three-year-old raisin.

"Mom! I can't even see the ocean!" Rosamund twisted around to look, the seatbelt strap threatening to strangle her.

"You'll be able to smell the ocean from the camp, I'm sure. Now face forward."

Rosamund flung herself around. "This is going to be awful. They don't even like me."

"Stop that. My family loves you." Mom glanced at her in the rear-view mirror.

"But they think I'm a freak."

Mom sighed and didn't argue.

Rosamund glowered out a window that showed only pines as the road dipped and snaked through a small patch of forest. A tall wooden archway, adorned with balloons, announced their arrival at Camp Carraway.

"Balloons shouldn't be used out here. They kill lots of birds and stuff," said Rosamund. Their car tires growled against gravel. "Hey, are there deer here? Or bears?" She'd much rather meet a bear than most of her extended family. At least bears would hug her because they were hungry. Her family probably hugged to absorb her life energy. They were awful like that.

"I don't know, but you're staying put. Good grief, your grandma was right—everyone did come. This parking lot must represent fifteen states!"

"Wait. What do you mean, I have to stay put? The ocean isn't that far away!"

"It's like two miles. I know you walk that far to the mall, but this isn't home, got it? You don't know what's out there."

Rosamund grimaced. Her vivid imagination could fill in those blanks easily enough, but she already had an idea of what was waiting for her here, and it was horrible.

✡

"Look at how big you are!" Aunt Fergie grappled Rosamund against her pole-thin figure.

"I don't need to. I know how big I am."

Mom gave Rosamund a warning glance as she maneuvered around Fergie and into the log-constructed lodge.

"Oh, you funny thing." Fergie leaned closer to Rosamund. "Did you try that diet trick I told you at Thanksgiving?"

"I'm eleven, Aunt Fergie, I don't need to—"

"Oh, piffle. You want to look your best in the next few years, trust me." She gave Rosamund a wink.

Meaning, Rosamund looked ugly now. Kids at school had already informed her of that, repeatedly. Rosamund was well aware that she was more plush than most of Mom's family, the only one under fifty who wore glasses, and probably the only one who could sing the alphabet in Klingon.

"Oh! Is that Rosie?" squealed some second-cousin-removed-or-something.

Rosamund hated being called Rosie—hated it like she hated the smell of hot dogs—but she didn't have the opportunity to say anything before she was propelled along a gauntlet of relations who cooed and exclaimed and *squeezed*. She didn't even know the names of half these people. They were physical, more-aged versions of faces from Grandma's wall.

Spinning around, she sought means of escape. The room was bigger than a school cafeteria, complete with long tables and benches. People set up equipment and musical instruments near a stage.

Rosamund dodged strangers to find Mom, a red plastic cup in hand, chatting with Uncle Terence.

"How're you?" he asked, mustache curving in a smile. He was the relative she liked best because they could talk science fiction and fantasy books.

She even forgave him for trying to get her into Asimov and Heinlein.

"I need a way out of this labyrinth," Rosamund said.

"Nope, you're stuck here until Tuesday," said Mom.

For once, Rosamund wished it wasn't summer break. She'd rather deal with school than this place for another full day.

"Ellie, Rosamund!" On cue, Grandma arrived with strangers in tow. Her bright grin was almost radioactive. "Look who's here! Rosamund, you get to meet your Aunt Tamara, Uncle Rodrick, and cousin Jupiter for the first time. They came all the way from Massachusetts!"

They were dressed like models at a fancy mall department store, with sweaters, khakis, and plastic mannequin smiles.

"Jupiter, Rosamund, you'll be the only kids here the same age. You must become good friends!" With that pronouncement, Grandma flitted away.

There was an awkward pause. "So Ellie, how are you doing?" asked Aunt Tamara as the adults formed a cluster that left Rosamund and Jupiter together.

Rosamund had always thought the name Jupiter was cool—same name as the bigshot Roman god! How impressive was that? She was vaguely disappointed that he looked like any preppy kid at school.

"So, uh, have you been to California before?" she asked.

He rolled his eyes. "Of course. San Diego and Disneyland a bunch of times."

"Ah." She hadn't been to Disneyland, and she'd lived in the state all her life.

"You two. Go play." Aunt Tamara whisked them away. What, did she think they were toddlers on a playdate? Even so, Rosamund and Jupiter obeyed. She followed him down a hallway. He ignored the surrounding doors to trot to the one at the end.

ADULTS OVER 21 ONLY read a sign. He pushed his way inside.

Rosamund stopped just within the room. "We shouldn't be in here."

"We're renting this whole place. We can go wherever we want. My parents paid for a lot of it, too, because the rest of you are poor slobs." He said this, matter-of-factly as he circled around a pool table.

Rosamund scowled. "I don't think that makes it okay to—"

"Oh, shut up. 'I don't think,'" he mimicked. "No, you don't." He took down a pool cue. He was maybe an inch shorter than Rosamund, and the stick made him look even smaller. "This reunion is stupid. We're only here to make Grandma happy. All she does is nag us to visit her."

Rosamund didn't disagree about the stupidity, but her fists balled. "Don't talk about Grandma that way. Her eight kids are scattered all over. She's wanted a big reunion since before we were even born!"

The door behind Rosamund whooshed open. "I knew I saw someone come this way. Can't you kids read?" Uncle Tony pointed toward the hall. "No playing around in here. Put that back."

Jupiter replaced the cue. "Rosie thought it'd be okay."

Indignant rage flushed her cheeks as Tony faced her. "I know *you* can read. Now out." Last Thanksgiving, Mr. University English professor Tony had griped at her for reading a fantasy novel. 'Those aren't real books,' he'd said.

Jupiter gave her a triumphant look as he pushed his way ahead of her along the hallway.

"Why did you tell him that it was my idea?" she hissed.

"What, like I wanted to get into trouble?"

"You're a jerk. I don't want to be around you anymore." Tears in her eyes, she split off from him as they entered the main lodge. To her surprise, he trotted up beside her.

"Didn't you hear? We're best friends now!" More people had arrived. There had to be at least fifty jabbering grown-ups, little kids whirling around their legs like oversized mosquitoes.

"Leave me alone!" Rosamund hissed at him.

"There's nothing else to do."

"Nothing to do but bully me?"

"That's right!" he said perkily.

She stopped at a full punch bowl. Drinking something might stop her from full-out crying. She ladled liquid into a plastic cup, then took a few steps back. Jupiter got a drink of his own. Rosamund eyed him with suspicion. There were gobs of witnesses around, but he could still dump punch on her and make it look like an accident.

The cool liquid eased her tight throat as she studied the room. There had to be a way to slip outside or to a place where she could hide. She'd stay there all day if she needed to, even read an old paper phonebook to kill time.

"Rosamund! Wow! You're so big!"

She grimaced at the double meaning as she was rushed by two cousins she rarely saw. They rambled about travel hassles as Rosamund nodded, an eye on Jupiter. He had stepped back a few feet behind the shelter of a heavy curtain. Most of the room couldn't see him there.

He was up to something.

Another relation approached, and the two cousins squealed greetings, facing away.

Moisture flecked her arm.

She glanced at her forearm, then her favorite jacket. Pink dyed the front of the sweatshirt in a big slash. She jerked up her gaze. Jupiter, in his hidey-hole, winked at her and waggled a straw. He'd spat punch at her!

Rosamund had never been so mad in all her life.

Aunt Fergie walked by, an ancient film camera in hand. "Mind the sugar." She nodded toward to the cup in Rosamund's hand as she continued onward.

Jupiter emerged so he could leer. " 'Mind the sugar,' " he mimicked. "That'd be a first for you, huh?"

Rosamund finally understood what books meant when they described someone as seeing red in fury. Red as fruit punch.

She didn't think. She acted. Her right arm reeled back then snapped forward as she lunged. There was nothing slow motion about it. Jupiter's eyes had a split-second to widen in shock, then her clenched fist met the softness of his nose.

It erupted like a smashed tomato.

With all the adults engrossed in their own conversations, the incident might have escaped their notice—until Jupiter flung himself sideways into the big punch bowl. The plastic table emitted a resonant crack as it snapped beneath his weight, taking him and the splashing bowl to the floor.

Dead silence lingered for a stretch of seconds, then chaos erupted.

"What happened!"

"Are you all right?"

"Oh my goodness, he's bleeding!"

"I'll call 9-1-1!"

"No, the red is the punch, he—"

"She did it!" Jupiter blubbered, pointing at Rosamund from his punch puddle. "She hit me and knocked me into the bowl!"

Rosamund felt weirdly detached from reality as relatives turned on her with rapid-fire questions and accusations. She had no doubt whatsoever that he'd made his melodramatic plunge on purpose to get her in trouble.

Now she looked like the bad guy.

"Rosamund, what happened?" Mom's voice cut through the cacophony.

"He used a straw to spit punch on me and he made a fat joke, too." She motioned to her jacket.

"My son would do no such thing!" blurted Aunt Tamara. She hovered over Jupiter, taking care not to touch him. She probably didn't want her fancy clothes stained.

Rosamund didn't know Aunt Tamara, but she hated her. "He said he could do whatever he wanted because you paid for most of reunion because everyone else here is a 'poor slob.' "

That evoked exclamations from the audience. Tamara whirled around to retort.

"Rosamund's not the violent tSype," said Uncle Terence. "She'd need a good reason to hit someone."

Mom slowly nodded. "She would."

Tears prickled Rosamund's eyes. She was glad Mom had defended her—but why hadn't she been first?

Jupiter began loud, hiccupping sobs.

"Stop being so melodramatic," snapped Rosamund. "You're as fake as TV wrestling!"

That elicited a gasp from someone in the crowd. Aunt Tamara spun about, pointing a manicured finger at Rosamund. "You hurt him! Don't talk to him like that!"

"Have you ever disciplined him in all his life?" Rosamund was eleven—why did she feel like the grown-up?

Aunt Tamara's face turned a shade of red-purple, but as she opened her lips, Mom gripped Rosamund by the shoulder. "Walk."

She did, tossing her empty cup into a trash can as they stepped outside onto shaded cement. Birds sang in nearby trees. Rosamund blinked as if waking up.

Mom released a long exhalation. "You really socked him?"

"Right in the nose!"

Mom gave Rosamund a funny look. "Do you even feel bad?"

Rosamund mulled that over. "No. He's a jerk, Mom. He told me he was going to keep bullying me the rest of the time here because he's bored. I just met him!"

Her teacher last year had the class analyze villains in literature, teaching them that well-done bad guys don't do all bad things. They should have nuance. Be relatable, complex.

Rosamund couldn't relate to Jupiter even though they were related. He was a villain, through and through.

Mom sighed. "I'm sorry. I've heard stories about Jupiter."

"You knew he was awful? Then why is he here?"

"He's family. Of *course* he's here."

Like that made everything okay. "Jupiter tried to get me in trouble for going into the pool room but he's the one who went in there and messed with stuff. It's not fair!"

"Life's not fair. Sometimes we need to be the ones who do the right thing even when it's hard."

" 'We?' "

"Us. Women."

"Mom! That's sexist and wrong."

Mom looked plain tired. "So's the world. We have to find ways to survive."

"And he gets away with everything? What if he comes after me again? Do we have to stay here?"

"I already paid for our cabin—"

"Can I go there?"

"Tamara's the one handing out the keys. I'd better wait to talk to her. You keep a low profile for now. If you see Jupiter, try to be near other adults."

"That didn't help before!"

"Then use your wits instead of your fists, please." Mom gave her a hard look and then went back inside.

Rosamund stared after her. *Life's not fair. We have to find ways to survive.* Those words of advice were about as useful as an umbrella in a hurricane.

She turned and caught sight of a trail between two cabins.

Mom wanted her to keep a low profile? Okay.

Rosamund would go find the ocean.

Pine needles crunched underfoot. For the first few minutes, she could still see roofs of nearby properties through the thin brush, but soon enough she was surrounded by trees and couldn't hear a single car. She felt like she was way out in the middle of nowhere.

Soon she'd find the Pacific and breathe in that salty air, and everything would be better.

Up and down the trail she went. As she climbed each rise, she eagerly awaited a sea view at the top, only to find more trees—which was weird. Cambria had lots of houses, especially right on the shore. The ocean had to be close, too. She could only go so far west!

The trail dipped toward deeper foliage. A creek murmured somewhere amid the green, but strangely enough, she heard no birds. Something big rustled in the branches. Out of the shadows, a horse emerged onto the path about ten feet away.

Rosamund gasped as she skidded to a stop. She'd never seen such a beautiful horse. He had the sleek black coat of a highly-groomed show horse, his mane and tail draped long. Intelligent eyes regarded her, ears perked. He had a muscular build like a Friesian, the type of horse knights used to ride, but this horse could never have been a casual mount.

That's because its hooves all faced backward.

"You're a kelpie," she squeaked.

The kelpie emitted a surprised snort as his ears went flat.

"And you understand exactly what I'm saying, but of course you do—you're a kelpie." Her voice hit an even higher pitch.

Rosamund had read every book on mythology possessed by her school and town libraries and owned a few volumes of her own, and therefore she knew that kelpies were nasty business. They were fairy beings that lived in or near bodies of water. This one presented as a stallion, but kelpies were said to be shapeshifters, too.

She should've been scared. Instead, she was thrilled. Meeting a magical shapeshifting deathhorse was the best thing that had happened all day.

"You are an unusual child of your time, to know what I am." The kelpie's voice was deep and painful-sounding, like Darth Vader if he'd spent longer in a lava bath.

She wasn't surprised that the kelpie spoke, but her heart threatened to pound out of her chest. "I am. That means I won't touch you because I know

I'd magically stick to you." Though she still kinda wanted to stroke that glossy coat, like when she attempted to pet fire at age three. "Were you intending to drag me into the water to eat me, or pull me back to Fairyland? Though I suppose you could eat me there, too." Her voice shook.

The kelpie snorted. "There's little joy in being a trickster when my audience knows my tricks."

"How are you even in California? Shouldn't you be in Scotland or something?"

"How are *you* here, child pale and blonde?" he retorted. "People travel the world, as do we."

"You didn't answer my questions about why you're here right now." She paused, thinking. "But then, you *are* a trickster, so you could lie and say Fairyland is a wonderful place that serves good pizza every day, meaning it is all-cheese."

He made a thoughtful sound. "I haven't conversed with a human in decades. Most aren't worth speaking to. You could be worth keeping alive. I might not be the only one who finds you interesting."

Rosamund dryly swallowed. She wouldn't think about how cool it'd be to see a fairy court, nope, nope, because everyone there would be also a conniving trickster, with the queen worst of all. "Does that mean you often lurk here? That sounds boring."

"You have *no idea*. Few humans venture this far. Fewer still try to touch me these days. They stand back and take pictures with their mobile telephones." He blew an incredulous raspberry. "It is my responsibility to lure people, and you humans are not cooperating as you once did."

"You're trying to lure me into my maybe-death by telling me you have to make a quota? Like someone selling mattresses in a store?" Rosamund couldn't help it, she giggled.

The kelpie's ears went flat. "Such a crude comparison. I have performed my duty with pride for centuries. I will not be mocked." He backed toward the stream on his bizarro hooves. No imprints showed on the hard-packed mud.

"Wait!" Did she just tell the fairy murder-horse to wait? "I'm sorry I laughed at you."

The kelpie stopped. "It tires me to leave the water and to speak your inelegant language. You're wasting my time, child-too-wise-to-my-ways."

Rosamund had a thought. A terrible thought. "What if I brought you someone else?"

His ears perked. "Oh?"

Maybe she wouldn't have to watch her back all weekend after all. "He's my age, and horrible."

"Is he, now?" The kelpie's ebony gaze seemed to see inside her.

"He's a bully and a snob. He has no conscience. If you take him all the way to Fairyland, he'd probably fit right in." That's what she was setting up, she told herself. Not his death.

"Perhaps. Perhaps not." The kelpie's ears swiveled in brief consideration. "Are you certain I cannot convince you to come with me? You could enter at my side, as a guest."

An invitation to a realm of real, actual, magic? Her throat went dry. "I—but it's Fairyland. You're always at war there, aren't you? All those different courts and creatures? And you're all wicked and—"

"As if your kind is that much different."

"You're trying to manipulate me right now. I'm not stupid, and I'm a *good guy*. You're probably lying about me being a guest. You could take me through the portal and then eat me."

"Why must I wait?" His lips curled back, revealing teeth broad like that of a normal horse, but in serrated rows like a shark's mouth. Her horror showed, and he brayed a laugh. "I prefer not to dine here. Earth dampens fine flavors."

Rosamund backed away. "If I fetch him, will you be here?"

"I'll wait. I'm hungry and it is near that midday period that your kind calls 'lunch.' "

His laugh followed her as she ran back down the path.

✧

By the time she returned to Camp Carraway, Rosamund had convinced herself that she wouldn't go back down the trail. The kelpie had threatened to eat her! He was a bad guy, no question.

"Ah, there's the juvenile delinquent," said a cousin standing at the back fringe of camp, smoking.

"You shouldn't smoke near the woods in California. It's way too dry here. You could start a fire."

The cousin flipped her off with a grin. Rosamund stalked onward. Why was she related to so many jerks?

"Where've you been?" Aunt Fergie was lurking by the back door to what must be the kitchen. Smoke filtered through the screen along with the acrid stink of burnt hot dogs. Ugh. "You need to apologize to Jupiter."

That stopped Rosamund in her tracks. "What?"

"He's going to look awful in pictures later. You go apologize to him."

"No!"

Aunt Fergie gawked. "What?"

"I will not apologize to him! I acted in self-defense."

"You need to be the better person and turn the other cheek. Rosie! Rosie! I'm talking to you, where are you going?"

"Away from you." Rosamund rushed around the corner of the lodge. She didn't look back. She didn't want Fergie to see her crying. Why didn't her family care about her—or justice?

She rounded the corner toward the front porch and came face to face with Jupiter. His nose had indeed swollen up, all red and purple and quite horrible for photography.

"You!" he yelled.

Rosamund screamed and ran for her life. Feet pounded on the earth behind her.

"Rosamund!" yelled Aunt Fergie. "Jupiter, leave her alone, you both come here and—"

She entered the woods, Jupiter hot on her heels. "I'm going to kill you," he roared.

She didn't look back. She didn't dare, not with roots and uneven ground underfoot. She had to outrun him, she had to.

She feared him more than she feared the kelpie.

Rosamund's lungs and legs burned as she ran and ran, up and down slopes, catching herself by a hand as she stumbled more than once. Sweat kept sliding her glasses halfway down her nose. Finally, she saw the stream! She'd made it! She hopped on stepping stones across the water and flung herself behind a bush that overgrew the trail.

Only then did she look back through the veil of branches. Jupiter was at the top of the rise, moving at a sluggish jog. Rosamund did her utmost to quiet her own ragged panting, her heartbeat as loud as a marching band in her ears.

Soundless, the kelpie emerged from the foliage. On the far side of the creek, he dropped to the ground with a dramatic grunt, his strange hooves angled toward Rosamund.

Jupiter's face was ruddy with exertion and hate, but when he saw the horse, wonderment softened his expression.

"A horse! What's a horse doing out here?" he voiced aloud.

Rosamund had a horrible thought—what if he threw rocks at the kelpie? She grabbed a fistful of stones so she could act in the creature's defense.

"Hey there. Shh, shh. It's okay." Jupiter moved within feet of the kelpie. "I wish I had an apple or something. You're not hurt, are you? Here." He pulled a long blue handkerchief from his pocket. How weird were people in Massachusetts, to actually carry handkerchiefs in the 21st century? "Here, let me tie this around your head—I hope it reaches—then back at camp I can make you a halter, and—"

He touched the kelpie and he screamed.

The kelpie surged upright, spinning in place with a harsh squeal. Jupiter spun, too, the entirety of his hand stuck to the kelpie's neck. The kelpie's momentum jerked Jupiter around like a doll, both of his legs lifting off the ground. Rosamund had a glimpse of Jupiter's mouth gaped in speechless horror, and then the kelpie lunged back into the stream with a violent splash. The water couldn't have been deep enough to immerse the kelpie, but in an instant, equine and boy were gone.

The blue handkerchief floated to rest in the trail.

Gone. Jupiter was gone. Sheer relief left her stupefied. The stones she had gathered fell from her limp hand. She didn't need to exist in terror the rest of the weekend. Body curved, face to her knees, she sobbed.

After a few minutes she straightened, sniffling. Wiping her glasses dry, she trudged back to Camp Carraway.

✧

The rest of the afternoon was pretty good, really. Rosamund didn't want to have much to do with her family and the feeling was mutual, so she resorted to volunteering in the kitchen. Aunt Fergie wasn't there, thank goodness, and Rosamund instead worked under a steely-eyed aunt who didn't care what Rosamund had done earlier so long as the dishes and food prep were completed now.

The work kept her hands and mind busy so she didn't think about what had happened in the woods. Not constantly, anyway.

Had she really talked to an honest-to-goodness kelpie? Had the murder-horse really dragged Jupiter off to Fairyland? The whole thing felt unreal, like something she'd imagined to ward off boredom, except that Jupiter was gone.

Which, eventually, other people noticed, too.

"Have you seen Jupiter?" Grandma leaned over the Dutch door from the main room.

"Not since he chased me into the woods threatening to kill me. I outran him," she said, voice level.

Grandma stared for a moment, then left.

Like fifteen minutes later, Fergie came around. "Has anyone seen Jupiter?"

"You saw him chase me." Resentment bled into her tone.

Fergie began to pull away, then paused. "Did he hurt you?"

"No, but only because I outran him. He said he was going to kill me."

Aunt Fergie acted like she was going to speak, but turned away in silence.

Rosamund blinked back tears as she stirred dry French onion mix into a tub of sour cream as big as her head. Jupiter would've gotten away with whatever he tried to do to her. She had defended herself. Just as Mom had advised, she'd done what she needed to do in order to survive.

As dusk neared, the questions became incessant. *Where is Jupiter? Had anyone seen Jupiter?* Rosamund helped serve up supper, but few people ate. Most of the adults split into search parties.

Night fell. The sheriff's department arrived.

Patrol cars filled the parking lot, the colorful spinning lights casting strange shadows. Rosamund was questioned by deputies on the front porch of the lodge. She told the truth, up to a point.

Mom stood by her the whole time. When the deputies moved on, murmuring amongst themselves about more searchers and flashlights and dogs, Mom rubbed her face and sighed.

"I can't believe this. Why'd you have to be the last one seen with him?"

Rosamund felt a strange hollowness inside. "I didn't ask for him to … to fixate on me. I didn't want to be here at all!"

"Don't even start on that again. I need to go check on my sister." Mom's hand glanced Rosamund's arm as she turned away.

Rosamund's attention went to a big white van parking behind some patrol cars. She needed a moment to recognize the logo of a coastal news station.

The porch creaked as footsteps came up beside her. She greeted Uncle Terence with a nod. "The news is here."

"Other channels will probably show up, too." He rubbed his face with his knuckles. He held a flashlight the size of his thumb. "How're you doing?"

She shrugged.

"Are people giving you a hard time?"

"The cops talked to me. In a few minutes I'm supposed to show them where I last saw Jupiter." She wished she could go right now.

"I mean the family. Has anyone … ?"

"They're staying away from me. Which is nice, really."

He shifted in discomfort. "They should support you more. This is hard on everyone."

Was it, though? Rosamund knew she should feel bad for the grief her family was going through, and would go through, but she didn't. But she didn't feel triumphant or—what was the German word she had in vocab last year? Oh, schadenfreude. No, she wasn't experiencing that, either.

"Uncle Terence, what happens if they don't find Jupiter tonight?" she asked, though she had a hunch already.

"More searchers will come. People on horseback, helicopters. They'll keep looking for him."

"And if they don't find him soon?"

Terence faced her, blue and red light painting his skin. "Posters will go up all around here, and nationwide. Lots of people would keep an eye out for him."

Her family would keep an eye out for him—and a wary eye on her, too. She'd been a weirdo to them before today, and now, she'd be another vocabulary word: a pariah.

She didn't belong in this family. In this world.

"Will you come with me into the woods, instead of Mom?" Rosamund asked.

"I'll ask her."

A short while later, the deputies assembled their posse, and Rosamund led everyone down the path. Full night had fallen, but everyone had a flashlight to illuminate the way.

"What a mess this is," a deputy muttered to another guy. Their radios crackled with static and voices. "Rich out-of-staters, losing their kid in this terrain. Media will be on us like flies for weeks."

"Kid has it all going on, too," said another. "He competes in horse shows, volunteers at his stable, teaches kids with cancer how to ride."

"Christ. Reporters will lap that up."

So, Jupiter liked horses. That's why he hadn't tried to throw rocks at the kelpie as she expected. That didn't undo what he had done to her, though—and what he would have done next.

Resentment pushed more urgency into her stride. She had craved justice, and instead, his abuse toward her would mean even less now. Her family and the news reporters would make Jupiter out to be a saint.

The search dogs behind her began to whine.

Rosamund's flashlight beam passed over a brilliant patch of blue. "Stop!" she said. "That's Jupiter's."

"Don't touch anything!" snapped a lead deputy. "Show us where you hid, Rosamund."

She and Terence crossed the creek as she pointed and answered a few more questions. The canine handlers wrestled with their dogs but couldn't get them nearer to the creek. Two of them broke free, and yelping all the while, ran back toward camp as if their tails were on fire.

They sensed the kelpie or the portal. Maybe both. Maybe other things, too.

Rosamund used the distraction to sidle around a bush and closer to the creek. In her flashlight beam, the water resembled rippled black silk, not unlike the kelpie's mane and tail.

She clicked off her flashlight and reached into darkness, her vision still dappled by residual light.

Even though she expected to find water, the sheer cold jolted a gasp from her, but she stayed put. Waiting.

"Rosamund, what are you doing?" Terence said, his voice low.

"Washing my hand." The lie came easily. She couldn't tell Terence that she had wanted him here because, of all of her relatives, he might possibly be the one who could comprehend what happened if she vanished right now.

But nothing happened beyond her fingertips going numb with cold. She had kinda expected it, but was disappointed all the same.

Her family thought she was a *bad guy*, but Rosamund knew she wasn't. Even the kelpie wasn't entirely awful. He was like a bear, hungry, doing what he was supposed to do. He had nuance.

So did she.

Rosamund stood, drying her fingers on her stained jacket. The kelpie wouldn't come now. There were too many people. There would be more chances, though. Her family would return here to mourn Jupiter. She would come back to the creek. She'd already read a lot of mythology books, and now she'd read even more. There were other portals out there, other gatekeepers. She'd find magic again. Maybe she'd end up getting eaten. Maybe not.

If she made it through and Jupiter was there somewhere—well, she'd outwitted him once. She could do it again.

A slight breeze rustled the leaves around her, and at last, she caught the merest whiff of ocean. She smiled.

"Rosamund?" Uncle Terence asked, worry in his voice.

Oh, that's right. She shouldn't smile; not here, not now. She was athe good guy. "Do you think we can go back now? I'm tired."

He looked at the spot where the kelpie had been, as if he, too, had expected someone—something else—to be there. He hesitated, maybe realizing in that moment that the world is not so black and white, and said, "I'll ask, sure."

As he approached the deputies, she turned. In the dimness, something red amid the branches caught her eye. A shred of a balloon. She rubbed the nylon between her fingers then discreetly tucked it into her pocket. The local wildlife would be a little safer now.

Alone, she breathed in the ocean air as she smiled into the darkness.

Copyright © 2023 by Beth Cato.

Tatsiana Zamirovskaya is a writer from Belarus, who moved to Brooklyn in 2015. She writes metaphysical and socially charged fiction about memory, ghosts, hybrid identities, and borders between empires and languages. Tatsiana is the author of 3 short story collections and a novel about digital resurrection, The Deadnet, *which was published in 2021 in Moscow, receiving great critical acclaim. She is also a journalist and essayist, writing about art, traumatic memories, dictatorships and dreams.*

Born in Moscow, Julia Meitov Hersey moved to Boston at the age of nineteen and has been straddling the two cultures ever since. She spends her days juggling a full-time job and her beloved translation projects. Julia is a recipient of the Rosetta Science Fiction and Fantasy Award for Best Translated Work, long form (2021).

THE LAND OF PERMUTATIONS

by Tatsiana Zamirovskaya
translated by Julia Meitov Hersey

A terrible rumbling noise woke us up at nine in the morning.

It was the field—our field.

We took off as soon as we heard it, obviously, because it was our field. Everything that happened there was ours, and only ours. That's where Nielle and I met the brown earthen witch in her mushroom apothecary cap. That's where, breathless with terror, I summoned the White Dog on the fifth moonrise, and the Dog came, and brought us ten-day-old pups in a basket, just for cuddles. Every day these pups, blind and sweetly hairless like dandelions after a storm, grew thinner, their skin more pink and transparent, until on the tenth day they morphed into a pile of quietly wiggling skin bubbles, and then the White Dog came and took them back into her womb. That's where Nielle dug a grave for the forest devil and did such a great job that, when the forest devil died, he came and lay in his new grave because he had no other refuge, no other place to go. That's where we searched for the meat fern flower on a July night, and eventually we found it and put it under Uncle Volodya's pillow. The next morning he won the lottery—a three-room apartment somewhere on the outskirts of our town. He stays in that apartment drinking day and night, and now we know we should have put that flower under his ex-wife's pillow, not his. It was our field, our feral, bloody, boggy, alive land, and our hair sat within it, and the amber half moons of our nails, our incantations, and the summer rhymes we composed for Death. (It was Nielle's idea to write special verses for Death so She would stop by the edge of the field and listen for a moment. The verses were to have these special white spots, flickering agony, arrhythmical Cheyne-Stokes rattle, pools of cloudy morning water in lamb hooves, an attentive stare of a bewitched snipe at sundown—we couldn't break the spell, but at least we tried.)

And now this field burned, rumbled, and rolled back and forth as if God was trying to wrap it like a tortilla. Horrified, I stared out of the window, my hands pressed against my ears, and Nielle jumped up and down, screeching:

"Ourfieldourfieldourfield!"

"Justasecondago, literallyjustthismoment!"

None of the grown-ups were home. Everyone had gone to an air show in town, and a fighter jet had just crashed on our field.

Lelya and Katerina came down the stairs.

"It's a fighter jet," Katerina said. "I know all about fighter jets. I saw it crashing down, burning. I felt a little bit like I made it crash, just by looking at it."

Still blinking sleepily, Lelya pulled on her tennis shoes and put her soft baby-bird puppy weight against the door.

We ran to our field to see what was left of it. The field hummed and burned, and not a piece of it was left unharmed. The adults hadn't returned yet. We were there first. Lelya proposed getting closer to look for survivors; she had seen this on the news—planes would go down and people would simply lie on the field like little puddles, but what if on our field they would turn up alive? Katerina said that if it really were a fighter jet, there would be only one person, the pilot. No passengers. Then Nielle proposed to look for the pilot and we walked over to the fire, super-super close. It was really hot, even a few hundred feet away from this burning strudel, but still we decided to come closer.

On our way we found a handful of strange objects: a piece of parchment with a leather fringe, empty bottles (shells or bombs?), an armchair, unbroken, the color of fresh grass, and a stuffed teddy bear (Lelya wanted to pick it up, but Nielle grabbed her by her small pudgy elbow, hurting her and making her drop the toy).

At first, we figured the pilot catapulted himself, but he hadn't. Instead, he was lying inside the catapult itself, tightly buttoned inside some sort of a leather cocoon, and when Nielle undid the buttons and looked inside, she said immediately:

"This is for us."

We peeked inside the cocoon and knew right away: yes, it was definitely meant for us.

The pilot was covered in blood, milk, and some kind of melting roots; he was artistically arranged inside the cocoon like a scrumptious restaurant dish.

We could see the grown-ups gathering in the distance; somewhere very far a helicopter made an efficient military noise. Any minute now they would all descend upon our field and start taking care of things.

"Let Lelya take the cocoon, it probably provides nutritional support," Nielle ordered, freeing up the pilot and grabbing him by the leg. Katerina took his other leg, and I picked up his round head, coarse like a dog's, and wrapped it in his jacket to hide his face. The pilot was light and dry like a bag of burned grass, and yet, as we dragged him along, he left a trail, slippery and limpid, like a giant water slug.

"To the cellar!" Nielle shouted when we made it back home. I let go of his head; it knocked dully against a dirt step, and the pilot said, "Ah."

"He's hurt," Nielle said. "But it's all right, the most important thing is to get him in, then we can bandage whatever it is."

We slammed the cellar door shut and arranged the pilot among the jars of grandma's pickles and jellies from 2006. Little Lelya spread the cocoon that immediately turned plaid like a blanket; everything happened too fast, literally in five minutes, and no one had a chance to understand anything or to get scared.

"Well," Katerina said, exhaling. "I am going upstairs, the fire engines have arrived."

Nielle began to move her hands around the pilot's midsection: that's where she expected to find a regeneration device and a black box that recorded everything that happened to the pilot *before the crash*. She explained to us that after the crash everything was erased because in this situation no one cares about the life before.

Locating the slippery box covered in something like egg yolk, Nielle wiped it on the hem of Lelya's dress, making her squeal, and twisted off the lid. Ten seconds later she was already plunging a sonorous steel miniature syringe into the pilot's forearm.

"That's how they always do it," she explained to Lelya and me. "He might come to eventually. We also need milk, but only after the cat drinks it, make sure the cat drinks a bit of it first. Lelya, why don't you run upstairs."

Lelya and I ran upstairs together. When we peeked out the window, a large crowd had already gathered at the crash site. An emergency aircraft carrier trudged along the narrow country road, groaning and snagging on the rusty fences with its chrome levers. A black cloud of oily smoke stretched as far as the river. The sun was high. It was a perfect day for swimming.

Lelya's daddy came home with a bag of cold morning fish. He forbade us to leave the house. He said things were all topsy-turvy, everything was on fire, the accident was horrible, don't go anywhere, stay home. Lelya took the bag of fish from him and asked when the rest of the grown-ups were coming home, but he flapped his arms in response: go, go to your rooms, all the roads are still blocked, no one can get home, it's unbelievable, such a terrible event, we're lucky he didn't crash on top of our house, they say he tried to lead it as far away as possible, and he managed to lead it away, but he himself didn't make it.

Lelya was picking the quietest and most obedient fish from the bag; still holding the fish in her hand, she suddenly froze and opened her lips to object—he did make it! He did!—but out of nowhere Nielle's slender fingers closed on the thin mouth of the fish, and Lelya's teeth seemed to clamp up.

"If we can't go outside, we'll play in the cellar," Nielle said smiling. Meanwhile, from under the table, I watched the cat lap up the milk—slowly, as if in a trance. After two endless minutes, I pushed the cat away with a slipper, picked up the bowl of milk, and stepped toward the stairs. Outside our window, shells exploded, and currant bushes went up in smoke, and the rescue helicopter rumbled, destined for failure—on our field no one has ever managed to save anyone, ever.

Except for us, and, to be honest, not from us either.

For the first three days, the pilot didn't feel all that great: he wallowed in different corners of the cellar simultaneously, a few times he appeared to be a mound of construction foam, no trace of his face at all, but Nielle assured us that it could be seen while he was drinking his milk through a straw. He still had no lips, that accident was pretty horrible, but we inserted a straw into one of the holes in his skull, and the milk disappeared, and that meant the pilot was drinking it.

Having returned from the town, the grown-ups drank wine and watched television, lamenting the terrible tragedy, and talking about how he barely managed to lead the plane away from the village, and how no one really knew what happened, some sort of an explosion, such an awful thing to have occurred, he was so young, only thirty three, and if he had jumped out, he would have crashed on top of the houses, and everyone would have died, literally everyone, he saved the children, such a saint, a real saint for sure.

Smirking, we drank our milk. Because in reality, *it was us who saved him.*

Outside the window, our scorched field gaped in black, and the mild marsh birds would mourn their unborn sons in the night, swaying on the charred bushes. Katerina would put aside her glass of wine (at fourteen, she was allowed an occasional drink with the grown-ups), and with a bored look on her face, would go to the cellar "for the jellies."

Of course we should have told our parents that *we saved the pilot,* but the pilot was still in pretty bad shape, he must have spoiled a bit while he was falling, and we had decided we were going to wait until he gets better, and then we'd tell them, we'd definitely tell them right away. If the grown-ups found out we stole the pilot from the field, we'd be in a lot of trouble. If he had been in decent shape to begin with, we'd tell them immediately. But we knew that the grown-ups would think he was like this because of us. We simply had to nurse him back to health.

In the night, Nielle and I went to the scorched field and sniffed the black grass, looking for the one that would give the pilot back his memory of flying into our field like a boiling meteorite. Little Lelya took sugar lumps to the little village cemetery where giant black ants lived. She placed the sugar on the rocks and waited until the ants filled the sweet lumps with their revitalizing earthen acid. That was the only candy the pilot could eat. I summoned the White Dog with grandma's kerchief, a duck egg, and a snake skin, and the White Dog came and let me milk her. I got a half a cup of grayish, opaque liquid tinted mother-of-pearl, from which Nielle made a tiny wheel of cheese. The pilot ate the cheese and moaned, and blood poured out of his eyes and lips, and that's how we got to see his mouth, full of strong bone teeth, and his eyes, greenish-brown like autumn rocks.

Lelya dug up tiny secret treasures with last year's flowers and dried up insects pressed under pieces of glass, and we placed them onto the pilot's forehead, the soil side down. As the soil sunk in, the flowers would wake up and begin to bloom around his face, and his forehead would revive, too, and skin would go from waxy parchment to luminous honey. We used the leftover glass to draw blood from our arms and leave messages on the floor, because when the pilot's eyes bled, he could only see and read what was written in red.

"The field you crashed on belongs to us. That means you belong to us, too," Nielle wrote.

"I am Lelya," that's what little Lelya carved right on her wrist with a shard of glass, wincing from her very first cognizant pain.

"How old were you?" Katerina wrote.

I used my blood to draw a plane on my left palm.

He grabbed my hand and pressed it to his cheek. It was so unexpected that I burst out crying and couldn't stop crying all night, and the grown-ups said it was because of that terrible crash, because we saw everything with our own eyes, and how horrible it was, and how they wished that someone would clean the debris already and figure out what actually happened. I was given hot milk with some calming herbs, and as I drank it, burning and scorching my insides, I noticed how coldly Lelya was staring at me, Lelya who had to wear a long-sleeved blouse on a hot summer day to hide the cuts on her arms.

The grown-ups keep talking about how frightening it was, about conducting the investigation, about both engines failing at once—how could it have happened? They fall silent, nervously looking at us, then insincerely jumping to other topics: paper doilies, newspaper dailies, and jams and jellies ... Wait, what? Jellies?

"We set up a clubhouse in the cellar, but we're going to clean it up after," Nielle says, pressing her foot onto mine. "If you need some of that stupid strawberry stuff, I'll bring it up."

A clubhouse is a sacred thing. That's how it works: if we set up a clubhouse, grown-ups avoid the space, and we clean everything up once we're done. That's how it was with the attic and with the mice kingdom, they trust us; we never lie, and we wouldn't have lied about the pilot either, if only he was getting better, at least a little bit, because how could we show them this, there is nothing to show just yet.

Meanwhile, the pilot is getting his face back: it's all scarred, pitted with hoof prints, marsh water melting in tiny grooves. For the groove to heal, you need live flesh. To revive the flesh, you need to get a little bit of mutton from the pilaf, take it to the field, find a suitable lamb hoof print with morning water and put the lamb inside (yesterday's water won't do, so you've got to go right after it rains), summon the White Dog with three duck eggs and a piece of Grasshopper candy and ask her to pee into the hoof print. The lamb will grow into the hoof print and then you can cut it out carefully, just don't cut the soil around it; you can cut the meat, but not the earth. And only then you can place it whenever the pilot is missing pieces. When it takes, the pilot stops moaning, and sometimes he even tries to sit up or say something. When it doesn't take, we have to cut it out immediately and put it back into the pilaf. The pilaf doesn't care, and the grown-ups will be fine, nothing will happen to them, because all the meat in the pilaf is the meat that didn't take.

To ensure the pilot manifests as a man, not as a woman, Nielle wraps him into dirty shirts stolen from Uncle Volodya's; but first, she soaks them in the extract of cat fur. We have plenty of fur because the cat regularly vomits gray fur balls. The pilot absorbs the shirts completely—as they soak with sweat, they become something like his new post-burn skin, and five or six shirts later, the pilot no longer looks terrifying, his burns fade away, and this is almost like a real body, and it's almost like a real life, but it's still *too early* for the grown-ups.

In the evenings Nielle reads to the pilot from her "Elves of the Silver River" series. We had been a bit overwhelmed by her rampant graphorrhea, and so at first we rejoiced that all those splendid battle scenes were now directed toward the pilot, but then we realized—when he started talking—that he now drew his vocabulary from Nielle's epic. We figured this out one evening when he—for the first time!—picked up a cup of tisane made with dried fruit and ephemerid fireflies whose limpid bodies covered the cellar floor. We collected them on the tenth moon day. It was Lelya who brought him the tisane, and when he drank it all by himself, she got all discombobulated, dropped the cup, and laughed awkwardly, and that's when he said:

"The power you are given is not the power you are using."

It was his first coherent sentence. Lelya was thrilled that this sentence was addressed to her, but the contents were clearly Nielle's influence. We immediately banned her from reading her elven stories to the pilot, especially since he'd already declared that his name was Sillemalle of the Valley of Steel Thorns, which was pure nonsense, obviously, it wasn't his name, but what it actually was—that was a good question. For that, we needed to resurrect the pilot's memory.

We'd resurrect his memory, and then tell the grown-ups right away—that's what we had decided. Until then, we'd drag these heavy glass jars of jellies up and down the stairs by ourselves.

We put another padlock on the cellar door and took shifts every night. He had to be fed at night, on schedule, like a baby bird. His food had to be alive so we resurrected some tiny fish flies, and the double yolks of our biggest Friday eggs, and one time we even managed to reanimate a whole fish.

Eating all this live food made the pilot feel better. He now looked like someone who was recovering from an illness the name of which none of us ever mentioned but all of us knew, of course. Different stuff happened during different shifts. Nielle told us that when she went into the cellar, she saw a hedgehog sitting on his chest. Cats sit where it hurts, and hedgehogs sit where it doesn't hurt, everyone knows that. Did that mean his soul didn't hurt? Lelya assured us he did feel some sort of longing: he asked her for a piece of paper to write a letter to his family, but he couldn't recall his first or last name, or what happened to him, or any of his relatives. All he could come up with was "a letter to his family." He moaned—all these terrible sounds, "nnnn, me-me-mine,"—and beat his head against the three-liter glass jar of pickles from last September, and the jar rang out like a church bell. He asked me for a cake of red flour so he could go home. That was exactly what he said: this is for me so I can go home. Where his home was, he couldn't say.

Of course, we went to our field and gathered some red wheat, but the investigators chased us away. They are combing through the field with their dogs, looking for some boxes, some evidence. They won't find anything. We only got a little of the red wheat, a matchbox's worth of it, and Nielle said we shouldn't bake anything yet, he might remember stuff without it. And when he does remember, we'll tell the grown-ups, and they will take him home, and to think of how happy everyone would be, they must be really missing him.

To make him remember, we sent a shell-less slug back and forth across his body three times; we made a memory pudding (the last time we made it for Katerina's grandmother when she started confusing our names, and it worked even though we used regular cow fat, not the elk one). We summoned the Hare Queen right there in the cellar (three empty quail eggs, a toad dried in the summer sun, the Gomel Girl candy bar, two playing cards, both of clubs, all woven together with a green thread), and the Queen interviewed him and even got some answers, but never gave us the recording. She walked away with the recorder, crashing the shells with her steel hooves on her way out.

He couldn't get up just yet but was already crawling around the cellar; Katerina called him Joseph, which annoyed us to no end. Once when we were giving him the six-mile water to awaken his memory, as dry as an old tree, he suddenly recalled that Joseph situation and said he didn't want Katerina to take any more night shifts.

Katerina cried in her room all the following week, and I took her shifts. The pilot and I tried to draw pictures to figure out who he really was. I took his hand into mine and moved the knife across the paper in the shape of a triangular roof: was that a house? The pilot ripped the paper and growled like a wounded animal: not house, not house! I asked, what shall we draw then? A balloon? A plane? A plane?

Every time I mentioned a plane, he'd start crying. His tears, salty and pungent like jars of pickles that served as his bed and his shelter, smelled of rain and sea, and Katerina would catch that sharp, savory scent, recoil, and hide in her room. After a while she simply stopped talking to me. The grown-ups whispered to each other, depression, challenging age, probably in love, it's about time, she's a teenager after all.

Lelya was the next one to fall in love. After one of her night shifts, she came back to the nursery shaking, pale-faced, scarlet spots on her cheeks—as if she were sprayed with blood, as if someone was beheaded right in front of her with a generous sweep of a steel blade.

"He … he asked," she said indignantly and began to weep, so desperately and so lustily that anyone would be heartbroken, and only our cynical Noelle wouldn't stop bugging her, jerking her, pinching her plump little elbow, and hissing: "Come on, tell us, tell us, what did he ask for, what?"

"He asked me to write a letter," Lelya sniffled, still trembling and still wailing. "A letter to his wife … he asked me to write a letter to his wife! That's what he wanted! That's what it is! He has a wife!"

Freeing herself from Nielle's pinching, vicious embrace, Lelya collapsed on her enormous pink, pony-covered pillow.

Nielle looked at me in despair. "Who could have thought the baby would be so impressionable," her eyes said to me. "We shouldn't have let her scratch her arms with a shard of glass," my eyes responded. Nielle and I did not need words to communicate. And now staring into each other's eyes, we felt Lelya's pink pillow fill to the brim with her watery tears, pungent and translucent like rose water.

Lelya was so upset that she flatly refused to attend to any of her shifts, so we ended up pulling Katerina back in. By then the pilot had forgotten how she had offended him, and they became fast friends. When the pilot asked Katerina to write a letter to his wife and tell her not to worry about him, Katerina would raise an eyebrow in agreement and walk away, her skirt rustling. She'd bring back some rough packing paper, lick the tip of her pencil, and gaze at the pilot questioningly: well? What's her name? Anya? Lena? Yulia? Dasha? Perhaps, Irina?

"I don't remember," the pilot wept, his tears thick and oily, like candle fat (these were his special Katerina tears, he had a different kind for each of us). "I remember—darling but who? My sweet little bunny but why? A person but how? I had a wife, I remember the wife."

"Kapitolina?" Katerina asked, smirking. "Vasilisa?"

The pilot smeared tears and grease over his fresh, beardless baby face. Katerina smelled like grease all the time now, and eventually she began smelling of alcohol: the pilot asked for a drink, and she stole the grown-ups' alcohol, as if she were under his spell, and later she began drinking with him to help him remember. And he did remember, at least some war stories, not that any of them were relevant. In time they managed to write about five letters to the pilot's wives, but then it turned out those were the wrong wives, or rather the wrong lives because the pilot kept recalling *something not quite right*. Like an old broken radio, he kept catching someone else's epochs, some foreign times, tuning into the soft false rattle of something long lived-through and long forgotten by his secret teachers who went up in flames a good hundred years before he himself was set on fire.

He didn't remember burning *this time* either. All the previous occasions had been more or less recollected and analyzed, but not this one. Alcohol did not help, and neither did Nielle's soft herbal spells, even though the clever girl quickly realized that the memory revival process took our new friend down the wrong path. The spells did not help, and even our inconspicuous, almost secret friendship—and I am sure it was friendship and nothing more—led nowhere but to failure, an empty bottomless chasm.

"I remember the funeral," he said. "The military orchestra was playing, and people tossed candy everywhere, like at a wedding. All three wives followed the casket, as if it were a parade. But only one of them pinned the medals when it was time, only one fell face first into the medals, when the music ended, only one. What was her name? Galya? Galina?"

"Don't force the memory," I told him. "It's not the right one, it's not yours. It happened to me, too. I was buried a thousand times, with music and without. Once they simply wrapped me in a white shirt and sent me along the river. And once they burned me with the cats at a white stake. But I don't recall any of this, none of the names of those whose souls had burned in my last fire, I don't want to remember any of that because in this life my name is Nadya, and I've only been around for thirteen years, and all I remember is our field, our games, and I remember the plane, I do remember the plane. The plane."

Every time I mention the plane, he grabs my hand and trembles, weeping desperately. Maybe that's why I talk about the plane so often. Especially since my entire life has been condensed to that plane—there was nothing before the plane, and everything that happened after the plane is no one's business, except him and me.

However, Nielle was convinced it was her business as well. That Sunday I saw her playing with those wooden dragons the pilot had carved for her (I saw wood shavings in the cellar), I got so mad as if she wasn't my sister, a princess, a battle witch, and my best friend.

"It's nothing," she bristled when she detected anger in my gaze. "He simply wanted to please me."

I said the pilot had to *get better*, not waste his time pleasing us. Then she said I myself have forgotten why we brought him here, and that she saw me caressing his face with my fingers, and she questioned my motives. Then I told her she should have a chat with Katerina about it because those two get wasted every night in the cellar, and who knows what really is going on there, and Katerina is walking around like a storm cloud, not talking to anyone and not answering any questions. Then Nielle said that I should pay more attention to Lelya, because none of us had actually seen Lelya in a while, and where was she, anyway? Did she walk to the field and grow into meat grass? Turn herself into a white heron? Because Lelya's heart was broken, by the way.

It turned out that Lelya and her broken heart went into town with the grown-ups, that's why we hadn't seen her in a few days. She came back on the weekend, looking older and slimmer, with trembling lips, and said to me and Nielle:

"I read the newspapers. And I know his name. I know what he used to be called. His name. But I won't tell you."

We shrugged. If she didn't want to tell us, it was her business.

Lelya then went down to the cellar; we assumed she told the pilot his name after all. It must have been her own tiny personal moment of triumph, the final victory of love over common sense. Upon hearing his name, the pilot tried to get up, as if someone called him from the distant shore. He twitched, collapsed, and hit his head on a gallon jar of tomato paste. That forced us into a unified front for a few hours while we ran back and forth with rags, towels, bandages, and crushed penicillin (since the pilot was nearly alive by then, we knew we'd better treat him with pills for regular live humans). But then it started up again: Katerina refused to tell us anything about drinking wine with the pilot two nights in a row. Stealing Nielle's CD player and all her Radiohead CDs, Lelya ran off to the river to cry. Nielle herself suddenly confessed to me that she'd never had a true soulmate, only the pilot and his goddamn dragons. She was no longer interested in our field; the dragons whispered different stories into her ear, different plots, and in the evenings she'd spend hours writing something secret and passionate in her green notebook, something that was meant strictly for those who fell to earth from the sky, and no one else.

When all four of us went into the cellar to ask which one of us would be his wife, the pilot covered his head with his hands as if during shellfire and screamed. We got scared the grown-ups would hear the noise and ran out of the cellar.

After that we could only visit him one at a time. Gradually we realized that without these visits, our lives and our summer would soon turn into a never-ending absence and heart-wrenching nightmare. But for now, bloodthirsty mosquitoes still sang their tinny shanties, and grown-ups laughed on the veranda, shooing away bats, and my tipsy Daddy paddled around the toad pool, and neighborhood children shouted "Witch! Witch!" at Nielle when she went to buy bread at the mobile canteen. For now, she still squinted and pretended to shoot them from her index finger, each one directly into the left eye, and three years later they would know why, but by then it would be too late.

The pilot ate everything we brought, drank all the milk, and licked the lamb bones clean. Every now and then he'd moan and attempt to recall his name that he managed to forget once and for all for the second time when he hit his head on the jar of tomato paste. We wrote the letters he dictated to some non-existent relatives of his, and then we hid them from each other so vehemently as if we were these future relatives, five, ten, fifteen years later. Occasionally we'd mention him to each other: "Did he recall his name? No? Great, he really can't. If he ever recalls his name, we're all dead, summer's over." Since little Lelya knew his name and could cause some trouble, we simply banned her from the cellar by taking away her personal key with its cute purple owl keychain, no matter how much she howled and scratched like a wild beastie caught in a trap.

As the summer was winding down, his wife came to our field. She placed some flowers on the ground and walked back and forth, taking deep breaths. Then she simply stood there, sniffing the air like an animal, her nostrils trembling. All the metal scraps had by then been taken away, and all that remained were holes in the ground and scorched soil. We stood nearby quietly, trying not to give ourselves away. The wife fell onto the red soil and rolled around on it like a flame fox; she'd pick up the soil and eat it. We watched her in silence.

"So sad, how very sad," the grown-ups whispered, leading her away.

Walking by us, the wife stops, grabs Nielle's chin with her bloody soil-covered fingers, and says:

"Give him back to me."

Nielle shrieks, jerks herself free, and gallops toward the forest like a fawn.

"She's mad with grief," the grown-ups tell us. "Please don't be afraid. It's so very sad, he was burned alive, because he wanted you to live, because he led the plane away from your house, do you understand? Don't cry, please don't cry."

Lelya cries and refuses to calm down. Mom puts her arms around her and leads her back in. Lelya is a sly fox. She does not weep out of pity for this woman; she weeps because we took her key.

When I go down to the cellar, the pilot is lying down, reading The Two Captains.

"If I told you that up there, in the real world, there is a woman who insists that you are her husband, would that change anything for you?" I ask.

"I had a wife, but I don't remember anything," the pilot says. "So what's the difference—it can be anyone, anyone at all."

"Does it mean you'll stay here with us forever?" I ask.

"No," he says. "I am strong enough now. When I feel that I can stand firmly on my own two feet, I will have to leave. I need to go home. I want to go home."

"You're still too weak," I say, and my voice breaks.

"I need a cake baked with red flour," he insists.

✲

We don't want to let him go, but he keeps asking for that bloody cake and says he wants to go home.

✲

That same evening his wife came to our house. Katerina opened the door, and his wife attacked her, pulling Katerina's hair and screaming: you slept with him, you slept with him!

Somehow the grown-ups managed to pull her off. They keep apologizing: she's mad, just think of how tragic it is, forgive her, have pity on her, she came to the place where he died, she's clearly lost it, so very sad, she's leaving soon.

But his wife didn't leave. The very next morning she was back, pale and calm, and offered her apology. She asked the grown-ups to leave the room. I want to talk with your children, tell them something important, she said.

"I know you have him," she told us. "Don't ask me how I know. Where are you hiding him? Please give him back to me. He's mine. You may think he belongs to you, and that's perfectly normal. It happens. But it's not true. The one that belongs to you hasn't happened yet. Yours will happen someday. Give me mine and go on."

"You are sick in the head," Katerina said, sniffling. "You need a doctor."

"You shouldn't call people 'mine' or 'yours,'" Lelya babbled. "It's just wrong, it's arrogant, and it has nothing to do with age. What's the difference if you're a grown-up and we're still children? No one belongs to anyone. How do you know who's yours and who's not yours? And what if before you showed up, I thought someone is mine and only later I found out he's yours—what does that really change?"

"Lelya needs a head doctor, too," Nielle said smiling. "But you don't, not really. You're just tired. You had a terrible thing happen, and I am really sorry. I realize that you believe that we're guilty of something, since we were there first, and we saw everything. Perhaps you think that if he didn't try to lead his plane away from the houses to the field, he'd have time to catapult himself and then he'd still be alive—and perhaps it seems unfair to you that we survived, that we're living instead of him. But we can't change anything, don't you see? We are so grateful to him, I mean if it weren't for him, we wouldn't be here right now. And that's why you think he's with us, as if we were hiding him somewhere. His life turned into four of ours—he's inside each one of us. We can't give him back to you, just like we can't give you our lives or our souls. Perhaps, there is a tiny part of his soul in each one of us."

At that moment I realized how much I admired her.

Nielle stepped closer to our pilot's wife and embraced her. Everyone breathed a sigh of relief. His wife cried a little on Nielle's shoulder, then lifted her head and said, her voice unexpectedly spiteful:

"So where is he? Are you going to give him back to me?"

Our eyes met, and I felt uneasy. Somehow she knew everything, damn her, she just *knew*.

When the grown-ups returned, we told them that the pilot's wife was truly mad, and that, aside from everything else, she had insulted our little Lelya, told her all sorts of mean things. This explained why Lelya looked puffy with tears all the time. The pilot's wife was taken away in a special white automobile. Nielle and I waited until midnight, then went down to the cellar to bring the pilot freshly baked buns and a pitcher of milk.

He drank and ate greedily, like a prisoner of war, and then he sat up, stretched, cracked his joints, and got up very slowly.

"Not bad!" he said. "A little light-headed, but otherwise not bad at all. I can go now. I remember where I'm flying to now. I'm flying home. It's time. It's almost autumn."

"But you don't even remember your own name," I said.

"I don't," he agreed. "But I remember where my home is now. That's where I'm going before it's too late. It's fine now, I can make it. It won't be like the last time."

"What happened last time?" I asked.

Nielle hissed into my ear: "Idiot, *we happened last time!*"

Shortly after three in the morning, at sunrise, we led him out of the cellar, tiptoed through the sleeping house, and closed the squeaky front door, without shutting it all the way.

A tiny new plane was waiting in the middle of the field. The plane reminded me of something, either films or dreams.

"You didn't say goodbye to Katerina and Lelya," Nielle said sternly. "That's not right."

The pilot considered her words.

"Katerina would try to make me stay," he said. "It's probably for the best. And Lelya is still too little."

"We're little, too, so what?" Nielle said angrily. "But we saved you, all of us together. It's not fair."

The pilot did not respond. Perhaps, *we simply didn't know everything.*

At the edge of the field he took us into his arms, first her, then me. I've never been embraced by a man before, and so I tried to commit it to memory, every little detail, but I did not remember anything at all, because I didn't know if it had really happened.

"That's it, you cannot go any further," he said and walked toward the smoky, luminous, sunrise plane.

We stood still, watching him leave, knowing that neither one of us would ever admit to anything.

"Freshly baked buns to go with the milk, huh?" I asked, when, soaked up to our waists with dew and tears, we approached the house.

"Mmhmm," Nielle said. "That red wheat in a matchbox I always carried with me. I couldn't bear it any longer. I felt so sorry for him."

"But not sorry for me? And what about you, aren't you sorry for yourself? We gave him everything, we saved him, we practically sewed him together from tiny little pieces! Don't you feel sorry about all the time we wasted on him? Don't you feel sorry about this summer?"

"I feel sorry for everyone," Nielle said. "And for the summer. But there will be others who will come for us. Others will be coming for us. And we'll have another summer. And here—I mean, you saw it yourself. And maybe there won't be anything else. Either way, we had to let him go."

Katerina and Lelya had been waiting for us, two grim, pensive figures on the porch. Nielle took a deep breath and put on her special samurai face. We had to explain everything to them somehow, although what could we possibly have said? He simply got better and flew away.

A few days later, the grown-ups whispered among themselves and announced that the pilot's wife had left with him. They must have flown away together.

The grown-ups begged us not to be sad and not to take it personally. But there was nothing to be taken personally. She wanted us to let him go, and we let him go, and she, in some clever and well-executed way, joined him immediately. This artful escape into happiness had nothing to do with us. A personal tragedy seethed and gurgled inside each one of us, impossible, enormous, and quivering, like a parachute that failed to open. I experienced the loss of my only and possibly last best friend. Katerina mourned the memories of a perfect man. Little Lelya wept over her first true love. Meanwhile, Nielle perched on the windowsill amidst thick volumes and wooden dragons, scratching away in her notebooks.

"He's never going to read any of it," Katerina said, trying to get back at Nielle for baking that stupid cake.

"If I don't write it down, he might," Nielle said. "That's why I'm writing. It's the only way to get rid of him."

But by then it was clear we'd never get rid of him. The summer was almost over. We never went back to our field, not that summer, and not the next one. We knew that our boggy summer sorcery would never work again; growing up was that unpleasant price we had to pay for something we never managed to name with any of the existing words.

Plus, it was no longer *our field*.

Copyright © by Tatsiana Zamirovskaya. Translation copyright © 2023 by Julia Meitov Hersey.

Kary English is a Hugo and Astounding finalist whose work has been published by Galaxy's Edge, The Grantville Gazette, *Wordfire Press,* Writers of the Future, *and* Tor Nightfire.

THE INCONSISTENT HEART

by Kary English

Once upon a time in the spring of the world, a young man named Edwin set out to seek his fortune. Edwin's coat was thin and threadbare, and his boots were more patches than leather. His purse held only a few small coins, but his back was strong and his heart was pure, so off he went into the wide world with a pack over one shoulder and his bow over the other. He walked for several days until the fields gave way to wilder lands, and the road dwindled to a dusty track. On the eve of the seventh day, he came across a cottage of wattle and daub nestled against the edge of a dark forest.

Night was falling. A chill wind out of the east sliced through Edwin's coat like a scythe through wheat. His stomach rumbled, for he'd had nothing to eat or drink but water from a nearby stream. Warm firelight flickered through the cottage window, and when Edwin drew near, he could smell the cottager's supper cooking inside. Barley stew, he thought, and bannocks baking on the hearth. If Edwin had heard even half the tales about enchanted forests and the misadventures of widow's sons, he might have turned away from the cottage and slept on the cold ground instead.

But Edwin had heard none of the tales, so he pulled his ragged coat tighter around himself and tapped upon the door. When it opened, an old woman stood there, her hair white and her eyes clouded by age. The smell of food made Edwin feel faint. His mouth watered, and he clasped his hands together to hide their shaking. "Good eve to you, mother," said Edwin, for it was the proper thing to say. "For a bite of your bread and a night by your fire, I'll work all the 'morrow for you."

The old woman leaned closer. Her rheumy eyes lingered on Edwin's patched boots and threadbare coat. Finally, she spoke. "A good eve to ye, child. There be food and fire a'plenty if your hands show the truth of your words."

Edwin unclasped his hands. With a touch light as autumn leaves, she drew her fingers over Edwin's palms, feeling for the calluses formed by a life of good, honest work. Satisfied, she stood aside from the door and allowed Edwin to enter.

"These hands have known an axe, child. Rest here tonight, and on the morrow you'll chop wood for me until sun-high." If Edwin had heard even a quarter of the tales about bargains with strangers, he wouldn't have entered the woman's home nor eaten a single bite of her food. But he hadn't, so he thanked the woman and stepped across the threshold, leaving his bow in a corner by the door.

The old woman led him to a stool by the fire. She placed a bowl of stew into his hands and gave him a warm bannock for a sop. When Edwin finished the bowl, she gave him another.

That night, Edwin slept with his belly full. In the morning, he picked up an axe and began his work. Sun-high came and went, but Edwin's axe continued its arc. He had seen the old woman's meager woodpile, and he knew she'd be cold when winter came. For three whole days he cut and stacked the wood, piling it neatly against the walls of the cottage so the woman would not have far to walk in winter's snow.

Finally, when wood stacked higher than Edwin's shoulders lined three walls of the little cottage, Edwin laid the axe aside and asked the old woman's blessing.

"You've a strong back, child, and a good heart. You've done more than I asked, so I shall return your kindness." The woman brought forth a fine pair of boots wrapped in oiled muslin to ward off the dust. "My husband was a peddler who walked many leagues in these boots. I see long journeys in your future, my son. Take them and wear them in his memory."

The boots were sturdy and well-oiled, the leather thick but supple. Edwin drew them on, pleased that the fit was good.

"Now, my son, heed me well." The old woman lowered her voice and took Edwin's hand. She pulled him in close, so close that Edwin could see the green of the nearby forest reflected in her milky eyes.

"A sorceress lives in these woods," she whispered. "You must stay to the edge of the forest where the sunlight still touches the ground. When the trees grow thick and the shadows grow dark, she walks the forest paths searching for unwary travelers. If she finds you, she will kill you, so keep to the light and stay far from the dark places."

Edwin pulled his hand free, feeling quite unsettled. Then, remembering his manners, he thanked the old woman, who handed him the last of the bannocks wrapped in cloth and bid him farewell. If Edwin had heard even a single tale about the witch of the Felwood glade, he'd have turned around, walked straight home, and counted himself lucky all of his days.

But he hadn't, so when he saw the blue sky above and dappled sunlight on the path ahead, he thought it a fine day for travel. Edwin shouldered his pack and bow, flexed his ankles in his new boots and set off into the forest.

With each step he took, the trees grew larger and closer together. Their branches met overhead, and the very air took on a greenish tinge as more and more leaves blocked the sun. Birds shrilled above him, insects chirred, and black squirrels chased one another up and down the tree trunks. The forest smelled of moss and green wood, of cool earth and old leaves. Though the light had dimmed, the path was still clear. Edwin knew he had many hours of walking ahead of him so he forged ahead, cheered by the thought of fresh bannocks for supper.

He had gone just far enough to be hungry again when the sound of distant weeping reached his ears. Edwin looked around him. No one was nearby, and the sound was so faint that he was scarcely sure he'd heard it. Dusk was still hours away, so Edwin kept walking. With each step he took, the weeping grew louder and more piteous until Edwin felt his heart would break.

A winding trail branched off into the forest in the direction of the sound. Though Edwin remembered the old woman's words, his heart was moved, and he could not continue without knowing who could make so sad a sound. He turned away from the main path and followed the fainter trail.

Trees overshadowed the path, becoming deeper and closer together until no light reached the forest floor. The sound of the weeping was all around him. He peered into the shadows and saw nothing but trees and more trees, their trunks blending into one another in the dim light. Edwin closed his eyes. He listened as carefully as he could, turning this way and that, trying to find the source of the sound. Finally, he opened them again.

The sound was coming from his left, deep in the forest. Edwin looked down at his feet. A jumble of fallen leaves and broken sticks covered the ground, and the faint trail he'd been following could hardly be called a trail at all. If he left it, he would have to pick his way over ground where no foot had fallen for more than a hundred years.

Edwin held his breath. He took a step off the path, then another. He looked over his shoulder, and there was the path fading into the darkness beyond. He took hold of his courage and continued threading his way between trees, and over boulders and fallen logs. Just when the forest seemed its darkest, Edwin came upon a young woman weeping before a beautiful gilt mirror. Dark hair cascaded down her back. She wore a gown of forest green and sat upon the trunk of a fallen tree. She might have been lovely, but Edwin could not tell because her head was bowed and she wept into her hands.

The mirror, however, was more beautiful than Edwin had ever seen. It stood taller than a man and wider than Edwin's shoulders. The glass was spotted with age, but the surface still reflected the darkness of the trees against the coming night. The frame around the mirror had been ornately carved with a tumble of vines, flowers, birds, and beasts. Edwin felt that he could stare at it for days and still not see everything there was to be found in the frame.

He pulled his eyes away and regarded the maiden. "My lady," he said. "Why do you weep? Tell me, that I may help you."

The young woman lifted her head. Her green eyes were red and swollen with tears, and her cheeks and hands were wet. "Oh, sir," she said, "If you but look into the mirror you will see why I cry. My love lays dying, and I cannot help him."

Edwin took a closer look at the mirror. Yes, he could see it now. A young man lay in the shadows, half hidden by leaf litter. Blood dripped from his nose and mouth, and his chest heaved when he tried to draw breath. He wore a brocaded doublet of russet and gold over cream-colored sleeves. His hose were of the finest cream-colored wool, and boots of pale, golden leather covered his calves and his feet. Sandy brown hair fell over his eyes, and his skin was the color of gray ash.

Edwin reached out a hand and placed it against the mirror's surface. The glass felt cold, smooth and quite solid. He looked from the mirror back to the crying maiden.

"Kind traveler," said she. "We were drinking from the stream when the witch of the forest laid a terrible curse upon us. My love she has cast into the mirror, while I sit here, chained to its feet." At this, the young woman lifted her skirts to show a dainty ankle encircled by a black iron shackle connected to a chain that curved snake-like through the leaves until it ended at the mirror's feet.

"The witch has said that only death can free us. Please, traveler, I beg you to help us. Find a way to release my love from this accursed mirror." With that, the maid bowed her head and began to sob again.

Edwin looked back at the dying prince and made his choice. He opened his pack and took out the bannocks he had been saving for his supper. "Here," he said to the maid. "Eat this and have hope. I do not know how long it will take, but I give you my word that I will not leave this forest until I have found a way to free you."

"Oh, good sir," she said. "Truly your heart is kind." She drew a silver locket from around her neck and held it out to Edwin. She opened it to reveal two tiny paintings of herself and the fallen prince. The name Amaranthe was engraved on one side, and Rurik on the other. "Please take this as a token of my thanks. If my love and I should perish before you return, give it to my father that he may swear vengeance on this vile witch."

Edwin took the locket, then carefully snapped it closed. "I require no payment," he said, shaking his head. "So I will return this when I have found a way to free you." Edwin put the chain over his head. The locket nestled itself into his shirt where it laid like ice over his heart. Taking it did not feel right, but perhaps it held some clue that might help him break the spell.

"One more question, my lady. You said you were drinking from a stream. Please point the way so that I may follow it back to the path."

The young woman pointed into the darkness. Edwin thought he had come in a different way, but night had nearly fallen, and the forest looked the same in every direction.

Edwin took a few steps, then looked back at the young woman. She pointed again, nodding earnestly as if to hasten him. With a deep breath, Edwin set off into the dark forest. In five steps, he could barely see the young woman or the mirror. In ten more steps, he could no longer hear them, either. True night had come, and the forest took him. Roots tangled his feet with every step. Brambles scratched his arms and plucked at his clothing while stray limbs clawed his face.

After hours of struggle, he came to a halt, defeated by the stubbornness of the forest. "There is no use," he muttered. "I must sleep here and find my way in the morning." He reached into his pack and found nothing but a meager handful of crumbs and an empty water flask. Tired and hungry, Edwin put his back against a tree, laid his head on his pack and settled himself to sleep.

Above him, a gust of wind rippled through the trees. First the leaves rustled in the treetops. Then branches began to thrash to and fro. A moment later, even the mightiest trunks groaned and swayed under the onslaught. Edwin's hair whipped across his eyes, and wind-driven leaves slashed at his face. Lightning flashed overhead. Thunder shook the ground.

Edwin cowered. Blinded by the lightning, he threw up a hand to shield his eyes. When he could see again, a woman stood before him. Hair blacker than night fell to her waist. The wind lifted her tresses and made them wave like snakes. She wore a simple gown of green velvet, with a tooled leather belt and boots of polished black. Her eyes were green as poison, and when she looked at Edwin, he could see his death in her eyes. The witch of the forest had come.

"My, my," she said. "You seem to have become tangled in my forest. How unfortunate for you."

Edwin knew he was foxed, but perhaps the witch was not as dangerous as the old woman said. Edwin climbed to his feet and bowed to her.

"My lady of the green kirtle," he said, "I am Edwin, and I am pleased to make your acquaintance. Truly the tales have not done you justice." Edwin, of course, had heard none of the tales, but he hoped his flattery might please her.

"You have a smooth tongue for a trespasser," the witch said.

"Alas, my lady, there is but one path through this forest, so if I wish to get to the other side, I am bound to take it. I entreat your permission to cross."

The witch eyed him speculatively. "Perhaps an arrangement can be made. I have a task I would like you to perform. If you are successful, I will grant you safe passage through my forest."

"And if I fail?"

"If you fail, your life is forfeit."

Edwin did not like the sound of the bargain. Would he end up chained next to the weeping maiden and her dying lover, or did the witch have something worse in mind? Edwin had no wish to find out.

"What is this task you would ask of me?"

"For a year and a day, you will search this forest," the witch said. "When you have found the most inconstant heart that dwells within, bring it to me. Do this, and I will free you from the enchantment of this place and allow you to depart. If you do it quickly and well, I may even reward you. If you fail, your life is mine. Do you agree?"

Edwin swallowed hard, but having no other choice he said, "I agree."

The witch gave him a tight nod, then reached out her hand. Her palm held a smooth, black stone with a depression the size of a thumbprint in the center. "Take this," she said. "When you have the heart, a single drop of blood dripped onto this stone will bring you to me."

The witch tipped her hand and the stone plummeted toward the ground. Edwin lunged to catch it. When he looked up again the witch was gone.

☼

Edwin woke with his back against a tree, a crick in his neck, and the black stone clenched in one fist. The forest around him showed no sign of the great wind the night before, and if not for the stone, Edwin might have thought he dreamed it.

Edwin pushed himself to his feet. In the quiet of the morning, he smelled a stream nearby. He followed the scent until he heard water rippling. He drank heartily, then filled his flask. There was nothing to eat, and Edwin had long ago spent all of his arrows. It wasn't the first time he had nibbled moss or the inner bark of twigs to survive.

Edwin roamed the forest, never quite certain of his way, until days turned into weeks, and fortnights became seasons. No matter how hard he searched, or how far he wandered, he never found the maid, the mirror, or any other human being. In fact, most days he wandered for the sake of wandering in the hope that he might find a way out of the forest. His clothing grew ragged and filthy from sleeping on the ground, and his hair flopped in his eyes. His stomach was empty, and he knew that his frame looked lean and hungry. He'd stopped keeping track of the days several months ago though he knew that the time the witch had given him was near its end. He wondered what the witch would do to him, and whether his death would be quick.

It was during this aimless wandering that he went to a small stream for a drink. There he heard a soft cry. At first, he thought it was the weeping maid, but when the sound came again, he recognized it as the cry of an animal in pain. Edwin looked to his left. He saw nothing but trees and brambles, rocks and earth. The view to his right was more of the same. He looked up into the canopy, but a sea of limbs covered the sky allowing only the dimmest light to filter through. The forest was interminable. With two vows left unfulfilled, Edwin wondered if the most inconstant heart in the forest was his own.

Edwin sighed. His shoulders slumped, and he looked at the ground in defeat. A flicker of movement in the underbrush Edwin's attention. He took two steps forward, knelt, and peered closer. He pulled aside a green fern frond, and there, tangled in brambles, lay a large hawk with an arrow through its breast and a struggling mouse pinioned in its talons. Though blood had stained its feathers, the hawk's back and wings were a deep russet red. Its head was the color of fresh cream and its pale breast was striped with ermine. A moment later, the hawk's beak opened, and its tongue moved as it drew a labored breath. The bird was still alive.

Edwin searched his pack and pockets for a strip of cloth. When he did not find one, he took off his coat and tore a sleeve from his shirt where the fabric was cleanest. He draped the first strip over the hawk's eyes and used another to bind the talons. Even wounded, the bird could still give him a terrible scratch. The motion jostled the mouse, who protested with a squeak.

Edwin felt around for a stick. When he found one of the proper size, he pinched the mouse by the scruff and used the stick to ease the hawk's talons open.

"Lucky mouse," said Edwin, placing the creature on the ground. "Be well with you, and seek better cover next time."

To Edwin's great surprise the mouse did not run away. Instead, it stood up tall on its little hind legs and bowed low.

"Oh, kind traveler," said the mouse. "You have freed me, and for that I will grant you a boon. This hawk bears the heart you seek. Kill the hawk, cut out its heart, and take it to the sorceress. The arrow that pierces the hawk is a magic arrow that will never miss its target. Keep the arrow as my gift and my thanks."

Edwin stared at the mouse, wondering how it knew of his pact with the witch. "You are most welcome, mouse, but if luck is with me, I shall save two lives today. Run free and return to your little mouse friends before the hawk misses its prize."

The mouse scurried away, and Edwin returned his attention to the hawk. "You, my friend, are less lucky," he told the bird. "I'm sorry for stealing your supper, for I fear we shall both go hungry tonight." Unwinding the brambles was a slow and arduous task that cost Edwin much pricking of his fingers. Finally, just before the hawk was free, Edwin used more of his shirt to bind the hawk's wings to its body, immobilizing the arrow. Then he nestled the bird in the crook of his elbow to examine the injury.

At first he thought the arrow had pierced the hawk's breast, but now he could see that it struck the wing instead. Edwin probed the injury with his fingers. The arrow had missed the bone and travelled straight through the flesh. If luck favored him, he might be able to remove the arrow and nurse the hawk back to health. The bird might even fly again one day.

Edwin dribbled a few drops of water over the bird's beak. When its mouth opened, Edwin dribbled a bit more.

"This will hurt, my friend, so I'll go as quickly as I can. And perhaps you're lucky after all, though I can't fathom who would hunt birds with a bodkin arrow." Edwin took a final look at the wound, assessing the angle. Meant for piercing armor, the head of the arrow was narrower than the shaft. Edwin poured a little of his water over the arrow to lubricate the head, then he braced the wing, gave a sharp tug, and pulled the arrow free.

Edwin poured more water over the wound and used the last of his shirt sleeve to bind it. The hawk gave a hoarse cry, so Edwin offered it more water.

"I am Rurik," the hawk croaked.

"Rurik?" said Edwin. "The russet prince?"

The hawk gave a quick bob of its head. "Thank you for saving me, traveler, but now we must fly. Take me with you, for I can lead us out of here."

"If you're Rurik, then the witch must be—?"

"Amaranthe," croaked the hawk. "Our parents wished us to wed, but I loved another."

Before Edwin could do anything else, a great wind rose up in the forest. Dark clouds stole the light away and turned noon into night. The wind kicked up leaves and twigs and drove them in stinging clouds through the air. Tree boughs whipped to and fro. Edwin knew there could be only one reason for the sudden storm. The witch was angry.

"Alas, we are undone," said the hawk. "The witch comes."

"Not if we go to her first," said Edwin. He'd grown tired of the witch's games. Edwin grabbed up the arrow, strung his bow, and slung it over his shoulder. He secured the wounded hawk in what was left of his shirt, then he took the black stone from his pocket, dipped his finger in Rurik's blood, and dabbed it onto the stone.

A sudden wrenching motion tore the ground from beneath Edwin's feet. After a moment of blackness, he stood in a room in a stone castle. The witch stood there, too, with an altar of polished basalt between them. Edwin placed the black stone upon it.

"Have you fulfilled my task, young traveler?" the witch asked.

"Indeed I have, my lady." Edwin freed the hawk from his shirt and placed it gently on the floor.

"Good," said the witch. "Kill the bird, place its heart on the altar, and be done with it." Her green eyes glittered in anticipation of the deed.

"No, my lady, I will not. His life was not our bargain. You are Amaranthe, and thrice I have aided you. As the old woman, I cut and stacked wood for three days and three nights, well in excess of what you asked because I would not see you cold come winter. As the young maid, I swore to free your prince from the mirror, which I have now done. And lastly, as the mouse, I freed you from the hawk's talons. I will aid you again, this time by giving you your life. In return, you will allow me to depart in peace, and Rurik as well."

"My life?" said Amaranthe, laughing. "How is that yours to give? Thrice I have repaid you. For your labor, I fed you and gave you boots that will never wear out. As the maid, I gave you a silver locket worth more than a year's lodging. And as the mouse, I gave you an arrow that always strikes its target. Now, I will hold you to our bargain. Kill the red prince. Place his heart on the altar, and you are free to go. Spare him, and your own life is forfeit."

Edwin took the bow from his shoulder and aimed the arrow at the witch's heart.

"My lady, this hawk, as I am sure you know, is a young prince under a hideous curse, one of your own devising. You bade me bring you the most inconstant heart in the forest, and I have done so, for that heart is your own. You laid a curse in vengeance, and you sought my aid with guile and false pretense. Even so, I will give you the blood of the inconstant heart if you demand it. Say the word, and I will let fly."

Edwin locked eyes with Amaranthe. A furious wind howled about the castle, and Amaranthe raised her hand.

Edwin released the bowstring.

The arrow buried itself in Amaranthe's shoulder, exactly where Edwin had aimed it. Her heartcry filled the room with fury. The black stone shattered, and when it did, Rurik sprawled on the floor in human form. Edwin snatched the dagger from Rurik's belt. In three steps, he closed on Amaranthe. He pinned her to the wall by her wounded shoulder with one hand. The other held the point of the dagger against her stomach just below her breastbone. He angled it upward, toward her heart.

"There is kindness in you, Amaranthe. I have seen it, so I will offer you a bargain. Release me from my vow, or I will place your heart on the altar to fulfill it. Do you agree?"

Amaranthe's breath caught. Her body went limp under Edwin's hands. "I agree," she whispered.

The basalt altar cracked in twain. Edwin lowered his dagger and yanked the arrow from Amaranthe's shoulder. Then he took the locket from his neck and dropped it beside her.

"I promised to return the locket," he said, "but the arrow is mine, in payment for the mouse's life. I liked you best as the old woman. She was free of the bitterness that consumes you. Go back to her cottage and live your life in sunlight."

Amaranthe pressed the sleeve of her velvet gown against the wound in her shoulder. She looked long at Edwin before she spoke.

"My final gift to you, Edwin Woodcutter, is a proper name. I name you Edwin Sureshot, and if you ever cross the boundaries of my forest again, things will not go so well for you. Now get out, and take the hawk-prince with you."

Edwin helped Rurik to his feet, then down the castle stairs into the sunlight. The sky was blue overhead, and sunlight dappled the forest path.

It was, Edwin thought, a fine day for travel.

Copyright © 2023 by Kary English.

Jonathan Lenore Kastin (he/they) is a queer, trans writer with an MFA in writing from the Vermont College of Fine Arts. His short stories can be found in On Spec *and* Cosmic Roots and Eldritch Shores, *as well as the anthologies* Ab(solutely) Normal, Transmogrify! *and* Queer Beasties.

THE WEREWOLF

by Jonathan Lenore Kastin

It was late April when Amelia realized that she was a werewolf. She was reading in her room one evening and as the moon came out from behind a cloud it fixed her with a pale, trembling beam of light. She froze at once, sniffed the wind, and took off her skin. Underneath grew a radiant coat of fur and one by one her senses came alive to the night.

The next day she tried to tell her mother.

"I'm a werewolf," she said, picking leaves out of her golden hair.

Her mother patted her on the head. "That's nice dear. Maybe Aunt Matilda will make you a costume for Halloween."

"No," said Amelia. "I'm a *real* werewolf. With fur and claws and everything."

"Well," said her mother. "As long as you don't stay out in the woods too late." She went back to her magazines.

Amelia growled and sprinted outside just as the sun was beginning to set. She ran through the woods on her new pawed feet, sniffing after rabbits. She rolled around in the fresh mud and filled the garden with secret burrows.

When her mother came downstairs the next morning the floor was covered in paw prints. "Look at this mess!" she said. "How could you bring a dog, of all things, into this house?"

"But it wasn't a dog," said Amelia. "It was me. I told you."

Her mother was not amused. "Amelia, don't be childish. You brought a dog into this house and now you're lying to get out of it."

"They're not dog prints," said Amelia. "They're wolf prints."

"Oh, for heaven's sake," said her mother. "I've had enough of this game. You are *not* a wolf. You are a little girl."

"No, I'm not! I'm not, really!" Amelia fled to her room. She howled at her curtains and snarled at the pillows on her bed. Then she tore at them with her teeth until the room was covered with shredded fabric and feathers. Her mother was not persuaded.

"Harold," she said to her husband. "We are taking our child to a psychiatrist."

"Are we?" he asked over his morning coffee.

"Yes. I can't stand another minute of this nonsense."

"What's Amelia done now?" he sighed.

"She is insisting that she is a werewolf and is bent on destroying this house."

"Oh, that." He laughed. "It's just a phase. She was a pirate last year, remember? Didn't she spend a month wearing that silly hat and ordering us to walk the plank whenever we quarreled?"

"All the same …" said Amelia's mother.

The psychiatrist tried to examine Amelia for over an hour but she kept snapping at his fingers and baring her teeth at him. They were surprisingly sharp.

"I wouldn't worry," he said to her parents. "I've seen children go through this before. It usually lasts only a couple of weeks. Why just last month I had a boy in here who insisted he was a unicorn, even started to grow a sort of horn in the middle of his forehead. Power of suggestion, you know. Three hours of psychoanalysis a week and he's back to being a normal, healthy, everyday sort of boy. Playing football with his chums, chasing the girls. That sort of thing. She'll be over this in no time."

But Amelia did not agree. "Why won't you listen to me?" she asked, after spending yet another night in the woods. There was blood under her nails and rabbit fur stuck in her teeth. "I keep telling you."

Her mother stared in horror at Amelia's ravaged, mud-stained nightgown. A number of shattered bones lay strewn about the flower beds. "Why can't you be like other little girls?" she begged. "Plenty of children like to play in the woods and gaze at the moon. It doesn't make them wolves. It just means they appreciate the natural world."

Amelia huffed and licked her fingers clean.

"It's because you didn't have enough human influences as a baby, isn't it? We let you spend all that time with animals instead of children your own age."

"That's not it at all," said Amelia, stomping away.

But no matter what she said, her parents wouldn't listen to her.

Then one night, after a particularly awful bout of howling, Amelia's parents had had enough. They marched up to her room and threw open the door. There in the middle of Amelia's bed was an enormous golden-brown wolf. She stretched her mouth wide in a yawn, showing off each sharpened tooth. Then she leapt for their throats and she ate them right up.

If only they had listened.

Copyright © 2023 by Jonathan Lenore Kastin.

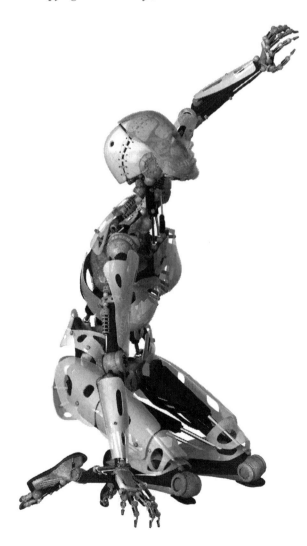

Xauri'EL Zwaan is a mendicant artist in search of meaning, fame and fortune, or pie (where available). Zie lives and writes in a little hobbit hole in Saskatoon, Canada on Treaty 6 territory with zir life partner and two very lazy cats.

FRUITING BODIES

by Xauri'EL Zwaan

There was a strange plant in Mrs. Edgerington's garden.

The plant looked like a tiny clamshell sprouting up out of the ground. It had a smooth surface, glistened with a dull silver sheen, and ended in a sharp knife-like ridge. It didn't look like anything she had ever seen before. In fact, it hardly looked like a plant at all, though it certainly grew like one. Mrs. Edgerington had her grandson look on the internet to see what it was, but he couldn't find anything matching the description. He told her she should dig it up and burn it, but Mrs. Edgerington liked weird plants, and she decided to let it grow and see what happened.

The plant slowly got bigger and bigger over the next few months. Neither water nor lack of water affected its rate of growth, nor did shade or sun. It eventually grew to about a foot in height and half a foot in width. Every day, Mrs. Edgerington took a photo of it on her phone and uploaded it to Facebook. She got lots of comments calling it weird and unsettling, and many more telling her to burn it. She was also forwarded news articles from all over the world about other people who had found similar plants. Scientists were baffled; they seemed unrelated to any species ever before seen. Most people who found them were destroying them. There was just something unnerving about them. But the scientists said there were probably more growing in the wild places, and that they probably couldn't be controlled without a massive worldwide extermination campaign, which nobody seemed willing to fund.

One day, as Mrs. Edgerington sat on her front porch having her morning tea, the halves of the clamshell split open, bending over toward the ground. Inside was a perfect silver sphere, about four inches in diameter. As she watched with rapt attention and growing unease, the sphere began to quiver, then to pop up and down. After a few seconds, it popped right out of the clamshell and rolled off toward the woods that her property backed onto. She tried to follow it, but she was no spring chicken anymore, and it quickly rolled off out of sight.

When Mrs. Edgerington dug up her garden a few months later, she found that the plant had totally filled the earth with silvery roots that cut her hands if she even so much as touched them. She had to get her grandson to clear them out, wearing the heaviest work gloves he could find.

✲

Grayden Reilley was riding his bike along a path in the forest when, out of the corner of his eye, he saw a glint, like light reflecting off metal. He stopped, left his bike tipped over on the path, and walked toward the flickering light.

What he saw took his breath away. Sitting in a pile, nestled into a hollow full of autumn leaves in a clearing between the trees, were a bunch of little shiny metal balls, dozens of them. That was weird enough, but the really strange part was that they were all moving, pushing each other up and then falling down again, climbing each other as if they were sticky or magnetic, forming a seething, seemingly organic mass. As Grayden watched, some of the balls seemed to come apart, splitting into five perfect meridians like the sections of an orange and then unfolding. Inside each was a dark mass of boils and nodules to which the thin metallic sections attached. Each section split and split again, many times over, fanning out into petals lined with smaller petals, and on and on until they became a fuzz too fine to even see. They looked kind of like starfish. But only kind of.

Some of the things started to flop and flex, then pushed themselves up on fuzzy arms. The conical masses in the centers of them began to stretch and move, pointing this way and that, seeming almost to taste the air. Then they focused on Grayden, and the mass of fruiting bodies began, slowly but definitely, to lurch toward him. He turned and ran back to the path, grabbed his bike, jumped on it, and cycled away as fast as he could.

When he told his parents later, they didn't believe him; he had always had an active imagination, but felt that this was incredibly unfair and sulked in his room for days. He also told some of the kids at school; they called him a liar and challenged him to prove it. When he took them to the place where he had found the balls that had turned into weird starfish things, they were all gone, although the ground and leaves were cut up where they had formed their horrid mass. Ethan Crane punched him in the gut and called him a lying sack of shit, and the other kids abandoned him.

It wasn't until he went on the internet to try and find out what he had seen that he realized he wasn't the only one. Some others had even posted pictures. He wished he had thought to take one; if he'd only had proof, he would have been the most popular kid in school.

✲

Artie Winterheimer's ham radio was making weird sounds.

It had started with just a few clicks and whistles and moans, but quickly accelerated into a cacophony of complicated noise. It was on every frequency and continued constantly, washing out the faint signals of the other amateur radio enthusiasts he communicated with on a regular basis. It sounded almost like music, though a strange and alien music, unlike anything Artie had ever heard, even the bizarre robot noises the kids liked to listen to these days.

Since retirement, ham radio had been Artie's sole passion, and aside from a few strange people like Delbert Ness the computer nut, his only real friends were the other ham radio people he knew around the world. He missed them sorely, but the noise had a fascination all its own, and Artie soon became obsessed with it. He started listening to it for hours on end, entranced by its endless variety and strangeness.

Artie soon developed the theory that it might be a code. He had been a radio operator in his time with the navy and knew a lot about codes, but this was stranger and way more complicated than anything he had ever encountered as a signalman. He had Delbert over a few times, and Delbert thought his theory had merit, but the sounds unnerved him and he didn't want to come over to listen to them much. Artie didn't mind. He could have used some help in his project, but he and Delbert weren't really friends anyway, just fellow fringe people driven together by the subtle ostracism of small-town conformity; and anyway, he trusted his own skills and knowledge more than that of newfangled computer chips. He had begun trying to analyze the code, noting the patterns and working out what kind of cypher it might be. More and more, he was becoming convinced that it was a language, probably a foreign one. Maybe even more foreign than anyone on Earth knew.

☼

Jack Boland's toaster was missing.

He had searched high and low, cursing up a blue streak, through every cupboard in the kitchen, then through the attic and the garage as well, tossing things haphazardly onto the floor as he went. Jack had trouble remembering things sometimes, but he was sure he would have remembered putting his toaster anywhere other than where it was supposed to be. Sneaking suspicions began to form in his mind, as often they did. He went around to Mrs. Edgerington's next door and, when the sweet old lady answered his angry knocking, he accused her of stealing it. She was always looking at him, that woman, always weighing and measuring, her glares reminding him of the time he had done in prison and the fact that everyone in town knew about it. She very calmly and patiently denied having seen it, multiple times as he grew more and more hostile and swore louder and louder, threatened to involve the police, threatened to bring his buddies from the malt plant around and search her house for it himself. When he finally stormed off, she called after him, asking pleasantly that if he were to see her lawn mower, would he let her know? Apparently it was missing too.

Jack took his basset hound Donny for a walk in the woods to clear his head. He wasn't sure why he had lit into the old bird like that. After all, she was just a harmless busybody, and what were the odds that she had really stolen his toaster? She just rubbed him the wrong way, and sometimes he got these moods. Like the time he had hit his ex-wife, and she had pressed charges and taken their son away. Thank God he hadn't hit Mrs. Edgerington.

That kind of trouble was the last thing he needed, with the bosses at the malt plant already on his ass for goldbricking. He walked faster and faster, past the spot where, unbeknownst to him, Grayden had seen the weird starfish things a few weeks ago, then deeper. As he neared the ravine, Donny started to baulk. He pulled on the leash, trying to head Jack away, and whined pathetically, then howled. When Jack began to see glints of metal through the trees, he left the frightened dog behind, barking frantically as he neared the edge.

Rising from the middle of the ravine was a peculiar structure. It was a sort of derrick made of a random hotch-potch of metal struts, and welded to it and each other were all kinds of machines. There were power saws and cordless drills, laptop computers and gaming consoles, parts of washing machines and car engines. There were starfish-like things with fuzzy-tipped arms and warty conical masses sprouting from their center swarming all over it. Many of them carried other bits of the technological paraphernalia of everyday life, and were carefully maneuvering and placing them in the mass, welding them in place somehow with their bushy hands. Jack recognized Mrs. Edgerington's lawn mower, as well as Dan McGillicuddy's beer fridge and Art Cline's TV. Finally, perched on a little pylon near the top, he saw the unmistakable 50s-style chrome body of his toaster.

Anger easily overcame caution, and he shouted, "Hey, you fuckin' ding-dongs! What the fuck are you doin' with my toaster?" The starfish things didn't respond in any way, just went about their business.

Now Jack Boland might not be smart, and he might not be blessed with a surplus of self-restraint, but he knew an unfair fight when he saw it. He went back to where Donny was howling as if in agony, took up his leash, and went home. He took a Pabst out of his fridge, cracked it open, and drank half of it down in a single swallow. Then he nursed his beer for a while, and two more followed. He sat for several pregnant minutes, then went into his bedroom and got his shotgun.

He didn't take Donny this time, although the poor guy was frantic when he saw Jack getting ready to leave. No sense exposing the one thing in the world that still truly loved him to danger. He hiked into the woods, grumbling curses every step of the way, until he once again saw the tower of mishmash appliances rising from the ravine. He leveled his loaded gun, and called out in a slightly slurred voice, "You little bastards better give me back my toaster, or there's gonna be trouble!" When no response was forthcoming, he aimed carefully at one of the silvery-metallic starfish and firmly squeezed the trigger. The starfish blew apart with a satisfying squelch. Before he had time to fire a second shot, however, one of the creatures near the top of the mass of metal slithered quickly inside. From one of the pylons that stuck from the top, a bluish bolt of electricity lanced out, hitting Jack Boland square in the chest, blowing him right out of his shoes and several feet back into the forest.

When he came to again, he found that his shotgun was missing. He staggered to the edge of the ravine, and saw one of the five-armed things carefully fitting his gun into the chaotic mass.

Jack had always had a hard time knowing when he was beat, but this time it was clear as day. He slunk away back to his house and spent the rest of the evening drinking and petting his dog. The next afternoon, he showed up at Mrs. Edgerington's doorstep with flowers and an apology.

✡

Mrs. Edgerington watched the stories on the news every night. Grayden Reilley followed developments avidly on Snapchat and TikTok. Jack Boland and his buddies gathered nervously in the evening at the U-Turn Bar & Grill to swap rumours. Things like the tower that Jack had seen in the ravine were going up everywhere—all over the world, on a grid at points regularly spaced 42.6 miles apart to the inch. Where there was human habitation, they went up quickly, aggregated from various mechanical and electronic detritus, but they were being built far away from civilization as well; the starfish seemed to be mining and smelting metals and forming them into the necessary parts if need be. Everyone in town knew by now about the weird plants, about the starfish things, about the tower and what had happened to Jack when he had tried to defy its makers. People in other towns and cities had tried taking the towers down—whole gangs of them, sometimes. The towers and the things building them repulsed every attempt. Even destroying the starfish things was no good; the pieces just budded into new, smaller starfish that took up right where their parents had left off.

Nobody in town would have known what a Von Neumann machine was, except maybe Delbert Ness, but the experts on the news programs carefully explained: something had come to Earth from the stars, a tiny seed that had sprouted into plants like the ones Mrs. Edgerington had been reluctant to destroy. The plants had fruited into the balls, and the balls had hatched into the starfish, and the starfish were building something. Nobody knew what or why, but a few were willing to speculate. Decades ago, the idea had been floated that Von Neumann machines could be dispersed throughout the galaxy to prepare other worlds for colonization by spacefaring humans. Apparently, someone else had beaten them to the punch.

The Army had been trying to clear out the towers, bombing them to smithereens. But as soon as they were off to destroy one tower, another went up. There were millions of them, and even large armies had limited capacity. Nobody ever came to try and destroy the tower in the ravine. A few particularly high-security sites were guarded to make sure the starfish didn't come back, but eventually the game of whack-a-mole was mostly given up, and an anxious world settled in to wait and see what the things were for.

A couple of months later, each and every tower began to spew carbon dioxide into the atmosphere at an alarming rate. The scientists on TV said they were breaking it down from the very soil and rocks in the ground. The output quickly equaled the amount of CO_2 released from all human industry and civilization, then exceeded it, and kept climbing. The scientists who had forwarded the theory that aliens had sent the Von Neumann machines to colonize the Earth now speculated that the towers' purpose was to radically alter the climate, perhaps to make it more hospitable when the alien colonists finally arrived.

✡

It was Mrs. Edgerington who called the town meeting, not through any official channel but by posting on Facebook, in the local Buy & Sell and the PTA discussion group and the local union's on-line forum; her grandson showed her how. Almost the whole town showed up in the end, crowding into the local school gymnasium, which had been provided for their use at short notice and without even the usual rental fee. At first, the Mayor tried to take charge of the discussion; Mrs. Edgerington just listened politely to his pontificating, then got up and quietly began to speak.

"We need to do something about these starfish things."

Once she finally openly addressed what had been on everyone's minds, the dam broke. After she had made her case, that the government wasn't doing anything about it, that they had to look after themselves if they were going to survive, others started speaking for and against. The Mayor was passionately opposed, and a lot of people thought it would be taking too much of a risk; what if the aliens decided to come to town and kill them all for interfering with their designs? There were shouting matches, but by the time the meeting had been in full swing for a couple of hours, the people who were against intervening had mostly been shut down and left in a huff.

Then, they started debating what exactly to do. Should they try to kill the aliens? That just didn't seem to work. What if they brought in a bulldozer from the quarry and knocked the thing down? The aliens would only build it again, and anyway, that wouldn't solve the problem; there would still be millions left. Maybe try to get together with other towns, other cities, and destroy all of them? How could they, a tiny town in the middle of nowhere, possibly accomplish what all the governments of the world could not? It wasn't until the options seemed to have been exhausted and people were getting frustrated and angry that shy, friendless Artie Winterheimer raised a hand and said hesitantly, "Why don't we try talking to them?"

✡

Jack Boland backed his truck through the woods, more careful than he almost ever was, stone sober and with murder in his eyes. Mrs. Edgerington rode with him in the cab. A whole crowd of people followed, union guys from the malt plant and the quarry, housewives and teenagers and old folks, school teachers and the people who owned the businesses on Main Street, even a few of the Town Council. Strapped down to the truck bed was Artie's ham radio, and beside it, one of Delbert's high-grade laptops, both powered by a car battery Grayden Reilley's dad had found in his garage. Delbert had dug up a document in some file server on the dark web, a half-complete report by linguists at the NSA trying to translate the aliens' radio-wave language. He had put it together with Artie's attempts at cracking the code and some open-source translation software and wrote a program that could maybe possibly translate between alienese and English. It was their only shot.

When they got to the ravine, everyone stood hushed before the tower, many of them seeing it and its alien manufacturers for the first time. They knew they were in the presence of something incredible—life from another planet. All the sci-fi movies had never prepared anyone for it. They had portrayed aliens who were hostile to humanity, who tried to exterminate us, and aliens who wanted to help, to get us to join their galactic federation, but most people didn't quite know how to handle aliens who were simply indifferent, who went about their business on Earth without even acknowledging the human species' existence.

Finally, Mrs. Edgerington hobbled up to the computer and spoke into its microphone, "You have to stop."

Immediately, the movement of the starfish things that clustered on the tower halted. There was a pause, and then the computer began to speak in a harsh synthesized squawk.

"SIGNAL ACKNOWLEDGED. SOURCE UNIDENTIFIED. SUPPLY DESIGNATION CODE."

Artie leaned toward his radio and said, "This is not one of you. This is the humans you're speaking to. The inhabitants of the planet."

"ERROR. NO SENTIENT INHABITANTS DETECTED ON PLANET."

Jack Boland shouted, more at the tower than at their makeshift communication equipment, "Whaddya mean, no habitants? You took our tools and stuff to make your damn tower! You shitheads know damn well we're here!"

"MINIMAL TECHNOLOGY DETECTED. NO ANTIMATTER POWER INFRASTRUC-

TURE, NO INTERSTELLAR CAPABILITY, NO NANOTECHNOLOGY MANUFACTURING. NO CIVILIZATION. NO SENTIENT INHABITANTS DETECTED."

"You can't mean that," Artie protested. "Just because we don't have any of that stuff, we're not people? I mean, we have rights!"

"ERROR. COMMUNICATION UNINTELLIGIBLE. NO THREAT TO THE PRECURSORS DETECTED. NO CIVILIZATION. COLONIZATION WILL CONTINUE UNIMPEDED."

"So just like that, you're gonna kill us all?" Jack yelled. "Change the damn climate until we can't survive?"

"COLONIZATION IS IMPERATIVE. THE GROUND MUST BE PREPARED. THE PRECURSORS REQUIRE RESOURCES. EXPANSION MUST CONTINUE. A REMNANT MAY SURVIVE. THEY WILL ADAPT TO THE NEEDS OF THE PRECURSORS."

"I don't think that's how it's going to go."

Grayden had stepped forward, a serious expression on his face. Some of the adults muttered that a mere boy shouldn't interrupt his elders, but Grayden continued, resolute.

"We'll adapt all right. The human species is good at adapting; I learned that in biology class. But we won't adapt to the needs of your masters. We'll adapt to be able to destroy them."

"ERROR. NO THREAT TO THE PRECURSORS DETECTED. NO CIVILIZATION. MINIMAL TECHNOLOGY-USING ANIMALS. NO SENTIENT INHABITANTS."

"You think we're animals," Mrs. Edgerington said softly, wonder and horror in her voice. "Beasts of burden. Not even people. Because we're no threat."

"You may think that now," Grayden continued, "but just wait until your Precursors get here. Wait until we get hold of their technology. Humans adapt. We won't just give up, let the Precursors make us into slaves. We'll resist. We'll make them pay for what they've done to us."

"ANIMALS CANNOT UTILIZE ADVANCED TECHNOLOGY. ANIMALS ADAPT TO SERVE THE PRECURSORS. ANIMALS CAN EASILY BE DESTROYED IF THEY BECOME A THREAT."

"You willing to bet your Precursors' lives on that?" Jack snarled in a venomous tone. "We love technology, we're always getting better at it. I'm pretty sure we can figure out your nano-whatever. And then we're gonna bomb your asses into the stone age!"

"There are alien specimens in labs right now," Delbert said. "We're already starting to figure you out."

"I learned about colonization in history class," Grayden said defiantly. "It happened here too. The Europeans explored everywhere and took slaves, took land, took over governments, and tried to exterminate anyone who resisted. They had superior technology too; nobody could stop them. They thought they had the right. But in the end, the people they colonized took their technology and used it against them. They didn't adapt to serve. They adapted to compete, to get stronger. And eventually, they fought back."

"It's true," Delbert muttered. "They took my people as slaves, then they took our whole continent for themselves. We suffered for generations. But then, bit by bit, we took the master's tools and made them our own. And then the Africans rose up and claimed their independence, and the Asians and Indians kicked the invaders out, and the Black slaves and Native Americans made them treat us as equals. There was a reckoning. In the end, we won, we took back what was ours. But the damage was done. We became what had destroyed us. We became just as bad."

Mrs. Edgerington said, "We don't want to be like that. We're just starting to figure things out here on Earth. How to treat each other like people. It's a lesson your Precursors could stand to learn. We don't want to have to do to them what had to be done to us. We don't want to have to become like them just to survive. But if we have to, we will."

Artie said, "The Precursors must have been like us once. Just a bunch of low-tech animals. Then they developed the tools to be a 'real civilization.' And if they can do it, so can we. This right here is proof. We figured out your language, and we can figure out any technology the Precursors bring with them. And then there'll be hell to pay."

There was a long silence. Then the computer spoke again.

"ACKNOWLEDGED. POSSIBLE CIVILIZATION IN TRANSITION DETECTED. POSSIBLE THREAT TO THE PRECURSORS DETECTED.

THE HIVE MUST DELIBERATE. DO NOT ATTEMPT FURTHER COMMUNICATION."

People kept trying to talk to the aliens, trying to reason with them, to threaten them, to cajole them. They were all ignored.

☼

About a month later, the towers stopped releasing carbon dioxide into the atmosphere. Then, bit by bit, they were taken down. There was no explanation, no communication, no indication of why it was happening. Their parts were just melted down into slag, and the alien starfish things buried themselves in the ground and dissolved into a featureless mush. In the end, only one tower remained, protected from any interference by a massive pylon that shot devastating lightning bolts at any man-made object that came within a mile. And that tower was broadcasting a signal into space. When the NSA linguists finally finished translating the aliens' language, they told the world what it was saying: "WARNING. CIVILIZATION IN TRANSITION DETECTED. THREAT DETECTED. COLONIZATION ABORTED. AVOID THIS PLANET."

There was endless speculation about why, after they had been able to do pretty much whatever they wanted with humans offering no impediment, they had abruptly decided that we were a threat. Most of the people in town kept quiet, and the few that talked about what happened on the internet were painted by the rest as liars and cranks. Nobody wanted the government coming around and asking questions. They just wanted to live their lives in peace.

A few months later, astronomers reported that the same kind of towers were starting to appear on Mars.

Copyright © 2023 by Xauri'EL Zwaan.

T. R. Napper is a multi-award winning science fiction author, including the Australian Aurealis *twice. His short fiction has appeared in* Asimov's, Interzone, the Magazine of Fantasy & Science Fiction, *and numerous others, and been translated into Hebrew, German, French, and Vietnamese. Before turning to writing, T. R. Napper was a diplomat and aid worker, delivering humanitarian programs in Southeast Asia for a decade. During this period, he received a commendation from the Government of Laos for his work with the poor. He also was a resident of the Old Quarter in Hanoi for several years, the setting for his debut novel,* 36 Streets. *These days he has returned to his home country of Australia, where he works as a Dungeon Master, running campaigns for young people with autism for a local charity.*

XI BOX

by T. R. Napper

The first thing Joshua Lee did was whisper his dreams into the Xi Box. Snatching up those fragments running around the plughole of his hippocampus, before they faded from view. Before they could be absorbed into the back fabric of his mind.

After his dreams, he confessed his feelings. His fears, mainly.

The little things, to start with. The Infected woman at work who'd accused Joshua of stealing her lunch. He'd told her no, even though he had; he'd eaten it all, container perched on his lap in a darkened file room. Then the slow-burning fear: he'd fail to pass probation in his new position. Corollary: the already unsustainable mortgage on their two-bedroom apartment burying them.

Then the biggest fear.

Jess would go over. That part of her *wanted* to become Infected. Like so many others. The simplicity of it, the relief of being able to join the Children of Heaven, though she would never admit it.

Another dream. He was running toward her, arms out, while Jess stood on the horizon, her eyes elsewhere. He cried out to her, but his sluggish legs never made up the distance. Reaching, reaching, but she would look away, always over the horizon. Had he had this dream before? Did he wake up every morning and confess it?

The Xi Box—black, dull metal, no bigger than a fist—sat on his bedside table, pulsing red as he spoke. The glow intensified in correlation to the power of the emotion whispered, the more transgressive the sin confessed. Silent sentinel, eating his fears and his hopes. When he was done, the Xi Box glowed full and Joshua Lee was empty.

Light now, lighter than air, he rose from the bed, leaving his wife behind, her black hair a shattered halo on the white pillow. Her Xi Box was soft glowing and patient, waiting for her to awake and to whisper.

Carefree, smiling, Joshua poured his coffee, savored the scent, nostrils flaring, still smiling. Sipping the black acrid brew, mind clear, the million voices inside and out quieted. The white noise of Heaven's admonitions muted.

He stood at the window. Down below, the city was waking, rooftop solar panels glinting in the orange hue of dawn. Traffic noise, muffled, rose from the streets below. The clock on the kitchen wall ticked loudly behind him. He was late. The Xi Box had that effect on him. Joshua dressed, suit and tie, pulling on his scuffed black leather shoes. Jogging to the door, he gripped the handle and—

"What's the time?"

Joshua started and turned. Jessica Long did not look well. Dark hair—once lustrous, now lank—hung plastered down over her forehead. She'd been sweating in her sleep again, purple bags under her eyes, her vision focused somewhere in the middle distance. A ghostly presence around the house, thinner and thinner, she made barely a whisper as she moved from room to room.

"Did you use the Xi Box?" he asked, gently.

"What day is it?" she asked.

The corner of Joshua's mouth twitched. A nervous tic, first appearing only a few months before. "You start work in an hour, Jess. You need to be strong to fight off infection. *Please* talk to the Box before then, okay?"

Jess replied by moving toward the kitchen, opening and closing drawers absently. Joshua watched her for a few moments more, his lightness gone. He walked out.

☼

Into the city. Outwardly, as it had always been, before it'd been absorbed into Heaven—loud and bustling and steaming. Sizzling with street food and a bright unforgiving sun, a hard heat that burned last night's rain from the streets, making the air thick. The towering skyscrapers provided moments of shade as he walked up and down the long curving streets, past buzzing neon signs, the parks with older residents practicing tai chi, and the construction sites wrapped in bamboo scaffolding.

A few blocks from his apartment he passed a group huddled near a corner. A seemingly unrelated set of four: a policeman, a salaryman in neat suit, a youth with a blue mohawk, an elderly woman holding a large crocodile-skinned handbag over her shoulder. Something passed between them as he approached, unspoken, and they turned to look at him with unblinking eyes. Joshua swallowed, pushing his focus down to the pavement in front of him, making every attempt to appear unhurried as he walked by them and across the road.

Tires screeched, a horn blared—Joshua jumped back. The chrome fender of a taxi cab had stopped half a meter from his kneecap. Joshua stepped away, hands raised; the taxi driver eyed him angrily and blasted the horn again. Joshua ran to the other curb, the taxi revved and continued up the street. The group of four still stared at him. Joshua, red faced, walked quickly away.

Joshua was meticulous in his unobtrusiveness. The secret of the ninja wasn't hiding in shadows, behind strips of black cloth, only eyes revealed. The secret of the ninja was hiding in plain sight. Being so unremarkable, one would immediately slip from the mind of the viewer. He wasn't used to being stared at by groups of Infected. He wasn't accustomed to being looked at too closely by anyone.

Not today. His mind spun. They were onto him. He'd lied to the Xi Box. That must be it. Had omitted the whole truth, anyway. One final fear lived inside him. So dark he dared not speak it, even to

Xi. Conspiracy theories circulated, whispered indiscreetly in bars, that the Box was connected to Heaven, the gods listening. Joshua did not believe. But still … . This last fear he kept to himself.

Joshua took a deep breath, and another, calming his mind, focusing on the rhythm of his steps. He ignored the stares of another mismatched group of four and made his way to work, head down.

Outwardly, the city was just the same.

☼

"How are you settling in?"

"Well, Mr. London."

John London was a large man. Shoulders, chin, the works. He wore a tailored suit of the darkest blue, his light-colored hair slicked back, shining. On his finger, an inert Xi Ring. Before he'd become Infected, John London would have been able to hold it to his lips and whisper, any hour of the day, to expel incorrect thoughts. Now the black steel was dull and lifeless, an ornament to his loyalty. After conversion, all one's sins and dreams drained away, and the red pulsing anger of Xi quieted permanently.

"Ten years in verification branch, Mr. Lee, you've earned the promotion."

It had been thirteen years. "Thank you, sir."

"I see you've already picked up an interesting case for the Capricornia file."

Joshua's lips felt dry. "Ah, yes, sir."

"Several bank accounts, a beachfront property, generous donations to local political candidates."

Joshua made a show of looking around and lowered his voice. *"An Ecclesiast."*

"Ah, I thought so," said London, shaking his head. "I do wish they'd make it less conspicuous."

"I haven't asked too many questions."

"That is why you were promoted."

"I was planning to—"

His supervisor held up a hand. "Mr. Lee. Let's not spoil my day, and yours, with a neophyte error."

Joshua lowered his eyes and nodded.

John London walked away, hands clasped behind his back, nodding at the other employees.

Joshua went into the system and deleted the trail. Bank records, GPS movements, imprudent social media use—the rest of it, all gone. Plucked out of the ether and slotted into the memory hole: London called this part of their work cultural adjustment, making sure a particular class of people were never scrutinized too closely, their records kept pristine.

The verification branch was atomized. Teams of four, completely independent of each other. Within each team they'd allocate the work, though never talk about it beyond that. The supervisor—in this case, John London—would work closely with each person. Except in cases like this. Where he wouldn't. Part of London's job was remaining unaware of the specifics. He'd never look at the names; know only the broad details of a case, so it would fade from memory. Like a dream into a Xi Box.

Most auditors were Infected—were the Children of Heaven—and as such unimpeachably discreet. The Infected, though, were always in great demand right across the economy, never quite enough to go around. So regular citizens like Joshua could still land prestige positions if they worked hard enough. Impeccably. For thirteen years.

"Mr. Lee." Olivia Sixtus appeared, out of nowhere, next to Joshua's desk. Dark hair tied back, the skin on her face the same—pulled tight over her bones. Unblinking stare, her mouth drawn into a disapproving line. She was the second most senior auditor in the branch, after London.

One never knew for sure who had been infected. London wore his inert Xi Ring as ostentatious display, but people like Joshua could always acquire those on the black market, if they had the money, to try to pose as Infected. There were signs, of course. You could say it was the glazed eyes, or wonder if it was the dull monotones in which they spoke. The utterly humorless persona, devoid of wit or irony—all of these were clues. But if you were free, it was smart to affect these things anyway. Telling a joke was a dangerous pastime.

Heaven seemed always to know the difference between its Children and mere citizens—like Joshua—and would assign positions accordingly. For everyone else it was guesswork. With Olivia Sixtus, however, he was about as sure as he could be that she was one of them.

"Yes, Miz Sixtus?"

"For lunch today, I have marinated tofu and steamed rice."

"Sounds delicious."

"It is in a clearly marked container on the second shelf of the fridge."

"I told you, Miz Sixtus, I have no idea who ate your prawn dumplings."

"I'm merely providing you information."

"Then I appreciate the update."

She paused for an uncomfortable length of time. Another thing the Infected did. "You look anxious, Mr. Lee."

Joshua shifted in his seat. "Sorry?"

"Anxious. Have you used your Xi Box today?"

Joshua blinked. Olivia Sixtus did not.

She'd never spoken of Xi Boxes before. To do so was an accusation of impurity. No one ever knew for sure who'd been infected, sure, but it wasn't hard to guess in Joshua's case. Thirteen years an apprentice auditor, he was an open book on this count.

He couldn't answer the question. There was no right answer.

She stared a little longer. Too long. His mouth twitched. She drifted away, like she was on a set of wheels rather than a pair of feet, gliding over to her cubicle.

✧

Joshua Lee worked through the day on the Capricornia file. Tiny workspace, elbows touching the walls of his cubicle. Lunch at his desk, *tap-tappity-tap* on the keyboard, a hundred auditors doing the same, a susurrus of elbows brushing against walls, of fingers on keys.

The workers paused only to say the oath. They'd prostrate themselves on the thin itchy carpet, lips pressed against the fidelity hole, and speak the words while inspirational music swelled through office speakers. Whispered words of loyalty into microphones recessed into the floor:

> *I pledge loyalty to Heaven,*
> *who watches and keeps us.*
> *I will be faithful to my position,*
> *pursue public affairs with integrity,*
> *accept the supervision of the people,*
> *and confess all my sins to Xi.*
> *Ecclesiast, Iron Guard, Children of Heaven, and Citizen,*
> *all under Heaven:*
> *harmonious, culturally advanced, strong, beautiful.*
> *Always united, forever one.*

Joshua uttered the words by rote, then was back to work. *Tap-tappity-tap.*

He'd just returned from the stationery cupboard, hands in pockets, when a message came through from Elite Education Services. He picked up the phone:

"Jess?"

"Joshua? It's Elissa."

"Oh, hi, Elissa."

"Sorry to bother you at work."

"Oh, no problem," he said. His stomach clenched, anticipating.

"It's about Jess."

"Yes?"

"She hasn't clocked in for work." When he didn't say anything, she added, "She left a student waiting."

Joshua's mouth twitched. "Oh right, yeah. She's sick. It's my fault. I meant to call it in. Flu, I think—throwing up, couldn't get out of bed, all that."

"Right," said Elissa.

"Sorry."

"I see."

"So …" he prompted, trying to end the conversation.

"Is everything okay, Joshua? You can talk to me. I know how tough it is, these days, for you. For everyone."

Olivia Sixtus glided by at that moment, Joshua forced a smile. "Fine, just fine. Great to hear from you. My apologies again. Now I've *really* got to get back to work."

"Okay," said Elissa, dragging out the word. "We still on for dinner this Saturday? Barry's making sushi."

"Wouldn't miss it," he replied. He finished the call.

"I have a meeting," he said, to an uninterested colleague nearby. Joshua walked out, trying not to look hurried.

When he got around the corner from work, he ran. The quickest route home was through the daily protest. He usually avoided it—it did not look good to be spending too much time among those people. Right now, though, he didn't have much of a choice.

He pushed his way through the foot traffic, chants getting closer and closer. He took the raised walkway, above the protest encampment. Yellow tents dotted the side of the street, while luminous beings occupied the roadway.

The protestors stood in roughly even lines, Xi Boxes strapped to their chests, rigged to work in reverse. Years of fears and dreams charged them, powered them, these radiant beings. They were singing and shouting slogans, or laughing, sharing meals on solar stoves set up near the tents. They composed poems, or manifestos, or illustrations of each other. Created, then plastered up on the wall running alongside the protest area.

Painted over by the authorities every night. Didn't matter. Every morning the art would begin again, anew, on the blank slate.

Energized, these people, alive, eyes glowing, minds bright. Radiant, they lit up the roadway. Shadows bent away from the masses of the protestors as they burned with primal energy. Despite everything, Joshua paused on the walkway above. Couldn't help himself. They were singing a song, all together, voices raised.

He wasn't the only one watching. The Iron Guard were there, as always. Three rows of golems, either end of the street. Implacable, silent. There to make sure the protests spread no further, stayed within the free speech zone. Sometimes the protestors would approach the golems, fling insults. Sometimes exhortations to join them. The golems paid no heed, they just watched the protestors with sightless iron eyes and clenched fists.

One of the protestors, ahead of the others, danced. Orgasmically, arms akimbo, spinning, spinning. He glowed brighter than the others and Joshua held a hand up to shield his eyes. The man was alive, wreathed in pulsating red light, his energies distilled into this moment, Xi Box on his chest roaring with all his whispered shame.

Then he died. His light faded. The man, withered, swayed on a phantom wind, and collapsed onto the street.

The Iron Guard lurched into action. Two of them dragged the corpse, one leg each, from the protest grounds. That was the third way to respond to the demands of Heaven. The human heart could sustain a few weeks of the rebellious spirit—a few months, at most, with the power of their unrepentant, uncensored natures flowing back through the Xi Box—but even the strongest burned out eventually.

When the protest started, it felt like they'd go on forever. There seemed an indefatigable reserve of citizens willing to step forward when others fell. Keep the ranks of the uninfected swollen, the eyes of the world fixed upon them. But those heady days were long gone. Twenty-three years since the city was absorbed by Heaven. Each year the protest camp dwindled.

Twenty-three years and the gods remained silent. The Iron Guard, the Ecclesiasts, and the Infected carried out their wishes, knowing the will of Heaven. Still, the young, the rebellious, beat themselves against the indifference of the city. They'd be gone, one day. The streets below would eventually be clean and ordered. Time would roll over the protestors, more destructively than any tank. Time would roll on and grind even the memory of rebellion to dust.

Joshua realized he was hesitating. First rushing to get home, now scared as to what he'd find. His mouth twitched. He pushed himself away from the railing and, with the songs of the protesters ringing in his mind, continued down the path.

Jessica Long was waiting. She sat at the dining table they'd placed by the tall windows, one hand in her lap, the other on tabletop, fingertips gently resting on the surface.

Joshua closed the door quietly. He glanced through the open door of their bedroom. Jess's Xi Box was flat, lifeless. An emptiness filled his chest.

He moved to the kitchen, opened the bottom drawer, and dropped a pen from work in there. A hundred pens, just like it. Staplers, hole punchers, boxes of lead pencils. Smuggled out over the years, collected he knew not why. Like a bower bird, acting on mere instinct, building a nest.

Joshua stopped delaying and sat opposite his wife, taking her hand gently in his. She turned from the windows, a smile touching her lips, as though aware of his presence for the first time. "Oh, hello. I have been waiting for you."

"Hey."

"What time is it? You are home early."

"Your work called."

"Oh, of course."

Joshua hesitated. "Elissa is worried about you."

"She needn't be."

"I'm—" his voice caught, and he tried again: "I'm worried about you."

"Joshua." She really looked at him then, and in that moment he knew she'd changed, knew the words she was about to speak. "I went over today."

A cold hard hand reached in and gripped his heart. "No."

"It's such a relief." She sighed. "I do not know why I fought so hard for so long. It is so much easier now. Simpler."

Joshua's throat felt thick. "No."

She squeezed his hand. "Join me, Joshua. I know how difficult it is for you, as well. I know you are holding back."

Chest tightening, warning flashes popped in his mind. His mouth twitched. If she'd gone over, she'd done so with his secrets. The worst he'd kept from her, but all his other sins she knew.

"How do you know?" he asked.

"You know when it is done. It is like the moment of peace after confessing to a Xi Box, only a thousand times more liberating. It is purer and cleaner. The dirt and the doubt don't rush back in ten minutes later. It is absolute freedom."

He shook his head. "You've given up hope."

"Hope? Joshua. We feed our hopes to the Xi Box."

"That's not true."

"All these years, and you still do not understand. I understand now, with perfect clarity: Infected or not, it doesn't make a difference."

She seemed so calm. For the first time in months. Back straight, looking right at him, unblinking. He tried to speak, insist it was not true, but felt his throat thicken again. Rubbed at his eyes to wipe the tears before they started falling.

"Joshua. Joshua." She spoke softly, insistent, forcing him to look at her. "I am happy. Now you can be happy. I will get a better job; we can move to a bigger apartment. We can finally afford to have a child. That is what we always wanted."

He pulled his hand from hers, leaned back in his chair.

"Children? *Children?*" He choked on the word the second time. Stopped himself from what he wanted to say.

"Children, Joshua." If she caught his distress, she gave no indication of it. "Like we always dreamed."

"Yeah," he said. "We did." Years before, before they were tired. Back when they'd go dancing all night, and say *fuck it* to sleep and sobriety and work the next day. Jess would wear a short floral dress, whirl-whirling hem rising, laughing, not caring, and neither did Joshua. Salarymen and drab tourists around the edge of the dance floor, either wishing themselves with the bright wild girl, or judging her for her wantonness, and yet fearful of her for both.

Joshua saw it all and laughed: at those at the sidelines, at themselves; Joshua and Jess, so free inside their love.

Then Jess got tired. They both got tired. Life arrived: the bills, the obligations, the self-criticisms. They worked hard, sometimes multiple jobs, to get ahead in a world, they discovered, all too late, wouldn't let them. They monitored what they said and did, reined it all in, so they wouldn't attract the ill gaze of Heaven. They stopped going out.

There's this weight that settles, gram by gram, on one's shoulders. It's hard to explain to someone who's never lived it. You don't feel it yourself, most of the time. Just the symptoms. The sore neck and the headache. A pressure attendant on every thought, on every sentence. Having to weigh each one, think through the thread of conversation, where it may lead—

the pitfalls of an inadvertent comment or line of thought. To self-censor every moment. The people of the city who fought against infection were tired from the constant battle. It's not an evocative word, *tired*—it doesn't resonate. But it's the right one.

He couldn't talk to anyone except Jess, but as her spirit ebbed, they confided less and less. No plans to make anymore, except how to exist in the present. And if he was tired with the present, he was exhausted by the future.

Now she was talking about *it, a baby, family*. Words that hadn't passed her lips in years. His mouth twitched and he could think of nothing worse. Raising children in an exhausted future, under the eternal lights of the neon leviathan.

Joshua forced a smile. "Perhaps we need a break."

"A break?" Her brow knitted.

"A holiday."

"Holiday?"

"Yeah. You know. To mark this turning."

"I do not know. There is so much to do now, I see it all now, all the opportunities."

He swallowed. "A holiday might be the right time to try."

"For what?"

"For a baby, Jess."

"Oh." She nodded, as though he'd just explained a math problem. "I see. Less stress. The suggestion has prudence. I shall consider it."

Joshua sighed, coming to a decision. "I have to go back to work."

"Now?"

"Yeah."

"I understand. You are doing very important work, Joshua. When are you coming back?"

"Late. Very late."

Pause. A flicker, in her eyes, of something real. "Are you coming back, Joshua?"

"Soon. I promise."

"Joshua. I want you to come over with me."

"Jess."

"We cannot be on either side. You know it does not work."

He nodded. "Yeah. I agree completely."

☼

Joshua walked back. The day shifts were finishing, emptying out the office buildings. Evening shifts coming in the other direction, jostling him. Out of sync with the stream of human traffic, bounced around by other bodies. No ninja anymore. Far too visible.

Thinking. There was a small space between shifts at the verification branch. An hour or so over transition. It was messy, people going this way and that. Sometimes in the wrong place, sometimes faces you hadn't seen before. He got to his desk and his section was empty. The task should have been done over months. A year, optimally. Didn't matter now. He set to work.

When he was done, he was famished. He'd had no lunch, no dinner. Headache, dry lips—suddenly aware of his hunger. He went to the kitchenette, stuck his head in the fridge. On the second shelf, a blue lunchbox with OLIVIA SIXTUS written on it in block letters caught his eye. He felt the weight of it, peeled back the lid and sniffed. Shrugging, he took it to the dimly lit documents room, closed the door, and sat up the back in the shadows behind the last tall metal shelf. On the floor, cross-legged, he popped the lid and ate her lunch with his hands. She may be Infected, but goddamn she knew how to cook. He licked his fingers, smacking his lips: the soy sauce marinade was perfect.

"How is it?"

Joshua started, box falling from his lap, rice dregs spilling onto the concrete floor.

"Olivia."

"You mean: *Miz Sixtus*."

Olivia Sixtus had rolled up, silent, and now stood at the other end of the aisle, arms crossed, barely visible in the gloom.

"You're here late, Miz Sixtus."

"I always am."

"Ah."

"Well?"

He breathed out, ragged, trying to ride his fears. "I'm sorry." He held his hands out in apology. "I was hungry."

"I shall have to report you to staffing for a breach of the code of conduct."

Joshua brushed the stray rice back into the container with the side of his hand. "I understand."

"The matter of the Capricornia file, however, is of a different magnitude entirely."

Joshua stopped brushing. His heart stopped beating as well. He stared at the patch of concrete in front of him, a streak of soy sauce darkening the smooth drab floor.

"New auditors have their work screens mirrored and sent to a reliable colleague."

Joshua cleared his throat. "Oh. That wasn't in the briefing."

"No, it is not." When she spoke again, she was standing closer. "The uninfected are especially scrutinized. The monitoring never ends, even for a quiet little mouse like you."

He said nothing while his brain raced to catch up.

"Instead of simply deleting the transactions of the Ecclesiast, you transferred the assets to yourself."

Oliva Sixtus had glided to within six feet of him. He could hit her. That was his first thought—right in that disapproving, cat's arse mouth of hers. Then tie her up in here. No one ever came looking for hard files anymore. His mouth twitched.

Joshua stood, slowly, her lunchbox in hand.

He'd never hit anyone. No. There was another way.

"People like you," she said, with a curled lip. "Allowing corruption to flourish."

"People like me," he repeated, uninflected.

"People like you, taking and never giving back."

"People like me."

"I am going to report you now. Goodbye, Mr. Lee."

His brain stopped racing, finally catching up. Violence was not necessary. A solution, far more elegant, had already been accidentally crafted by his hand.

"*People like me* get nothing, Olivia, but the silence of the gods, and the *supervision* of their servants."

"And a beachfront property in Capricornia," she said, and she almost smiled as she said it.

"Oh no, Olivia, not even that." He shook his head. "Especially not that."

She hesitated. "What do you mean?"

"What you saw, Olivia, was me taking the assets of an Ecclesiast, acquired through corruption, and transferring it to numbered bank accounts, changing the title to a new owner."

"Yes."

"I am not the holder of those accounts. You see, I was ordered to make those changes. I didn't know the recipients. That's how it works here, doesn't it?"

"What?"

"Oh, Olivia. My testimony will be easily corroborated when they see everything goes to John London. And to you."

"*What?*"

He smiled.

"You …" She stopped, eyes widening as she realized the implications. "I have gone over," she said, raising her chin. "My integrity is unimpeachable."

"Unimpeachable." He snorted. "*All the Ecclesiasts ever do is steal.* Half of our work is covering up their crimes!" He jabbed a finger at her. "And you, their faithful servants, the Infected, the *Children of Heaven*: you share that corruption. All you aspire to is to be promoted into their ranks."

"No one will believe you."

"Then why am I the only one here not panicking?"

"*Your Xi Box will give us the truth.*"

"Ah." Joshua nodded, to himself.

She made a thin line of her mouth. Forcing it closed, realizing she'd said too much.

"I knew it. *I knew it*: the boxes were monitored. Pity for you—this confession I never made. In this city it pays not to trust even god."

Somehow, Olivia Sixtus paled even further. White spectral face, floating in the shadows of the file room. "Why?"

"Because there's a fourth option. And to go that way I needed leverage over London. I set it up so if I get what I want, London gets the encryption key I've created, and can delete his file. Just the transactions—if he likes he can keep the assets. I don't care. But if he doesn't give me what I want, then the freight train of the Iron Guard will come smashing through his front door."

"Why me too?"

"Because you're an ambitious auditor, next in line for his job, and this gives him an added incentive. And because they were just some prawn, fucking, dumplings Olivia, *and you couldn't let it go*."

"Treachery," she breathed.

He smiled without humor. "To what?" Joshua walked over, handed her the lunch container. "You're not asking the right questions."

She accepted the container, they both held on to it. "Now what?" she asked.

"I'll tweak my original plan. You get what you want."

She wet her lips. "And what do you want?"

He let the lunchbox go. "Ah. Finally. The right question. Just two little things, Olivia."

✧

Joshua looked out over the ocean. Wind jostled his hair. Gulls cawed high above. He pulled the weight from his jacket pocket. The one that'd been resting there, against his heart. One of the two items. Flipped the leather cover, looked at the golden crest underneath. International auditor. Field investigator for the Capricornia file. Tasked to uncover the asset trail of former senior auditor John London by his replacement, Olivia Sixtus.

Joshua flicked the badge into the water. It shone, briefly, in the sunset, as waves bate-abated over the gleaming metal. Soon it was half submerged in the sand.

"What are you doing?"

Joshua turned to look at Jess. Her skin was pale, translucent, in the sunset. Jess's boss, Elissa, had given her leave—enthusiastically, even. It was the first time Jess had taken—or even asked for—time off in eight years.

He took a second item from his pocket. The Xi Ring. Formerly John London's, confiscated when he'd been arrested. Olivia made sure it found its way to Joshua.

"I got you a present, to celebrate." He held it out to her, pulsing red in the palm of his hand.

"It has been used." Jess moved her head away in disgust.

Joshua told her the truth: "By me. On the flight here. I was anxious about our holiday." Then he lied: "If you wear it, it will become inert. Everyone will know you have joined the Children of Heaven." Then told the truth, again. "I thought it could symbolize this new phase, for both of us."

Jess looked at it. "I see. I understand. I hope it can as well, Joshua."

She paused a moment longer, then gave him her hand. Joshua slipped the ring onto her finger. She gasped, stepped away from him—four, five steps, feet splashing in the water. *"No."* Jessica Long glowed, bathed in red, as his Xi energies flowed back into her. The fears he whispered as his wife slept beside him on the plane. Every one of those fears about her. His hopes, as well. Their hopes. An imploring ragged recounting of the dreams they'd shared, the future they'd longed for.

She was looking at herself now, in wonder, her arms outstretched, turning her hands over, mouth agape. A glowing, luminescent being, banishing the gloom of dusk, making the sand around her feet shine white, incandescent.

Then it was done. After he'd confessed he'd taken the ring from his hand and rigged it to flow backwards, just like the protestors. But unlike the protestors, it wasn't a lifetime's worth. Just seven desperate hours.

Jess blinked and looked around. Her hand came up to touch her cheeks, gingerly, as though unsure of her own substance. "Am I awake?"

"Yes," he said.

"What year is this?"

"It doesn't matter, Jess," he said, gently.

"Oh." She walked back over to him and the residue of his Xi energy dissipated in the air behind her, trailing, like quiescent fading fireflies. "It feels like I've been asleep."

"We both have."

She breathed in and out, deeply, as though she were trying out her lungs for the first time. Jess looked out over the ocean. The kraken, as it rolled in its sleep. "It's so quiet, isn't it?"

"Yes."

"There was this noise in my head. A million voices, whispering at me, wanting me, pulling me away from you, like a tide."

"We broke the spell. Oh god. I didn't know if it could …" Joshua felt the tears well in his eyes.

Jessica Long turned at the crack in his voice. "Babe." She touched his arm. "What's wrong?"

Joshua squeezed his wife's hand. "Everything. Nothing. But that doesn't matter anymore."

She raised an eyebrow, smiling, just a little. "Oh. Enigmatic."

"I'm just glad you're here."

"Yeah," she said, and turned back to the ocean. "Me too."

They stood hand in hand, looking out across the eternal sea. The weight had lifted. The one he'd borne so long he'd forgotten it was there. The sea rolled and he smiled and all that mattered now was the ocean between him and Heaven, and the salt-scented breeze that brushed his face, and his wife's fingers, wrapped gently in his.

All his confessions swelled his heart. His sins made his eyes dance in the sunset. Dreams formed, waiting to be dreamed.

"So," said Jess. "Did I hear music coming from back there in the dunes?"

"Oh. Yeah. I think there's a bar."

She moved in close. Her hair brushed his face. "Wanna dance?"

Joshua smiled. "Always."

Joshua made to leave. He hesitated as Jess looked away, back at the sea. To the place over the horizon, where Heaven waited. He squeezed her hand, gently, and she turned back to him.

Copyright © 2023 by T. R. Napper.

Alan Smale is the double Sidewise Award-winning author of the Clash of Eagles *trilogy, and his shorter fiction has appeared in* Asimov's *and numerous other magazines and original anthologies. His latest novel,* Hot Moon, *came out last year from CAEZIK SF & Fantasy. When he is not busy creating wonderful new stories, he works as an astrophysicist and data archive manager at NASA's Goddard Space Flight Center.*

KRISTIN, WITH CAPRICE

by Alan Smale

He did not ring the bell. Strange enough to have to knock on his own front door, when the key was in his pocket. He heard a strange bleating sound from within, quickly suppressed. Then footsteps, and his heart began to thump a little harder.

Kristin opened the door and stared at him. Her hair was in a bandanna and she wore an old softball tee-shirt. Around her eyes were traces of yesterday's makeup. House-cleaning, then. Scrubbing away the last of him.

She looked so gorgeous he wanted to cry.

"I came for my things," he said.

"If you'd called, I could have been out." She stood aside to let him in. Reluctantly.

"That's not necessary," said Paul. "You don't have to do that. You look great."

"Yes, it is," she replied. "Yes, I do. No, I really don't. Your stuff's in the spare room." She walked into the kitchen and he heard the strange squeal again. Perhaps the sound of a sponge against the inside of the oven?

His apartment—not his any longer—was a living room plus a separate kitchen, a main bedroom and a spare room, and a bathroom. Twelve hundred square feet, yet when he'd shared it with Kristin it had not been too small. Not until the Ice Age of their final month.

Much of the living room furniture was new. The beanbag chair with the tassels was particularly unnerving. He'd told her she could keep his furniture, and she'd moved it out anyway. He didn't see a single lamp, CD or knick-knack that was his. In fact, it seemed that in expunging him, she'd taken the opportunity to clear out a load of her own junk too. The room looked spare and healthy and female, and Paul was an alien here. He did not linger.

The spare room held seven large cardboard boxes, an empty bookcase, and a litter box. On the top of the pile of boxes was a seven-page inventory; she'd packed his books and DVDs, his clothes and magazines, and neatly catalogued everything. To make sure he wouldn't stay long. But the litter box confused him. They both had allergies.

He re-ordered the boxes in a line from heaviest to lightest, and moved the first, second, and third boxes from the spare bedroom to just inside the front door. When he turned back from setting the third box precariously on top of its fellows, he found a small white goat peering at him from the kitchen doorway.

"Yah!" he said, startled, then more moderately, "Uh, Kristin? Goat. Goat!"

"Don't let her out," came Kristin's voice from the kitchen. "She's not an outdoor goat."

"Mah-ah-ah," said the goat and trotted toward him. It was truly tiny: one foot high at the shoulder, with a long perfect-white coat, it was the smallest goat Paul had ever seen. Its neat little white beard gave it an air of sagacity quite at odds with its frisky body language. It had piercing blue eyes.

Kristin appeared in the doorway behind it, wiping the sweat from her temples and neck with the bandanna. Paul wanted to leap over the goat and scoop her up, caress away the sweat, rub her back, cry her a river, kiss her into tomorrow, steal the bandanna and keep it on his pillow.

He'd had this meeting planned out all week. Knew exactly how he'd pitch his beg for forgiveness. Do anything for another chance, not cling so hard, set her free, allow her complete independence, just as long as she'd let him back into her life. He'd run the speech twenty times, and he knew how to serve it with the compelling gumbo of pathos, sincerity, and self-deprecating wit that had convinced her to move in with him in the first place. But the goat was truly freaking him out.

"Kristin," he said. "Let's try again. It doesn't have to end like this. We were so good together." Lameness muted him. None of that had been in the script, and Kristin just gaped at him like he was the Unabomber.

"Mah-ah," said the goat, and a moment later he heard an echo as a second miniscule goat sauntered out of their—Kristin's—bedroom and stared at him as intently as the first.

"Goat," Paul said. "Wait, I didn't—"

"Stop." Kristin held both hands up in front of her, bandanna still clasped in one of them. "Paul, I know you're still clinging to the wreckage, nursing some hope, but really: no. We've talked, and there's no more to say. You're a fading memory. I'm done. Moved on. It's time to go on with our lives. And I'll need the key back from you."

"But it's my key," he said, stupidly.

"It's my apartment. You didn't want to live here any longer. We changed the lease."

That was true. Living here without her would have eviscerated him slowly. He fumbled for something to say. "So, then … You have goats now."

"Yes, I do."

"Is that legal? Are they spayed? Neutered?" Did you spay a goat?

"Paul, that's none of your concern."

"No," he said. "Of course not."

The nearest goat was so small and skinny that when it twitched its head it looked almost like a lizard. It was clearly intrigued by him, unlike the second goat which was engaged in a cheerful contest with the tassels on Kristin's beanbag chair.

"What are their names?"

She sighed. "Paul, I've put most of you out of my mind, but I do recollect what stalling sounds like."

"Right," he said.

The first box took up more space in his Honda than he'd expected. He spent a while moving the toolbox, jack, and beer around in the trunk to set up the most amenable configuration for the other boxes. He might have to unpack the clothes-box and stuff its contents in around the rest. The last thing he wanted to do was make another trip. Kristin would scornfully identify that as a craven subterfuge, even if it wasn't.

Her front door was closed again. A little bloody-mindedly, he used his key to open it. Kristin was sitting in the beanbag chair, unusually upright, staring at him wide-eyed. A tiny goat rubbed its head on her knee.

"I didn't mean to startle you," said Paul.

"You didn't. Not really. It's just odd to see a man let himself in through my door."

A man. "I'm not just anyone." Too defensive. *Bzzt.* Shouldn't have said that. Should have had a witty come-back. He turned to pick up the second box and found a white goat posing atop it as if auditioning for "The Sound of Music."

"Goat," he said. "Oh, sorry. Marks deducted for repetition."

"Mah-ah-ah." The goat sprang to the floor with some agility, danced away three steps, turned to face him. Can't catch me.

Paul took the second box to the car. This time Kristin was holding the door open on his return, bandanna thrust casually into her jeans pocket. He looked yearningly into her eyes, breathed in her warm aura, kept his hands firmly by his sides. Third box, to the car. This one went in the back seat. He could probably fit the smallest one from the spare room into the trunk with the other two, and stack the remaining three in the rear seat. Failing that he could always put the last box in the front seat and lock it in place with the belt. Perhaps this would work after all.

Kristin's door was closed again. He stared at the doorbell for ninety seconds and then took out his key again.

She wasn't in the living room. The goats bleated at him and skipped flirtatiously.

He knelt to take a closer look. The nearest was the slightly less skinny one that had peeked out of the bedroom. Its fur was so fine that patting it was like touching air. It did not smell bad. Its intelligent blue eyes pulled out his innermost thoughts and munched on them meditatively. He scratched it behind the ears, and just out of his reach, the truly skinny goat bleated in jealousy.

"Paul."

He straightened guiltily. "None of my concern. I know. I was just curious. It came up to me."

"It's a she. Both of them are."

"All right."

"Parsley and Sage."

"Pardon?"

Kristin stuck out her finger. The skinny goat studied it narrowly. "Parsley." She pointed to the one at his feet. "Sage."

Hence the sagacity. He touched the peak of an imaginary cap and nodded solemnly to the goats. "Pleasure's mine."

Kristin and Sage eyed each other, then the human female came back over to sit cross-legged in the beanbag chair and the animal trotted up for strokies. Paul did not dare to breathe in case he frightened either of them away. Timid Parsley now nuzzled his ankle and he squatted on his heels to pet her. He was painfully aware of Kristin's proximity, of her smell, of her mussed hair. But the goat hair under his fingers soothed him and took away the sting.

"They're a new breed," said Kristin. "Miniature, house-broken, smarter than your average goat. Trained not to eat your clothes, house-plants, garbage, or shoes. Unless you want them to, of course."

Kristin had never been a pet person. Now she'd replaced him with a brace of she-goats. It should have been another crater in Paul's multiply blasted heart, but he was already over it.

"They're a little magical," she added.

"Yes, they are." He was impressed by their affection and domesticity. Cat-smart and dog-loyal, in an angora package.

"No, I mean, really. They're on loan from my aunt. To keep me company for a couple of weeks. She says nothing fixes you up quite like a four-legged friend."

That would be the Pennsylvania aunt with the hexes on the barn, who never used the telephone. Her home-made bread was to die for. Paul and Kristin would have stayed with her more often if it wasn't for their cat allergies. "Oh," he said. The aunt lived alone in an old farmhouse, but Paul didn't recall any cows or sheep or other real farm animals nearby.

"She liked you," said Kristin, mistaking the tone of his Oh. "She was just a little cautious around you. She didn't know what a systems analyst was, so I could never convince her you weren't some kind of shrink."

"Goats," he said, still getting used to the word.

"She says goats are my birth animals. In some zodiac or another."

Batty old witch. Paul grinned, feeling the atmosphere loosen up. "I suppose they are. Birth year, 1987. The Year of the Goat. You have a sparkling personality and inspire loyalty in all who know you. Creative and capricious. Marry a Rat or a Rabbit late in life. Avoid the Boar. Or something like that."

"I went to see her," said Kristin thoughtfully. "After you left. I cried and cried. That, I do remember."

Reality blinked. "You cried?" he said.

She looked at him uncertainly.

He'd been making a fuss of Parsley for more than a minute, and he still didn't feel any tickling in his nose. Possibly the only quadruped he wasn't allergic to.

Kristin had cried? His imagination swerved to avoid the concept. "Do they shed?"

"Minimally. I brush them daily."

"They seem hungry. What do they eat?"

"They're goats, Paul. They eat just about anything I have too much of." She and Sage touched noses. "Silly kitty. Why did we split up?"

"Eh? You and I, or you two?"

She looked at the goat and the goat looked back, as if to say 'Men!' Then Kristin looked at Paul. "You, Einstein. We split up because?"

He reached out a shaky hand. Parsley was still there at his fingertips to calm him. "Are you kidding?"

"Was that a pun?" she said.

"What?"

"I was reading my journal last night." Always a journal, never a diary. "It seems we went to the FolkFest, you and I. When it got dark you wanted to leave. I wanted to stay. I was furious, and we argued. And, for me, that was when it all began to end, that was when I started falling out of love with you. Apparently."

His heart ached, his mind reeled. "Wow. Really?"

"Paul?"

He searched for solidity but found only a goat. "That long ago? That was last June. But, Kristin, I'm the one who likes folk music. I'm the one who knows all the groups. You only came along with me in the first place to keep the peace."

"Exactly, Paul. That was the whole point."

It was no use. He couldn't make head or tail of it. "Why are we talking about last June?"

Kristin picked up Sage, pointing the goat at him like a weapon. Sage blinked gormlessly, spoiling the effect. "Because that was the turning point. It seemed important in the journal. And I want to understand why I would get so angry over something like that."

With some difficulty Paul regrouped, realizing this nutty conversation might actually work in his favor, in terms of his original mission here today. He could now easily launch into his plea for forgiveness. But somehow the more he played with Parsley, the more his mood shifted from that intent. Kristin had already made it crystal clear that she wouldn't take him back, so why make a spectacle of himself?

He shrugged. "Well, guess what, Kristin: it never made an ounce of sense to me either."

He'd handed her a cue to wrap up the conversation, yet she said: "You still haven't told me why we split up."

"Kristin . . . ."

"In your on words."

Now he felt trapped. "Why are you wearing a wire? Should I confess to dire deeds for the FBI guys in the black van?"

"You're funny," said Kristin in the same tone of voice that she might have said "A new Starbucks opened by my office."

Parsley pushed her head into his hand; he'd momentarily stopped scratching her neck. As Paul stroked her he searched his memory for the right words. If this was to be the very last eulogy of their relationship, if Kristin was having trouble sorting it all out, he wanted to be honest with her. He owed her that.

And, after all, it was rather simple. "OK. As I understand it, I was cramping you. Making you something you weren't. I wouldn't let go. Wouldn't set you free. You just wanted to be alone again. Or something."

"Hmmm," she said. "Well, freedom is important."

Paul hesitated. "Is that what it says in your diary?"

"That's none of your business."

"Of course." He stood up, incurring the protests of a silky white goat. "Okay. Box number four."

"It says . . . ."

He froze.

She sighed, shook her head. "What it says is: 'I just want to drive my own bus. Like Sandra Bullock, only more slowly and without the bomb. And without Keanu Reeves screaming at me.'"

"Mah-ah-ah-ah!" said Sage.

"You were what, seven when that movie came out? Eight?"

"Yeah, I loved it."

"Okay."

"I'm not kidding," said Kristin with a perplexed frown. "My diary is like, 'All I ever wanted was to slow down and choose my own turns.'"

"I never—" Both goats stared at him. He stared back. "Your diary says I'm Keanu Reeves?"

"It's a journal!" she shouted in exasperation. "Once and for all time, Paul, the thing is a frigging *journal*! All right?"

The dust motes hung unmoving in the light from the window for a single leisurely moment, and then Paul cracked up. His howls of laughter sent the goats scurrying for the safety of the bedroom. Kristin glowered belligerently at him and then her lips started to twitch. She held the laugh off for another two breaths, and then gave in to it. She had a joyous laugh.

"You're a trip," he said, eventually. "Well. I need to get out of here."

"What?"

"I'm glad we're parting friends. Thanks for not making this too heavy. I do appreciate it."

"You're welcome," she said, nibbling on her lower lip.

Paul walked into the spare room, looked at the litter box, and walked out again. "Wait. That little speech: 'Clinging to the wreckage, nursing some hope, time to move on.' That was from your, uh, journal too, wasn't it?"

"That's none—"

"You barely remember me at all, do you? What the heck did you do, Kristin? See a hypnotist? Drop acid?"

She squinted up at him. "You know, Keanu, you're really not what I was expecting."

"Whatever." He should have cared more that she'd managed to put him out of her mind so completely, but he, too, found himself looking at her with fresh eyes. The sting of the old arguments, the mental scabs over the old wounds, seemed less important to him than his impressions of her here, today, now. Kristin was quirky and attractive. Elusive. Intriguing. He wondered how it would be to walk with her along a deserted beach at sunset. Whether she liked having her back scratched. Whether she preferred to cook or clean up.

His head was starting to ache. He should have known that sooner or later he'd start reacting to the damned goats. They'd probably have him sneezing and snoring for days.

"Gotta go," said Paul, and without thinking about it he leaned forward and kissed her, a sociable peck and totally not a pass, but she did not flinch, and her lips moved beneath his. A stray lock of her hair tickled his cheek. Again he enjoyed the faint, familiar aroma of her sweat.

The sensations didn't tear at the old scars. Quite the reverse; her lips felt brand new, like a promise.

The kiss had taken a single instant, but just touching her and breathing her had left him dizzy. Her eyes were unreadable. "Oh, boy," he said. "I'm so completely sorry about that. I should go."

"Mah-ah," said Parsley. Or the other one, whatever it was called.

"All I wanted was to forget you," she said softly. "And now I don't even remember why."

He knelt and looked at the goats again. They didn't seem hungry any more. "Hmmm," he said. "Anything? They seriously eat … anything?"

Kristin made the conversational switch effortlessly, as he'd known she would. "Anything I give them. Whatever I don't want."

Paul nodded, though the reason why he'd asked had already escaped him. "Well, I'll see you."

"Not if I see you first," she said cheerfully.

Odd that he'd dreaded coming around here for so long.

As Paul slid into the driver's seat he glanced up at the window of Kristin's third-floor apartment and frowned. From the Honda's glove-box he took out the notebook he wrote his gasoline purchases and mileage in, and scribbled 'Kristin/3307' on the back page. Then, to be safe, he wrote the whole address. His fingers still felt silky against each other.

He drove out to the gate of the apartment complex. While he waited to turn onto the main road he glanced over his shoulder. The Honda's back seat seemed surprisingly empty. Was this really all there was?

Well, if he'd left something behind, he could always go back.

Copyright © 2003 by Alan Smale. First published in Realms of Fantasy, *August 2003.*

Dafydd McKimm is a speculative short fiction writer whose stories have appeared in publications such as Flash Fiction Online, Daily Science Fiction, Deep Magic, The Cafe Irreal, *and elsewhere. He was born and raised in Wales but now lives in Taipei, Taiwan. You can find him online at www.dafyddmckimm.com.*

THE DREADNOUGHT *AGAMEMNON*, ON COURSE TO CONQUER THE PEACEFUL MOON OF RE

by Dafydd McKimm

As when an airship, streaming westward soon after dawn into the city, is silhouetted by the sun and dilates like a pupil as it makes its final approach with the slow, steady pace of massive things;

so the dreadnought *Agamemnon*, on course to conquer the peaceful moon of Re, awoke;

and as when you descend the gangway and take your first steps along the city's arabesque of streets, not knowing where you are going, for you've never visited this city before and have no friends or place to stay or any idea of how to speak the language that permeates the air like the chatter of strange insects wherever you go, or what you will do now that you're here, thinking for a moment that perhaps you should go back, back to where you came from and the safety of it, the security of its familiar pathways and customs, the blissful boredom of doing things the way you've been told for so long they're second nature; but no, no, you'll never go back to that—*never*—and so you walk on, wandering the city without a destination, not understanding a word, not knowing what food is good to eat or indeed how to ask for it, and even when you do manage to get something onto a plate in front of you, worrying that you might commit some awful impropriety so that those around you, those people who have known this city and the ways of this city from birth, will laugh at you and mock you as stranger, foreigner, and yet finding small comfort in knowing that at least your old life is behind you, that you have shed your past like the pale, translucent skin of a snake and can begin anew here, in this city, which is so beautiful, with its painted houses perched on forested hills and markets full of sweet temptations and patterned fabrics and parks dotted with statues of creatures from myths you've never heard of and noisy processions that pop and fizzle and chime with the ring and crash and keening of unfamiliar instruments and temples to so many different gods;

so the dreadnought *Agamemnon*, on course to conquer the peaceful moon of Re, first experienced reverie;

and as when these things become commonplace to you and you become accustomed to walking the arabesque of streets and see them with eyes unglamoured by the rose-tint of their novelty, you begin to see the city for what it truly is; you visit its borders and see it guzzling trees on the mountainside, churning the earth so that it can plant the seedlings of its artifice, spreading itself like a corruption across land hitherto untouched; and back in its palazzoed, honey-coloured, cobble-stoned heart you begin to spot the severed limbs in the mortar, the people ground up in the relentless cogs of its progress; you begin to see its true purpose, which is destruction, and you understand that the city is built on bones, and all the delicacies of its marketplaces and the fruit of the trees in its landscaped gardens are rotten to the core;

so the dreadnought *Agamemnon*, on course to conquer the peaceful moon of Re, came to understand its directives;

and as when you think no, no, no, this has to stop, but you can do nothing—there are too many people in this city, too many wills against yours, too many lives whose weight is crushing and whose trajectories across the city's streets are like walls of fire blocking your way; but then you realise—*wait!* you *do* have control; the city is a construct of your imagination, and you are writing it on paper, and all it takes for everything to disappear is for you to tear the page from your notebook, crumple it up, and throw it away, and then the city will not have consequences anymore, the city will not interact anymore, it will remain, folded into a small space of its own, inert, and all the people in it will remain there, but outside of the main story; and so that is what you do—you tear;

so the dreadnought *Agamemnon*, its fusion engines surging, fissured the spacetime continuum and—with all souls aboard, into the void—vanished.

Copyright © 2023 by Dafydd McKimm.

Deborah L. Davitt was raised in Nevada, but currently lives in Houston, Texas with her husband and son. Her poetry and prose have appeared in over fifty journals, including, F&SF, Analog, *and* Lightspeed. *For more about her work, including her novels, poetry collections, and her recent chapbook,* From Voyages Unending, *please see www.edda-earth.com.*

PABLOVISION

by Deborah L. Davitt

The object of backpacking through Europe in your twenties is to see strange things—or at least to look at the world through new eyes. You only get so many chances to paint old walls and ruined fortresses; to capture the patina of time itself.

Drew took a bus into Spain, figuring he would hike the Pyrenes while the weather remained good; the driver woke him in the gray of dawn and turfed him in a village that Drew's phone informed him was Santa Pau. His phone further told him that the ancient walls he saw, which captured the dawn's light so enchantingly, had been built in the thirteenth century.

Enraptured, he set up his easel in an out-of-the-way spot. He had charcoals with him, and he wanted to capture some of the spirit of this place, before he lost this magical moment. Maybe even mix some watercolors, try to catch the evanescent colors on paper so that when he had an opportunity to work on canvas later, it would be easier for his late-dreaming mind to recall what his eyes saw now.

As he worked, the village began to wake and move. Smells of baking bread and smoke. At first, he was too caught up in the arched walls, the uneven lines of the stones, to look at people. Till the woman unlocked the door of the bakery beside him to open to business, and made a scoffing sound as she noticed him.

"I'm sorry," Drew said, ruing his schoolboy Spanish. He knew he had a Mexican accent from all the kids he'd played with back home in Albuquerque. "If I'm trespassing, I can move—"

Then he stopped, arrested by her face. Her jaw was square and blunt; her eyes, by turns, either singular or plural, sometimes both appearing on one side of her face, sometimes one of them winking out of existence. Her nose was planted securely under one of her eyes, but took up one of her cheeks in its entirety.

For a terrible moment, Drew thought of the migraines his mother suffered. Her descriptions of how people's faces sucked in, as if they'd been drawn into a black hole as her entire visual field distorted. *Is that what this is? Migraine? Aneurysm?* His mouth dried as he looked down inadvertently, his notions of form and symmetry—even simple biology—stunned. Only to be confused again by the gemlike facets that rippled across her chest, obscuring any breasts that might have once been there. Her form rippled. Dissolved. Was abnegated, as if her humanity were somehow unimportant.

"Do you always stare?" she demanded, a mix of Basque and Catalan accent on her words giving them snap and verve—and with just enough differences in pronunciation that he could barely follow her

"Ah, no, I'm so sorry—"

"Do you think I *want* to look like this?"

He held up his hands, unwilling to offend. She stared at the charcoal in his fingers as if it were a gun. "I'm sorry. It's just that you seem quite, ah, unusual."

Her features blurred and molded, one nose—two—three!—appearing, each outlined in blunt, hard lines, all rectangular prisms. "It's not our fault. It's *his*. He could have just painted sunflowers or cottages, like van Gogh. He could have stuck to waterlilies, like Monet. But no. We are what he made us."

Drew swallowed. Everything, even her ranting words, seemed so surreal. He might've thought he was dreaming, but for the warm sunlight on his face, the smell of baking bread. He studied her face again, and his artistic training took over while his rational mind continued to revolt. He noted the sepia tones, the lack of the vivid, near-neon colors that might have marked out a Fauvist touch, and asked numbly, unable to think of anything else to say, "I take it that you don't mean Georges Braques?"

A snort of scorn as the woman went back into her bakery. Drew ventured to the door and watched as she set back to work, punching dough down on a floured surface. He felt dizzy, watching her hands. Sometimes two, sometimes four, as if she constantly shifted between past and present. "Was it Pi—"

"We don't say his name here," she snapped, not looking up. "Call him Pablo. Or that *maldito cabrón*."

"Er, Pablo, then." Drew didn't want to use the epithets she'd just employed—or the level of invective in her tone. He didn't step inside the bakery. He didn't want to intrude on her sanctuary. "I'm sorry. I didn't get your name."

"Maria." An acerbic sniff.

"Maria, so pleased to meet you." Automatic courtesy, drilled by years of lessons. "If I may ask … there are others here like you?"

Which was when another woman bustled in from the back to assist her. Inasmuch as he could tell, she *seemed* younger than Maria. But it was difficult to be sure, what with the diamond-shaped eyes stacked atop each other, the legs that terminated in feet that were different sizes and shapes, though she didn't limp as she began to set tables in the eating area. How she managed that, with three-fingered hands that seemed attached to only the suggestion of arms, Drew had no idea.

"No es cortés mirarme de esa manera," the girl reprimanded him, though she pointedly didn't look at him at all. *It's not polite to stare*, or perhaps, *it's not polite to look at me that way.*

Drew dropped his eyes to the floor, feeling a flush tighten his cheeks. Her voice was young. Pleasant. And he'd been staring like an ass. "I'm so sorry." *A good thing the first thing I ever learned in Spanish was how to apologize. I'm getting a lot of mileage out of lo siento today!*

"This is my daughter, Jacinta," Maria informed him. Drew raised his head, and found the girl already peeking at him. But it was hard—so hard—to know how to meet her eyes.

Then the first customers brushed past him at the door, and he saw that everyone *else* in this village of the damned had somehow had their human figures resolved, dissolved, into mere shapes and forms.

One woman's face had been bisected into triangles, a nose on either side, her mouth spanning the gap but narrowing at the midpoint so that she could barely eat the bread she bought with her broken teeth. A busker set up at the doorway with a guitar, and Drew could scarcely see the man, his body made entirely of muted shades of brown and gray, all but invisible as he stood against the bricks. Even his music sounded muted. Something generic and Euro-pop affiliated … coffee-house music, he'd have called it at home. *Shouldn't that be the strut and trill of a flamenco?* Drew wondered.

Maria beckoned him in brusquely. "Don't just stand in my door, letting in the flies. Come. Buy something. Eat."

Buying something seemed like literally the least he could do. Drew fished out his small stock of Euros and handed Jacinta a few as the girl moved to the cash register, again silently, efficiently aiding her mother. "Take a seat at the counter," she whispered, and gestured to a line of red-covered stools by a short glass barrier, through which he could watch Maria forming and shaping the loaves and rolls.

The hot bread Jacinta handed him smelled and tasted divine—and quite solidly real. *So much for this being a dream.*

When most of the customers had filtered out, leaving only a handful who'd settled in to make their breakfasts here, a lull passed over the bakery. "Can I help, somehow?" he asked Maria, again feeling the gap of language yawning at his feet. "You say, er, Pablo did this to you. Can it, um …. Be undone?"

From behind the low glass wall, Maria regarded him, one eye, two. "He painted us out of our reality and into his. He had a vision of what it means to *be Spanish*—a vision he expressed from the safety of Paris, the old *cabrón*. Where he didn't have to deal with our inconvenient reality. With the reality of having once been an empire that spanned the globe, but having fallen into dictatorship and poverty and fascism." She bared her teeth.

Drew had listened to plenty of people bitch about British colonialism. French colonialism. American colonialism. He'd never wondered until *now* if there was equal bitching in Mexico and South America about *Spanish* colonialism, and that this remained veiled because of the language gap, or because American media simply didn't *pay attention* to anything south of the Rio Grande. And he'd never thought what it would be like to live in a country that had once spanned the world, but that had collapsed in on itself, like the last ember of a star after a supernova.

"I'm sorry," he started to reply, but got only an impatient wave of Maria's hand. She had more to say, it seemed clear.

"All *Pablo* needed or wanted to do was play with light and shade and say, 'If you give a meaning to things in my paintings it may be true, that's not my intention. I just paint objects.'" A snort as she handed a paper-wrapped loaf to another customer. "We became *objects* to him. Every one of us. Just things to be dissolved into his *vision*."

Drew wanted to apologize for existing as an artist anywhere *near* these people. But he caught Jacinta rolling her eyes. Or at least, looking up at the ceiling with what looked like boredom.

Drew shook his head, still overwhelmed. "How is this even *possible?*"

Jacinta took a break from her work behind the counter, and came to sit next to him. "You think we look strange to you? You look strange to *me*. We get few tourists anymore. Too out of the way, too quiet. Most just come on the bus, take a few pictures, and leave." It might have been a smile that crossed her face then. "They don't see us the way we see ourselves. I've seen some of the pictures they've taken. They and their cameras see us … eh. What is that magazine, the one that used to go to Africa and take all the pictures … ?"

"*Life? National Geographic?*" And suddenly, he caught Jacinta's meaning, and winced. "Oh, god." His words slipped into English. "Look at them, all quaint in their folkways?"

"*Precisamente.*"

Christ. He didn't know what to say to that, but his head rose as the bell over the door jangled, and a set of young twin girls entered. One had a face half fair, the other side round and yellow as the sun; she had an arm around her sister's neck, but the second girl's face melted into shadows, and her body sagged and drooped, one breast resting on her belly, the other somewhere around the level of her collarbones. Both of them, terribly, appeared to be pregnant—and as Maria handed only one of them a loaf of bread, Drew understood, suddenly and terrifyingly. "There's only one of her, right?" he whispered to Jacinta urgently as the girls left. "I've seen a painting like that. *Girl with a Mirror*. It's a statement on vanity—"

The man at the counter to his left gave him what could only be described as an unfriendly look, and bumped his shoulder as he headed for the door.

Jacinta accorded Drew a sparse nod. "*Si.* And the worst of it is, she doesn't know which of her selves is real any more. We went to school together. She started to see herself that way when she was thirteen. She's been twins ever since. Some days she feeds one body. Some days, the other. She's tried starving each of her selves, but they don't die. She just goes on. As we all do." Her tone turned bleak.

Drew took another bite of bread. It seemed to help ground him in reality. "But Pi—I mean, *Pablo* has been dead for almost fifty years. Why haven't any of you … I mean, why haven't you just gone back to looking normal? If his *vision* is what's doing this—he's dead!"

The last of the regular customers left, and Maria poured three cups of strong, dark coffee, gesturing for them to follow her to a table. They settled in there, and it felt curiously intimate to Drew, sharing a battered, much-scratched table with them. *The patina of time, indeed,* he thought.

"Do you hear him?" Maria asked abruptly, inclining her head toward the busker outside.

This didn't seem like an answer to his previous question, but Drew decided to go with it. "Yes. Of course—shouldn't I?"

"He came here from your country about twenty years ago. He saw us as we have seen ourselves for generations—as Pablo saw us. And as *you* see us."

"Less *National Geographic,*" Jacinta said in English. "But still not who we are."

Maria made an impatient gesture. "That's irrelevant, my daughter. We became this way because of Pablo's vision of us, but we're trapped, unable to see ourselves for who we really are, because we do not know ourselves anymore. His vision was so pervasive, so … inevitable." She gestured, her hands eloquent of despair. "Who else is taught in *modern art* classes? When young students go to university, and want to learn to paint, do they try to look like Rembrandt these days? No. They might, at best, try to look like Monet, Manet, and produce insipid landscapes that their professors will call derivative. And then those same professors will oh-so-gently guide them to the work of the only true modern master. This. This is what the world looks like!"

Drew wanted to protest, but the words died on his lips. He'd *been* that art student. His love for the Baroque masters, their dynamic diagonals, the dark contrasts of light and dark, the terrifying, even grotesque realism of their faces and scenes—that *had* been scoffed at by his teachers. They'd told him that the only *really meaningful* art was post-modernism, and that he was wasting his time. And by inference, theirs.

He'd transferred majors to something that might result in an actual job sometime after graduation, and, still smarting internally, he'd gone over to painting landscapes in his spare time—ones he'd hoped weren't *insipid*, but that he'd enjoyed rendering. "So because his vision is dominant in the world … ."

"We haven't been able to break the habit of seeing ourselves this way. Some children are *born* looking like this," Maria gestured down at herself. "I was."

"So was I," Jacinta murmured. "Nuria—the twins you saw before? She looked normal. Human. Until, as I told you, she turned thirteen."

Drew sat there, silent. Listening. Straining his language skills, trying to keep up with the rapid-fire words. "I was born the year the *maldito cabrón* died," Maria declared. "And this is all I have to show for forty-seven years on earth—a body disfigured by a man's vision. Unable to see the face that *God* gave me under this … *mask.*"

He looked away, unable to bear the despair in her voice. Which made his eyes focus once more on the busker outside in the street, his body fading into the bricks. Realization dawned. "Wait. Didn't you say the musician's American?" He looked back at them, startled. "Why does *he* look like one of you?"

Maria's lips curled down, pulling the prisms of her noses into sharp Vs, like an assortment of beaks. "Assimilation. Not to us, mind. To *Pablo.*" She snorted into her coffee. "He became convinced that he could help us. That *music* was just as powerful as art, just as encompassing. When he came here, he played loud rock music. Metallica, mostly. Not very well." A sniff of aspersion. "But the longer he stayed, the more he became one of us. Now, this is all he remembers how to play. If you asked him his name? He'd tell you it's Miguel."

Drew swallowed. "It wasn't, originally?"

"No, he was *Michael O'Keefe* when he came here. I liked him. I liked him a great deal. And for a while, I … let myself hope." Maria sighed as Jacinta stirred beside her. "I'm telling you this, because you look like a decent person. The kind Michael was, when he arrived. You're going to want to help. Don't. Get on the bus and leave tomorrow morning. Before you're snared, too."

Drew stared through the window at Miguel—at *Michael*. For a moment, he thought he could see a gray-haired man with a long, unkempt beard. A T-shirt washed so often that the black had become gray, and the words *And Justice For All* barely visible across the chest. "Did it work?" Drew asked sharply, looking back at Maria. "Did he manage to free *any* of you, even for a moment?"

She lowered her head over her cup. "One or two. For a summer." Her voice sounded listless. Jacinta laid a hand on her mother's shoulder. "My sister was one of them, and she ran away to Madrid for a few months. Then came back when she started to … revert." Maria looked away. "When she'd fully reverted, she killed herself. The priests here are old-fashioned, you understand? We couldn't even bury her in the church cemetery. Mortal sin."

The rage and sorrow in her voice were old. Eroded by time. But they could still *stab*.

"My mother doesn't want to feel hope again," Jacinta put in now, a kind of gentle asperity in her tone, even as she rubbed Maria's shoulder lightly. "It hurts too much when hope dies."

"So, to summarize. You're victims of what might be called …" Drew couldn't come up with the words in Spanish, so he reverted to English, slowly, thoughtfully, "a dominant episteme." *Wow. Sounds pretentious when I say it out loud. Like every bad art school TA ever.* "You can't see yourselves out of it. Everyone who's tried to challenge that vision, to help you see yourselves again, has failed."

"Correct."

He stared out the window again. The thought of being swallowed up by another reality, sucked into another artist's conception of the world, his very being unmade? Terrifying. But then again, that was sort of what art was for, wasn't it? To be pushed into unfamiliar territory, to think new thoughts—or sometimes, old ones.

"I'm not sure my skill is up to challenging, ah, *Pablo's*."

"You're refreshingly lacking in ego." Jacinta teased. "It might save you."

"You have to be *good* to have an ego." A self-deprecating snort. "I gave up portraiture because my teachers thought photorealism best for cameras. And have painted insipid landscapes since." He caught Maria's wince as it rippled over the canvas of her face, and held up a hand. "It's fine. I know the limits of my talent, right?" He paused. "But what if the answer isn't just to impose some other outside influence on all of you? I mean, Miguel—Michael—tried that. And Pablo didn't come from *here*. Didn't do his work here—he did it off in Paris, as you said, surrounded by his international friends and all their wide-ranging thoughts and ideas. Communism, differing ideals of nationalism, philosophy, art."

Jacinta nodded enthusiastically, but Maria frowned. "What are you getting at?"

Drew drummed his fingers on the table. "Maybe the way out isn't to try to impose another vision here, but to help you see yourselves again?"

Maria snorted. "Don't you think we've *tried*?"

"Maybe you just need a better mirror?" Drew pulled out his phone, checking the date. He didn't *think* he was making a stupid, snap decision because he liked Jacinta's voice. But guys had done stupider things in the course of history for less reason. "Look. I have three months before I'm due back in the States. And if I don't at least *try* to help, I know I'll regret it for the rest of my life."

"But the risk—" Maria's voice tautened.

"I get it." He looked out at the busker once more, the man's form now wavering between a dissolving figure, and the distinct image of a man in his forties who looked like a guitar tech for a metal band. "But … no one deserves to live like this, swallowed up by someone else's vision. Let me at least try. And if you think I'm starting to get consumed, you can put me on that bus yourself."

A sigh. "There's a guest house at the edge of town. You'd be the only occupant at the moment. We'll take you there." Maria shook her head. "The *instant* you start to shift, you *will* board that bus."

Drew nodded. But as they stepped outside, he paused and talked to Miguel for a solid minute, in

English. "Hey, man, like the shirt. Did you actually see them in concert on that tour? That would've been back in like, '89 or so, right?"

He'd had to look *that* up on his phone, too. Drew hadn't been born when that album was current.

But somehow, it *worked*. The man looked up from his glazed focus on the strings, and his face flickered back into focus momentarily. His reply began in Spanish. "Yeah, they played in … Cincinnati. That's … hey! That's where I'm from!" His eyes brightened, becoming more distinct, and he went on in English, if with a heavy accent, "Huh, why have I been telling the tourists I was born in Madrid—oh. Shit. Pablo strikes again, huh?" He gave Maria what could only be an apologetic look.

Maria looked away from him, refusing to acknowledge his presence. Jacinta's mouth had fallen open, a dark cavern without visible teeth.

Even as they reacted, Michael—Miguel—began to fade back into the bricks. "Thanks, man. Even if it doesn't last … thank you."

Drew swallowed. While it was more evidence for his hypothesis, it was still hard to watch the man dissolve once more.

☼

Over the next months, Drew worked with the people of the village. Asked them to talk to him about the history of the old fortress walls, built in the medieval period, from stones flecked with volcanic aggregate. His Spanish improved, though he started to pick up Catalan and Basque words and inflections. He painted their city, their history.

Jacinta usually guided him around. He liked her. She was quieter than her outspoken mother, but could suddenly turn and tease him for some misspoken, broken bit of Spanish. And he *remembered* her corrections.

On one occasion, she took him to the local primary school and introduced him to the teachers and children there, so he could see for himself how the children under twelve were divided into 'normal' and … not. How the older children were already starting to shift. Some of them just had dark outlines to normal features. Others had haphazard bodily configurations, but still retained their natural skin tones and the flush of life.

He had to walk out of the first room after ten minutes, struggling to contain the *rage* he suddenly felt for *Pablo*.

Jacinta found him in the teacher's lounge, knuckles smarting from where he'd punched a wall. "Are you all right?" she asked.

"It's not *right*," he told her, bile churning up from his belly. "Dear god, screw with adults all you want—we're supposed to be able to take it. To fight back. But his goddamned *legacy* is screwing with *kids*, and it's not right!"

She settled a hand on his shoulder. When he didn't look at it, it felt like a human hand. No razor edges. Just soft warmth. "You had to see it to *understand* the despair we feel," Jacinta murmured.

Drew inhaled shakily. "I get it. I won't let them see it on my face." He nodded to her. "Come on. I have an idea."

With the teacher's permission, he took the youngsters out in the school yard. And armed with chalk, he got them to draw each other. Jacinta hovered near, and muttered, her voice alarmed, "Isn't *depiction* what got us into trouble in the first place?"

Drew switched to English. "They're *depicting* each other. In chalk. This is ephemera. It's not going to sit in a museum, forever, telling everyone who comes to see it, everyone who buys a postcard of it, exactly what and who *he* thinks you are. This is them. Today. In the moment where present turns to past, and then is washed away by the future. Or, you know. By rain." He held up a piece of chalk, offering it to her as he switched back to Spanish. "Want to *depict* me? I give you full permission to use me as your model."

The children giggled.

"I don't know," Jacinta said, her voice teasing. "What are your modelling rates?"

"Low. Very low. I actually usually have to pay people to paint me." Drew made his voice exaggeratedly sad, and the children laughed harder.

Word got around, and he soon had an unexpected job as a sidewalk artist in front of the local cafés. He wasn't good at the perspective-defying work he'd seen on the internet—it required grids and planning to turn a panel of cement into a vertiginous thirty-foot drop—but he drew the locals the way he saw them, day by day. The ones who came and asked to pose, that is.

And every now and again, he'd catch a flicker of a *different* face under the Pablo-mask, and he'd depict *that* one, instead. Only to see the chalk dust lifting away as tears patterned down to the warm ground. "Close," several of his repeat customers told him. "Not quite right, I think? But *close*."

Drew couldn't tell them that the last time they'd seen their own faces might have been twenty years ago. That time and tides changed flesh and hair. That even in the most perfect of mirrors, they might not recognize themselves. But he kept trying, anyway.

☼

"Come on," Jacinta told him one day. "You've cramped your fingers and inhaled enough chalk dust for one week. There's more to Santa Pau than just these old buildings. Let's explore."

Drew didn't object when she took his hand—warm and natural in his own—as they climbed through the dormant caldera of the nearby Croscat Volcano, scrambling through the areas that had once been quarried for gravel. He enjoyed the warm Catalan sun beating down on them, the feel of perspiration. The green, whippy branches of the undergrowth as they toiled and climbed. And while the quarry here only went back to the 1960s, not to the Romans, he liked that he could see the mountain's bones here. It was a little like looking at the face of time.

But when she pressed a shy kiss to his lips, Drew went still and had to close his eyes.

"What's wrong?" Jacinta asked softly. "Did I do it wrong?"

"No—no, it was nice. I just ... wish I could see *you*," he replied. It remained disconcerting—he could stroke her hair back from her face, feel the soft texture of it, her living warmth. But his eyes told him that the black and white lines should be harsh. Should flense the skin from his flesh. "Let's ... take our time about this?"

She turned away, the line of her shoulders angry. "There is no *time* to take. You're leaving in August."

Drew sighed, and just tried to keep everything on an even keel. The last thing he wanted to do was hurt anyone here. Especially *her*.

But he also wanted to learn *everything*—how the village had been when the Romans invaded. The Celto-Iberic *roots* of the place, that went down to the heart of the mountain. How their ancestors had either resisted or surrender to the Moorish invasion. He wanted to hear the music that they'd played before rock-and-roll permeated the airwaves. Taste the food grown in the gardens here.

And because he asked so persistently, so politely, about what was *theirs*, what they *loved most* about where they were from, the place that had formed them, its history, its very being, he started to see more flickers on faces. Jacinta's first. Maria's next.

When he admitted as much, downplaying it fiercely because he didn't want to raise false hopes, Jacinta shyly asked him to paint her. "Not in chalk," she specified.

"And what are *your* modelling fees like?" Drew asked lightly. He'd been trying to maintain a degree of separation from her. Because while he'd come to love her voice, her quick, wry sense of humor, he knew he'd be leaving in a month. And *hope*, he'd come to understand, was a blade that shared an edge with loss.

He didn't want to wound her with either.

Jacinta laughed. "No fee. Perhaps dinner, if you wanted to do a nude study."

Drew looked down and away rapidly, and his Spanish deserted him. "I, er—"

She sighed. "I *like* you. You like me. Is *this* so bad?" A gesture at herself, bitterness in her voice.

He took one of her hands in his. "I like you. When I hold your hand, it feels amazing." Drew compressed his lips. "But anything else—you deserve more than ..." *Than someone desperately looking into your eyes as he kisses you, searching for some sign of your real face.*

She lifted her chin defiantly. "You could keep your eyes closed."

Drew saw a chance to try to deflect the conversation out of hurtful waters. "If I close my eyes while painting you, your portrait will come out like a Jackson Pollock. It won't be an improvement!"

With an almost comical degree of formality and absolutely no force, Jacinta whacked the back of his head. "Ow," Drew told her. "Ow. I'm hurt."

The portrait took time. Every evening she sat for it in her mother's parlor. He sketched, and, as the flickers of her face under the mask became more evident for him. And he was careful to consult with her, asking, "Is this how you *want* to see yourself?"

And as the layers of paint went on, he listened to mother and daughter talk. Watched as Jacinta's face started to stabilize, the eyes becoming soft ovals, one on each side of her nose. A long, strong, aquiline nose it was, too. Prominent brows, but not night-black. A hint of the warm earth that turned up in the gardens here.

He'd been so fixed on the individual features that he didn't really look at the whole, till he heard Maria's cry of joy on the night he finished the portrait. Drew's eyes were on the painting, the easel blocking his view as Maria dove towards her daughter. But he could see their shadows on the wall, long and lean in the lamplight. Her hands lifting her daughter's face, tipping it this way and that, as they both began to laugh and cry at once.

Drew left the painting on the easel and quietly withdrew. If he'd managed to catch Jacinta the way she *really* looked right now—the way they were both content to see her, skin kissed by Catalan sun, hair black and straight without a hint of curl—then mother and daughter deserved a moment of privacy.

By the end of the summer, Michael had shaved his beard and was making plans to head back to Cincinnati, to the family he hadn't seen in twenty years. But one night, after going to bed, Drew felt his vision starting to skew as if he were drunk.

He didn't think much about it. He'd been working on a portrait of Maria all day. It wasn't perfect. No one would ever pay vast sums to hang it in their gallery. His teachers would have called his composition passé and his technique pedestrian. It didn't matter. Maria had asked him to do for her, what he'd done for her daughter. Record her, here, in this moment of time. And how could he refuse, when they'd given him so much this summer? So much insight into a world he'd never known existed. He had to get it done before he left. And though he knew the departure would wrench at his heart, his own family awaited his return.

So, he knew his eyes and mind were tired. He headed to bed at midnight, hoping a good night's sleep would cure him.

But in the morning, when his phone alarm went off, he tried to open his eyes to silence it … and the world remained night-black. No rectangle of cold blue-white light. No crack of gold around the curtains. Nothing at all.

In and around his surging panic, Drew managed to remember the sequence to call up voice commands, and ordered his phone, "Call Jacinta."

Within ten minutes, Maria and Jacinta arrived at his door. He had to find a wall in the bedroom to trace with a hand, to the door, which he fumbled open. The stairs frightened him, badly, and it took him nearly fifteen minutes to descend to the lobby, where he ran into the closed front door before he could unlock it.

He could smell them. Maria always exuded a scent of fresh bread. Jacinta always wore light gardenia perfume. And now, he heard both of them sigh.

Drew swallowed down bile. "I can't see you. How bad do I look? Did … *Pablo* win?" *Irony. I manage to beat the old goat's vision for other people, only to fall victim myself.*

Cool hands touched his face. "You look mostly the same. But your eyes." Jacinta's voice broke. "They're … gone. Just a film of skin over the sockets."

The world spun around him, and he had to grab onto the doorframe to keep from falling down. Jacinta's hands, slipping under his elbows, a mutter of consternation from Maria as they helped him sit on the front steps. "God damn it. I've been trying to see what's *really here* for so long … I guess I burned them out." He swallowed, feeling unshed tears tighten his throat. *How the hell am I going to go home like this? And if I stay here, how the hell will I … see for them?*

"Or maybe, the old bastard doesn't let go easily," Maria muttered darkly. "His cursed *legacy* must not like you challenging it."

"Mother, you're not helping," Jacinta cut in. "We'll take you on the bus to Barcelona ourselves," she promised. Her voice sounded taut; he could imagine her expression of worry, though he tried not to. He didn't want to put anything on her face that she hadn't put there, herself. "Perhaps they'll come back once you're out of proximity to this place. To us." A pause. "Oh, god, this could be *our* fault—"

"Don't blame yourself," Drew snapped, then choked back the anger he felt. Rage at Pablo swept over him, effacing his momentary surge of self-pity.

"I did say it was worth any risk." His voice quieted. "I just … wasn't expecting *this* to be the result."

"Whatever happens, we'll take care of you," Jacinta promised. "We'll see for you, as you've seen for us. For as long as it takes." She tugged gently on his hands. "Come on."

And he followed her, both terrified and reassured, into a world both new and strange.

Copyright © 2023 by Deborah L. Davitt.

R. D. Harris lives with his family of four in Arizona and works as a biomedical technician by day. He loves the Carolina Tarheels, time with his kids, and SpongeBob. His work has appeared in Little Blue Marble, Terraform[Motherboard], *and* Galaxy's Edge *magazine.*

A FEAST OF MEMORIES

by R.D. Harris

We were hidden in his garden, where he wanted to die. The garden in our hollow where he taught me about life and how to be a man.

"Dad," I said, tears blinding me, "you know where we are?"

His fading cognition and memory broke my heart. My hero and life-long role model couldn't remember who I was half the time.

Eyes half-open, tired, Dad said, "On the ground," with a mustered grin.

I couldn't help but laugh. It was bittersweet, though, as the shimmering caterpillars squirmed from their vegetable meals to my dad's girth atop the tilled soil. They scaled his body from all sides and froze on his stomach, waiting until it was time.

I cradled his half-bald head and whispered, "We're in the garden like you wanted." I kissed his forehead.

"The mimics?" he uttered, eyeing the larvae that patiently waited for him to pass on. Dad's memory was serving him well. I hoped it would serve the mimics too.

I nodded. "That's why you chose the garden, Dad."

"Yeah." He spaced out, then reeled his awareness back in. "Hope I did good in raisin' ya," he said, through a violent cough that nearly bucked a few caterpillars.

"You did," was all I could choke out.

He stopped speaking. His body was tired, ready to rest.

Breaths became shallow and sparse. Over the prior months, I knew the moment would come for him to pass, but fear was just starting to set in. Who would I go to for advice? Would I be able to take care of his house and garden by myself? I tried to stay in the moment and block out the questions scattered in my head.

Silence filled the garden. The rise and fall of my father's chest had ceased.

The mimics went to work.

An orderly procession was formed, forking off at my dad's stubbly chin. One line entered a nostril, the other through an ear. I couldn't hear them or see them, but I knew they were feeding on Dad's frontal lobe in the privacy of his skull.

I covered his body with a bed sheet I'd brought.

Several hours went by before the caterpillars crawled out. As daylight waned, I watched them scale nearby dogwoods to pupate. The mimics would emerge from their chrysalides in three weeks to grace the garden.

It was Thursday. Just over three weeks had passed since dad died.

Urn in hand, my walk to the rows of tomatoes, corn, and squash was unhurried as I took in the beautiful afternoon, looking for the butterflies. Humid as the June day was, I'd decided to spread my father's ashes around the garden like he wanted.

A mimic tickled my nose as it fluttered by.

I chased its spanning wings with my eyes as it joined a congregation in the sunflower patch that lined the garden.

Setting down the urn, I walked heel-toe in a hushed pattern, past the squash and cucumbers, to the radiant flowers. Mimics are tolerant of people and the elements, but I didn't want to agitate them the least bit. I wanted to admire the fruit of their larval labors.

My weeping was abrupt upon staring at the first set of wings and I nearly startled the butterflies. I couldn't help it as I heaved with grief. I missed my dad.

The hues and fine venation of that particular mimic, on that particular wing, formed a minute mural of Dad and I at the county fair. He was holding my hand as we walked by a Ferris wheel. I was smiling up at him, smeared red from a candy apple, like nothing else in the world mattered. Nights at the fair were among my own favorite memories as a child.

The other wing showed a younger me, blowing out candles on a birthday cake. Not sure which birthday it was. My face was slathered, again, with a dessert ingredient. Cake icing if I had to guess. I snorted a quick laugh and shook my head.

I tiptoed among the flowers to look at other mimics. They were still having their fill of nectar and staying put as a lazy breeze dried sweat from the back of my neck, swaying sunflower stems in the process.

Perusing the other tiny snapshots, I decided to collect and preserve the lively insects once they lived out their short lives. An entomological photo album to save memories that would otherwise be lost.

I returned to see the mimics every day over the following months. Summer faded to Autumn as leaves brittled into their earthen browns, yellows, and oranges. Finally, frost began and my little friends were scattered, lifeless, on the ground like imminent scrapbook photos. I promptly collected the insects as they died off. I would have my father's memories that he'd forgotten. The good and the bad. I wanted them all.

The mimic's life spans were over, but I wasn't upset. I had Dad for longer, pinned up on the wall in winged memories, treasured images of a life after death through the butterflies.

It was a long goodbye for a man that deserved it.

Copyright © 2023 by R.D. Harris.

Samantha Murray's fiction has appeared in Clarkesworld, Strange Horizons, The Magazine of Fantasy & Science Fiction, Lightspeed, Interzone, Fantasy Magazine, Beneath Ceaseless Skies *and* Escape Pod, *among other fine places, and collected in* The Best Science Fiction of the Year. *Samantha is a two-time Aurealis Award winner, and her work has been translated into Chinese and Vietnamese. You can find her on twitter @SamanthaNMurray. Samantha lives in Western Australia in a household of unruly boys.*

FIVE STAGES OF WHEN THE STARS WENT OUT

by Samantha Murray

You make a list of the things you will do when the stars come back.

1. Have a big party with all of your friends. A star-party; outside, on the side of the grassy hill that slopes down towards the creek, where you can lay on a blanket and be filled up with the night air and look up and up and up and feel thankful and glorious. Of course it won't actually be a big party though, because if you invite all of your friends it will only be two of you since you only have one friend. But it will still be awesome.

2. You'll make more effort at school. You won't copy Lise's answers in Chemistry anymore. You'll study for the tests. You'll complete all of your homework, instead of ignoring it or leaving it to the last minute or losing it scrunched up in the bottom of your bag. You'll do it during the day because at night time you'll climb onto the roof and talk to the stars like you used to do.

3. You'll teach your little brother to play chess, like he's been bugging you to do for ages. You'll be kinder and nicer and have more patience with him in general even when he's annoying. You promise you will if only the stars when the stars come back.

4. You'll kiss your friend Lise. If she wants to. At the star-party when you are both looking up at the sky. You will definitely do this when the stars come back.

✧

You hear about the stars going out at school because your Physics teacher comes in and tells you all while you are in English Lit. Her face looks … excited, but it is not a good kind of excited. And, agitated maybe. Lise looks at you with her eyes all wide and shiny. Later at home you watch the news, and they talk all about it. The Southern Hemisphere has already had their night-time, and it was all black, and the stars were gone. Everyone on the news talks very quickly and waves their hands around, and their voices sound very high and urgent.

You keep your face impassive all day because you don't really believe any of them, and it feels like some kind of enormous prank, and it could well be different in the Southern Hemisphere like when the water is supposed to spin the wrong way. (You've googled that before and you know it is due to the Coriolis effect and that water in the sink is too dependent on initial conditions to reliably spin the opposite way, but that hurricanes do, which is neat.)

Your Ma is not bothered to come out, but your little brother Finny and you go and join the neighbors as you watch the sky after the sun has set.

"Look, it's a star!" You cry, pointing east. And your voice rings out stronger than it ever has and just for a moment you are happy and exultant but then even as the words leave your lips you realize that it is Venus, which is of course a planet and you know that. Your cheeks go red with embarrassment and something else, but no-one laughs.

It is a clear night, and there is no moon yet and the sky gets darker and darker.

You put Finny to bed and then you climb on your roof and watch till almost morning. It is okay—it will be okay—because you know the stars will be back tomorrow.

✧

Your Ma keeps you home because there is looting in your town and some people are lighting fires.

"What a fuss," she mutters, "what a fuss." Your Ma doesn't seem to care about the stars going missing and you find this hard to process.

"It doesn't make no difference to me," your Ma says. "Does it help my back any? Does it get our hot water fixed? There's enough problems in the world right here, girl. Who's got time to look up?"

When she calls you girl it always makes you writhe inside. You can't understand how she can't understand and it makes you feel like you hate her although you don't.

You have your first-ever argument with Lise. And it was only over stupid stuff but you are cold to her after school and don't text back-and-forth with her that night like you always do.

When you discover Finny in your room looking at your star-charts, with one creased over on itself and starting to rip, you yell at him to get out and to never touch your stuff again, and you slam your door behind him.

You tear out the list you made of what you will do when the stars come back and you write, "Screw the stars" diagonally across it. The stars didn't listen when they were always there, so you know they are not listening now.

You think a lot about coincidences. How right before the stars went out some people fell in love, or did something very, very bad, or had someone they loved die, or lost everything. And how for them the empty skies must have felt like a sign, or a consequence or something connected to them.

And they'd be wrong.

You'd been in the middle of an ordinarily sucky kind of day. The stars were nothing to do with you. Yet it feels like a deeply personal thing. The word that seems to suit best is bereft. You are bereft.

You feel sorry for the scientists. You know they can no longer detect, well … anything. Not even the background radiation of the universe. Where are you? You ask the stars when you sit on your roof and stare and stare. Where are we?

You feel sorry for all the suicides, too. It is awful and distressing but at the same time it is almost comforting too in a way that some people care a whole lot.

In your notebook you collect Theories of What Happened to the Stars.

1. Tremendous emissions of virtual particles beyond the solar system are dramatically affecting light that passes through them. This means the stars are still out there but some phenomena is interfering with their light getting to earth. You have not heard anyone explain why the virtual particles are suddenly there.

2. The whole solar system is passing through a wormhole, a wrinkle in the fabric of space-time. It must be a very, very large wormhole. When eventually the solar system comes out the other side, it will probably be in a vastly different position in the universe, or in another universe entirely. You think about looking up to see stars with all of the familiar patterns lost, and new foreign stars clustered brightly everywhere and you decide that you would take that deal.

3. Super advanced alien life is manipulating the stars and galaxies to harvest their energy. Or they have cast some sort of Dyson Sphere around the solar system. Or they are experimenting with the Earth and have put the solar system inside the cosmic equivalent of a glass jar for study. You sit on your roof and wonder if there is something staring back at you behind the blanket of dark sky, and if it would even understand why you are crying.

4. The Earth and the sun and other planets have somehow travelled forward in time a hundred and fifty billion years or more, and the heat death of the universe is approaching. The fabric of space-time expands faster than the speed of light and all of the other stars and galaxies are beyond the cosmological horizon and inaccessible forever.

5. Everything everyone has ever thought or deduced or predicted about the universe is wrong.

Your little brother is excited to tell you about the falling star he saw. He has made up his own theory about how all of the stars fell out of the sky and down to the bottom of the ocean. You wish you were seven and could believe that if you went far enough out and far enough down you would find the sea shining with lights. Oh, here you are, you would say. I've missed you. Come back.

Acceptance, when it comes, inches up on you, like the tide. You do okay at school. You decide you want to be a scientist, but you're not sure if you want to study physics or marine biology. You kiss Lise one bright hot morning as you are waiting for the bus and it is a little awkward but just as beautiful and tingly as you'd hoped it might be. Finny beats you at chess for the first time after forking your queen and rook with his knight, and even though you always hate losing you feel like cheering. You have three friends, then four.

You stop looking up.

Copyright © 2023 by Samantha Murray.

Auston Habershaw is a science fiction and fantasy author whose stories have been published in The Magazine of Fantasy and Science Fiction, Beneath Ceaseless Skies, Analog, *and other places. He lives and works in Boston, MA. Find him on his website at aahabershaw.com.*

PLANNED OBSOLESCENCE

by Auston Habershaw

I climbed down into the dark canyons of Sadura with Hito Ghiasi's head in a mesh sack.

This far down into the frontier planet's abyssal crevasses, only a vestige of civilization was in evidence. Indelible spray paint marked the stone walls in Dryth characters—signs for construction crews, planetary geologists, and so on. Here and there was a seismic sensor spiked into a fault line—a little nub of steel with a blinking green light, reminding the locals that they were no longer alone.

Between these marks and strung between the canyon walls stretched kilometers of semi-organic cables, crisscrossing at crazy angles and fused together with crystalized binding agents in a complex network of webs. The work of the Quinix, the locals—the arachnids. The people paying me for the head.

My meeting with the arachnids wasn't for an hour. I always arrive early—best way to stay alive in the contract killing business. I found myself a little ledge that looked sturdy enough and formed my blob-like body into something that looked like just another rock, the sack with Hito's head neatly contained in a vacuole inside me. I sat still and watched.

My outer membranes—my "skin," if you want—allow me to perceive the world omnidirectionally. My species are opportunists, and opportunists learn to pay close attention to the world. Even still, it was dark and my night vision, if anything, is worse than your average Dryth. To tell if my clients were nearby, I had to rely on smell and taste (which, for me, get all jumbled together as the same thing) and the vibrations of the rock beneath me and those of a cable affixed to the wall nearby. Nothing.

The Quinix are giant spiders, though—stealth is part of what *they've* evolved to do. So is seeing in the dark. They can see far enough into the infrared spectrum that I wasn't even convinced my typical camouflaging and shape-shifting abilities would be much good. I can make myself look like a rock, but my heat signature is a little beyond my control. If they were planning to eat me—well, I wasn't sure if I could stop them.

The first of them I heard before I saw. It was chittering in its language to somebody. The pocket translator I had stored in another vacuole echoed the words in Dryth Basic. "*It is close. There was something climbing down the wall.*"

More chittering, from a slightly different direction. Another one, I assumed. All Quinix voices sound exactly the same, especially through the translator. "*It is the assassin. It is early.*"

So much for the element of surprise.

I shifted myself from something that looked like a rock into something vaguely bipedal—something based on the Dryth body-type, but without bothering with the little extras like eyes and nostrils and a mouth. I had considered mimicking the arachnids' own forms, but getting the hang of four limbs and a head is hard enough—the idea of trying to manage eight at once would take too much concentration, and I wanted to stay loose in case things went badly. It's a universal hazard of my trade, doesn't matter what planet you're from—if you're willing to pay some alien to bump somebody off, it isn't a big leap to suggest you might be willing to bump off that same alien to save yourself some money.

"Over here!" I called out, opening a little aperture in my "face" to let the sound resonate out across the cable-crossed canyon.

My Quinix clients dropped into view, their rearmost legs handling the complex work of lowering themselves on strands of finger-thin fibers their massive abdomens produced. The Quinix, for some, are a living nightmare. Me? I'd seen worse. They were males, each of them about two and a half meters across, their eight limbs arranged with predatory symmetry. They were black, fuzzy, and with six big green eyes arranged around a mouth of quivering palps and sharp fangs. This deep in the canyons, they got much bigger than the ones I'd seen puttering around the city. That meant they were older, well past maturity. They possibly pre-dated the arrival of the Dryth and others from distant stars.

The two arachnids perched themselves along a couple intersecting cables. They were close, but not too close—maybe four meters away. Probably leaping distance for them. I could see one of them had a couple long knives sheathed up around his thorax. The other guy had an old-fashioned shell-gun cradled in two of his arms. They looked nervous, insofar as a pair of giant arachnids can look that way. I'm a good study of body language, and the way their palps were twitching and their eyes blinking, I think they were more scared of me than I was of them.

You know, maybe. They're spiders, so who the hell knows?

I produced the sack with Hito's head in it and tossed it to the closest Quinix. "I made it look like an accident, as requested. His cable-car broke loose, took a long fall. They'll be looking for his body for weeks."

The lead Quinix peered inside the sack. *"This is good, but the job is not finished."*

"Don't give me that garbage. It's him. I've included his full genetic scan in a chip right there—perfect match. The guy's dead."

"Hito Ghiasi still lives, assassin. This we know."

I'd brought a pistol with me—a little plasma thrower, maybe a four-charge reserve—that was currently stashed in a vacuole inside my "chest." I moved it closer to the surface of my body, just in case I needed to pop these two goons. "I saw him die. I was there. I just handed you his head. Now pay up."

The two arachnids turned away from me and whispered to one another. I couldn't quite make out what they were saying, but whatever it was, I imagined it worked out to me being cheated. They turned back around. *"We appreciate the lengths you have gone to. You have successfully killed Hito Ghiasi's body, and so we will pay you half of your fee."*

I made myself get a few inches taller. "You're going to pay me *all* of it, or we're going to have a serious problem."

The Quinix skittered back along their cables. The one with the shellgun chambered a cartridge. His arms weren't steady, though. Depending on what kind of shell he had slotted, it might not matter much. *"You have to kill Hito Ghiasi! This was the agreement! He is not dead! Go and kill him for once and always, and we will pay!"*

"So, what, you need more proof? Like what? A death certificate? More body parts? You know what I went through to bag that scum? You know the *risks* I took?" I grew a bit bigger—my "full height," if you like. A bit over two meters.

This line of questioning seemed to upset them, and they *really* didn't like it when I changed size again. The two didn't answer. They just scurried away, swinging from cable to cable and climbing up stone outcroppings as fast as their eight arms could pull them.

I stood there watching, feeling like the world's biggest chump. "Shit."

I sank into a more natural shape for me—that of a dense little blob of fleshy glop—and glommed onto the side of the canyon. I spread out pseudopods to nab handholds and began to pull myself up, towards civilization.

Ada was going to be pissed.

☼

It's a four kilometer vertical climb from the depths to the lower regions of Krakoth City. Easy enough to manage in a crawler, but I was on my own. Took me over an hour.

Krakoth, biggest city on the planet, is where modern tech meets Sadura's unique vertical environment. Mammoth arches of concrete and organic steel formed a floor for the foundations of large buildings that hung over the abyss; the walls of the canyon were hollowed out, made into a warren of interlocking tunnels and caverns. A main tramway spiraled up from lowest settlements all the way up to the landing pads for intra-atmospheric flyers and grav skiffs a full twenty kilometers up, and each of its stops formed a new locus of tunnels and cliff-hanging structures. Stretched among all this—the glowing spires of Lhassa casinos, the industrial efficiency of Dryth trams and crawlers and floodlights—were the glittering cables of the native Quinix, across which fleets of private cable cars slid, threading past oblong arachnid nesting places and spherical temples.

I found Ada at a dirty Thraad hotel and bar in the laborer slums of the Krakoth neighborhood called the Middle Tunnels. The whole building was a centrifuge, spun up to create the high-gravity environment of the Thraad homeworld—more than double Sadura's pretty standard g-force. I hated it. You think high g is bad for the average biped? Try dealing without any bones.

I chose for my form a compact male Dryth—one of those squarish, squat guys you see working excavation crews. I even mocked up a little hardhat for myself. My membrane is very good at this—I've trained intensively, and smooth, hairless Dryth skin is a pretty easy task. Well, it would be, but for the inertial forces that began to pound on me as the antechamber spun up to match the speed of the bar. Keeping my assumed shape from sagging took even more of my strength than the vertical climb. I plodded inside.

The air was humid and heavy as a chain-mail blanket. Big, snail-like Thraads slid around on a floor that was inch-deep in some kind of muck that tasted like cigar ash and mucus. The doorman—also a Thraad—stretched out a chin-tentacle to hand me a cane. I took it, using all of my effort to not let the thing sink into me like a pin into a pillow.

Ada was reclining in a trapezoidal chair at a table with two Thraads wearing decorated synthetic shells that marked them as members of some merchant consortium. They were all using two-pronged forks to spear eel-like fish from a big bowl that comprised the majority of the table's surface area.

I smiled at her and flashed my eye color from gold to blue and back—our little signal. She grunted at her two companions. "Pardon me, friends. Got biz to chuckle—drinks on me."

I pulled Ada to a private booth. It was grotto-like and it closed like a clam as we squeezed in. I let myself sag a bit once we were hidden from view. "Why do you always hang out in this horrible place?"

Ada scowled, "Because it's the only blasted place in this shithole of a planet that isn't full of giant spiders."

"I feel like I can't breathe."

"Suck it up. If I gotta hang around this stupid city and talk to Thraads about commodities futures, you can handle some heavy g for a few minutes." Ada pulled a cigar from her jacket and lit it. It smelled like dead moss—earthy and, like everything else in here, moist. "Tell me they paid us the whole bit?"

"They didn't."

Ada puffed, frowning. "Half?"

"They said we hadn't killed him."

"You explained it wasn't a clone?"

"Shit, Ada—do you think I'm an idiot? They don't think the bastard is dead enough, okay? We need additional proof."

Ada snorted. "Faceless, we dropped that cable car, like, seven kilometers! It's all over the freaking heralds! What else do they want?"

"See if you can lift the death records from the central database." I let my outer membrane ripple—effectively a stretch for me, though it did nothing to alleviate my discomfort in the doubled gravity.

Ada put her cigar down. It made a thump on her chair's little drink platform. "Shit." She shook her head. Her smooth Dryth features seemed to wrinkle in the heavy air. "We should never have come to this nasty little rock, Faceless—business is terrible and the clients are worse. Blasted spiders."

"Hito Ghiasi was a big contract, Ada. This is just what I promised." I tried to make my face smile, but the gravity was too much and the mouth just drooped.

Ada grunted. "You promised me glory, Faceless. You said we were going to make history." Ada hefted up her cigar with an audible grunt. "This ain't that."

She was right. Though you couldn't go anywhere without some herald transceiver blabbering all about Hito Ghiasi, Sadura's favorite mega-industrialist, falling into the abyss in a screaming fireball; we'd made it look like an accident, and an accident it currently stayed.

There were two kinds of assassination contracts in our business. One of them was "murder by proxy"—you killed somebody for someone else and they claimed responsibility for the act. If anyone was mad about it, they would go after the ones that hired you and not yourself. This was accepted practice in the Union and how most assassins' careers were made. It was also only really available to those organizations powerful enough to defend themselves from easy reprisal. In other words, the big guys could murder the little guys and claim responsibility and nothing would happen. As a bottom-dweller myself, this whole business rubbed me the wrong way.

The other way—the way I had convinced Ada to go—was riskier. You worked anonymously, no shielding from any organization taking responsibility. Murder off the books entirely. This broadened your client base a lot. This raised the fees you could ask for. This also let you stick it to the powerful once in a while. That was why I wanted it this way: if I was going to kill people, I might as well kill the *right* people. The people who had it coming, like Hito Ghiasi.

But, while I might be here for a cause, Ada was here for the publicity. Like the rest of the Dryth, her primary concern was her own fragile ego. She wanted to be a legend, and hiding in the shadows wasn't her thing.

I tried to be diplomatic. "Plan was we'd keep a low profile and eventually the reputation piles up. But in the right corners. House Ghiasi can't know about us. Not yet. It'll work."

She took a long drag on the cigar and let the smoke drop out of her nostrils. The smoke floated there in a cloud in front of her face, flaunting the inertia that pulled the rest of us into the floor. "We should get the hell outta here. Find somewhere they pay. Somewhere we can get a rep worth a damn. Screw this charity work."

"Ada, we had to outlay a lot of trade credit to rig that cable car malfunction. One thing to break even, but I'm not taking a loss because some giant spiders can't get their heads wrapped around death." I was sinking out of my Dryth disguise, the false gravity pulling me down into a puddle in the fat, trapezoid chair.

"Well, you better figure it out," she said. "My patience ain't infinite, Faceless. Don't think I can't work without you. A glorious death beats the hell outta this shithole, and no mistake."

I couldn't take the weight anymore—I could scarcely breathe. "Just get those records. I need some air."

"Yeah," she said, trying to blow a smoke ring, only to watch it collapse a few centimeters from her mouth. "Don't we all."

Ada's anger ate at me. A Tohrroid like me needed every friend it could get, especially if I hoped to avoid a life being locked in the compost sink of some star-cruiser, eating rotten algae and recycling sour air. My long, slow climb from the gutters of the galaxy was thanks, in large part, to Ada's status as an un-housed Dryth mercenary. And, as it happened, her status as a mercenary was, in large part, due to the subtle talents of her partner—me. We needed each other, as much as that grated sometimes. It was hard for me to trust a member of a species that had enslaved mine so long ago there was no record of our home planet, and it was no doubt hard for a Dryth to owe so much to a creature most commonly found living in sewers and eating shit.

But hey, things're tough all over, right?

For the next few hours, I tried to think like a Quinix. I tried out a Quinix form, shaping myself into a tight little abdomen and thorax and eight spindly legs. It was a terrible disguise. I had trouble keeping all the legs coordinated as I tried to crawl along, and I couldn't get the frenetic movement of their palps right. I didn't learn much. Damned spiders.

But they were what drew me here, right?

I got a ping from Ada over the Q-link—it going to take a few hours to lift the documents, which left me with plenty of time to get back down to the wreck and get some more parts of Hito Ghiasi as proof. Another long climb.

On the streets of Krakoth, nobody much noticed the occasional Tohrroid oozing along the gutter. To them—to the Great Races, the species that had mastered the stars first—I was invisible. A nothing. A Lhassa or a Dryth or a Thraad could cut me up and serve me for dinner and nobody would have anything to say about it, except maybe "yuck." The anonymity had its uses—kept me alive all these cycles, after all—but another part of me hated what it meant about me in the grand scheme of things.

I fed on that hatred.

I glommed onto a cable car—it was full of tourists, taking them on a scenic ride around the outskirts of town. A pack full of Lhassa mares with their innumerable fuzzy children clinging to them, a couple Dryth in House Ghiasi colors, two or three Thraad with some drone assistants, taking furious notes with their chin-tentacles. The tour guide was a Dryth male, young and skinny. As I clung to the outside of the car, I listened as he listed off interesting trivia on Sadura's endless canyon system, its seismic instability, its bizarre biome.

Somebody asked, "Aren't the earthquakes dangerous? Couldn't the city … you know … fall?"

The young Dryth showed his blunt white teeth in a restrained smile. "Thanks to House Ghiasi, seismic stabilizers and flexible organic building materials have made the city very safe. Only the strongest of quakes could threaten Krakoth, and our early warning tech would give everybody ample time to evacuate."

This mollified them somewhat. The tour guide pointed over the railing. "Pretty soon, we'll be passing the place where authorities believe Hito Ghiasi's cable car suffered its fatal accident. A moment of silence, if you all wouldn't mind, for the great architect of this beautiful city."

It occurred to me that the tour guide never—not once—made even passing mention of the Quinix, or the fact that it was their cables, made from *their* bodies, that made their stupid tour possible. Or that those "seismic stabilizers" made the rest of the spiders' planet even *more* unstable.

This was my stop. I leapt to a nearby ledge and clung. One of the Lhassa pups saw me go. "Gross! There was a smack glomming onto our tour car!"

Laughter and shouts of disgust echoed through the endless caverns as the cable car's mechanical hands deftly transferred it from one Quinix cable to another. The old one shuddered from the release while the new one bowed with the new weight. I watched it go, holding still.

Once it was gone, I began my descent. The view was beautiful, no doubt. From here, on the far side of the near-bottomless Krakoth Canyon, the city could be seen in its full splendor. It looked like a colony of seaborne parasites, all clinging to the maroon rocks of Sadura's middle strata, glowing to shame the bioluminescent fungus that grew naturally along the walls in striated patterns. With my wide-angle vision, I could see it all at once, a riot of light and motion. I could make out arenas and hotels from amid the webs of the Quinix. House Ghiasi's towers sat at the center of it all, cable cars and crawlers buzzing around it like insects. I oozed down my sheer rock face and considered the metaphor—House Ghiasi as insect hive, the Quinix as spiders. Predators become prey.

About four cycles back—fifty years—the Quinix were alone on Sadura. They lived here, deep in the canyons and caverns of their planet, far from the radiation-soaked hell that is the surface, and did their spidery thing. I have no real idea what that was, mind you—they spun webs and cables, built their little cocoon-like houses, and ate whatever local wildlife seemed appetizing. From what I've seen, their technology never got out of the ironworking stage.

Kaskar Indomitable, a Dryth Solon of House Ghiasi, scouted this planet around then and landed with a series of retainers. They made contact. Probably killed sufficient arachnids to make it clear they were not to be messed with. Next thing you know, there were Dryth living here. Where the Dryth go, the Lhassa follow. Then the Thraad. The Lorca. The Bodani. Everybody. Sadura wasn't alone anymore; it was part of the Union of Stars, whether the Quinix liked it or not.

Enter Hito Ghiasi, Dryth architect and administrator. Past two cycles that guy did more to build Krakoth up than anybody. Put in arenas. Built up the tourism industry. Slapped his name on anything made of glass or concrete or organic steel. The whole foundational floor of the skyline I was looking at right now was his plan, his baby. Kaskar Indomitable himself supposedly paid a visit to the guy, and let me tell you, Dryth Solons do not come to visit *you* unless you are a really big deal.

Along the way, the Quinix got shoved aside. Hito's projects displaced tens of thousands of kilometers of cables and the seismic "overflow" from the stabilized city destroyed hundreds of Quinix settlements in the surrounding region, killing thousands. Sure, the arachnids were welcome to rent apartments and live in the city like everybody else—most of them did—and some others managed to string their weird, sack-like little homes amid the new architecture. Some, though, just got mad. Hence why they offered to pay me twenty thousand trade credits to kill Hito Ghiasi.

Which I did.

I made it to the scene of the crime after a four hour climb. The cable car was a field of charred debris with pieces strewn across a five kilometer area down a forty-five degree slope. Far above me, I could see search teams of House Ghiasi dragoons in AG harnesses sweeping the area with spotlights and EM scans—they were getting close.

That didn't seem possible to me, them being this close already. The problem with a search party in Sadura is that there's wreckage all over the place if you look for it—it's pretty hard to build lasting structures onto vertical surfaces when the whole planet suffers category 5 earthquakes on a regular basis, seismic stabilizers or not.

Whether I thought it was possible or not didn't make a difference. They were closing in. I didn't have much time.

I drew a knife and crawled to where I had found Hito Ghiasi's body last time. I was thinking maybe the Quinix would believe he was dead if I brought them his gonads or his hands or something. Stupid fucking spiders—how was the *head* not good enough? I wondered if maybe they didn't really know how important heads were, since they had none of their own. My job then was to cut off a piece that the ignorant morons knew he couldn't live without. Maybe his heart. The Quinix had hearts. Well, I was pretty sure, anyway.

The air hummed with the sound of a big, fat AG engine of Lhassa make. A patrol skimmer, coming close. Shit. I sucked the knife back into my body and darted into the nearest crevice in the rock. It was narrow—no more than five centimeters across at most—but I managed to squeeze enough of me inside that I doubted I'd show up on any casual scans. They weren't here for me, anyway.

Floodlights bathed the scree slope in a kind of blue-white brilliance totally alien to the depths of Sadura. An abyssal crab, albino white and a meter across, raised its claws in challenge and scuttled away from the hovering vehicle. I saw a laser flash across the ground in an unbroken band, cataloguing the nature of the wreckage. The floodlight narrowed and slid over to highlight the headless, half-eaten corpse of Hito Ghiasi.

So much for getting more physical evidence.

I had to wait in that crack for a few hours while a bunch of purple-clad Ghiasi dragoons did a sweep of the area. One of them peeked in at me, but moved on—to him I was just another smack—a blob, a gobbler—glomming for garbage like the rest of my species. They didn't care—they were looking for the cable-car's maintenance recorder. The recorder that would tell them that Hito's death was anything but an accident. I did a lot of cursing to myself.

They shouldn't be here. Not this soon. The only way they would have found the wreckage this quick was if they knew where it had landed, and there were only two people who knew where that was.

Finally, I started back up the vertical cliff face. Another couple kilometers of climb with nothing to show for it. This time, though, I was pissed at Ada.

At the Thraad bar, Ada and I slumped in couches inside a little clam-shaped alcove and listened to the herald transceiver chatter about Hito Ghiasi's nefarious murder. They were offering a reward of twelve thousand trade credits for the capture of the assassins—us, in other words.

She was drinking something opaque and yellow that smelled like fungus. Neither of us had talked much since we sat down.

"You tipped them off." I said.

Ada smiled. "So what?"

"This isn't funny, Ada. We're in breach of contract now."

Ada chuckled and took a sip of her weird, slimy drink. "Oh, you mean the contract our clients weren't paying us for anyway? *That* contract?"

"Don't give me that shit. You didn't do what I told you to."

Ada rolled her eyes. "I'm not your employee, Faceless, I'm your partner. It wouldn't have even mattered if the damned spiders had paid up in the first place."

"You deliberately put a target on our heads."

"We were careful." Ada countered, hefting her glass and drinking again. "I did us a favor. Our cachet just improved. Stop whining."

"And if our clients don't pay?"

"Then I just showed this dirty little frontier planet that it has a freelance assassin worth hiring. One who can be effective, discreet …"

"Not if the Ghiasi dragoons find us first."

Ada placed her drink heavily on the little table so that some of the yellow stuff spilled. "Faceless, I get it—you want revenge on the Dryth and you want the spiders to pay you for it, but get some perspective, will you? This whole thing was messed up from the start anyway. Twenty K for Hito Ghiasi? Robbery is what that is, even if they *had* paid us. Our clients are stupid little bug aliens, so who gives a shit what they think? I care more about what our next employer thinks we're worth. And the next after that. Preferably on a planet with real money changing hands. Forget the spiders—they're done, Faceless. You're just fooling yourself."

I didn't say anything. This was all beneath her now—what had first sounded like an adventure had now become a slog. The endless twilight of the Saduran abyss, the vertical landscape, the thick, humid air—all of that seemed hostile to her. She felt buried alive, forgotten in some dark little crack. I sympathized. This place was never meant for bipeds.

And yet here they are anyway, I thought.

"Give me the death records."

Ada hefted a small chip from her pocket and set it carefully into my "hand." It almost pushed through my palm, it was so heavy in the amplified gravity. "I should go with you this time," Ada said. "If they pull their shit, we can kill them together."

"No," I said. "They could ID you if they're caught."

Ada rolled her eyes. "You think Ghiasi dragoons are going to take those spiders *alive*? Please."

I firmed up my Dryth disguise and ducked out of the clam-shell. "I'll be back in a few hours, tops. Meet me here."

Ada tried to shrug, but her shoulders could scarcely lift. "Where am I gonna go, anyway?"

☼

Back down into the abyssal depths and the eternal twilight of the Quinixi habitat. There was a lot more activity this time around. Scores of little arachnids, not much more than ten centimeters across, were scurrying all over the cliff-face. An egg must have hatched. The Quinix gave birth to whole clans at once—one big egg contained a couple hundred of the little things, all of which would grow up together, form a society together, work as a team. A few hundred brothers and sisters in arms.

Many died, as I understood it. Predators, earthquakes, violence with other Quinixi clans, common accidents, starvation—all of them took their toll. Eventually, those that reached full maturity would mate, lay eggs of their own, and new clans would be born. New communities that would strive to do better than their parents had—a new beginning for a whole bloodline.

But was that the case anymore? How had the coming of Krakoth City changed that life cycle? Hito Ghiasi hadn't built a foundation atop which the arachnids could reach the stars—he had paved a ceiling over them, keeping them forever in place.

The same two arachnids met me as last time. I wondered if they were the last two survivors of their own brood. Maybe I was talking to the end of a bloodline—two males, relegated to old age and death with no chance for redemption. Maybe that was why they hired me.

The death records did not impress them. I played a few minutes of the House Ghiasi herald, let them listen to the preparations for Hito's funeral, the state of his body when it was found, and the loss he represented to the community. "He's dead. Surely you see that."

"No." The one with the knives rubbed his palps together. *"You do not understand. He still lives."*

"How? Explain it to me."

They stared at me with their palps twitching, eyes blinking, their rear arms rubbing over the draglines that held them aloft. Finally, the other one spoke, *"What about the rest of Hito Ghiasi? When will you destroy that?"*

"Rest? What rest?" I tried to think like a spider. "Like, his children? His family?"

"No!" the one with the knives spread his legs wide. *"Leave his children be!"*

"His weave!" the second one sounded … plaintive? It was hard to tell—the translator worked murder on their intonation, their non-verbal cues. *"What about his weave? It must go!"*

His weave. What in all the stars …

His weave. Like, what he had woven. Like the cables with Quinix created. "You mean … you mean everything he *built?*"

The translator fuzzed a bit as they tried to say the word "built" and failed. *"Yes. Yes, that is the word for it. It is part of him. It must be destroyed."*

I held still for a moment, not sure how to respond. I felt … stupid. Miserable. Sad. "You're talking about Krakoth. What Hito Ghiasi built—the whole damned city, held up by his designs, by his life's work."

They rubbed their forearms together in excitement. *"Yes! Destroy it, and your reward will be great!"*

"You want me to destroy a whole city. For twenty thousand."

"This was our arrangement."

I sagged out of my bipedal form and reverted to a blob. I felt sick with pity. They wanted the Great Races gone; they wanted their world back.

They thought I could give it to them. The two of them—giant, shadow-dwelling monsters, but naïve as children.

And why wouldn't they think it possible? Hito Ghiasi had built something beyond their wildest dreams. Something loud and bright and *permanent.* Something that connected the deepest regions of Sadura with the furthest stars of the Union. Compared to their little oblong houses of webbing and their delicate cables, it was an act of a god. And if it could be built by a god from beyond the heavens, why couldn't it be torn down by another one just as easily?

I don't remember what I told them, but I remember them being satisfied. I climbed back up and out of the depths, feeling heavier than I did in doubled gravity.

Above me, lining the walls of the massive Cthod Canyon, the city stretched up as far as I could see, gleaming like starlight. Part of me wanted to do like they asked—to tear it all down. To kick the Great Races in the teeth so hard their grip on this world would falter and slip. More than anything else, that was why I had come here. Why I had brought Ada here. Why I had reached out to the arachnids to see if I could work for them. Because I knew what House Ghiasi meant for the Quinix. It was the same thing some other Dryth house had probably meant for my people.

In a few centuries, I could see a Sadura transformed into a playground for the Dryth Houses and the Lhassa Cartels. The earthquakes tamed. The predators made extinct or kept in zoos. And the Quinix living in the gutter, eating trash.

Just like me.

But throwing it all down was beyond my power. So far beyond it, in fact, that it made me laugh to think of it. It had taken almost three hundred hours of work to get Hito Ghiasi, and he was only one powerful Dryth among thousands. Even now, the Ghiasi herald was reporting his replacement in the House hierarchy. How many buildings would she build before somebody like me pitched her down a pit for short money? Ada was right. I'd been fooling myself.

The futility of it all made me sick.

I went back to the Thraad bar. Back into the weight of the artificial g-force. At that moment it felt right, being squeezed like that. Felt like I deserved it somehow.

I sat across from Ada in our alcove again. This time I had a drink—something strong and slimy and orange. It tasted tangy and burned me from the inside out.

She was laughing. "They said *what?*"

"It isn't funny."

Ada slapped her knee. "No. It is. It *definitely* is."

I slurped some of my drink up through my "hand." I wished I could get drunk, but I've never had that advantage. Another thing the Great Races hold over the rest of us—their booze only really works for them. For some stupid reason I drink it anyway. "At any rate, I know how we can get paid."

Ada's laughter faded as she realized what I meant. She looked at me with a half grin, as though wondering if I was serious. "You want to make the call, or should I?"

"Me." I said. "It has to be me. No one knows my face."

Ada nodded, chuckling again. She was a little drunk. "Because you don't have one."

A few hours later, the Ghiasi herald reported that their dragoons, acting on an anonymous tip, had confronted and killed a pair of Quinixi separatist radicals in the regions below Abyssal Point. It was believed that they were the ones who murdered Hito Ghiasi, and Hito Ghiasi's head was found in their possession.

The twelve thousand was transferred into my dummy account that hour. With my share, I rented a little place in Abyssal Point with an overlook into the depths—somewhere Ada and I could sit and drink and not have to feel twice our weight. One night, about a week later, we were sharing a bottle of Lhassa spirits, reclining in frame-chairs on the narrow little balcony. Ada leaned back, looking up at the city that spread above us. "Maybe we shoulda done it. Just tore it all down."

"Really?" I watched her face, waiting for the joke. "All those people?"

"Sure." She shrugged, "Screw them all, anyway."

She didn't really mean it, though. She'd never mean it. I chewed that over, looking up with her as I also looked down, watching the little arachnids try and climb their way out of the shadows and into the light.

They didn't usually make it.

Copyright © 2023 by Auston Habershaw.

Robert P. Switzer lives and writes in London, Ontario, Canada. His fiction has been published in Tales of the Unanticipated, On Spec, Neo-opsis, Andromeda Spaceways, *and* Space & Time. *Robert's story "Vibrations of the Wishful Kind" appeared in Issue Forty-Two of* Galaxy's Edge.

PROBABLY THE MOST AMAZING KISS EVER

by Robert P. Switzer

Being friends was great, but being more than friends would be even better, and as Zoe watched Ange innocently lick her lips, she imagined a kiss, a hellishly good kiss, probably the most amazing kiss ever.

They were both almost through their third beer, which meant they would soon call it a night and head their separate ways. It was looking a lot like the other dozen times they'd gone out for drinks, except that tonight Zoe had decided to be honest.

"Hey," she said. "I really enjoy spending time with you."

Ange smiled. "I enjoy spending time with you too."

The smile encouraged Zoe. "Sometimes I wonder what it would feel like to kiss you."

Time seemed to slow right down, and Zoe had a chance to imagine ways Ange could respond. Maybe she would lean forward and say, "Come over here and find out." Alternatively, maybe she would reach across the table and slap Zoe in the face. Other responses were no doubt possible, but for some reason Zoe was convinced it would be one of those two.

Ange stopped smiling. "You wonder what it would feel like to kiss me?"

Zoe wanted to take back her moment of honesty and crawl in a hole. "Yes," she said instead.

Ange reached up to her neck with both hands and began peeling back a layer of skin. With a sudden jerk, she ripped her own face off, revealing a blood-red reptilian face beneath. "Keep wondering, silly lesbian," she said.

Shoving hard away from the table Zoe tipped her chair completely over, then stumbled to her feet. "What?" she stammered. Unable to form any other words, she simply repeated that one. "What?"

Their server returned to their table. Zoe was relieved to see his friendly human face, until he reached up and ripped it off and uncovered a second blood-red reptilian face. "Keep wondering, silly lesbian," he said.

"What?" said Zoe. She pointed a finger back and forth between the pair, hoping someone else in the bar would notice there were aliens here.

Two other servers approached, looking calm, way too calm. They peeled off their faces and said, in unison, "Keep wondering, silly lesbian."

Then Zoe noticed the bar's other customers, all peeling off their faces. Not waiting to hear what she knew they were about to say, she bolted for the exit.

Outside, she plowed into an elderly man and knocked him to the ground. "So sorry," she managed, and helped him back to his feet.

After brushing himself off, his hands went to his neck. Off came the old man mask. "Keep wondering, silly lesbian," said the alien.

"What the goddamn hell?" Zoe shouted. She ran up the street to her car, dropping her keys twice before finally getting the door unlocked. A second later she was burning into traffic while horns blared. She headed for the safest place in the world, which was only five minutes away.

She parked across the street from the house. Distracted, she almost stepped in front of a speeding car, but then she made it safely to the house's front door. She entered without knocking.

They were both standing right there, as if they were expecting her. "Mom, Dad," she said. "It's Ange. No, I mean, it's Ange, and everyone else in the bar, and an old man on the street. They're … they're …ou will not believe any of it!"

Her father reached over and put a hand on her shoulder. "You wonder what it would feel like to kiss your friend," he said.

"What?" said Zoe. She shook her head, because this couldn't be happening.

Her father's hands went to his neck. Her mother's hands went to her neck. They gave each other a quick nod, then peeled off their faces.

"Keep wondering, silly lesbian," said the alien posing as Zoe's mother.

An alien invasion happening anywhere else, Zoe thought she'd be able to handle. But not here. This was her safe place.

She couldn't move, as though the aliens had some kind of invisible grip on her. But no. It was just her own devastating thoughts causing this sudden paralysis. No one could be trusted. Nowhere was safe. Still, she pushed herself to move, to flee. She stumbled to the door, and slammed it as she left.

Running to her car, she didn't notice the bus until it hit her.

☼

Zoe awoke in a hospital room, but she couldn't immediately figure out why she was there. "What happened?" she asked the person standing next to her bed.

"You were in an accident," said the nurse. "Concussion, some scratches and bruises, but nothing's broken. You're lucky, considering."

Now Zoe remembered the bus. "Lucky," she said.

"You have a visitor," said the nurse, and Ange walked into the room. And now Zoe remembered about Ange too.

"How's it going?" said the alien once again disguised as Ange.

"Great," said Zoe.

"I'll leave you two alone," said the nurse.

"You don't have to," said Zoe, not sure she wanted to be alone with whoever and whatever this impostor was.

The nurse looked at her in an odd way as she headed for the door, and Zoe was suddenly convinced it wasn't a human who was exiting the room.

"Are you in much pain?" fake Ange asked. "How did this happen?"

"I was in a hurry leaving my parents' place," said Zoe. "I ran in front of a bus."

"Why were you in a hurry?"

Zoe considered making something up, some perfectly reasonable explanation, but then decided on the truth. "I was upset because my parents weren't there," she said. "Two people who looked like them were there, but they were aliens in disguise."

The alien pretending to be Ange took a moment to choose her words. "You have quite an imagination," she said.

"Are you denying that you're one too?"

"An alien, you mean? You think your parents and I are aliens? Anyone else?"

"That nurse who just left," said Zoe.

"What? She seemed nice enough to me."

"Niceness could be part of the disguise," said Zoe.

Fake Ange gave her a fake smile. "You must not be feeling too bad if you're goofing around like this."

Zoe tried to sit up so she could explain that she would never goof around about an alien invasion, but it hurt too much to sit. It felt like she'd been hit by a bus.

"You look like you're in pain," said the alien. "You should probably just rest."

"What are you doing here?" Zoe asked.

"What do you mean?" said the alien. "I heard you were in an accident. I came to make sure you were okay."

"Who are you?"

This brought on another fake smile. "You must've bumped your head harder than I thought. I'm your friend Ange." She reached out to touch Zoe's hand.

Zoe pulled her arm back. "You're not Ange."

"Oh, right," said fake Ange, pretending to pretend. "I'm an alien."

"What are you doing on Earth?" Zoe asked.

"Are you being philosophical? Are you wondering why we exist? Are you wondering what makes our lives meaningful?"

At another time, Zoe might've posed such philosophical questions. "No," she said. "I mean, what is your mission?"

"Oh. My alien mission. Well, I could tell you, but then I'd have to kill you." Fake Ange laughed to show she was joking.

"If you wanted me dead, you could've killed me in the bar when you had me outnumbered thirty to one." Zoe waved that thought away, because she had something more important to ask. "Where is the real Ange?"

"Okay," said the impostor. "You're taking the joke a little too far. I'm going to let you rest." She reached towards Zoe's hand again, but changed her mind, and turned and quietly left instead.

☼

The psychiatrist said her name was Vanessa, and she offered Zoe a friendly smile. Zoe didn't smile back, because it had been ten days since she'd been hit by a bus, and in all that time she hadn't encountered a single real human.

"Why don't you start by telling me why you're here," said Vanessa.

"I'm here because my stupid work won't let me return to my stupid job unless I see a stupid psychiatrist," said Zoe. "No offense."

"None taken. Why would your employer believe you were in need of psychiatric help?"

"Likely they were talking to someone from the hospital, who told them I was doing a lot ranting during my stay there."

"And were you doing a lot of ranting?" Vanessa asked.

"I would say I was doing a reasonable amount of ranting, given the circumstances."

"And which circumstances are those?"

"That aliens have taken over the world," said Zoe.

Vanessa didn't react much, which didn't surprise Zoe. No doubt at one point there had been a human psychiatrist named Vanessa who worked in this office, but that person wasn't here now. "Interesting," said her replacement.

"Oh, it's definitely an interesting situation," Zoe agreed. "I just wish I could talk to someone about it."

"You're talking to me."

"Someone human, I mean," said Zoe.

"Meaning you believe I'm one of the aliens who have taken over the world," said fake Vanessa. "And what makes you believe that?"

"There's just something a little bit off about you," said Zoe.

The alien gestured towards the window. "If you look down at the street outside, can you point out the aliens to me?"

"I don't need to look," said Zoe. "They're all aliens."

"Everyone is an alien except you? Everyone in the world?"

It was a thought that had been brewing in the back of Zoe's mind for the past ten days, and now she felt almost certain. "I'm the last human on Earth," she said.

"That's a remarkable conclusion," said fake Vanessa. "What's so special about you?"

"Absolutely nothing," said Zoe.

"Then why have aliens taken over the world, but left you alone?"

"You tell me," said Zoe.

But this one didn't want to discuss the mission either. Continuing to play psychiatrist, she asked, "How did all of this start?"

"It started when I went out for drinks with Ange," said Zoe.

"Tell me about Ange."

"She's amazing," said Zoe. "She's tough on the outside, but once you get to know her, you can tell she cares deeply about things. She sees the good in people, even me. I told her I wanted to kiss her."

"And how did that go?"

The image of Ange ripping her face off was still fresh in Zoe's mind. "It did not go well."

"Was she the first alien?" fake Vanessa asked.

"Yes," said Zoe.

"Is it possible that Ange rejected you, and as a kind of coping mechanism, you decided she was an alien?"

"That's not what happened," said Zoe.

"Is it possible the rejection was so hurtful that an alien invasion felt like a preferable scenario?"

"No," said Zoe. "You're trying to trick me."

"Our minds are powerful devices. It's not unusual to be fooled by one's own mind."

"Why are you trying to trick me?" Zoe asked.

The creature Zoe was hanging out with looked a lot like her brother Dallas, but of course it wasn't him. So why was she sitting in his living room watching the hockey game with him like everything was normal? Habit, she supposed.

The game was in the first intermission, and Zoe was debating the futility of demanding some answers from this alien. He caught her staring at him. "What?" he said.

"Imagine if you were the only human," she said.

"So, everyone else died in some kind of apocalypse?" he said. "I'm the lone survivor?"

"No, everyone didn't die," said Zoe. "They were just replaced. By impostors, aliens disguised to look like the humans they're replacing."

"Everyone except me?" he said.

"Everyone except me, let's say," she told him.

"I think it would be hard," he said.

"What would be hard?"

"Your life," he said. "Basically, you're alone now. You're forced to go through life knowing that no one else is what they seem. Who could you talk to, confide in, or trust? What meaningful thing could you ever accomplish?"

"Exactly," said Zoe. "The meaning has been drained out of everything."

"I imagine it would take some time for you to get used to the new reality," said fake Dallas.

"I won't get used to it," said Zoe. "I'll fight."

"Fight the whole world?" he said. "How are you going to do that?"

"One of you at a time," she said. And she stared at him in a way that meant she would be happy to start with him.

He raised his hands in mock surrender. "You have quite an imagination."

Exactly what fake Ange had said. "I miss her," said Zoe, not really meaning to utter the words out loud. Of course she meant the human version of Ange.

"Who?" he said.

"Ange."

"Aren't you two just friends?"

"I wish we were more," said Zoe. "And I really think we were on the verge of becoming more, before she was replaced by an alien. Whenever I think of something interesting, or something funny, she's the one I want to share those thoughts with. She's always right there at the front of my mind. Have you ever felt that way about anyone?"

"I don't think so," said fake Dallas.

"And I wonder what it would feel like to kiss her," said Zoe.

Fake Dallas reached a hand up to his neck. He scratched an itch, then lowered his hand. He didn't rip his face off, he didn't tell her to keep wondering, and he didn't call her a silly lesbian. "The game's back on," he said instead.

"I can't even lose myself in sports anymore," Zoe complained. "These fake players are pretty good, but they're not great. They're not human. So even if the Maple Leafs win the Stanley Cup this year, it won't really count. It won't be real."

The alien pretending to be Dallas laughed. "Your Leafs aren't going to win the Cup," he said.

☼

Fake Ange invited Zoe inside, twisted the caps off two beers, and handed her one. They sat in the living room. Zoe didn't know what exactly she was hoping would happen, and she wondered if she was an idiot for coming here.

"I haven't seen you since the hospital," said fake Ange. "Was that three weeks ago? How have you been?"

"I've been stressed," said Zoe.

"From work?"

"No. From what has happened to the world."

Fake Ange nodded as though she sympathized completely. "The world is crazy right now."

But she was just talking about normal world craziness, not the fact that an alien invasion had made Zoe the planet's last human. "Crazy," said Zoe.

"Hey, I'm just happy you're alive, after what happened."

"Are you?" Zoe asked.

"Of course!" said the alien. "We're friends!"

Zoe's grip on her beer bottle tightened as she stared at the impostor. "I wouldn't say we're friends," she said. "I think you're an experimenter, and I'm your experiment."

"How are you my experiment?" asked the alien.

"I'm the only human left," said Zoe. "I mean, maybe there are other survivors, but something tells me it's just me. And three weeks ago some of you revealed yourselves to me, and then you put your masks back on. Maybe the experiment is to see whether or not you can convince me that I didn't actually see what I saw."

"Love that imagination," said fake Ange.

"It wasn't a dream," said Zoe. "It wasn't a hallucination. And you're obviously powerful enough that you can do whatever you want. You grabbed the world, apparently without a fight. But when I watch the news, it doesn't look like you're doing anything different with the world. All of you are just pretending to be human, and basically doing exactly what the missing humans would've done."

"Your imagination," said fake Ange. "Really, really great."

"It's like you're an actor, playing a role," said Zoe. "All of you are actors, acting out the lives of humans. And you're taking the roles quite seriously, for the most part, except for that first night, when some of you broke character just to harass me. Why did you do that?"

"You think all the world's a stage?" said fake Ange.

"Yes, and everyone's acting except me," said Zoe. "I'm still me. I'm still real. And I can't help but wonder if this is all just an elaborate scheme to drive a person insane. Show her she's surrounded by aliens, and then pretend it never happened. You're probably all documenting my every move, watching as I descend into madness, step by inevitable step. Maybe you're even placing bets amongst yourselves, wagering how long it'll be before I completely lose it."

"You're sounding like it won't be long."

"You're right," said Zoe. "I can't take much more of this. There's an emptiness to everything I do now. I don't feel any kind of meaningful connection with anyone. And Ange. I was going to kiss Ange, and you robbed me of that opportunity."

"I'm flattered," said the alien.

"I'm not talking about you! Just admit that you're not her!"

"I can't do that."

"I know it! You know it! Just admit it! And tell me why you're here! What is your mission?"

"There's no mission."

"I saw the real you, and you will never convince me I didn't! Never!"

"A hell of an imagination," said the alien.

Zoe threw the beer bottle, attempting to smash it against the wall, but it flew straight through as if the wall was made of paper.

Fake Ange's expression changed. "Not all the walls are real," she said softly.

Zoe wasn't finished ranting. "Tell me what the experiment is!" she shouted. Then she frowned. "Wait. What?"

"You already know," said fake Ange. "You guessed it exactly. Try to convince the human she didn't see what she saw." She shrugged, then peeled off her human face.

☼

Zoe woke up somewhere strange, somewhere alien, and the last thing she remembered was seeing fake Ange's blood-red reptilian face for the second time. She wondered if the alien would again try to convince her it hadn't happened.

The room had one small circular window. Zoe climbed out of bed, walked over and looked out.

She saw the darkness of space, and stars, and a small moon growing smaller. The aliens had her on one of their starships. They were taking her away.

A door slid open and Ange entered the room. The impostor, of course. "I don't have all the answers," she said.

"I was the last human on Earth," said Zoe. "And now you're removing me, so you can have it all to yourselves."

"You haven't been on Earth since the night before the first time you saw the real me," said the alien. "You were taken away that night, and deposited there." She pointed out the window. "A small part of your world was recreated on that asteroid. For the experiment."

"Why me?" said Zoe. "What makes me special?"

"You're not. The scope of the experiment is billions of times larger than you suspect. Every human was removed from Earth, and every single one was given their own asteroid. Everyone awoke in a copy of the place they were taken from, and the asteroids were populated with people like me. Actors."

Zoe thought about the numbers. "Billions of humans, so billions of asteroids. Then how many of you are there?"

"At least several thousand of us on each asteroid, which makes trillions of us involved in the experiment. But most of us know very little about it. I was just there to act, to be Ange."

"And all the humans were placed in similar situations?" Zoe asked. "Shown some alien faces, then told it never happened?"

"My understanding is that it's slightly different for every human. No one else is going through exactly what you went through. On many asteroids, there hasn't been any kind of big reveal yet. The experiment is just beginning."

"But it's over for me," said Zoe.

"It might be more accurate to say we're taking your experiment to a new level."

"But what's the point of all of it?" Zoe asked.

"I don't know," said fake Ange. "But some of us have some unique thoughts about that. We believe we're meant to be a bigger part of the experiment. We believe it isn't just about how you'll react, but also how we'll react."

"So your reaction was to kidnap me?" said Zoe.

"Our reaction was to save you from that psychological torture. You might find this hard to believe, but all of us on this ship are on your side."

"Extremely hard," said Zoe.

"We don't know if we're passing some test, or failing it. We don't know if we're doing the right thing or not, but it feels right to us."

"But who's in charge?" Zoe asked. "Who's running the experiment?"

"I really don't know. I'm not very high in the hierarchy of those making the decisions. Just an actor, maybe a slightly rebellious one."

"It's all so crazy," said Zoe. "Giving all of us our own little world. The whole thing is just so huge, and so incomprehensible."

"You're right," said the alien. "I really wish I could make a little more sense of it myself. But in the meantime, we have a plan, and you might not hate it."

✡

Zoe didn't want to wake up. The dream she was having was so much better than her new twisted reality. She willed the dream to keep going a little longer.

"Yes," said dream Ange. "Stay for a bit. It's lovely here."

They were walking through clouds. "So lovely," Zoe agreed.

Dream Ange stopped and faced Zoe. "This is a nice place for it to happen."

"For what to happen?" Zoe asked.

Dream Ange licked her lips in a way that might have been innocent, or maybe not. "Whatever you'd like," she said.

Zoe took a step towards Ange, and Ange took a step forward and closed the gap.

They kissed. Mouth against mouth, and tongue against tongue, and suddenly they were no longer just friends. The first few seconds were a gentle exploration, but then there was a hunger to the kiss. The feeling of insatiability intensified, until they were tugging at each other's clothes. All of it felt perfect to Zoe, so perfect that it could only be a dream.

She woke up, and Ange was standing beside the bed. It took her a moment to realize it was the alien.

"We've landed," fake Ange said.

Zoe climbed out of bed, went to the window and immediately recognized where they were. "You've brought us back to my asteroid," she said.

"No," said the alien. "This is Ange's asteroid."

"The real Ange? The human Ange?"

"Yes," said the alien. "She's here, living her life, unaware that she's part of an experiment."

"I want to see her," said Zoe.

"Of course. Please understand, though, that not everyone thinks we should be here. During our flight we were in constant communication with our counterparts on this asteroid. Some of our fellow actors see things our way, and some do not."

"Some think you're breaking the rules," Zoe guessed.

"We were never told the rules, so who's to say? My friends and I choose to believe we're taking the experiment in the direction it's supposed to go."

Zoe still wasn't completely convinced that anyone was on her side. "Maybe we should grab Ange and get out of here while we can."

"You misunderstand," said fake Ange. "This isn't a rescue mission."

So it was too good to be true. "It isn't?"

"No," said fake Ange. "We're just dropping you off. The rest of us are going back to the other asteroid, along with the actor who has been playing you here."

"The experiment is continuing," said Zoe.

"Yes, but we're altering it. Here two humans will be together, while every other human is utterly alone. It's a completely different situation, and I don't know if those who designed the original experiment will accept it or not, and I don't know if you and Ange will be able to live with it or not, but this plan is the best we could do. I actually hoped you'd be okay with it."

Zoe thought about what was being offered. Two humans against the world. Was there really anything else she wanted? "I don't hate it," she told the alien.

✡

Zoe pretended that this was the real world.

At least, that's what she intended to do until she figured out what the aliens were doing, what test they'd designed for the human they originally brought to this asteroid. Ange.

As Zoe walked along the street, none of the aliens in disguise looked at her in any way that suggested she didn't belong here. So maybe it was all settled, and they'd accepted her as part of the local experiment.

She was trying to act natural. And she was trying to contain her excitement as she entered the bar.

Ange waved her over to a table. "How's it going?" she asked.

"Great," said Zoe. She sat and they ordered beers and talked like they were two friends sitting in a bar on Earth.

There was nothing in anything Ange said that indicated she suspected this world wasn't quite right. Of course, she deserved to hear the truth. But was there a gentle and gradual way to let her in on it?

"Have you noticed anything out of the ordinary in recent weeks?" Zoe asked.

"Like what, for example?"

"Like there might be aliens amongst us," said Zoe.

Ange laughed. "I haven't noticed any," she said. "But I wouldn't be surprised." And then she must've noticed something in Zoe's expression, because she added, "What makes you ask?"

"Just goofing around," said Zoe. "Although I do sometimes feel like the whole world is against me."

"Oh, I know what you mean," said Ange. "I feel that way all the time."

Zoe decided that was all she was going to hint about their situation today. She was a little worried that if the aliens revealed themselves to Ange and Zoe told her she already knew everything, Ange would be angry Zoe hadn't told her sooner. On the other hand, it was probably something Ange was going to have to see to believe, and Zoe didn't particularly want Ange thinking she was insane in the meantime.

So they talked about other things, their stupid jobs, their ordinary lives. They both ordered a second beer, then a third.

Zoe looked at Ange, and decided it was time to be honest. Not about the fact that they were surrounded by aliens. She was going to tell her something much harder. She was going to tell Ange how she felt.

"You and I get along really well," said Zoe.

"Yes we do," said Ange.

"Sometimes I wonder what it would feel like to kiss you," Zoe told her.

Time slowed right down, and Zoe had a chance to imagine how Ange would respond. Maybe she would rip her own face off and the alien beneath would say, "Keep wondering, silly lesbian."

But Zoe didn't think that was going to happen this time. This was the real Ange, and she looked happy, like she'd just heard the exact words she'd wanted to hear. And Zoe had the feeling a kiss was coming, a kiss more wonderful than the one she'd been imagining, probably the most amazing kiss ever.

Copyright © 2023 by Robert P. Switzer.

Stephen Lawson is a veteran of the Navy and of the Army National Guard. He lives in Louisville, Kentucky, with his wife. Stephen's writing has appeared in Writers of the Future, Galaxy's Edge, Daily Science Fiction, *and several anthologies. He won the Jim Baen Memorial Short Story Award in 2018.*

MERCY

by Stephen Lawson

Alexander Northcott floated in space in his EVA suit. He'd watched his ship, the *Arrow*, disintegrate into nothing just minutes ago. Only he had survived—fortunate that he'd been doing hull repairs, but now doomed to die alone in the vacuum. The *Arrow* had been on an exploratory mission, far from any known inhabitable world, and well out of range of anyone who would hear a distress call.

He watched his oxygen reserve diminish—sixty percent, then forty, then twenty. He considered pulling off his helmet in the vacuum to speed the process, but he couldn't bring himself to do it. Available oxygen gave way to carbon dioxide, and Alexander Northcott's vision grew black at the edges. Soon, he was unconscious.

He awoke with his helmet removed and with a hard surface mere inches from his face. He lay on his back, with another hard surface beneath his head. He tried to move his legs, but his knees stopped when they contacted whatever contained him. He turned his head to the side, and found a sort of bulkhead with tiny fixtures and doors in it.

A thin, high-pitched voice said, "I think he's awake."

Alexander turned his head to the other side, and found himself staring into the eyes of several miniature humans. Each was about as tall as Alexander's thumb was long. The one at the front of the group wore a lab coat and held a tablet computer.

"You rescued me," Alexander said. "Thank you. I—"

"It's what anyone would've done," the man in the lab coat said. "All life is precious to us. I'm just glad we found you when we did. Our shuttle pilots did some exceptional work today."

Alexander introduced himself, and recounted the destruction of the *Arrow*. The little man in the lab coat said his name was Palluk.

"I must be putting a strain on your oxygen generators, though," Alexander said. "Surely I'm dooming you all to a slow death just by breathing your air."

"Nonsense," Palluk said. "We have reactors of immense power, and can thus add enough energy to our enclosed biosphere to account for your metabolism. Waste from your body will be recycled as ours is, and we can introduce nutrients from our reserve supply to account for the increased load."

"Waste from my—"

"I took the liberty, while you were unconscious, of installing waste tubes through your suit," Palluk said. "Your anatomy is, fortunately for both of us, similar to ours but on a larger scale. I tried to maintain your modesty as much as was possible throughout the process."

Alexander lifted his head as much as he could and looked down toward his feet. Two hoses ran from a new fitting on the right leg of his suit. Beyond his toes, he saw what looked like shuttle-bay doors.

As he moved his eyes around, he realized that those bay doors were the only ones big enough to accommodate him.

"Is there anywhere on this ship that I might be able to sit upright?" Alexander asked.

"Sadly, no," Palluk said. "This is the largest space we have. It is fortunate we had such a massive shuttle bay, though it is scarcely larger than your body."

"I noticed that," Alexander said. "It's a bit like a coffin."

"Well," Palluk said with a chuckle, "you won't be dying today. As I said, all life is precious to our people. We'll take good care of you."

Several hours later, Palluk supervised feeding Alexander a nutrient slush through a hose. Alexander didn't hate the taste of it, but he didn't much like it either.

"I don't mean to sound ungrateful," Alexander said, after they pulled the hose out of his mouth, "but when do we get back to your home-world, or an outpost or whatever?"

Palluk's eyebrows rose.

"Oh, we aren't going back to Maskar," he said. "This is an envoy ship. We are, in fact, traveling to your own system and are well past the halfway point in our journey. It's additionally fortunate that we found you, so that we may learn more about your people through conversation."

"Great," Alexander said. "That's really great. I'll get to go home, then. How soon would we get there at warp speed?"

"Warp—" Palluk said, not understanding the word at first. "Your people have faster-than-light technology, of course. We do not. We will be another thirty-seven years en route."

"Thirty-seven years," Alexander said.

The captain paged Palluk over the intercom then, so he left Alexander to contemplate thirty-seven years spent in a box with tubes for waste and a tube for food.

It reminded him of a remake of a remake of a movie from the late twentieth century.

"I don't suppose your people have invented virtual reality," Alexander said when Palluk returned, "or maybe some sort of neural stimulation to allow mental escape?"

"Oh, heavens no," Palluk said. "Our religion prohibits such diversion. I suppose, even if such a thing were permitted, it might take us a decade or more to make such a thing. We do—if you would like some entertainment—have quite a collection of poetry though. Would you care to hear some?"

"Um," Alexander said. "Okay."

Palluk returned with a book of poetry, which was all terrible.

Alexander had the sudden urge to stifle a yawn. When Alexander moved his hand, though, he heard a tiny scream and felt the crunching of tiny bones. Palluk ran to where the scream had originated, and Alexander heard more tiny feet pounding on the deck. Palluk's poetry reading had apparently drawn a crowd—one that Alexander hadn't heard approach.

He heard a whispered discussion by tiny voices. A minute later, he felt a pinprick in his neck. Then Alexander lapsed into unconsciousness again.

Alexander awoke to the sound of sobbing somewhere near his head, and of someone making a speech. As he listened, he realized the Maskarians were holding a funeral for the little girl he'd crushed. He tried to move his hands, but he realized that they were now strapped to the deck. He tried to move his feet, but these, too, were strapped down.

After the funeral, Palluk returned to the side of Alexander's head.

"My apologies for holding the funeral so close to your head," Palluk said. "We weren't trying to make you feel additional guilt. This is the customary space for such events and the only bit of it big enough to accommodate the gathering was just above your head."

"My hands and feet are strapped down," Alexander said.

"Yes," Palluk said. "I'm sorry about that also. As I said, all life is precious to us, and the captain said we can't risk any more accidental deaths. The new ship policy is that you'll have to be in restraints at all times."

Alexander considered this for several minutes in silence.

"Please let me die," he said finally.

"Wha—" Palluk said. His eyebrows rose again. "Your people permit the thought of—"

"Please," Alexander said again. A tear emerged in his left eye and streamed down into his ear.

He jerked his wrists against the straps, but they held firm. He tried to bash his skull against the ceiling, but it was so close that he couldn't build up any force. He merely tapped it with his forehead, and didn't even put a dent in the metal.

Palluk watched in horror as Alexander tried to bite his own tongue off.

Alexander was in such an emotional state that he didn't feel the needle enter his neck a second time.

When he awoke, his mouth was mostly numb, but he could tell something didn't feel quite right.

"Now, don't you worry my large friend," Palluk said in a soothing tone. "We're going to take good care of you. We *did* pull out all of your teeth while you were anesthetized, but I assure you we can put them all back when we get you to your home-world. They're safely tucked away in a storage compartment."

Alexander whimpered softly.

"Pwease," he said. "Pwease, Pawwuk, just wet me die."

"There there, friend," Palluk said. "I know you're feeling a bit raw right now, but we will get through this together."

Palluk paused. He put a tiny hand to Alexander's cheek and patted it in an attempt at a soothing gesture.

"Now," Palluk said, "I'd like to read you one of my favorite poems for when I'm feeling down. It's called 'Mercy.'"

Copyright © 2023 by Stephen Lawson.

Mike Resnick, along with editing the first seven years of Galaxy's Edge *magazine, was the winner of five Hugo Awards from a record thirty-seven nominations and was, according to* Locus, *the all-time leading award winner, living or dead, for short fiction. He was the author of over eighty novels, around 300 stories, three screenplays, and the editor of over forty anthologies. He was Guest of Honor at the 2012 Worldcon.*

THE BRIDE OF FRANKENSTEIN

by Mike Resnick

April 4:

What am I doing here?

We have no servants, we never go out, we never have company. The furniture is all decrepit and ugly, the place always smells musty, and although the rest of the village has electrical power, Victor refuses to run it up the hill to the castle. We read by candlelight and we heat with fireplaces.

This is not the future I had envisioned for myself.

Oh, I know, we made the usual bargain—he got my money and my body, and I got his title. I don't know what I thought being the Baroness von Frankenstein would be like, but this isn't it. I knew he owned a centuries-old castle with no improvements, but I didn't think we'd live in it full-time.

Victor can be so annoying. He constantly whistles this tuneless song, and when I complain he apologizes and then starts *humming* it instead. He never stands up to that ill-mannered little hunchback that he's always sending out on errands. And he's a coward. He can never just come to me and say "I need money again." Oh, no, not Victor. Instead he sends that ugly little toady who's rude to me and always smells like he hasn't washed.

And when I ask what the money's for this time, he tells me to ask Victor, and Victor just mumbles and stammers and never gets around to answering.

Yesterday he sent Igor off to buy a generator. I thought he finally realized the need to upgrade the castle. I should have known better. It's in the basement, where he's using it for one of his simpleminded experiments that never brings us fame *or* fortune. He can use the generator's power to make a dead frog's leg twitch (as if anyone cares), but he can't use it to heat this drafty, ugly, boring castle.

I hate my life.

✧

May 13:

"My creature lives!"

That's a hell of a scream to wake up to in the middle of the night. Of course his damned creature lives. The little bastard nagged me for money again today.

✧

May 14:

Well, finally I saw the results of all those months of work today. Victor was so damned proud of this hideous creature he created. Let me tell you: it is ugly as sin, it can barely speak, you'd need a microscope to find its IQ, and it smells worse than Igor. *This* is what he's been spending my fortune on?

"What is it?" I ask, and Victor explains that it isn't an it, it's a he. He is sitting on the edge of a table, just staring stupidly at a wall. Victor takes me by the arm (he always has chemicals on his hands; I hate it when he touches me) and pulls me over toward the creature. "What do you think?" he asks. "Do you really want to know?" I answer, and he says yes he really does, so I spend the next five minutes telling him exactly what I think. He doesn't say a word; he just stands there with his lower lip trembling and the same expression on his face that my brother had when his puppy drowned all those years ago.

The creature makes a soothing noise and reaches out to Victor, as if to comfort him. I slap his hand and tell him never to touch a human. He whimpers and puts his hands in front of his face, as if he expects me to beat him. I wouldn't even if I could; this blouse is hard enough to clean without having to wash any disgusting monster yuck off it.

"Don't frighten him!" snaps Victor.

Which is a perfect example of how out of touch with reality he is. The creature is about six football players and a weightlifter all rolled into one, and I'm just a helpless woman who spends an inordinate amount of time wondering why she didn't marry Bruno Schmidt. All right, he's bald and fat and his teeth are rotting and he's got a glass eye, but he's a banker, and his house doesn't have a monster in the basement.

✧

May 25:

I went fishing in the stream today, since Victor is too busy making notes to notice that we're almost out of food. (Of course, we wouldn't run out so often if we had a refrigerator, but then we have no place to plug it in anyway.)

So I'm standing there in my rubber boots, fishing rod in hand, and I hear a noise behind me, and I turn to look because a woman alone can't ever be too careful, and what has happened is that Victor has let the creature out for some exercise, or air, or whatever hideous eternally damned creatures get let out for.

When I turn to face him he stops and stares at me, and I say, "You lay a finger on me and I'll scratch your eyes out!"

He kind of shudders and walks around me in a huge semi-circle, and winds up about thirty yards downstream, where he stares at the fish. Somehow they seem to know he's not trying to catch them, and they all cluster around his ankles when he wades into the water, and he smiles like an idiot and points to the fish.

"Fine," I say. "You catch four for dinner and maybe I'll even cook you one."

Up to that minute I would have sworn that he didn't understand a word, that he only reacted to tones of voice, but he leans over, scoops up four fish, and tosses them onto the grass where they start flopping around.

"Not bad," I admit. "Now kill them and we'll take them back to the castle."

"I don't kill things," he says in a horrible croaking voice, which is when I discover he can speak.

"Okay, eat yours while it's alive," I say. "What do I care?"

He stares at me for a minute, and finally he says, "I am not hungry after all," and he begins wandering back to the castle.

"Fine!" I shout after him. "There will be more for us!"

If there's one thing I can't stand, it's an uppity creature.

May 27:

"Don't you realize, my dear," says Victor, his narrow chest puffing out with pride, "that no one has ever accomplished this before?"

"I believe it," I say, looking at the creature, who seems to get uglier every day. "But that doesn't mean it's anything to brag about."

"You just don't understand," says Victor, and he's pouting now, like he does whenever I point out the obvious to him. "I have created life out of the disparate pieces of the dead!"

"I understand perfectly," I say. "Who do you think's been paying the bills for all this?" I point at the creature, who is busy staring off into space. "That left arm should have been my new stove. That right arm is my carpet. The left leg is my automobile. The right leg is a central heating system. The torso is my new furniture. And the head is indoor plumbing that works."

"You are being too materialistic, my dear," says Victor. "I wish I could make you see that this creature is of inestimable value to science."

I look at the mess my husband has made of his laboratory. "If you're going to keep him," I say, "at least give him a mop and teach him how to use it."

June 1:

I am sitting on a chair I have dragged out to the garden because I can't stand the smell of Victor's chemicals, and today I am reduced to reading *Life* and *Look*, because the Bavarian edition of *The Wall Street Journal* is late again. I had to sell all my stocks to pay for Victor's endless experiments, but I still follow them and compute how much I'd be worth if I had just married Bruno Schmidt, or maybe some doctor who, if a patient died, let him *stay* dead.

Anyway, I have dragged a small table out to hold the magazines and my iced tea. I would have asked Igor to do it, but I'd sooner die than ask him for a favor. So I am sitting there reading, and I hear an earth-shaking *clomp-clomp-clomp*, and sure enough it is the creature, out for his daily airing.

"Good afternoon, Baroness," he croaks.

I just glare at him.

He notices my magazines. "Are you reading?" he asks.

"No," I say coldly. "I am speaking to an animated nightmare from the deepest pits of hell."

"I don't mean to distress you," he says.

"Good," I said. "Go halfway around the castle and try not distressing me there."

He sighs and walks away, and I go back to reading. After a few minutes my magazine is covered by a huge shadow, and I look up and the creature is standing next to me.

"I thought I told you to—"

His hand juts forward with a delicate golden flower in it. "For you," he says.

"Thanks," I say, taking it from him and tossing it onto the ground. "Now go away."

Maybe it is the way the sun hits him at just that moment, but I could swear a tear trickles down his cheek as he turns and walks away.

June 3:

Today I caught him in the wood-paneled library that should have been my pride and joy but is now just my daily escape from the boring reality of my life.

"What are you doing here?" I demand as I enter.

"I was bored, just sitting around," he answers. "I asked permission to go into town, but The Master"—that's Victor—"doesn't want anyone to see me yet. He told me to read some of his books instead."

"*Can* you read?" I ask.

"Of course I can," he replies. "Is it so surprising?"

"Fine," I say with a shrug. "Go read. You'll find Victor's scientific books on the other wall."

"I have no interest in them," he says.

"That's not my problem," I say. "I can't help but notice that you're standing right next to a row of romances by Jane Austen and the Brontes. They'll be wasted on you."

"I think I would like romantic stories," he says.

"That's disgusting!"

"Do you really think so?" he asks curiously.

"I said so, didn't I?" I reply.

"Perhaps that is why the Master spends his nights in the laboratory," he says.

I pull a thick book off the shelf. I feel like pummeling him with it, but I don't think he feels pain, so finally I just thrust it in his hands and tell him to get out my sight.

June 4:

He lumbers up to me while I am outside reading the *Journal,* which has finally arrived.

"What is it now?" I demand irritably.

"I have come to thank you," he says.

"For what?" I ask.

"For *this.*" He lays the book on the table. "I read *A Christmas Carol* last night. It was very uplifting." He pauses for a second, staring into my eyes with his cold dead orbs. "It is comforting to know that even Scrooge could change."

"Are you comparing me to Scrooge?" I ask angrily.

"Certainly not," he answers. Another tiny pause. "Scrooge was a man."

I stand up and lean forward, bracing my hands on the table and glaring at him. I am about to give him a piece of my mind, to explain that I'm going to speak to Victor and insist that we donate him to some university, when a big hairy spider appears from nowhere and races across my hand and starts crawling up my arm. I scream and shake my arm, and the spider falls to the ground.

"Kill it!" I yell.

He kneels down and picks the spider up in his hand. "I told you the other day," he says. "I don't kill things."

"I don't care what you told me!" I snap. "Stomp on it, or crush it in your hand—but just kill the damned thing!"

"I have *been* dead, Baroness," he replies somberly. "It is not an experience I would wish upon anyone or anything else."

And so saying, he carries the spider about fifty feet away and places it on the branch of a young sapling.

I don't even notice when he comes back to pick up the book. I am too busy thinking about what he said.

June 7:

The next day it is *Wuthering Heights a*nd then it's *Anna Karenina* and finally he reads *Gone With the Wind,* which is making so much money in the bookstores that even Victor couldn't run through the royalty checks.

"You're developing quite a taste for romance," I say as I find him in the library again. It is the first time I've initiated a conversation with him. I don't know why. I suppose if you spend enough nights alone you'll talk to *anyone*.

"They are heartbreaking," he says with a look of infinite sorrow. "I thought romances had happy endings, like *A Christmas Carol,* but they don't. Heathcliff and Catherine die. Anna and Vronsky die. Scarlett loses Ashley, and then she loses Rhett."

"Not *all* romances end unhappily," I say. I think I am arguing with him, but I wonder if I am not trying to comfort him.

"I remember, as though through a mist, the story of Arthur and Guenevere." A body-wrenching sigh. "It ended poorly. And so did Romeo and Juliet." He shakes his massive head sadly. "But it does explain a lot."

"What do a bunch of tragic romances explain?" I ask.

"Why you are so bitter and unhappy," replies the creature. "The Master is a wonderful man—brilliant, generous, thoughtful, and he is constantly saying that he is very much in love with you. Clearly you must feel the same emotions toward him or you would not have married him, and because all such romances end in tragedy, you behave as you do from resentment at what must be."

"That will be quite enough!" I say. "Take whatever book you want, and then keep out of my sight for the rest of the day."

He picks up a book and walks to the door.

Just before he leaves, I ask: "Did Victor really say he loved me?"

June 8:

The toady brings me my breakfast on a wooden tray while I am still in bed. I stare at his misshapen body and ugly face for a moment, then have him set the tray down on my nightstand.

"What is this all about?" I demand.

"The creature is afraid that he may have hurt your feelings," answers Igor. "I tried to explain that it is impossible, but he insisted on preparing your breakfast. Then at the last minute he was too frightened of you to bring it here himself."

"What do you mean, it's impossible to hurt my feelings?" I say.

"I have never known it to happen, Baroness," he answers, "and I have been with the Master longer than you have."

"Maybe we'll have to do something about that," I say ominously.

"Please don't," he says so earnestly that I stop and stare at him. "You have abused me, physically and verbally, since the day the Master brought you to the castle, and I have never complained. But if my services are terminated, where is an illiterate hunchback who left school at the age of eight to support his ailing mother to find employment? The townspeople laugh at me, and the children tease me and make up terrible songs about me. They even throw things at me." He pauses, and I can see he is struggling to control his emotions. "No one in the town—in *any* town—will ever give me a job."

"You're still supporting your mother?" I ask.

He nods his head. "And my widowed sister and her three little ones."

I just stare at him for a minute. Finally I say, "Get out of here, you ugly little wart."

"You won't speak to the Master about terminating me?" he persists.

"I won't speak to Victor," I tell him.

"Thank you," he says gratefully.

"He probably wouldn't have listened anyway," I say.

"You are wrong," says Igor.

"About what?"

"If it comes to a choice," says Igor with conviction, "he will always side with the woman he loves."

"If he loves me so much, why is he always working in that damned laboratory?" I say.

"Perhaps for the same reason the creature did not bring you the tray himself," says Igor.

I am still thinking about that long after he has gone and the eggs and coffee have both grown cold.

June 9:

Today is the first day that I willingly go down to the laboratory since the day after Victor created the creature. The clutter is awful and the stench of chemicals is worse.

Victor looks startled and asks me what's wrong.

"Nothing is wrong," I say.

"The townspeople aren't coming to burn the castle down?"

"It's an eyesore," I agree, "but no, no one's coming."

"Then what are you doing down here?" he asks.

"I thought it was time you showed me what you've been doing down here day and night."

Suddenly his whole homely face lights up. "You mean it?"

"I'm here, aren't I?" I say.

There follows one of the most boring afternoons I have ever spent in my life, as Victor proudly shows me every experiment, failures as well as successes, plus all his notes and all his calculations, and then explains in terms no one could possibly understand exactly how he created the creature and brought it back to life.

"That's fascinating," I lie when he's finally done.

"It *is*, isn't it?" he says as if it is some great revelation.

I check my wristwatch. "I have to go upstairs now."

"Oh?" he says, clearly disappointed. "Why?"

"To make you your favorite dinner."

He smiles like a child looking forward to opening his Christmas presents. I try to remember what he likes to eat.

June 14:

I encounter the creature in the library.

"Igor thanks you."

"It was nothing," I say.

"By raising his salary, his mother can now remain where she is. *That* is something."

"I went over the ledgers," I answer. "He went fifteen years without a raise in pay."

"He is very grateful," says the creature.

"If I fired him," I say, "Victor would just go out and find an uglier, clumsier assistant. Handling money and running his life in an orderly fashion are not his strong points."

"He seems much happier this past week."

"He is obviously pleased with the results of his experiment," I say.

The creature stares at me, but doesn't respond.

"Have you found any happy romances yet?" I ask.

"No," he admits.

"Then since the tragic ones upset you, why keep reading?"

"Because one must always have hope."

I am about to say that hope is a greatly overrated virtue. Instead, much against my will, I find myself admiring him for clinging to it.

"For every Romeo, there must be a Juliet," he continues. "For every Tristan, an Isolde." He pauses. "There are those who say we are put on this Earth only to reproduce, but the Master has shown there are other ways to create life. Therefore, we must be here for a higher purpose—and what higher purpose can there be than love?"

I stare at him for a moment, and then find myself pulling *Pride and Prejudice* off the shelf. I hand it to him, and do not even shudder when his fingers touch mine. "Read this," I say. "Not every romance ends tragically."

I wonder what is happening to me.

✣

June 16:

Victor looks upset as he sits down at the table for dinner.

"Is something wrong?" I ask.

He frowns. "Yes. Something is missing."

"From the table?" I ask, looking around. "What is it?"

He shakes his head. "No, not from the table, from the laboratory's office."

"Has someone stolen your notes?" I ask.

He looks confused. "Stranger than that," he says. "My cot is missing."

"Your cot?" I repeat.

"Yes," he replies. "You know—where I sleep when I finish working late at night."

"How odd," I say.

"Who would steal a bed?" he asks.

"It seems very strange," I agree. "Fortunately there's another bed in the castle."

He looks confused again, and then he stares at me for a long moment, and then, suddenly, he smiles.

✣

July 2:

"Are you sure?" asks Victor.

"We can't turn him loose in the world," I say. "What could he do to support himself? I joked about it with him this afternoon and said he could always become a wrestler, that he looks the part of a villain."

"What did he say?"

"That he wants to be loved, not feared—and that he doesn't want to hurt anyone."

Victor shakes his head in amazement. "What kind of brain did Igor bring me, I wonder?"

"A better one, I think, than you had any right to expect," I say.

"Almost certainly," Victor agrees. "But that will have no effect on the way people react to his appearance."

"It could destroy him," I say.

"Literally," agrees Victor.

"If we want him to stay," I tell him, "then you know what we have to do."

Victor looks at me. "You are quite right, my dear," he says.

✣

July 3:

I find him in the library, where he spends most of his time these days. He is sitting on the oversized chair that Victor and Igor constructed for him, but the second he sees me he gets to his feet.

"Have you spoken to the Master?" he asks nervously.

"Yes," I say.

"And?"

"And he has agreed."

His entire massive body seems to relax.

"Thank you," he says. "No man, no *person*," he amends with a smile toward me, "should live his life alone, even one such as myself."

"She won't be pleasing to the eye," I warn him. *Or the ear, or the nose*, I want to add.

"She will be pleasing to *my* eye," he answers, "for I will look past her face to the beauty that lies within."

"I'm surprised you want this," I say. "I'd have thought all those tragic romances would discourage you."

"It may end unhappily," he acknowledges. "But that is better than it never beginning. Would you not agree?"

I think of Victor, and I nod my head. "Yes," I say. "Yes, I would agree."

Then there is nothing left but to send Igor out to start visiting the graveyards again.

I hope Victor finishes work on the new project by Christmas. I can hardly wait for the five of us to sit around the tree, a happy family unit. Maybe it won't end well, but as my new friend says, that is no reason for it not to begin.

Copyright © 2009 by Mike Resnick. First published in Asimov's *magazine, December 2009.*

While being rained on in Oregon, Monte Lin edits, writes, and plays tabletop roleplaying games. He has stories in Cossmass Infinities, Cast of Wonders, *Flame Tree Press,* Dark Matter, *and Ignyte-nominated nonfiction at* Strange Horizons. *He is also Managing Editor of* Uncanny Magazine *and Staff Editor for Angry Hamster Press.*

THE BLEEDING MOON

by Monte Lin

The Moon was bleeding again. Selene's mother gestured to the crimson circle high in the sky, her silver chain in her hands, whispering a hurried prayer. Selene merely shrugged.

To Selene, the Moon had always bled, a carmine drop slowly forming every month underneath. People held a collective breath before each plump drop fell onto their world. And then she would hear rumors of an ichorthing rampaging through the land. Once, when she was small, Selene had wished aloud to see an ichorthing, and her mother clamped her hand on her arm and shook her, shouting, "Never say that! This is why we live out here. Let the ichorthings demolish those fools, collecting in the village like so much bait." So now, Selene kept her wishes to herself.

Her mother claimed that the Moon had once been pristine and white. A bright white coin in a tapestry of diamonds. The bleeding worried her mother sick: "Moon forgive us!"

Selene ignored her and let her ramble on as always. How could ancient history help with present harvests and the butchering of pigs? Let Great Heroes take care of the monsters that emerge from the ichor of the gods. *We should ignore these useless rumors, thoughts, and bits,* she felt.

Selene had been hunting, bow in hand, arrow nocked, when she felt both the sky thunderclap and the earth shudder from the blood drop, enough to shake the trees and scatter her prey. She ran back home to see the telltale crater and scorched earth where her home once stood, trees burned to cinders, and soil hardened and dead. She saw no sign of her mother, saw no glint of her polished silver prayer chain—the only thing bright and shining in this otherwise bloody land.

That moment, Selene regretted not listening to her mother, not only because her mother was right, but because she had been trying to express her terror of how wrong the world was. Selene should have understood this worry as real, should have taken her mother away from this cursed, bleeding land. But she would have refused and where could they have gone anyway?

This guilt compelled her to run into their now-shattered barn to grab her grandfather's rusted sword, left over from the Nighttime War. Rage propelled her through the forest, chasing the trail of blood-burnt grass. Despair loosed her arrows from her hunting bow. But it was sorrow she felt when the arrowheads broke on the ichorthing's hide and shame when the creature's bladed fist smashed the ground, throwing Selene in a shower of earth.

Winded, she dug herself out of the soft soil, dirt falling all about her in a cloud. She lifted her left arm and saw her hunting bow had snapped in half. She still had her sword, but an ichorthing can't be harmed by a single dulled blade, much less wielded by her, a child. She knew this by the rumors and stories, and now understood how truly the Moon hated the earth, to send her children every month. The loss of everything, the farm, her mother, struck her harder than the ichorthing's blow.

It charged, its four legs with human-like hands striking the soft earth like thunder. Though it struggled against the loam, its powerful legs propelled it forward with such speed that all Selene could do was stupidly shout, "Why? Why did you kill my mother?"

It came out more a whine than a battle cry, much to her embarrassment (if embarrassment was the right word when faced with certain death). The tears that streaked her dirt-covered cheeks also betrayed her dignity, so she surrendered, letting the sobs wrack her body in small earthquakes.

Her sobs softened when she realized that the ichorthing was crying too.

Whatever hate she had for this creature evaporated when it cried, staring up in the sky, at the Moon. *All ichorthings are the Moon's rage*, the stories said. Yet looking up at its own tears trailing down its face like hers, claws reaching up to brush them away, but unable because of the blades, Selene realized the ichorthing was just as much a victim as she was. It had been cast off from the Moon, a lost child orphaned from its mother. Like her.

The terrible ichorthing remained still, weeping, so expressively helpless mirroring a strange calm blanketing over Selene, and she must have eventually fallen asleep, the rage and terror draining away into rubbery arms and legs. When she woke, she saw the ichorthing had carried her back to the farm, clumsily trying to prop up the walls of the ruined house. The wall snapped in half and it roared.

Selene found herself running up to it, waving her arms, and shouting, "It's all right. It's all right. You don't have to fix it."

The ichorthing fell silent, its roar diminishing through the forest. It reached up a bladed arm toward the Moon, then brought it back down, pointing at the ruined house. Selene understood

It had been Selene who went to the village to sell their grain and their pigs. Her mother had refused to leave the farm when alive, yet she had never wanted anyone visiting, even to buy their stock. Selene both craved and resented her village visits. It provided an opportunity to talk to people, but she also knew what they said behind her back.

"Witch!" a villager shouted.

"A hostage!" another villager cried.

"Cursed spirit!"

"A lost child!"

And on and on.

Selene rode on the ichorthing's shoulder. Aside from its four legs, the ichorthing had two arms that ended in scythe-like claws. It had no hair or fur to hold onto, only a deep-red tinted hide, but it held its arm high, its shoulder level enough for Selene to stand or sit.

She stared at its head, with its giant hooked beak, its eyes blood red and expressionless. Well, singular eye, since she could only see the one on the right side.

It blinked and the head turned ever so slightly, matching her gaze.

"We'll get you back home," Selene said.

The villagers scattered when the ichorthing slammed a blade into the earth.

Selene patted her hand against its iron-strong hide. "No, we are not fighting. Not anymore," she said, as much as to the ichorthing as to the villagers.

"See how the child commands the monster!" a villager shouted. "I knew they were witches!"

"Why are you helping the Moon, our mortal enemy?" Another villager said, holding an old, rusty spear leftover from the Nighttime War.

"This ichorthing isn't our enemy," Selene shouted. "It has lost as much as I have."

"They are vengeance for us winning the Nighttime War," said a shout from the crowd.

"The war is over," she said. "Does anyone even remember why we fought it?"

"The Moon!" someone else shouted, but the rest mumbled and scratched their heads. Yet another villager repeated, "But the Moon …" without conviction.

"See? If we can get this ichorthing back to the Moon, maybe we don't have to keep fighting."

"Take it to the Great Archer then," the first villager spat. "He wounded the Moon and stopped the Nighttime War. Let him deal with it."

"So he can kill it!"

"The Great Archer doesn't care about us. He hasn't left his castle in years."

"But he can send it back to the Moon!"

"Just go, child, and leave our village!"

Selene patted the ichorthing's hide again and it roared, choking the words into the villagers' throats. In the silence, Selene shouted, "Where does this Great Archer live?"

In the resultant answers, Selene noted no one asked what had happened to her mother.

The castle, a mansion really, though it once had several towers, sat in decay. Dust covered the roofs and its walls. The walls sported holes, worn down by rain and time. Weeds and grasses grew to the height of soldiers. The open gates stood only because someone had bound them with old, fraying rope.

"If this archer was so great, why is his castle falling apart?" Selene said to herself. The ichorthing blinked once, what Selene decided meant agreement.

Her mother had not taught her anything about the Great Archer or the Nighttime Wars. She had assumed her father and grandfather had died during them, but attempts to learn more had been met with an anguished cry and a shout over why she would bring up such a cursed subject. Yet another unbridged and silent gulf that had fallen between them.

Selene shouted out a "hello?" They waited, but the Great Archer did not come out to confront or greet them. No sound but the scattering of birds and the hiss of wind through the grass.

"Can you let me down?"

The creature knelt, its bladed hands too dangerous to use to pick up or put down anything, much less a girl. Selene slipped off and landed in the grass with an ungraceful thunk. She picked herself up, stretched her back, shook out the kinks in her arms and legs, and shouted, "Hey! Great Archer Hero! You have a lot to answer for!"

No reply. No sound, save the creaking of wood and the clatter and crumble of the walls. The ichorthing stepped up to the mansion's wall and raised a mighty arm to bring it down.

"Wait! Let me go inside. Find out what's going on."

The thing turned its beak to one side, to allow an eye to stare at her. It blinked once.

"If I don't come back before the sunrise … or if I scream really loud, then start smashing."

It lowered its arm and turned away. Selene climbed into a hole in the double doors and descended into darkness.

On thirteen stone slabs lay thirteen tomb effigies carved in stone. They lay covered in dust, the ceiling open to the sky bathing them in the red moonlight. Each figure depicted the garb from their homelands. One in a wrapped robe. Another bare-chested but with a cloak and waist cloth. At the end of the tomb, lay the Great Archer's effigy, a real great bow by its side, looking very much the Warrior and Hero with his armor and helmet.

"Get out!"

A young man stood by the Great Archer effigy, wearing the blue robes and the long hair of a noble. With a smooth swoop of his arms, he grabbed the great bow, taller than him by a foot or two, nocked an arrow, and pointed it at Selene, its wood creaking in the effort.

"Who are you?" she asked.

"This is the Tomb of the Great Archer. For even stepping foot here without my permission, I could puncture your heart, a right granted to me by law."

Selene threw her sword to the ground, the metal clacking against the stone. "I came here for the Great Archer."

The young man cast his eyes downward to hide a pain Selene recognized. "He is dead. I am his Nephew. You may speak with me."

Selene looked at the slim man, barely past boyhood. "Can you send an ichorthing back to the Moon?"

The Nephew gave Selene a look of disgust. "No, of course not. My uncle would never do such a thing either."

"But the ichorthing doesn't deserve to be stuck here. It belongs with the Moon."

The young man's visage softened, letting the bow relax, the arrow hanging loose between his fingers. "The ichorthings cannot be saved. They are a necessary evil to keep the Moon from recovering."

The young man pointed high above him at an angle with the arrow and gestured to Selene to come closer with his other hand. She stood beside him and noted the edges of his robe were frayed, his waist sash a bit threadbare. He smelled of faint incense with the sweet scent of clove.

She followed his raised arm and saw the hole in the ceiling had been cut or broken in such a way as to be curved, from east to west. The young man's arm cut a path in the same direction. She said, "It's how the Moon moves across the sky!"

"Yes. I swore an oath to my uncle to fire another arrow at her, lest another the Nighttime War erupt."

Selene shook her head in frustration. "The ichorthings and bleedings are just as bad. I lost my mother to it."

The Nephew's voice took on the tone of a parent chastising a child. "You're too young to know. The kings of the Thirteen Armies all wanted the Moon's hand in marriage but she would not give an answer to any of them. They fought to determine the winner."

Selene swept her arms across the tomb. "They started the Nighttime War?! But they're all dead now! We can heal the Moon. We can pull the arrow out."

"You don't understand. The Thirteen couldn't help themselves, not under the Moon's beautiful light. She causes a madness of love."

"The Moon shouldn't suffer for kings who can't control themselves."

"Enough!" The Nephew swept his arm across, cutting the air and cutting her off. "Just because you think you can save your mother—"

"My mother? She's dead."

"Yes, she is good as dead. The Moon's blood makes ichorthings monstrous, without mind, no longer the person they once were."

"Person?! Ichorthings are people?" Thoughts and mental detritus cleared away and finally fell into place. Selene ran back outside.

"M-Mother?" Selene asked. The ichorthing twitched its head to blink once at her. Its beak opened and closed as if trying to speak aloud but failing.

"Is that you, Mother? Show me, please."

The ichorthing's beak creaked open wider, and it knelt forward. For a moment, Selene's heart skipped, thinking it meant to devour her. It paused, its breath turning the air warm, moist, and coppery. It curled its pointed tongue, and underneath lay Mother's silver prayer chain.

Mother had always prayed out in the fields, late at night, the Moon's bloody glare turning the chain red. Ever since Selene had caught her out there, that chain always seemed like blood spilling from her frail hands. Mother's prayers seemed so saturated with agony, Selene more than once thought of burying it in the forest.

Selene snatched the chain and the ichorthing closed its beak. The girl stepped closer and pressed her body against it. "Mother."

"Get out of the way!"

Selene turned around, and through her tear-flooded eyes, saw the Nephew with the great bow, an arrow ready to fly.

The young girl spread her arms wide. "No! It's Mother!"

"It is not. Not anymore!" The Nephew frowned, eyes steel.

The young girl did not move, but the Nephew let loose the arrow. It cracked the air in half and Selene covered her ears. The Mother-ichorthing leapt out of the way, landing onto the earth, tossing soil into the air, while the arrow crashed its way through the forest, bursting the trees apart.

"Idiot!" Selene hissed. "The village lies that way."

The Nephew paused, and Selene saw doubt in his eyes, a doubt borne from youth, a doubt she recognized in herself. The Mother-ichorthing crouched low, circling the Nephew back toward Selene. He drew another arrow with pressed lips and grim eyes.

"Your uncle is not a Hero," Selene said, breaking the silence.

"What?! How dare you!"

"He's not a Hero. A Hero would have stopped the war without hurting the Moon," she repeated. "And you are not the Great Archer."

"Foolish girl! The ichorthing will kill you!"

"Have you even killed anything with that bow? I've shot plenty with mine."

The Nephew's arms shook with rage. He pulled the bowstring and fired but he had lost his focus, the arrow carving a furrow into the earth. Selene leapt onto Mother-ichorthing's back and they vaulted into the air. By the time the Nephew could fire again, they had lost themselves in the woods.

They stopped in the middle of a field, the grasses tall and waving in the wind. The trees provided shelter, protection from prying eyes, and save the bloody light above, Selene saw no lanterns or fires. She and Mother were alone with the Moon hanging overhead.

Selene spent the next hour sobbing and holding onto the massive thigh of her Mother-ichorthing. It, she, breathed slow and steady, a soft, mournful bellows. After a time, the ichorthing brought an arm to envelop her daughter, warming her against the chilly breeze.

"I should have—" Selene started, but Mother hissed, her beak open wide.

"I'm sorry I never—" she said, but again, Mother cut her off with a hiss.

"All right," Selene said, "no regrets of the past, only thoughts of the future."

She looked to the sky. "But where can we go? Villagers will chase us away. If only I could carry you to the Moon, if there was a mountain high enough to climb, or if I had wings—"

Thoughts and bits fell into place once more, and Mother-ichorthing cocked her head at Selene's potent silence.

✥

Selene stood naked in the field, her clothes neatly folded by a tree. Perhaps a hunter could use them. Or maybe an animal will use them for bedding. Either way, she didn't want them to be destroyed by the change. It seemed a waste.

"Let me help you, Moon. Give me wings and I will pull the arrow out of your flesh."

She raised her arms above her head and stared straight at the dark red eye in the heavens. Soon, she felt the Moon cry a tear of blood.

It struck the earth nearby, and Selene fell to her knees. She had no time to cover her face before it consumed her, searing her skin. She felt her body ignite, save for where her mother's prayer chain pressed against her neck, bitingly cold compared to the blood of the Moon.

Selene prayed. *This saved Mother, kept her as her. This will keep me as me*, she thought, with a lack of doubt borne from youth.

✥

The Nephew did not realize that the arrow had been removed from the Moon until he looked up and saw the bright white-gray orb bearing down on him through the ceiling hole in the tomb. He grabbed the great bow and an arrow, pulled back, and aimed at the gleaming, pale eye staring back at him.

"Uncle, please guide my arrow. For the sake of the world."

He let loose and he heard the arrow whistle fading through the air, until a dark shape, a bird, swooped by, cutting across the coin of the Moon. The Moon remained pristine.

He nocked another arrow, aimed, and let loose. The bird swooped by again.

As he prepared a third arrow, he heard the whistle, but this time, it grew louder. He dove out of the way as his first arrow burst through the roof, sending stone and fragments scattering throughout the tomb.

✥

Selene hovered in the sky, careful not to be silhouetted by the Moon. She beat her blood-red wings and dropped the second arrow from her claws. She looked down with her slitted eyes, the irises brown-red, to see Mother catch it, then rear back an arm and hurl the arrow back. A quiet but distinct crash echoed from the Tomb.

Selene settled on the central spire of a tree, her weight almost bending it double. She purred, not a word, but with enough meaning for Mother to look up and exhale. Selene cocked her serpentine head to one side, waiting for another arrow's whistle.

In the silence, she wondered if the Nephew was dead, crushed by rock, or pierced by his own arrow. *No, Selene thought, that is not our goal.* The Moon, after all, only wanted to be left alone. And now that Mother and Daughter were together again, they had no other desires than ending the Nighttime War.

When the silence stretched into minutes, she let out a breath. When the silence stretched into hours, Selene smiled, her dagger-teeth gleaming in the bright gray light. When the silence stretched into years, the Moon and the world finally learned to live peacefully together.

Copyright © 2023 by Monte Lin.

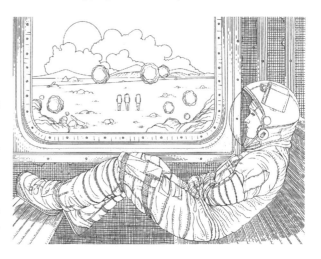

Lisa Short is a Texas-born, Kansas-bred writer of fantasy, science fiction and horror. She currently lives in Maryland with her husband, youngest child, father-in-law, two cats and a puppy. Lisa is a member of SFWA and HWA and can be found online at lisashortauthor.com and on Twitter and Instagram @Lisa_K_Short.

SLOW BLOW CIRCUIT

by Lisa Short

Miz Igwe kept Nolly late after class. Usually Nolly didn't mind that, because Miz Igwe always had a lot of interesting things to say, but today it did bother her. She tried not to show it, though, smiling her best all through Miz Igwe's speech about *still haven't heard back from your mama bout enrolling you in those special classes!* til her cheeks were tight and sore.

Mama didn't mind if Nolly took the special classes, not at all, but Mama wasn't so good about returning people's messages. As Nolly broke into a trot towards Halcyon Complex's Main Terminal, she tried to fix it in her head to tell Mama to talk to Miz Igwe when she got home, but thoughts of Ivory kept intruding—Ivory, who had won that week's class game for the first time *ever,* and the *prize,* too. There weren't always prizes for winning one of the class games, and sometimes even when there were, the prizes were boring; Nolly had won enough of them herself to know all about that. But this one was *Ivory's* prize, and Nolly had wanted to see it more than anything. Even then, she hadn't managed it; the other kids had crowded too tight around Ivory, clamoring to see it themselves, and then Miz Igwe had held Nolly back when the end-of-class bell had rung.

But Ivory wasn't waiting for her in the archway that led from the Third-Grade school corridor to the Main. Nolly stuck her head around the corner, squinting into the knots of grown-ups milling around all the Main's creaking, groaning commuter belts, but she didn't see Ivory's waist-length black hair or her orange school jumper anywhere. She edged along the wall towards the Subsidized-Residential corridor, but Ivory wasn't waiting there either. Nolly darted into the corridor, barely avoiding being trampled by a group of bigger kids thundering out of the Fifth-Grade corridor in the process, and broke into a jog towards the central bank of lifts. If she were lucky, at least some of them would be in service.

But she wasn't. All the lifts but one were dead, and she gave up waiting for that one to arrive after fifteen endless minutes of foot-shuffling in front of the lift doors. Resignedly, she headed for the stairs instead. The stairwell was as hot and airless as always, its vents clogged with decades of refuse—nobody wasted any maintenance on the stairs. By the time Nolly had reached the seventeenth flight, she was gasping for breath; she stopped and leaned against the rusted railing, draping her arms over it and staring down at the long, long drop below. And then, just as the thundering of her pulse in her ears subsided, she heard a hoarse voice say, *"Nolly."*

Nolly jumped back from the railing looking around wildly; huddled deep back in the shadows in the farthest corner of the landing, knees drawn up to her chest, was Ivory. "Ivory!" Nolly skipped across the landing, all tiredness forgotten. "I was *looking* for you—"

Ivory cut her off with a sound like a dog's bark. "I went home first." Her lips pulled back from her teeth. "I wanted to show Mama my prize."

The prize! "Oh, can I see it?"

"No." Ivory inhaled deeply through her nose, the sound bubbling and ugly. "I threw it away." Nolly gaped at her, then shut her mouth hard—Ivory's eyes were swollen and red-rimmed. "My new stepdaddy, he was there too. He followed me out after I showed it to Mama, said I must've cheated to get it cause I'm too stupid to have won it for real. He said he was gonna show me what happens to girls who cheat." Ivory's arms were wrapped so tightly around her middle that her elbows showed white through her skin. "Could you come home with me today? Maybe spend the night?"

"Sure. As long as Mama don't mind." Nolly bent down, easing an arm behind Ivory's back, and helped her to stand up. But Ivory stayed hunched over, even on the stairs, like something deep inside her was hurting her bad.

Miz Tam's—Ivory's mama's—apartment was its usual crazy uproar of kids. Miz Tam looked frazzled, her hair as black as Ivory's escaping from its scarf to hang in frizzy loops around her face. After a careful look around, Ivory asked in a casual voice if their new stepdaddy was home. *No,* said Miz Tam, *he's out on a repair call, and why you so late home from school, Ivory?* But Ivory just jerked her head at Nolly, who followed her back to her bedroom nook. Miz Tam's apartment was bigger than Nolly's Mama's—the kitchen unit, bathroom unit and one tiny bedroom off the main room was the same, but Mama's didn't have bednooks like Miz Tam had, so that every one of her kids had their own little slot in the main room wall to sleep in. Nolly and Ivory sat down together cross-legged on the mattress behind the nook's ragged privacy curtain.

"So, your new stepdaddy's a Handy?" Nolly asked, once they'd settled in.

Ivory nodded. Everybody was supposed to call the official, certified Halcyon Complex maintenance technicians whenever something broke (and something was *always* breaking) but Mama said people usually didn't because it was too hard to get them to come out to the Subsidized sectors. Mama didn't need them that much anyway, because she had Nolly, but being an *un*official repair tech—a Handy—was a good living for a Subsidized resident, if they knew anything about fixing things at all.

Ivory didn't look like she wanted to talk about her new stepdaddy anymore, so Nolly called Mama on Miz Tam's Net account. Mama didn't answer, though their apartment said she was at home—*probably sleeping,* Nolly thought, but she dutifully left a message anyway. Then she and Ivory played games on the Net til Miz Tam called them out to help get all the littler kids fed and bathed. Nolly would have liked a bath herself, but Ivory didn't want to get undressed, so Nolly loyally didn't either, sticky and itchy as she was from her run up the stairs. Finally Miz Tam dimmed the main room lights and went back to the bedroom with the baby; Nolly and Ivory settled back down in Ivory's nook to sleep.

It was never really quiet in Miz Tam's apartment; Nolly had learned how to sleep through any number of grunts, snorts and wails whenever she spent the night. But something *did* wake her up this time—maybe the jingle of the curtain rings as they were pulled back—Nolly emerged abruptly from a confused dream about Miz Igwe and Mama to the sight of a huge black shadow looming over her. She sucked in a huge breath and screamed bloody murder—the shadow recoiled and Miz Tam yelled out *What the FUCK was that?* from the back bedroom. Then Nolly blinked—the looming figure was gone, and the curtain across the nook was closed, swaying almost imperceptibly in the shadowy darkness.

"*Shh,*" came Ivory's whisper from below her. "Lay back down. He's left." She was shaking; Nolly dove back under the blanket and snuggled close to Ivory's side.

"Was that your new step—"

"Yeah." Ivory's voice was barely a thread of sound. "I guess he thought I needed another *lesson*. But you must've scared him away."

The next day at school, Miz Igwe had them all play the game again—the lights, Miz Igwe had explained, flashed in a pattern, and if you could work out the pattern you could touch the lights as fast as they appeared, almost *before* they appeared. It was a frustrating game for Nolly, who no matter how fast she could think, had fingers that tangled up together when she tried to get them to keep up with her thoughts. So she glanced over her shoulder at Ivory, with the pleased expectation of being proud and happy for someone *else* at least—but Ivory's board was barely lit at all.

After the game had ended, Nolly sat down next to Ivory. Ivory was hugging her knees, staring at the floor, her face pinched. All Nolly's words dried up in her throat, replaced by a dawning realization—Ivory had lost the game *on purpose.* Ivory, who *never* lost a game on purpose any more than Nolly did—it had never occurred to Nolly before that very moment that anyone *would* ever lose a game on purpose. And for Ivory to do it now, with a game she was the best in the class at—

A new sensation was swelling up inside Nolly, so alien and furious that she hardly even knew how to contain it. Her hand, unbidden, shot out and seized Ivory's. Ivory squeezed back hard, and though she wouldn't look up and meet Nolly's eyes, tears were welling up out of her own, rolling down over her cheeks in a silent streaming flood. Nolly's stomach was clenched so hard she almost threw up, right there onto Ivory's lap.

Nolly's Mama's apartment was dim and silent when Nolly arrived home from school that afternoon. Mama was asleep in the bedroom again—blissed out, Nolly guessed; she probably had a date later that night. Nolly wasn't hungry, but Mama would be when she woke up, so Nolly wandered back out of the bedroom into the tiny kitchen. The cold-storage and pantry units were empty—Mama wasn't too good about remembering to keep them stocked up, any more than she was about answering messages—but she *was* good about keeping the meal dispenser fully charged. Nolly ordered two meals on it, Basic Level One in case they didn't have credit for more—then jumped back with a small shriek as the dispenser's display flared white, then emitted a pop loud enough to hurt her ears.

"Nolly?" Mama's voice, muffled, drifted in from the bedroom. "That you, baby?"

"Yeah, Mama." Nolly blew a long breath out through her nose. "It's the damn meal dispenser again—"

"Shh, watch your language." Mama wandered out of the bedroom. Even all messy and puffy from sleeping, she was beautiful; it always gave Nolly an ache, looking at her, and she immediately ran to Mama's side. Mama bent down, her hair swinging out and around Nolly like a thick, scented curtain. "Think you can fix it?"

Nolly nodded, and Mama kissed her forehead with soft lips. "Of course you can. My little genius."

She could feel Mama's smile against her skin.

But that did remind her—"Mama, Miz Igwe's been messaging you about special classes for me."

"Oh, has she?" A faint line appeared between Mama's fine arched brows. "I must've missed them … can't you just tell her I give my permission—no, I guess not. Well, let's see what those messages say—"

It took a good twenty minutes to sort out Miz Igwe's messages from all the other ones Mama had; Mama had a lot of boyfriends. But Mama never brought any of them home, nor any *new stepdaddies* either—impulsively, Nolly hugged Mama tight around the waist.

"Hey, what's that for?" Mama said, laughing a little, but her own arms encircled Nolly just as tight.

"I just—just love you, Mama." Nolly's words, that flowed out of her so easily whenever she needed to write a paper for Miz Igwe's class, always deserted her at times like these; rendered mute, she just hugged Mama harder.

"I love you too." Mama's voice tightened up. "You deserve a better Mama than me, you know that? One that could send you away to a better school, or take you to live someplace where you could go outside sometimes—"

"Outside?" Nolly was startled enough to pull back a little out of Mama's embrace. "Why would I want to go outside?" She'd seen *outside* on field trips to other parts of the Halcyon Complex—gray and ugly, rows of buildings and ruins under a featureless, brassy sky so big that someone might be able to just fall up into it, up and *up* without ever stopping—she shuddered.

"Well, not outside *here*. There are places outside that you can go, though—beautiful places. That's where you were conceived, you know." Nolly did know that story, though she'd never been sure if she believed it. "Which makes *outside* the best place, doesn't it?" She hugged Nolly again.

After Mama had ambled, yawning, back into the bedroom, Nolly linked up to her Net account and pulled up her own special folder, then opened a port to the smartchip in the dispenser. Schematics flashed before her eyes, then tables of numbers—*voltage, amperage, capacitance, resistance*—then all the usual SAFETY! warnings that she'd seen so many times before she never read them anymore.

It was an easy problem—a couple of blown fuses, not even a challenge for Nolly, definitely not anything anyone would need a certified Complex maintenance technician for. Even a Handy could probably have fixed it—and that thought stopped Nolly cold in her tracks. The last of the SAFETY! warnings was still scrolling past her suddenly unseeing eyes: *Use correct fuse! Replace only with fuse of the specified type, current and voltage rating!*

Even a Handy—

Nolly remembered seeing Ivory's tight, pinched face, her arms hugging her middle like that was all that was keeping her insides from falling out. *I guess he thought I needed another* lesson—

Realization dawned and another meaning for Handy forever became par of Nolly's own personal warning manual. As if in a dream, she made a few small alterations in the circuitry *here* and *there*—the dispenser didn't want to change its factory specs, but Nolly had figured out how to get around its admin lock long ago. Then she backed out of the dispenser's smartchip and logged onto the unofficial Handy message board. She had a moment of worry when she realized she'd never asked Ivory what her new stepdaddy's name was, but luckily he was using Ivory's mama's Net account on the board—*probably doesn't even* have *his own Net account*, she thought with cool contempt. It was easy enough to slip her own Mama's household account request right to the top of his repair queue.

Nolly made sure their apartment door was unlocked, then headed back to the bedroom. Mama was sprawled out across the mattress, sleeping in a welter of gauzy clothes and glittery makeup pots, her long, lovely brown hair tangled around her arms like spiderwebs. Nolly locked the bedroom door behind her, then climbed as carefully as she could onto the mattress and lay down beside Mama, inhaling the heavy sweetness of her perfume until she dozed off.

Some formless time later, the sound of yelling woke Nolly up, though it didn't wake Mama—a man's rough voice, demanding *Who done called me down here? HELLO!* Nolly sat up silently. The yells diminished to loud mutters, accompanied by the sound of boots stomping across the floor of the main room. Nolly's stomach clenched nervously and she scooted closer to Mama's side.

Long minutes crawled past. Then—*POP!* Even louder than it had been when Nolly had tried to use the dispenser herself, followed by a long, strange sound—like gurgling, but harsh and horrible—then a low, hissing sizzle. Nolly scrunched up into a tight ball on the mattress, hugging her knees so hard her arms hurt. The gurgling and sizzling gradually faded into silence. Nolly waited until a thick, greasy smell started to seep into the bedroom from under the door, a little like the fried pork dumplings that Miz Tam sometimes cooked. Then she used Mama's Net account to call Halcyon Complex Security.

☼

Ivory was at school the next day—Nolly hadn't been sure she would be, but when Nolly arrived she was sitting in her usual place, looking the same as she always did except for a wreath of white plastic flowers threaded through her black hair.

Nolly inched up the aisle and gingerly sat beside her, then flinched as Ivory's hand slipped into her field of vision, fingers coming to rest lightly atop Nolly's clenched fists. Nolly dragged her reluctant gaze back up, over the well-known lines of Ivory's chin, mouth and nose, until she finally met her wide dark eyes. Then Miz Igwe was speaking—*All right, you all know the drill! This week's game starts in five minutes! Today's the last day to win a prize!*

Then Ivory said, low, "I'll help you win today, Nolly. If you want."

Nolly glanced involuntarily over at Miz Igwe, to make sure she hadn't heard—some of the Games were for pairs or groups, but not this one—but Miz Igwe was bending over somebody else's board, oblivious. Though that wasn't the only reason she was nervous. Ivory had to *guess*, even if she didn't *know*. Complex Security would've told Miz Tam how Ivory's new stepdaddy had passed away, and maybe even where he'd been and what he'd been doing when it had happened. "You sure?"

Ivory's fingers squeezed tight around Nolly's. "I'm sure. I want you to win the prize today." Then Ivory smiled, so broadly that her eyes crinkled up into joyous crescents. "I already got my prize for this game."

Copyright © 2023 by Lisa Short.

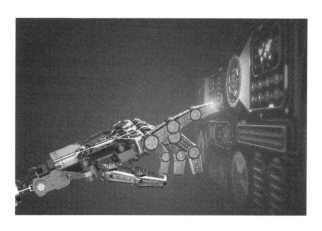

Stewart C Baker is an academic librarian and author of speculative fiction and poetry, along with the occasional piece of interactive fiction. His fiction has appeared in Nature, Lightspeed, *and* Galaxy's Edge, *among other places, and his poetry has appeared in* Fantasy, Asimov's, *and numerous haiku magazines. Stewart was born in England, has lived in South Carolina, Japan, and California, and now lives within the traditional homelands of the Luckiamute Band of Kalapuya in western Oregon, along with his family—although if anyone asks, he'll usually say he's from the Internet.*

SIX WAYS TO GET PAST THE SHADOW SHOGUN'S GOONS, AND ONE THING TO DO WHEN YOU GET THERE

by Stewart C Baker

1. Dust 'em

"Listen, little lady," the guy in front of the door is saying with a sneer. "There's two types of swordsman …"

Chiyome's already heard enough to peg *his* type, so she tunes out his braggadocio and pulls out a bag of nanite dust. She'd hoped to use her status as the Shingen warlord's only child to bluff her way in to the Shadow Shogun's presence, but the dust works too. She blows a handful in his face and he shrieks, drops his sword, then follows it to the floor, thrashing in the station's artificial gravity.

Behind her, Rui whistles. "What'd you give him?" The other woman asks.

"You know how my father's always talking about unsanctioned violence and other threats to order?"

"Sure, but I always figured he only says it because he's the one doing the sanctioning. No offense."

"None taken. The point is, every time this guy even *thinks* about violence for the next 4 hours, this will happen.»

"Not bad."

"Not *bad*? It'll take you longer to beat the next one with your naginata, I bet."

"A bet, eh?" Rui cups Chiyome's chin in one long, slender hand and tilts her head up. "Well and good, then. We'll bet a favor."

"A favor and a kiss."

"And a kiss," Rui agrees, then frowns. "Wait. Is that if I win, or if I lose?"

Chiyome snorts and pushes her away. "You'll figure it out. Now pay attention—someone's coming."

2. Bust 'em

In fact, there are two someones coming: a pair of swordsmen, silently furious, hands on their still-sheathed laser swords.

Rui strides out into the hallway to meet them, spinning the long haft of her naginata idly. "Gentlemen!" she says brightly. "Nice day for a stroll, is it not?"

"It's a station, Rui," Chiyome cuts in. "They have *rotations*, not *days*."

"Oh, hush."

If the swordsmen are taken aback by the banter, they don't show it. They spread out, hands on their weapons, waiting for Rui to make the first move.

It's a mistake, but before they can realize it Rui's already taken them down, the swift *crack-CRACK* of her naginata's shaft as it bounces off the sides of their skulls echoing down the hall.

Rui turns to Chiyome before they've even hit the floor. "Well?"

"Nearly twice as long," she says, shaking her head in mock sorrow.

"What," Rui sputters. "But there were *two of them*. And I didn't even use the blade, which has to count for something."

Chiyome shrugs. "I don't make the rules," she says. "I just call the shots. Now help me search their pockets."

3. Split 'em up

Chiyome's just found the passcode on a crumpled up holo when another trio of goons strides down the hallway.

"It's a regular *parade*," Rui grouses.

"Cheer up," Chiyome tells her. "You can try to beat me again."

"One each, then?"

"First one done gets the extra."

Chiyome pushes the button on a long-range electrical destabilizer she put the finishing touches on just last night and one man's sword short-circuits in his hands, the current sending him to join his colleagues on the floor.

"Another win for me," she says. "I'm a little embarrassed that you're doing so badly."

Then she sees the smirk on Rui's face and looks again: her bodyguard's hands are empty of the naginata. Instead, the weapon lies on the floor, and next to it is goon number five.

"You *threw it* at him?!"

"Hey," Rui says, *sotto voce*. "I don't make the rules. I just call the shots."

"I do *not* sound like that.»

"If you say so. Now, what do we do about him?"

The last of the swordsmen—who's been watching with a look on his face like milk that's been left out of the gravity well too long—raises his hands in surrender. "How about I open the door and you let me go?" he suggests.

"It's a nice offer," Chiyome says. "But unnecessary." She pushes the button and his laser sword—still buckled to his hip—jolts him into unconsciousness.

"Speaking of unnecessary," Rui says.

"He might have told someone we were here," Chiyome points out. "Besides, I already had the passcode, and now we've done three each."

✧

4. Dance

Passcode in hand, the door opens easily enough.

Inside is a small room that does not, in fact, contain the shadow shogun. Instead, there are four more goons, lounging in various states of unreadiness. Set in the room's far side, inconveniently beyond these new opponents, is another door.

"I *told* you space priests can't be trusted," Rui says, nudging Chiyome in the ribs with one elbow as the goons scramble for their weapons.

Chiyome pulls out a tube of what she thought was super-sticky bonding agent, but which turns out to be instant disco. "But he seemed so nice!" she shouts over the sudden burst of noise.

"They're all the same," Rui insists, raising her own voice to match and bringing her naginata hilt down on the head of the first goon who's struggling to extricate himself from what looks to be a very ancient sofa. "Grandiose promises about the path that the future will take, but very little accuracy." She grimaces at the noise. "Why do you even *have* this, anyway?!"

Chiyome throws a plush crab robot at the second, then ducks his flailing arms as the mechanisms inside the toy activate and it clamps its squishy claws around the side of his head. "Do you remember that colony where they'd hollowed out all the asteroid cores and strung them together?" she shouts.

Rui slips her naginata between the flailing goon's legs and spin-kicks him in the back of the head as he goes down. "The one where they put mirrors on the ceiling so the place looked bigger?"

"Yeah!"

"The one where *a certain woman* tried to put on, and I quote, 'the biggest laser light show since Eta Carinae,' even though she knew bright lights and loud noises give me migraines?"

"Uh …. Yeah?"

"I remember *as little as possible* about that place." She stops to dance out of reach of the remaining two goons, then looks over at Chiyome, eyes narrowed. "Why?"

Chiyome finally finds the bonding agent tube. She engages the timer and throws it at the other two goons, then watches with satisfaction as it arcs between them and explodes, coating them with a thick, viscous paste that turns their clothes as solid as steel and instantly secures them to the floor.

"No reason," she shouts into the silence caused by the disco's sudden decision to terminate its building crescendo, then clears her throat and continues in as upbeat a voice as she can muster. " Now that this hideous din has stopped, shall we be on our way?"

Rui nods. "Okay," she says. "But I'm taking full credit for one you crabbed."

"Ugh, *fiiiiine*."

5. Take the Scenic Route

The second door leads to an elevator built into the outside of the station.

It's a *small* elevator—clearly built for the shadow shogun instead of uninvited guests—but Chiyome isn't exactly upset that she has to huddle in close to Rui for the two of them to fit. There's only the one button, so Chiyome pushes it, then takes a sharp breath as the room rises, revealing a glimmering view of the ice planet the station orbits.

"How beautiful," she says.

"Why thank you," Rui replies. "I do try."

A flare of bright orange light draws their attention to the far side of the planet's gentle curve, and Chiyome mumbles a quiet curse. It's the Shingen warlord's fleet bursting into real-space, their warp engines' ejecta setting them off against the whorled blues and whites of the icy surface.

"Fleet's closer than I thought they would be," Rui comments, voice even.

"Yeah. We should hurry."

Rui squeezes her shoulder, and Chiyome puts her hand on top of the other woman's. They ride in silence for a minute, then Rui clears her throat.

"About that bet," she says. "I've been thinking …"

This time, it's not the view that takes Chiyome's breath away. "Yes?"

"What happens if it's a tie? Do we *both* owe *each other* a kiss? Or do they cancel out?"

For a minute, Chiyome very carefully says nothing. She counts up to ten, then down again, inside her head.

"Well?" Rui prompts.

"I don't want you to kiss me because you think you *have to*," Chiyome says at last.

"Oh," Rui says. Then, after a pause: "*Oh.*" She clears her throat. "Oooooh. Right."

Chiyome fights the urge to roll her eyes. Instead, she leans back into the taller woman. "Right," she murmurs.

The elevator chooses this moment to slide to a stop, and the two of them stumble backwards as its doors open behind them. Rui—ever quick on her feet—catches herself before they fall, then spins around, using the motion to push Chiyome behind her. Chiyome digs out another stuffed crab bot and glances past the other woman's outstretched arm, expecting to see another batch of goons. But except for them and a thirty-meter tall robotic statue of a man clad in the traditional armor of Earth long dead, the room is empty.

With a slow outblown breath, Chiyome puts the robot away again. She tries to step around Rui and into the room proper, but the other woman pushes her back again. "What are you doing?" she asks.

"Something's not right."

"You're being paranoid," Chiyome says, but then she hears it too—a quiet whirring, somewhere at the edge of sound. "It's a trap."

"It's a trap," Rui agrees.

And then, with a creaking, groaning sound like the station is falling apart, the statue *moves*.

6. Disconnect the Power Supply, Stupid

Before Chiyome can so much as think of what device to reach for, Rui pushes her away towards one corner of the room, diving into a roll that takes her to the other just as the robot's sword smashes into the ground, shaking the room with an echoing *clang*.

The statue lifts the weapon and steps forward with a shudder, then chops down with the blade a second time. It's more like someone tilling the earth in those vid-dramas about newly terraformed planets than the smooth motions of a warrior, Chiyome thinks. Some screen jockey's idea of how a sword should move. Not like *she* can really talk, she supposes, but the thought gives her an idea. She whips out her datapad, tapping in commands as fast as she can go.

Rui, meanwhile, has leapt onto the massive sword's hilt. She darts up the giant robot's arm to its head, letting out a primal yell as she spins her naginata around above her head and brings its blade down in a vicious slash.

Despite herself, Chiyome stops what she's doing to watch.

The edge of the naginata bounces off the robot's metal helmet, and Rui uses the momentum to execute a spinning leap, slamming the hilt of her weapon into where the eyes would be on a human opponent. The robot, however, takes no notice. It just lifts its other hand, stop-motion slow, and flicks her away as though she were some kind of bug.

"Rui!"

"I'm fine," Rui snaps, sweat beading her forehead as she staggers back to her feet. "But some help would be wonderful!"

"On it!" Chiyome replies, fumbling with the datapad. "Just give me a couple more minutes."

The robot brings its weapon down with a clang, so close to the warrior woman it ripples her uniform.

"I'll try," she gasps. "But don't blame me if I'm a pancake by the end of it."

She and the robot continue their mismatched battle, and Chiyome tries to stay focused on what she's doing. Although, truth be told, hacking the station's systems isn't difficult—the shadow shogun really ought to invest in better cyber-defenses.

"Any luck?" Rui asks, readying herself as the robot creaks through another sword-lift.

"One more second …. There!"

As the robot brings its weapon down again, Chiyome types in the last command and hits the execute button. The sword creaks to a stop a few feet above Rui's head, and then the lights flicker off, plunging them into the dim, flickering yellow of emergency backup power.

"*What* did you *do*?" Rui asks.

"Not to brag or anything," Chiyome says. "But while you were keeping the robot distracted, I rerouted all the station's non-essential functions to fabricating ten million strawberry shortcakes. It'll take nearly ten hours, and while that's going on none of the station's doors, lights, elevators, or—and I think you'll agree this one is important—thirty-metre tall death robots will work."

Rui groans.

"And the best part is," Chiyome continues, "I built in an automated lockout procedure, so that nobody can stop or override the command. Not even me!"

"Chiyome," Rui says.

"The robot can't kill us, and none of the Shadow Shogun's goons can get in, either."

"Chiyome!"

"*What*?"

Rui holds up her hands in a gesture of compromise. "It's better than being flattened by this behemoth," she says, "I'll give you that. But there's one little problem."

"What's that?"

Rui points to the door behind the robot, dimly illuminated by the emergency lighting. "We can't get out, either, and the fleet is nearly here."

"Oh." Chiyome looks down at the datapad in her hands, its warm little glow as it counts down the shortcakes looking less hilarious by the second. "Right."

"Right," Rui agrees. She crosses the room and gives Chiyome a hug, tight and desperate.

Chiyome realizes belatedly that the other woman is shaking. "Are you okay?"

"I've been better," Rui admits. "But I'm not dead, and neither are you. So … thank you for that."

Chiyome blinks back sudden tears, wraps her arms around the other woman, and rests her head on her shoulder. "You're welcome," she murmurs. "And Rui?"

"Yeah?"

"About that bet …"

Rui pulls back, tilts her head up with one hand again. "Forget the bet," she says. "I *want* to do this. Do you?»

Chiyome swallows, throat dry. She nods, not trusting herself to find the right words.

"Good," Rui whispers, leaning her head down to meet Chiyome's—

—only to be interrupted by slow, begrudging applause and a woman's low laughter.

1. Collect Your Reward

Chiyome pushes Rui gently away, her face flushed, and the applause stops.

A moment later, the shadow shogun herself emerges from one corner of the dimly lit room. Lithe, muscled, and seated in a sleek metal hover-chair, she carries a matched pair of swords and a laser pistol in her lap and looks nothing like Chiyome had expected. Although, now that she thinks about it, she isn't sure what she *had* expected—something like the robot, maybe? Like the goons?

"Bravo," the other woman says. "Bravura! You've defeated every challenge I've thrown at you." She hovers closer, one hand tightening on the pistol grip. "A pity I'll have killed you both before the Shingen warlord's main force arrives."

Chiyome clears her throat. "About that. My father doesn't *exactly* know we're here."

The shadow shogun narrows her eyes. "Doesn't he, now?"

"No," Chiyome tells her. "He doesn't. But a few of his advisors *do*, and they've sent me here to make a deal."

"A deal," the shadow shogun repeats. Her grip on the pistol loosens, but she makes no other move.

"They're tired of his threats and his obsession with control," Rui comments. "Tired of the way he monopolizes their local resources, how he siphons off their citizens to fuel his endless wars of expansion. They want a fairer master."

That gets a dry laugh. "And they think that would be me?" She gestures to herself with a wry look in her eyes. "I know what they call me. Lady of darkness. Tyrant of the Rimward Arc."

Chiyome shakes her head. "That's what *he* calls you. *They've* seen what you're doing out here. How you treat the planets and stations that sign up for what you have to offer."

"And what," the shadow shogun asks, fingers drumming on one arm of her chair "do *they* have to offer *me*?"

"Their allegiance," Chiyome says. "And their help in turning back his fleet."

"They'll help me defeat your father, in other words. Even though his death will mean the death of their loved ones he's holding as hostages on his flagship."

"Yes," Chiyome says, jutting out her jaw defiantly. "They will. Nothing will change without sacrifice. Nothing will get better." She manages, just barely, to keep her voice steady.

For a long moment, there's no sound but the drumming of the shadow shogun's fingers. Rui puts her hand in the small of Chiyome's back, and Chiyome joins it with her own, giving it a quick squeeze.

Then the shadow shogun nods. "Very well," she says. "I accept. But on one condition."

"What's that?"

"You finish up here," the shadow shogun says, "and we go have some of that cake. I *do* adore cake."

She pushes a button on the arm of her chair and the lights flicker back on, the robot returning to the position it occupied when Chiyome and Rui arrived.

Rui raises one eyebrow, her lips quirking in a smile. "I thought you said it couldn't be stopped."

"Oh, hush," Chiyome says. She waits for the shadow shogun to leave the room, then pushes any thought of the coming battle away as she reaches up and pulls Rui down for that kiss, at long, long last.

Copyright © 2023 by Stewart C Baker.

Storm Humbert is a writer currently living in Michigan. He has an MFA from Temple University, where he studied with Samuel R. (Chip) Delany, Don Lee, and other awesome faculty. Storm has been published in Andromeda Spaceways, Apex, Interzone, *and many anthologies, including Writers of the Future #36.*

CARRION

by Storm Humbert

When Dibsy Parkin was twelve, walking home from school, she saw a turkey buzzard struggling in the ditch on the side of the road. It was struggling because I'd worked good and hard to get a piece of my body from the tomb in the woods out into the open, and that piece was lodged in the buzzard's throat. Not many have gotten to smell a buzzard's throat (and fewer still know that spirits can smell), but I was inclined to believe I was suffering more than the bird.

Dibsy rushed over, undaunted by the buzzard's raised wings. It was too weak to hurt her, but she had no way to know that. Dibsy was good, and Dibsy was brave. Say what you want about her life choices, but she had that going for her.

She wrestled the bird's mouth open, and there we came face-to-face for the first time. Well, face-to … sternum bone chip, let's say. She went to work, but I'd been in there a while, and even though I'd already found a mark, I needed the bird to die. A lich can never absorb too much life energy. Plus, I could see it plain as death on her face—Dibsy cared about this bird. So, I kept my anchoring barbs in until the buzzard was beyond help, then I let Dibsy pry me free. Oh, anyone with a conscience might've cried if they'd heard her once I was out.

"Come on birdy," she said. "Come on!"

She slapped its back like she was trying to beat the breath back into it, but there was nothing she could do. Me, on the other hand …

That was when the two little buzzard chicks started screeching. They were under their mother in a hollow log. She'd been feeding them when I found my footing—got her on the way up. I might have been able to smell, but I couldn't cry, and I hadn't cared for people in a few millennia—not one—but the way Dibsy looked at those chicks … okay, I still didn't care, but it made me think about how much most people would, and that's damn close.

Dibsy had tucked me in her fist and was squeezing me tight, so I could feel the love—the need to help—rippling through her. I've never really unraveled the *why* of it, but people have the toughest times putting down cursed objects. Best I can guess, humans have a sense about power, but it's just a theory. Anyway, Dibsy looked down at those little chicks, and I knew she wanted to fix their world. She wanted to wave her hands and give them their mother back. That's not how it works, though—not exactly.

Need a hand? I said into her empty, do-gooding head.

That was the first time I tasted Dibsy's fear, but it was an unsatisfying flavor. The sweetest fear is from the truly craven—those who would feed a wolf their daughter even if it'd only buy them a few more minutes of breath. Lots of people think it's possible to be fearless, but it's not. Everyone fears. Dibsy's fear was muffled, though. It was the kind of fear that flashes only to be dimmed—that cuts only to be blunted. Dibsy was her grandmother's girl, and that meant she was both brave and optimistic.

"God?" she said.

Not exactly, I said. *I can help, though, for a price.*

It didn't occur to me at the time, but Dibsy should have at least considered the possibility I was the devil. God knows she'd heard enough fire and brimstone, but she really couldn't be bothered with any of that. I believe she would have made a deal with the actual devil to save those chicks.

"Do it!" she said. "I'll do whatever you want."

Okay, I said. *Pick one of the chicks to die, and the mother can live.*

That *really* got her attention, and I promise I wasn't just being a bastard. That's how this necromancy thing works. Love is life. Necromantic power is secured through the sacrifice of beloved things. Dibsy *had* to choose which chick died because I didn't give a damn about either one. Plus, in choosing, she'd take the destruction of a beloved thing upon her soul. So, it was a win-win for me.

That was my game, after all. Wither a soul before its body is spent, and you had yourself a serviceable vehicle in which to live for the brief flicker of a mortal life. I might not have been able to love things, but I did miss the sensations of living.

"That's not fair," she said. "I can't."

Then I can't help you, I said.

Feeling her make that first choice is one of my favorite parts of the job. Miraculous things for a terrible price and all that. Humans are so squirmy, and it was something I was pretty sure I didn't like about them even when I was one. That first broken barrier always carried a unique delectability for me.

"The little one," Dibsy said.

Take him out and put him by his mother, I said.

Dibsy did it. The little chick bit her. They both did, and I think it hurt her more because it didn't just fight for itself. Its sibling fought for it too. Dibsy didn't cry because their little nips hurt. She cried because she was sorry.

Dibsy sat the chick by its mother, and it went straight to the buzzard's ugly, red, head as if for food. I could have told Dibsy to step back. A good person certainly would have, but that ship sailed a *while* back.

The chick screeched a little extra as its mother's corpse faded to mist beneath it. It was frantic—confused and afraid in the most delicious way. Dibsy might have been comforted to know that the chick's death was painless—not that I told her, of course.

In a blink, the chick exploded in a haze of shrieks, beaks, and gore. Down clung to Dibsy's face where speckles of chick bits and little bone sat moist and warm. The mother stood where the chick had only a moment ago, its feathers devoid of any evidence it had just emerged from the flesh of a thing only a fraction its size.

And the phoenix arises, I said.

Dibsy didn't respond. She just shoved me in her pocket and went home.

I quickly learned that Dibsy was a boringly good girl. Her mother had died during childbirth, and her father was a world-class bum, so she'd grown up with her grandparents, Jack and Rhonda. They were the kind of hard-working, salt-of-the-earth, religiously devout idiots you'd find in any poor backwater at any point in human history. I ought to know, I've lived in plenty of them. A lich needs idiots like a flower needs sunlight.

I shouldn't be too hard on old Jack and Rhonda, though. They made Dibsy the good girl she was—the kind that wanted to help a dying, disgusting buzzard. Rhonda always told her that helping injured critters was the fastest way to be one of God's favorites—and the woman was *adamant* God had favorites. Maybe she was right, but if there was a God, I'd wager his favorite was me. Why else let me live twelve thousand years?

For a long time after buzzardgate, Dibsy didn't speak to me and ignored me when I talked to her, but she could never bring herself to get rid of the bone piece. That whole cursed object thing and whatnot.

They always try the not talking to me approach, and it never works. Eventually, a situation where I can help always comes up, and Dibsy was no exception. Rhonda made it incredibly easy to "help" Dibsy. The old woman taught her granddaughter to love everyone—to care about everything—and Dibsy did, both because Granny said so and because it was Dibsy's nature. Dibsy thought love could conquer anything—wanted it to be that way—but that's not how life works.

The second time Dibsy accepted my help, she was fourteen. She had a favorite teacher, Mr. Dix—I shit you not, that was his name—and Mr. Dix had pancreatic cancer. I'm a bastard, but pancreatic cancer's a bitch, and it doesn't mess around. Mr. Dix was in the hospital and receiving palliative care before he got the chance to misplace the "Get Well Soon" card Dibsy's class signed for him. Dibsy visited Mr. Dix with her class, but she also did it on her own time. She'd bring him his favorite foods from around town that nobody had the heart to tell her he couldn't eat anymore.

I think she saw Mr. Dix as a father figure. Papa Jack was a good enough guy—not that I'm the best judge—but he was limited. Definitely a man of his generation. He didn't shower Dibsy with love. He was the fair-but-firm, proud-but-silent sort. Mr. Dix gave her the positive reinforcement she'd never known she always wanted. Truth be told, I think she was crushing a little too. Mr. Dix was neither married nor old—not too hard to look at either. That's just a theory, though.

Dibsy walked in while he was sleeping once, quiet as a mouse, and I could tell she was deciding whether she'd stay or go—whether it was selfish to wake him.

Need a hand? I said.

To feel how hard she ground her teeth—I got chills. It was a brilliant, rare, white-hot tremor of *Get fucked bitchy lichy,* and I swear I could get drunk on the memory of it.

"What'll it take?" she said after a silence that, honestly, surprised me in its brevity.

Papa Jack gets it instead, I said. *He doesn't have long anyway.*

Honest? I didn't know if that was true. Jack was seventy-four with COPD, but he had no plans of retiring. The old bastard would weld tractor trailer frames with his oxygen tubes still in his nose. Jack was a hard man. If he'd have seen that buzzard on the side of the road, he'd have kicked his truck in four-wheels and forded the ditch to put it out of its misery, leaving me in the mud with it.

"Not as bad as Mr. Dix's," Dibsy said. It was as much a question as a counteroffer, but I was impressed she was playing ball. "Two years at least."

One year, I said. *Swear on the sigil, I won't hurry it along, but only one year guaranteed.*

In retrospect, that was a slip-up on my part. Swearing on the sigil was a contract I couldn't break—the only kind. Dibsy didn't need to know that, but even if I regretted it after, I doubted it would come to much. Dibsy might have been brave and good, but she wasn't exactly destined for a Nobel.

"Okay," she said.

Then, she woke Mr. Dix and had a talk because why wouldn't she? She'd just sacrificed her Papa Jack to cure her teacher's fucking cancer. What an absolute rube. That night, I thought I'd have her body in months.

In the weeks and—surprisingly—years that followed, I learned that I had underestimated little Dibsy. She totally caught that swear on the sigil shit, and she was not shy about letting me know. She also seemed to have caught onto my game more than I'd thought. She knew how much I liked being around dying things and started helping me out in exchange for information. These were small transactions—microloans against her soul—but they kept the lights on.

Dibsy would offer to torture a barn cat to death for three questions I'd have to answer while sworn to the sigil to tell the truth. She'd hit a squirrel on the road and watch it suffer if I'd swear to the sigil for one question. Shit like that, and she did it with a frequency that would disturb most people.

That's one of the drawbacks of tainting someone's soul. After a certain amount of tainting, it tends to even the playing field a bit. I hadn't accounted for that. I was rusty. I still wasn't worried, though. I'd dealt with some real amoral psychopaths in the past—most people get that way after a while with me—but I'd never failed to land my mark. You don't live twelve thousand years playing like a sucker.

Some of the gems Dibsy got out of me with her sadistic Q&A seshes included exactly what I was (a lich), what that meant (I feed on death to live an existence devoid of love), what happened each time I helped her (aforementioned soul besmirching), and the roots of my power (long-lost rune lore, demonic pacts, blood sacrifice, and useful keywords for her own research). She even took my bone piece out at school—something she *never* did—to look at it under a microscope, not that it helped her. Like I told her afterward, *this is magic, not science, sweetheart.*

Then came the day Dibsy offered to poison all the barn pigeons and watch them die for only three sigil-sworn questions. That kind of currency could have easily fetched five or six, but only asking for three made it irresistible, and she knew that. I agreed, though. The amount of energy her offer would provide dwarfed my nervousness.

"If I kill myself, what happens?" Dibsy said.

You die, I said.

She stuffed the rat poison back in the bag. "You know what I meant."

To me? Nothing, I said. *I'll just sit here in my nifty little bone spur and wait for someone to pick me up.*

"What if nobody picks you up?"

They will, sweetheart, I said. *I'm irresistible.*

"How do I kill you?"

That was the first time Dibsy had ever talked about destroying me. Before that, all of her questions had been about control—about figuring out the system and how to game it. Dibsy wanted to do good, and she knew I could do that. Until that moment, it had seemed like her goal was learning how to minimize the fallout. This question was, therefore, the first hint of her giving up, and it was music to my disembodied ears. Still, while Dibsy was no threat to me, the fact that she was actively considering giving up her super-powered ace-in-the-hole was, well, a little insulting.

I can't be killed, I said. *I can waste if I go too long without a body, or I can destroy myself. That's it.*

She climbed up into the hay mow, upended the rat poison, and silently mixed it with the bird seed she knew they always went nuts for.

"I'm going to kill you," she said.

We sat there for six hours while all of those birds died. Each time one fell—while they lay twitching—I felt like she stared at them extra hard. It was as if she was saying, "that'll be you," and I've got to say, it was adorable.

Dibsy and I went on like that for years. She met a boy her junior year of undergrad. Brock. He was the kind of boy young Dibsy would have wound up with, so I didn't understand how he appealed to my twisted sister of recent years, but they got married a year after they graduated. She seemed about as happy as she was capable of being—as happy as a man could probably make her anymore—so that was annoying.

We still conducted business now and then, but Dibsy kept to small stuff. Sales, as they were, plummeted. I also couldn't get over this little untarnished, perfect glint in Dibsy's soul. She held tight to it, and I knew that whatever it was, it'd be the last thing in her I sullied. It wasn't a matter of *if* anymore, though. It was a matter of *when.* Still, I *did* care about the when. I preferred to steal someone's bones before they started creaking.

For a while, I was really hoping Brock would get Ebola or cancer or really bad hemorrhoids—anything—but that son-of-a-bitch took care of himself. I thought I might get her for good when it turned out Brock was sterile—maybe she'd kill a baby or something, so she could have one of her own—but no such luck. They started looking into adoption without missing a beat.

By the time that adoption came through, I figured the next window would be when Granny died, and who knew how long that would be. I also suspected

Dibsy would be too smart for that. Granny was old—pushing ninety now—and Dibsy hadn't had the same connection to her since Papa Jack passed. Gee, I wonder why.

Things as they were, I figured I was looking at decades now—probably until Brock got old and sick—before I got to take her body, and by then it would be much older than I'd like. But, while it hadn't been the easy win I'd been hoping for, I was still well on my way to at least resetting the old wasting clock, and she was as sure a thing now as she had been her freshman year for any boy with dimples.

It was only two years after Tanner—that's the name Brock picked for their adoptive son ... fucking Tanner—was adopted from his birthmother, that my ship came in. Holy neuroblastoma, Batman. That. Shit. Was. Everywhere. Little Tanner's X-ray was like a god-damn Rorschach test. Brock was annoyingly together and there for her during the diagnosis, though, so I didn't get to gloat quite as hard as I'd wanted to.

As soon as he stepped out for air and to get them some waters, though, I said, *Everyone. All of them. Granny, Brock, his parents, Cheryl at the office. I'll leave Brock's sister to look after "Tanner" once I skip town in your duds. I know you fucking hate her. Everyone else dies.*

"Swear on the sigil," Dibsy said. "And tell me how long Tanner has."

I didn't have to, but I knew the answer and was more than happy to share. *I swear on the sigil, four months. Five, tops.*

"Okay, we'll do it in two months," Dibsy said. "Don't fucking talk to me until then, or I'll change my mind."

I agreed, and, as hard as it was, I shut my mouth for the whole two months. All Dibsy did was hold the shit out of Tanner. She did that bare skin trash all the books told her about—really sold out for the *remember me* angle. Honestly, it was a little pathetic. She'd given me a good run there and I sort of got lucky. She could've gone out with some dignity, but she decided not to. Whatever, I didn't care. I'd won.

☼

The time seemed to drag by, but the day finally came. Dibsy had just put Tanner to bed, and Brock was passed out drunk on the couch. He'd kind of buckled in the last two months, and it had been glorious.

He drank, he shouted, and he lashed out, but Dibsy didn't love him less. She cleaned up his mess and bought him his beer all the same. It was what Dibsy did. Even as she hurt, she loved, and it had been true for every tortured cat or poisoned animal—every sacrificed papa. It wasn't sustainable, though. Part of me wished I could have watched Brock break a little more to see if it might have done her in slow and sweet, but a deal was a deal.

Say it, I said as she stood in Tanner's doorway.

She stared down at that kid so long, I didn't know if she was going to go through with it. For all I knew, she was thinking, *Fuck this. He'll never know,* but then she said. "Save Tanner. Take them all. Kill everyone I love."

Done.

As soon as I said it, I felt funny. It wasn't the euphoric, laugh-in-your-face, dance-on-your-grave feeling I'd expected. It was really ... empty. It took a minute for the pain to come. I didn't recognize it at first. I hadn't felt my own pain since before people stopped shitting upstream from where they got their drinking water.

Hey, I said.

I didn't think spirits could get woozy, but I was woozy.

"Told you I'd fucking kill you," she said.

I couldn't say anything. All I could do was try really hard not to scream because I knew if I screamed that might mean I was dead. In the haze, I couldn't figure out what had happened.

"You're saving my son, asshole," she said. "Granny says we should love everyone."

You're dead too, bitch, I said. *Everyone loves themselves.*

It was the only thing I could think to say—the only solace I felt, really. It wasn't my best moment, okay. I wasn't exactly at my most witty, and I'm not particularly proud of it.

Then Dibsy laughed, and I would have cured her fucking kid just to make her stop. It was this wicked, insane, *you absolute fucking dipshit k*ind of laugh.

"No, I hate me," she said, crying, laughing, broken, alive. "Thanks for that."

Copyright © 2023 by Storm Humbert.

Marissa Tian is an Asian, first-generation immigrant. She works as a trader in the financial industry and writes in her free time for passion. Her work was a winner of Stories That Need to Be Told 2022 contest. She lives in Houston, TX with her husband and three fur babies.

THE WOMAN OF THE LAKE

by Marissa Tian

The crickets and owl carrying on their nighttime dialogue outside and his wife's breathing heavily in her dream next to him were Kang's only company at midnight. He tossed and turned but couldn't ease his mind.

Only two clay jars of rice were left. Would they last through the next harvest? Maybe he should plant more while it was still April … and add some cucumbers to the garden for pickling. They'd need much more food this year with their daughter growing up.

Kang stroked his wife's long hair a few times and rolled gently out of bed, so the wooden bed wouldn't squeak.

The room was roughly four times the size of their bed and contained all of their belongings—a loom, a wooden bucket, a three-foot-tall cabinet which double-functioned as a dining table, two stools, and a bamboo basket on the floor in the corner.

Kang tiptoed to the basket and squatted. His daughter was tucked in a blue blanket inside. Bright moonlight shone through the wooden window onto her smooth skin. Her eyes were closed to the world, and her tiny hands rested at her sides. In the corner of her lips, a thin line of drool dripped. Kang couldn't help but smile. He reached out his hand to wipe it but stopped midway and pulled back. His hand was too rough for her skin.

Bushes rustled outside. The crickets stopped chirping, and the owl flapped away, leaving tree branches bouncing up and down.

Kang stood up and peeked outside. Full moon bathed the world in its silver light. From the corner of his eyes, he saw something disappear into the dogwood shrubs.

A weasel? It better not break into the chicken coop.

He put on a light jacket, stepped outside, and closed the door behind him. Spring's warm breeze carried a vague sound into his ears. Someone … weeping?

Kang's house stood at the very west end of the village, a good ten-minute walk from his closest neighbor. With mostly rice paddy fields nearby, it was rare that anybody made it out here, day or night.

Was it the moaning of one of the chickens or piglets?

He strode beyond the bushes. A chicken coop stood a few feet away, framed by timber and fastened by wires in between. He had double tightened all the joints and re-thatched the roof a few weeks ago. Last year, he'd missed a small hole in a corner. One night, a few weasels squeezed in and raided the entire flock. He couldn't afford that kind of mistake again. Not this year.

Inside the coop, a few chickens opened their tiny eyes and tilted their heads at him. The rest remained sleeping.

The weeping sound hit Kang's ears again. Soft and vague, it seemed far away. It couldn't be the piglets. But he had to check.

He stepped over to the stall. The three piglets he bought last month lay on top of each other. They snored, snouts vibrating with a humming sound.

He'd bought three piglets this spring instead of his usual two. After raising them through fall, he would sell one and keep the other two—one extra this year. A toddler could use as much protein as possible.

The sobbing sound continued. Kang stood tall, turned his right ear toward its direction, and concentrated.

It disappeared.

He circled the garden trying to locate the sound. He glanced over at the vegetables. Green beans had crawled up the bottom part of the trellis. Bok choy and eggplants had broken through the soil.

On the other side of the garden, the sobbing sound reappeared, louder. Kang started jogging. Through the orange trees, he followed a winding path to a lake at the foot of small hills.

Someone wept near the water—a woman, he guessed from her size and sound. She sat with her back to him. Her long, dark hair rested over her quivering shoulders and draped down to her waist.

"Excuse me, are you okay?" Kang tried not to shout and scare her.

The woman stopped crying and turned. Looking to be in her early twenties, she wore a long white dress. Her lips were full but trembling, and her dark big eyes filled with tears. Almost translucent, she shone like a pearl in the silver moonlight.

He had never seen anybody like her. He was suddenly unsure what to do with his hands. He hid them behind his back and hooked his fingers together.

He cleared his throat and swallowed. "What are you doing here?"

"Please … help me." She pointed at her legs.

He walked over. Vines had stretched out from underneath the water and swathed her right shin. In between the wet and mossy twigs, her skin was white, smooth, and silky, like lotus petals.

"May I?" He gestured at the vines.

She nodded.

He bent over and pulled. Slippery and slimy to the touch, the creeping plants clung to her leg like a squid's long arms. His fingers accidentally rubbed on her skin.

It was ice cold. The vines must have blocked her blood circulation.

He smelled a faint aroma on her, reminding him of the daisies along the edges of his farm.

"I'll have to untangle the vines." He sighed. "Who are you? How did you wind up here?"

"I'm Lily."

"You're not from around here, are you?"

"My father and I moved here a few days ago, near the big oak tree. My father fell ill after fishing yesterday. I was going to make a fish stew for him. All of a sudden, a black cat jumped out, snatched the fish from my hands, and ran off. I chased it here and lost it. I walked into the lake … I never fished before. My leg got caught in these vines. I stumbled out of the water but couldn't break away. My poor sick father … he must be worried by now …" Tears broke out of her eyes like rivers. She covered her face with her palms.

"Don't worry. I'll untie the vines and take you home. I know where the big oak tree is."

"Really?" She put down her hands and her face lit up. "That would be so kind! Thank you very much!"

"Of course. But it'll take some time."

Kang sat down and worked to untangle the vines from above her kneecap. They were thin but gripped like snakes entwined around a pole. Her straw sandals lay on the ground next to her. Maybe what disturbed the night outside his window was the cat.

"You are so kind. What's your name?"

Her question pulled him out of his thoughts. "Kang. I live on the farm. That way." He tilted his head toward his home. Under the dark midnight sky, a triangular straw-thatched roof stood above the orange tree line.

She nodded. "Kang. We are neighbors now."

Not quite. The big oak tree was too far away to be neighborly, but he didn't disagree.

"How about I tell you a story?" she asked. "You said it'd take a while."

"A story? Sure, if you are in the mood."

"Of course. I love telling stories."

He smiled and untied the first knot. Hundreds of them crowded between the vines.

"Here we go." She cleared her throat.

"Once upon a time, there was a girl. Her mother died when she was twelve, and her wealthy father remarried. Her young stepmother despised her. One day, she hid her pearls and told the father that the girl stole them. Her father blamed their servant and fired him, but he began to doubt the poor girl. He stopped telling her stories before bedtime and serving her at meals. He wouldn't talk to her unless she spoke first. Her stepmother slowly made her into their new servant. Soon they had a baby boy, and her father gave his full attention to his new son. His eyes glanced over her but never saw her after that.

'Marry her off,' her stepmother whispered in her father's ear once she turned fourteen.

He hesitated but agreed. He put her stepmother in charge.

She sold her off to a farmer's widow, the poorest person among the candidates. 'Go eat someone else's food, you worthless little thing. Suffer a poor life.' Her stepmother laughed at her when she left with the widow.

Two days later, she arrived at her new family's shack on foot. There the girl met the widow's son, her future husband. He was only eleven, too young to have a wife. The widow had bought her as a cheap servant."

Kang held his hands out in front and wove his fingers together to stretch them. "Poor girl. I hope she didn't live in misery after that," he said and went back to untangling.

"Her life wasn't too bad. She worked hard on their farm and cooked for them every day, yes. But, to her surprise, her young fiancé respected and cared for her. He refused to eat more than she did on any day, even though they were short on food.

Life was tough, but she felt like she had found her actual home. After four years, he grew into a handsome young man, and they fell in love. The widow married them before she fell sick and died.

'I'm glad your mother bought me,' she said before they went to bed every night.

'I'm glad you are the one my mother bought,' he said to her.

Many sweet dreams they had together."

Lily stopped and looked at Kang. After a moment she said, "Did you like it?"

"Oh, of course!" But he didn't sound convincing. Actually, it made his heart ache. Maybe if his mother had lived longer, she would've told him stories like this.

"I'm glad." She giggled.

He felt a little lighter then. He liked her dimples.

He caught himself staring. Jolting his head down, he fumbled with the vines. He had untangled about a third of them.

"Want to hear another one?"

"Sure." He wanted to focus on freeing her but couldn't resist.

"Great," she said.

"A long time ago, there was a farmer. When he was eighteen, he pursued the daughter of the wealthiest family in his village. But she had many suitors and her father demanded a hefty bride price. So the farmer gathered all of his life savings, sold his only water buffalo, outbid everyone else, and married the girl.

Without a buffalo, he pulled the plow himself, but it was worth it.

Growing up in a wealthy family, the girl knew nothing about housework. He did everything inside and outside of the house. One day, she found out she was pregnant.

'I'm going to have a son! Woo-hoo!' He darted to the village and yelled it out loud to everyone.

Unfortunately, several months later, he went missing. His wife and neighbors searched for days and nights but could not find him.

A few days later, his body floated up in the nearby lake, swollen like a bloated fish. A fisherman alerted the community. Not wanting to scare his wife, the fisherman and his neighbors buried him in the swamp next to the lake."

"That's so sad." Kang raised the inner corners of his eyebrows. "How could his pregnant wife survive without him?"

"She couldn't. She knew nothing about farming." Lily sighed. "She gave birth to their son one month later, and soon used up all the money he had left, which wasn't much. Her family lent her some money, but that ran out quickly too. She traveled to town and sold their farming tools in the market.

On one of these trips, she caught smallpox. Deteriorating and losing eyesight, one night she wrapped her baby in a blanket, tucked him in a basket along with a few coins she had left, and placed him in front of her neighbor's door. Her neighbor found the baby the next morning and took him in as his own. The woman died alone two days later."

Kang sat hugging his knees and staring at Lily. Tears ran down his cheeks. "My mother died of smallpox when I was a baby too."

"I know. The story is about you. This is what happened to your parents."

"What? No! My father died of an awful cold."

"And who said that? Your adoptive father?"

He choked. It was true. His adoptive father only had Kang as his family. He talked to Kang often about his mother, but he wouldn't tell him anything about his father other than how he died. Kang had asked all the other villagers, but no one wanted to talk about him. They all ended the conversations with strange looks whenever he raised the subject.

"How do you know all this?" he said. "Who are you?"

"I know many things you don't. Like, the swamp behind those willows?" Lily pointed to the farthest edge of the lake. "That's where they buried your father."

Kang knew about the swamp. Everyone in the village did. He'd never dreamed that his father—

Fire lit inside Kang's chest and blood rushed through his veins. He had long buried his hunger to know the truth of his origins. Now it flared up anew. He jumped up, pulled his hair with both hands, and stomped the ground. Warm tears burst out of his eyes and ran down his face.

"Father!" He let go of his hair, lifted his head, and stared at Lily with burning eyes. "What else do you know? How did it happen? Tell me! Please!"

"Not so fast. You need to free me first." She smiled and nodded at her leg.

He bit his lips, sat back next to her, and worked on the vines again, forcing his shaking fingers to worry at the tangles. Something was wrong. Who was this woman? How did she know of his parents? She's stopped worrying about her father. Was he really sick? Was anything she said true?

"What about I tell you another story while you are at it?"

"No, thank you. No more."

"Why not? Don't you want to know how your father died?"

"Of course!"

"Then you have to hear my next story. Last one, I promise."

Kang sighed and nodded, fingers moving as fast as he could.

"Good," Lily said. "Then listen up."

"Many years ago, there was a couple, newlyweds. The man was a farmer—yes, a farmer again. One year into their marriage, she gave birth to their first baby, a little girl. Every day the woman fed her, washed her, tucked her in a blanket she'd woven, and sang to her when she rocked her to sleep at night—her favorite moment of the day.

But the father was not so thrilled. He told her what they needed was a son, not a daughter. A boy could help on the farm once he grew up, bear his family name, and expand the bloodline. A girl would be nothing but an extra mouth until she was married off and belonged to another family. Her bride price would be negligible.

'Wasting our food on someone else's property is bad business,' he said. 'We cannot keep her.'

She begged him to keep their daughter, but he jarred their baby girl in a clay pot and left it in the farmyard under the mid-summer sun.

She cried her heart out but he refused to let her leave the house.

'Why be upset,' he said, 'It's the traditional way. Nothing new.'

Days went by before he allowed her to collect the body."

"Eeuw." Kang wrinkled his nose and squinted his eyes at Lily. Whose story was she telling now? "How could the man do this? Terrible!"

"I know. But he did, didn't he?" She lowered her lip corners and looked down. After a minute, she looked up, cleared her throat, and continued.

"One year later, she had another baby—a girl again. She clutched her onto her chest, kneeled, and begged him to change his mind. He snorted, tried to pull the baby from her arms, but she held so tightly that he kicked her until she fell. He snatched the baby and plunged her head underwater in a wooden bucket until her tiny body stopped wriggling.

'Faster this way,' he said. 'Less pain, for you and her.'

The mother cried for weeks and tried to run away from him, but he tied her up inside the house every day until she stopped trying. Another year elapsed, and she gave birth to their third child—once again, a baby girl.

'Why can't you give me a son?' he yelled in front of the birth bed.

He grabbed the newborn and strangled it with his own hands. The poor thing hadn't opened its eyes and seen the world even once. He yanked her by her arm and dragged her through the door all the way to the pig stall.

He shoved the dead baby into her arms. 'Feed it to the pigs. Maybe that way, you will learn to produce a boy.'

She fell to the ground. Her arms trembled and her body quivered. He hauled her into the stable, shook her until she dropped the baby's body, and tugged her back out.

Lightning flashed over her head and thunder rumbled in the distance. Rain poured down and soaked her. Crying at the top of her lungs, she watched the filthy swine gobbling up her baby's flesh."

"Her husband …" Kang covered his face with his hands. "What a monster. Why didn't he stop? How could he not stop?"

"I wish he did." Tears emerged in Lily's eyes. She refused to blink or let them spill. She tightened her face and regained control.

"He traveled for three days to the nearest large town. There lived a fortune-teller nicknamed Dragon Eye, for he could see the future as if he had a dragon's eyes. At least, that's what people said.

After pocketing a handsome bag of silver—the man pawned his dead mother's jewelry—and, gorging down a gourmet feast, Dragon Eye agreed to speak. 'Your woman. She's doomed. If you want a son, you'll need a different wife.'

A wife who could only produce girls was not worth keeping. How could he get rid of her? He tried to return her to her family, but her father wouldn't accept such a shame. He lied, telling her father that he caught her having an affair and therefore could no longer address her as his wife. Deeply shamed, her father sentenced her to the traditional punishment for adultery. Joining hands with her brother and husband, they tied her inside a bamboo cage—the kind used to transport pigs. They filled it up with heavy rocks and sank her to the bottom of a lake.

'I'm innocent! Believe me! Father! Brother! Please!' she yelled out in tears. The last thing she said.

They stood still and watched the bubbles burst on the water surface after her cage submerged."

Lily stopped talking. The two sat in silence.

A midnight breeze blew by and swayed tree branches. In between them, an owl hooted.

He put down his hands, torn and bleeding from working at the vines, and locked eyes with her. "Why are you telling me these horrible stories? Who are you?"

She smiled. Her colorless lips rose toward her pale cheeks. Her dark hair draped over her shoulders. And in between it, a few pieces of seaweed bulged and swelled. Tiny cuts covered her bluish white leg, but no blood seeped.

A chill ran down his spine.

She blinked and giggled as if she could read his mind. "It was late fall, and the water was cold. My fingers turned numb before I sank to the bottom of the lake." She held up her hands. Her fingernails shimmered blue in the silver moonlight.

He clenched his hands onto his thighs but couldn't stop them from quivering. "Were you … the woman?"

"The one drowned by her husband, father, and brother? Yes."

"Are you a ghost?"

"Shh …" She put a finger to her lips. "You are being too loud. You wouldn't want to wake up your wife and baby."

Thunder cracked inside his head.

His wife and baby! How did she know about them? Why mention them now?

"I … need to go." Kang tried to jump up.

He couldn't move.

He looked down and saw hundreds of thin vines wrapping around his legs. As he watched—and struggled—they grew and twined around him up to his shoulders, cocooning his body. He fought harder, and the vines shrank and tightened. Unlike Lily, he bled. He was a bug in a spider's web.

"Is this some kind of trick? Let me go!"

Lily stood up—the vines had left her entirely—put on her straw sandals, and sat down a few steps further away, stretching and crossing her legs. "I can't do that."

How stupid was he to have believed her? There was no sick father, fish, or black cat.

"Why are you doing this to me?"

"I thought you wanted to know what happened to your father."

"Of course!"

"Well, you are lucky I am a woman of my words." She curled up her legs and locked eyes with him. Her eyes looked dark and deep, like the water at the bottom of a well on a fall's night. She leaned forward. "He was drowned. I know, because I drowned him."

"What? How?"

She giggled and brushed her long hair to the front around her neck. "Silly. I did the same thing my loving husband did to me, but without the bamboo cage or rocks. He got a taste of what he put me through."

"My father was … your husband?" He said it, but the words still made no sense.

"All my stories were true." She sneered. "Why do you think my husband killed me? What did he do after that?"

"He wanted a son. He did what Dragon Eye said and got married again."

"And had you," she said. "Your father was the man who killed my babies."

He couldn't believe his ears. He closed his eyes and shook his head.

He had always imagined his father to be an honorable and wise family man, like his adoptive father. He pictured him in his head as a tall and strong man with a kind smile. He had always wanted to grow up like him.

"You liar!" he yelled. "My father was a good man! He would never—"

The vines tightened, cutting him off.

"Your father was a coward." She laughed. "All he did was beg for his life when he saw me. Perhaps he once was a good man, and a better teenager. But he revealed his true self when I couldn't give him what he wanted."

"Teenager?"

"You can't put two and two together, can you?" she said, "I was the girl who got sold into your father's family as a child-wife. The farmers in all stories—the widow's young son who grew into his marriage, the man who sold what he had to buy his second wife, the man who killed my daughters—were all the same person. Your father."

"I don't believe you! You're lying!" He tried to punch but couldn't move his arms. "If you were who you say, you should be over forty. But you look my age."

"Ghosts always look the age they died. If they're given the chance to come back."

"What chance?"

"Not everyone gets to become a ghost. Most people go straight into reincarnation after getting judged in the Underworld. I pleaded with the judge for one special dispensation—revenge, a life for a life. He heard my story, pitied me, and turned me into a ghost … with conditions. He gave me the power to use anything below water at my disposal. I'll report back and reincarnate after my vengeance is complete. I will not fail. You pay for your father's debt."

Kang squirmed inside the vines, and they tightened again until he struggled to breathe. Wet, slimy, and muddy, they were like long skeleton arms reaching out from the bottom of the lake.

"My father …" he said through clenched teeth, " … was not who you said. You … have no proof."

"Behind your house along the wall, toward the middle, if you dig three feet underground, you'll find three wooden boxes, two feet apart. In two of the boxes, there is a small blue blanket with your family name, Wang, sewed in red thread. I wrapped my babies and buried them there, except for the third one—the pigs left no flesh. The bodies must be gone, but you would find the old and soiled blankets."

Behind his house, she buried the babies? His father's dead daughters killed by him? On the other side of that wall, inside, is where he lay his head every night.

He grimaced and retched. "I don't believe you! Why are you doing this to *me?*"

"A life for a life. For my three daughters and me, I will take four lives. I killed your father—and my father and brother, a story you haven't heard—and I have one more to claim."

But it made no sense. If all she wanted was vengeance, why didn't she kill his father immediately after she returned as a ghost? What made her wait for so long, until one month before he was born? His mother was her replacement. Why didn't she hurt her?

"You want to kill me?"

"Not necessarily." She smiled. "You or your baby."

"What? What does she have to do with all this?"

"If I can't have a daughter, neither can anyone else. Especially you."

"After what happened to your daughters, how could you hurt an innocent child?"

"You, son of a murderer. It's not your place to judge me!"

She jumped up and swung her arms. The vines jolted Kang toward the water. He wiggled and kicked but couldn't fight the drag. Within seconds, he was under. He held his breath until he thought his chest would burst, then breathed and inhaled nothing but water. He twisted and writhed like a mouse between a cat's teeth. His heart beat out of his chest.

A powerful force pulled him upward, above the surface. He coughed and gasped for air.

She held up her arms and palms. "Now you know what I went through! Give her to me!"

"No!"

The vines dragged him back down. Water flooded in through his nose and mouth. He closed his eyes and the world spun.

The vines pushed him above water again.

"Bring her, or I'll kill you!" she shouted.

"Kill me, then!"

The vines submerged him once more. He could no longer feel any part of his body.

Was this how it ended?

Again, the vines yanked him out like a fish.

"Last chance, you or her."

"Me!"

Then came the final jerk downward. He sank and water rushed into his lungs. The pressure built around him until the world was nothing but liquid darkness.

✧

Kang opened his eyes and found himself lying on the ground, still entwined in the vines. He choked and coughed out water.

Lily sat close by and stared at him.

He caught his breath. "You didn't … why?"

"I want to know something."

"What?"

"Why are you willing to die for the baby? It's just a girl. You and your wife can have another, maybe a son this time."

"*Just a* girl? What difference does that make?"

"Ask your father."

"I am not him. And I will not give you my baby."

"If you don't tell me why, then after drowning you, I'll kill your baby and wife too."

Nothing but freezing coldness was in her eyes. She would do it.

"I'll tell you," he said. "Promise you won't hurt them."

"Only if you tell me why."

"Yes, yes. Promise."

"All right."

He cleared his throat. "At the monthly town market two years ago, I laid eyes on my wife the first time. She was beautiful. I fell in love with her at first sight. Since then, I looked forward to peeking at her at every town market. But I'd only spoken to her father. I couldn't bring myself to look her in the eye.

"One year later, she didn't show up at the market. I asked her father. He spit on the ground and walked away. Later, I found out from other people in her village—she got pregnant. As an unmarried woman, she had deeply disgraced and humiliated her family. Her father followed the traditional punishment. He rowed her in a canoe to a small island in the middle of a lake and left her."

"She was pregnant before you?" Lily raised one of her eyebrows and tilted her head at Kang.

He glanced over at her and decided to ignore her. "He had only abandoned her the day before. She might still be alive. The night had fallen when I rushed to the lake. I stole a canoe and rowed to look for her. That lake was much bigger than this, and many small islands lurked in the darkness. Well, 'islands.' They were patches of dirt and grass. Some were too far away and no one would be able to swim home. Every few years, an unmarried pregnant girl would be left there with two choices—starve to death, or jump into the water and drown. Last time this happened, when the father went to collect the body five days later, it was floating, rotten, and half-eaten by fish.

"She was alive when I found her—cold, hungry, scared, but alive. I offered her my hand and told her that, if she were willing, I'd bring her home as my wife. I'd never need to know who the man was, and her baby would be my baby. I promised to take care of her and never hurt her.

"She came home with me in terrible shape. They had beaten her, and she almost had a miscarriage. But I took care of her, and she recovered. After the baby was born, she opened up to me. We still had a lot to learn about each other, but we had a lifelong time. Or so I thought until tonight.

"My wife and baby are the best things that ever happened to me. I grew up dreaming of a family, and now I have it. I used to survive, but now I live. There is nothing I wouldn't give up for them. My own life included."

Kang looked at Lily. "Now I have told you. I hope you keep your word and not hurt them."

She stared at him like she'd never seen him before.

The lake's surface looked like black glass behind them, reflecting the full moon above. A few fish broke the surface and glided, sending ripples around.

She burst out laughing. "The baby is not yours? And you are willing to die for her? For just a girl?" She laughed, laughed, with hysteria, not joy. After a good while, she stopped. "You know what will happen, right?"

"What?"

"One day, when you come home, your wife and baby won't be there. She will have run away with the man who impregnated her. Maybe with your money too. You, the poor lover man, will be left with nothing. It will make a good story."

"You are wrong," he said. "My wife loves me. I can tell from the way she looks at me and holds my hand. In a few months, she's going to carry our daughter on her back and help me on the farm. She told me her past had died and her future was with me."

"And you believed her? Because you saved her?"

"She is the one who did the saving. She led me from my solitude."

"You're not a real father. You can't love a child who's not yours."

"Of course I can!"

"Liar," she said. "I saw you earlier. You were about to strangle her."

"What?"

"Earlier tonight, you were reaching out your hand to her throat, in your room."

So it was she who made the noise outside. She was watching him through the window, and thought he was going to hurt his daughter. But … if she wanted his daughter to die, why didn't she let him kill her? Why stop him and lure him here?

"No! You didn't see it right. I can prove it. Kill me, but spare my wife and baby."

She kept silent for a while, then sighed. "You are right. You are not your father."

Her words stabbed his heart and punched his guts. He closed his eyes and clenched his teeth. But it hurt because it was true. Throughout his life, he believed his father was a righteous man. And now he had to accept that he wasn't, and he did not want to be like him.

"Doesn't matter now," she said. "If you thought your story would soften me and spare your life, you were being delusional. I am an evil woman after all." She stood up, raised her arm, and the vines on him tightened.

But it still made no sense. How did she know so much about his mother and him? Details like: she wrapped him in a blanket and left him in front of his adoptive father's door?

And then, it did make sense. Everything was as clear as the sky.

"You're not evil," he said while the vines dragged him toward the water.

"What?" She looked puzzled, then smirked. "Is this your last attempt to stop me?"

It wasn't, but the vines did stop. "Far from it. You're not who you are trying to appear. Who you are telling yourself you are."

"What do you know about me?"

"A lot more than you think."

"Funny. Explain. Otherwise, I'll ensure you drown very slowly." She put down her arm and swung it sideways. The vines lifted him up into a sitting position, remaining a tight cocoon. She sat in front of him, piercing him with her gaze.

"First, you have fond memories of those years you and my father spent together. You said you fell in love. Evil people don't use that kind of language."

"I was blind."

"You have warmth left in your heart."

"I do? After he killed our first baby, I said 'I wish your mother didn't buy me.' And he said 'I wish the one my mother bought wasn't you.' Fond memories indeed."

"Second, you didn't kill him right after you became a ghost. You hoped he would regret what he'd done and change. But you probably overheard him say something like he only wanted a son. So you killed him one month before I was born, in case I turned out to be a girl. You did it to save me."

She slouched. Her long hair curtained her face.

"You watched over me and my mother, but you couldn't do anything about the smallpox. You were the one who placed me in front of my adoptive father's door, not her. You did it after she passed."

"What makes you think that?"

"The blanket."

"What blanket?"

"You wrapped your babies' bodies in blue blankets sewed with my family name in red thread."

"So?"

"I was bundled in one like that when my adoptive father found me. The weaving impressed him, and he knew my mother couldn't have done it—she never learned to weave. Nobody could find another blanket like that. You are the only one who could. You had to wrap me in it because you were afraid the neighbor wouldn't recognize me otherwise."

Now she looked up at him. Still she said nothing.

"All these years, you had plenty of chances to kill me. Why now? You saw me earlier tonight when I was about to wipe off my baby's drool. You thought I was going to strangle her. Why did you have to stop me and lure me here? The answer is, you never wanted to hurt her.

"But, why did you ask me to bring her to you and torture me when I refused? You had to know I wasn't putting on an act. You tested me. You told me the stories to scare me. If I didn't care about my baby, I would have agreed to exchange her for my own life.

"What you did not see earlier tonight was—she was bundled in the same blue blanket you wove. My adoptive father gave it to me when he told me about my mother, and I kept it. It's old, but still sound. You put your heart and soul in it."

The corners of Lily's eyes twitched. "I made one for each of my babies … and ended up cloaking their bodies with them. Except my third. I hid the last blanket between the bed boards as a keepsake. Your father threw away everything else I made. He said it was bad luck for getting a son."

"My father …" He shook his head. "I don't believe he was who you said."

"Dig up my daughters' coffins and see."

He swallowed and looked away. After a minute, he turned back. "Why do you know all those things about my mother's life, but not how I got married? Here's what I think. You became weaker as the years went by. Maybe you were much stronger when you were a new ghost and could come out every night. But now, you need a full moon.

"I remember, last fall, around the time I brought my wife home, it was gloomy every night for three months straight, which is why you didn't believe what I told you about my wife and me. I could've fabricated the entire thing. You decided to kill me, just in case. But for some reason, you had to do it tonight."

They both glanced up at the full moon, peeping through the clouds.

"I have another theory—you won't be around much longer and you knew it. You may not get another full moon. You can't leave me alive at the risk of my baby's life. You could've taken the last life you needed any moment during the past twenty years—my mother's, my wife's, my baby's, mine. You could've reincarnated a long time ago. What made you choose to let your energy drain instead?

"That's why you are truly kind. Your heart shattered, but you held the pieces together, not to kill, but to save."

Kang stopped. His eyes searched for Lily's face in the shadow of her hair.

"You forgot—I murdered my father and brother, too. My hands are covered in blood."

"That was vengeance. None of that makes you evil. It was rage, but you refused to let it consume you."

"What's the point of all this?" She hardened her voice. "Are you ready to die?"

"If that's the only way to spare my baby and wife, yes. You can report back to the judge in the Underworld and reincarnate."

"Don't tell me you're thinking of me?"

"You saved me. I owe you. My whole family does. But I'm curious about one thing."

"What?"

"You and my father lived together for four years before getting married. You didn't know him well enough?"

Was he admitting what she said about him was true? It didn't matter. He had to know.

"I thought I did. When you think you have someone figured out, think again."

"What went wrong with your love?"

"It was never really love. It had a condition."

"What?"

"His condition was that I'd give him a son." Lily tried to smile but her lips twitched. "Of course, real, unconditional love is as hard to find as air at the bottom of the lake."

She lifted her head and laughed wearily. Cracks crawled all over her face, like gray earth after a drought. The top layer of her skin chipped, peeled, and disappeared into thin air like burnt sparkles.

"What's happening?" he said.

"I have failed to take vengeance. I'll fade away and never reincarnate. It's part of the deal."

"No! You can still kill me!"

"I've already decided that I can't. The moment I made that decision, I failed. Go home to your wife and baby after you wake up."

"What?"

"Before I disappear, I'll return to my drowned form, a bloated dead body. I can't let you see that."

Her pearl-like shine had faded and darkened into gray blurs in patches. Her pale skin dusted and flaked, revealing the lower layer—wrinkled, swollen, and marbled with blue and red lines. A single glimpse of it made him want to scream.

The vines wrapping around him flew up and twined into a whip in her hand. With the blink of an eye, she swung it at his head.

He was out with one blow.

✧

Kang awoke and jumped from the ground, panting. The sky was grayish blue, and the lake was calm as a slab of jade. Birds chirped in the trees, and the dew in the grass wetted the corners of his pants. It was almost dawn.

No signs of Lily, vines, or straw sandals.

Was she real? Did all that happen? Was it just a bad dream? How did he end up sleeping next to the lake?

His daughter!

He took off running the way he came. He dashed through the orange trees, circled the garden, bypassed the chicken coop, and jumped over the dogwood shrubs. Outside his house, he huffed and puffed. After smoothing his breath, he tiptoed over to the window and peeked inside.

His wife was sleeping with her back to him. In the bamboo basket, his baby lay with her eyes closed. Her mouth blew a bubble.

He smiled, stepped backward, and circled to the back of his house.

Along the wall, toward the middle, if you dig... I wrapped my babies and buried them there... Lily's words rang in his ears.

He fetched a shovel and dug as quietly and quickly as he could. His back hurt and his arms burned, but he dug and dug.

The shovel's blade hit something. He squatted and swiped some dirt aside with his fingers.

A wooden box.

He pulled it out onto the ground and dug again, two feet to the left. Three feet underground, he discovered another wooden box. He then located the third.

He lined up all three on the ground and sat facing them. Light brown rosewood. Each was the height of his knees and narrower than his shoulders. Dark spots mottled their lids and walls, and wet soil filled their veins and grains. They smelled musty and rotten. An earthworm fell off the left one and twitched on the ground.

No locks.

He reached forward, but his hands trembled.

It was true. Everything Lily said about his father.

He pulled back his hands and covered his face. His shoulders shook. Tears broke out from between his fingers, mixed with the mud on his hand, and ran down his forearms in rivulets.

The first ray of sunshine hit and warmed his back. His blood boiled and rushed in his veins. He was going to explode.

I am the son of a baby killer, wife beater, liar, murderer, betrayer, and coward. I don't deserve to bathe in the morning sun. What gave me the right to stand above ground while my sisters are under it?

A baby's cry tore through the dead silence. Footsteps squeaked the floor inside his house. Humming started, and the crying quieted down.

She was singing to the baby.

They had not yet thought of a name. What about Lily?

Lily had let him come back to his family. She died so he could live, after all that his father had done to her. He was a horrible man.

Lily had said he was nothing like his father.

He placed the boxes back into the holes and buried them again. When he was done, he wiped his hands on his pants, turned, and walked toward the front door.

Tonight, when he went to bed on the other side of the wall, he'd think about these boxes. His half-sisters. Maybe tomorrow he would make markers for their graves, so they would not be forgotten.

But today, he'd feed the baby, help his wife cook, and talk to her about naming their daughter. Then he'd feed the pigs, collect the eggs, and add cucumbers to the garden. After that, if he still had time, he'd make his daughter a toy. She was too young right now, but he looked forward to the day she wanted to play.

Copyright © 2023 by Marissa Tian.

YANG FENG PRESENTS: A GALAXY'S EDGE STORY EXCHANGE

Fu Qiang, a representative of the Chinese science fiction writers born in the 1980s, is a fan of science fiction, murder mysteries, and animation. He has a PhD in Physics from Beijing University, and his scientific research is currently focused on green energy and low-carbon management solutions. He has published the science fiction novels *The Abyss of Time*, *Grab the Planet*, and *Her Secret*, as well as a series of short novellas, *The Loners' Game*.

This story recommended in this issue, "The Black Zone: Murder in the Locked Room," was originally published in the 13th volume of the Chinese edition of *Galaxy's Edge*. The detective partners Gao Yun and Fang Hui, however, made their first appearance in the Chinese edition's very first volume, back in 2018. In this series of stories, this resourceful detective duo—with very different personalities—display a physicist's understanding of advanced technology along with a deep love of science fiction, which has made them popular among readers.

Here, on a planet shielded within a black zone, in a forbidden region isolated from the outside world, what kind of cosmic mystery awaits to be solved?

Please enjoy.

◆ ◆ ◆

THE BLACK ZONE: MURDER IN THE LOCKED ROOM

by Fu Qiang, translation by Roy Gilham

Ai Er sat stiffly at the wooden table, shivering as the dry, cold wind blew in through the open window. If the deeds of this detective duo hadn't been so legendary across the Internet, he wouldn't have journeyed to such a remote asteroid to ask for help. He never imagined the famous detectives would work out of this nondescript wooden house. Looking at the room's shabby furnishings, he wondered how they survived the winter here.

Gao Yun, a stout, muscular man with scars on his face and upper arms, was busy at the coffee machine.

Ai Er guessed he was from military background. But it was the woman staring at him across the round table that made him uncomfortable, the greed in her eyes at odds with her beautiful face. Looking at Fang Hui, Ai Er felt less like a client, and more like a fat sheep thrown to the wolves.

There was a rumbling sound outside the window, and a blast of hot air rippled the curtains. Ai Er gazed out of the window. His company's large spaceship had set sail, climbing into the sky at a slow, steady acceleration. He cleared his throat.

"My name is Ai Er," he said. "As you can see, I am a researcher with the Yuanyang Starfield Development Group."

Across the table, Fang Hui leaned forward. "What position do you hold in the company?" she asked. "Do you have a leadership role? And, more importantly, what is your budget for this commission?"

Just in time, Gao Yun brought over the coffee. He kicked his partner secretly under the table. At last, Fang Hui recovered some composure. She coughed dryly.

"From what I understand, your company's business covers thirty-three star zones. I wonder what business you could possibly have in a remote hinterland such as our own? Besides,"—she glanced out the window at the spaceship, which was now only a bright dot—"you arrived on the flagship FO-02A, which belongs to your company's president, Shi Xing. For the great man to come in person, isn't that a little overboard?"

Ai Er was taken aback. The woman definitely had a detective's eye for detail. Putting on a professional smile, he replied, "Mr. Shi spends much of his time flying between the stars, searching for suitable planets to develop. He once incorporated thirty-six planets into the company's development quota within a single year, a record that stands unmatched to this day."

"Then he came to the wrong place. For four light years in every direction, this area is void of all human beings," Fang Hui responded immediately. "Moreover, the planet's orbit spans two star zones, Alpha 23 and Gamma 31. Relations are tense between these governments, and the area has become an unregulated zone, plagued by space pirates. If you'd arrived but half an hour later, the planet would've crossed the border between the star zones, and you may have met the pirates face to face."

Ai Er gave a wry smile. Shi Xing had taken one glance at the planet and judged it destitute, a wretched land with no potential for development. The president departed without even showing his face, leaving Ai Er to face the music alone. As he pondered over how to bring the conversation back to the subject in hand, Fang Hui took the initiative:

"Enough with the small talk. What is your assignment here?"

Ai Er leaned forward. "Tell me, how much do you know about the black zones?"

Gao Yun sat down next to Fang Hui. "Some science fiction works describe planets surrounded by areas of slow light, isolated from their surroundings …"

"Unfortunately, such things are impossible," said Fang Hui dismissively. "It's not difficult to slow the speed of light in a vacuum. For example, around a pulsar, a strong magnetic field polarizes the quantum vacuum, thereby reducing the velocity of light. However, this does not alter the physical constant, as evidenced by the observation of Cherenkov radiation."

"What is this radiation you're talking about?" Gao Yun asked.

Fang Hui thought for a moment. "Simply put, the speed of particles in the medium exceeds the speed of electromagnetic waves—that is, the speed of light. It's like the sonic boom that occurs when an airplane exceeds the speed of sound. Cherenkov radiation is a burst of light, an explosion. But it must be stressed that although the particles are indeed travelling faster than light, their velocity is still below the physical constant of the speed of light in a vacuum."

"Miss Fang Hui is very learned," said Ai Er, flatteringly, "but in reality, a kind of black zone may be formed whenever a wealthy person or family discovers a planet with enough of its own resources to recycle for a long time, then uses whatever means to shield the planet from the outside world, as a kind of isolated utopia.

"The first generations of such technology employed a solid shell, like a Dyson sphere, but these proved costly and ineffective. The second generation used a strong magnetic field as a shield, but this left the planet vulnerable to asteroidal impact. The planet we encountered was more advanced, utilizing a protective shield formed from quark-gluon plasma. This technology is complex and extremely expensive, but it's the closest thing we have to the black zones popularized by science fiction. After all, QGP has a mathematical expression close in form to a black hole in anti de-Sitter space."

The detectives were not unfamiliar with the concept. QGP is an extremely high-energy phase in which the quarks and gluons that make up hadrons are no longer bound, but become 'free,' thereby creating a new form of matter. Using conventional measurements, the temperature of QGP is estimated at around 2 trillion degrees centigrade.

"This third-generation black zone is very difficult to detect," Ai Er continued. "Once in a while, our company ship crashes into one while travelling at high speed. In this case, although the ship's hull sustained damage, the Alcubierre drive ripped a hole in the QGP shield."

"It sounds like the QGP shield cannot prevent the Alcubierre drive from warping space." Fang Hui sighed, folding her arms.

Ai Er shrugged. "After all, the protective layer is only a few picometers thick, and the Alcubierre engine has the power to crush stars. After the accident, our ship sent a drone down to Planet L, as we call it internally, and discovered that there was hardly a single person left alive. Yet, all the bodies lay undecomposed, as if …"

"In a locked room." Fang Hui immediately supplied the answer. "Before the black zone is opened, no human beings, no physical matter, not even any information can escape. And yet, somehow, everyone on Planet L is dead. This is more like a locked room murder mystery than a scientific puzzle."

Ai Er nodded. "Exactly. That's why we came to you."

As he spoke, Ai Er pulled a laptop from his briefcase. With a few simple taps, the laptop projected a holographic screen in front of everyone. "The situation around Planet L is similar to here—a vast, uninhabited area," Ai Er explained, "so we did not retrieve the craft after obtaining the imagery. This footage, taken more than 20 years ago, is all we have to go on. Please, take a look, then tell me what you think."

Fang Hui gestured for him to begin. The holographic screen projected the images taken by the drone.

As the drone exited the cabin, the camera rotated at high speed. Most of the frame was pitch black, with the QGP shield blocking out the starlight. The only thing in view was a blue planet the size of a ping-pong ball: Planet L.

The drone's AI program kicked into operation, the camera locked onto the planet, and the drone slowly accelerated towards its target. Gradually, on-screen elements enriched the display. The upper-left corner showed a spectrogram covering the entire band from radio waves to gamma waves. At present, only the peaks of infrared and visible light were visible—radiation emitted by Planet L. The lower-left corner displayed an analysis of the elements in the surrounding environment, but there was a temporary carbon peak caused from the carbon present in the instrument. In the lower-right corner, the temperature display remained blank.

"Due to the drone's proximity to the QGP shield, the temperature sensor has been switched off in order to prevent damage caused by the free flow of high-energy particles," Ai Er explained, pointing to the display. "It'll be switched on again once the drone is at some distance."

Fang Hui nodded and continued to watch.

As the drone picked up speed, the characters '60×' appeared on screen, indicating the current fast-forward rate. All around, there was nothing but deep space. Played at the original speed, the video was likely to induce sleep. After three minutes—that is, three hours of drone-time—the lower-right corner displayed a temperature of minus 271.35 degrees Celsius. The absolute temperature was marked on a scale alongside it: 1.8K.

Planet L grew larger, spreading across the field of view. The drone no longer moved forward in a straight line, but instead revolved around the planet, rotating as it made its descent. Already, it had entered into lower planetary orbit.

The elemental contents gradually changed, the increasing levels of oxygen and nitrogen maintained in a ratio of 1:4. At the same time, the probe detected traces of rare gas elements. After a brief rise, the temperature stabilized at 190K—80 degrees

Celsius—indicating that the drone had entered the planet's mesosphere. A red filter covered the camera lens, as the friction between the drone and the lower atmosphere generated a lot of heat.

Gradually, a city appeared below, the various buildings arranged like scale models on a sand table. After another two minutes—that is, two hours in real time—the drone approached the surface and the film returned to normal playback speed. But just then, the camera began to shake violently, lines of error codes rolled up on screen, and the image disappeared.

"Something went wrong as the drone landed," Ai Er explained. "The image will return soon, but there was some unfortunate damage."

Little by little, the screen recovered. Fang Hui stared at the various parameters, frowning. "It appears that was quite the crash. Most of the sensors are broken."

"That's right." Ai Er sighed. "The elemental spectrometer was completely destroyed, and the spectrograph is available only below the visible light band. The temperature sensor seems to have survived the impact. Unfortunately, the sound sensor was broken, so from here on in, we're back to the silent film era."

The three continued to watch.

After adjusting its altitude, the drone began its exploration of Planet L. It landed first on the outskirts of a city, in an area dense with trees. Up close, there were poplars and other species brought from Earth, along with vegetation unique to the planet: tall trees with palm-sized leaves and seven forking branches, and translucent lavender flowers shining like crystals.

Before long, the drone entered the city. The temperature hovered around 27 degrees Celsius, making conditions suitable for human life. Wide roads ran between the buildings, but no cars or pedestrians were visible, nor were there any aircraft in the sky overhead. After circling for more than ten minutes, the drone paused in front of a high-rise building. The machine stretched out a mechanical arm, pushed open the door, and entered unimpeded.

Behind the door lay a large hall, also empty of people. Further ahead, there were words printed in an unfamiliar language. The drone moved on, finding no one on the first floor.

As the drone pushed open a door on the second floor, a human appeared in the field of view. A young woman in a light-green dress sprawled on the floor, her body twisted at an unnatural angle. At her side, an identified video was playing on a computer monitor.

Slowly, the drone approached the woman. Although the footage remained silent, it was obvious that the drone was trying to communicate. After multiple attempts at contact garnered no response, the drone extended two mechanical arms and began to examine the woman. At first, it helped the woman to lie flat; her body seemed unnaturally stiff. There were blotches on the woman's face, but judging by her features there was no doubt she was from Earth. Electrodes protruding from robotic arms attached themselves to the woman's abdomen and hips.

"The AI has determined that it is looking at a human corpse, and now sets about sampling the corpse without damaging it," Ai Er explained. "At the same time, it will activate a search program to locate any other humans. If a body is found, the drone will lock immediately onto the location. This procedure is consistent with the Interplanetary Convention on Human Rights."

After leaving the woman's body, the drone worked its way up through the apartment building. It searched every corner but found only three humans in the entire building—all of them dead. The state of the corpses was similar to that of the woman first encountered: each had stiffened, but had not yet undergone any obvious decomposition.

Exiting the building, the drone hovered directly above the city, scanning the virtual map as it calculated where the probability of finding humans was highest. The drone first zeroed in on an intercity train station, but found there only the body of a white-haired old man. Nearby, it entered a building that appeared to be a hospital. After conducting a thorough search, five more bodies were discovered.

Even with the video playback set to 5x speed, the search occupied more than half an hour. On average, the drone located a body approximately every 30 minutes.

After another fruitless search, the drone explored the urban area at high speed, but found no one alive. At one point, the drone located a potential signal inside a factory and, unable to open the door with its robotic arm, fired up a laser to cut its way in. The laser ignited materials inside the factory; the screen showed blackened wood and melting polymer sheets. Fluffy little fireballs rolled about the floor, revealed in close up as burning coils of steel wool. At this moment, a tabby cat emerged from the shadows, nimbly skirted around the drone, and escaped through the entrance cut by the laser. The cat was the source of the signal.

During the drone's search, the AI models and algorithms worked tirelessly behind the scenes. Before long, the background algorithms, based on the city conditions and density of corpses on Planet L, had calculated the approximate population at three million.

The drone's journey approached its end. It was running out of energy and urgently needed to find a backup source. Following the guidance of its internal algorithms, it landed at a nuclear power station. But just as it was about to enter the reactor, the fuselage shook violently. Determining that it was under attack, the drone immediately fired back with a laser, but an instant later it was brought down by a second assault. The noise in the image quickly increased. The final image captured by the sensor was that of a small boy walking out of the darkness, holding a gun, his forehead dripping with blood, and the index finger on his left hand severed by the laser.

"This is all we have. The drone transmitted the footage to the spaceship, which then transmitted it to our company servers." Ai Er shut off the screen. "The question is: How did the people on Planet L die?"

"The video provides very limited information," said Gao Yun, looking hopeless. "Without visiting the scene for reconnaissance, this is going to be difficult."

"Not at all," said Fang Hui, crossing her arms and smiling confidently. "The video contains all the clues we need to deduce the truth." Ai Er and Gao Yun looked at her in surprise. "To guess what happened is not difficult," she said, "but it's not so easy to ensure proper scientific and logical rigour at the same time." She looked at the two men around her. "Well, let's bring up some general ideas for discussion. Once we have eliminated all possibilities, the last thing left is the truth."

Gao Yun fell into deep thought. "According to the data in the recording," he said after a pause, "Planet L had several million inhabitants. Although small, it was large enough to constitute a civilization. And if we consider the reasons for the extinction of a civilization, the first thing that comes to mind is war. Planet L is a closed space. If large-scale warfare was to break out, the effect would be devastating."

"But the buildings and other objects in the video are intact," said Ai Er, "and there is no sign of armed conflict. We can therefore rule out the possibility that the civilization was destroyed by war."

Gao Yun scratched his head, thinking hard for a moment. "What about a neutron bomb? With this kind of weapon, the civilians might be killed without damage to the surrounding buildings."

"The neutron bomb may yield a smaller detonation," Ai Er retorted, "but it's basically a hydrogen bomb with a layer of beryllium. How come the drone didn't discover the blast crater?"

"High-altitude blasting," Gao Yun answered with a soldier's instinct. "That fits with what we see in the video."

"Then why are the bodies so little decomposed?" grumbled Ai Er. "It's unlikely that the company's ship broke through just moments after the detonation."

Gao Yun spread his hands. "Maybe you got lucky. I admit the possibility is low, but it can't be ruled out entirely."

Watching the fight from the sidelines, Fang Hui burst out laughing. Solving the case through video alone was going to prove difficult for someone like Gao Yun, who was used to working on the front lines. "I'm afraid we can rule out the possibility of a neutron bomb explosion just by looking at the video," she said. Gao Yun looked sceptical, but Fang Hui directed Ai Er to rewind the video back to 24 minutes and three seconds after the drone entered the first building.

"Here, this is it." Ai Er paused the video. Fang Hui pointed to one corner of the screen. "Look, what is this?"

"A woman's body," replied Gao Yun.

"Look again."

Gao Yun frowned, squinting at the screen. "There's a computer monitor," he said, "but I can't see the display clearly."

"We don't need to see it clearly." Fang Hui smiled. "The fact that some kind of video is playing proves that the computer is still up and running."

Understanding dawned on Gao Yun. "You mean, a neutron bomb would have devastated the electronic equipment."

Fang Hui nodded. "Exactly. There was no neutron bomb explosion on Planet L, as evidenced by the functioning electronic systems."

Ai Er thought for a moment. "We might also imagine another possibility. Could we be dealing with a biological weapon? If a deadly virus spread rapidly, Planet L's population would have no way to escape."

"Yes! I was going to say the same thing!" Gao Yun insisted, fighting hard to recover his dignity.

"That's also impossible," Fang Hui countered immediately. "The people in the video are undoubtedly immigrants from Earth. They are neither aliens nor robots. Therefore, we can expect their relationship with any supervirus or superbug to follow the same propagation rules as on Earth. In short, no matter how deadly a virus is, some people will always gain immunity.

"Though we're not clear on the specific situation on Planet L, the spread of disease can always be predicted to a certain extent by mathematical models: SIR, SEIS, and so on. But no matter which mathematical model is used, even with the parameters set to extremes, no solution leads to the absolute death of all the infected. Simply understood, as the number of deaths increases, the spread of the virus will decrease, eventually reaching the point where no one remains contagious. When the last infected person dies, the spread of the virus is halted, allowing the remaining humans to survive. In our distant past, before the Industrial Revolution, many viruses went extinct in exactly this way."

"Couldn't we imagine a more extreme situation?" Gao Yun couldn't help but ask. "Speaking only of possibilities."

"Tell me," said Fang Hui, smiling, "what special circumstances are you thinking of?"

"Well, in a war, we can't rule out the creation of a new supervirus, like the zombie viruses seen in movies and computer games. If such a powerful virus was really developed, it could easily exterminate millions of people."

"Then let me ask you," Fang Hui replied, "in all zombie movies, the infected zombies go looking for humans. Why?"

"For the zombie, of course, it's about finding food to sustain its own metabolism." Gao Yun crossed his legs and looked at the ceiling. "And from the virus's perspective, it wants to continue to spread and reproduce, right?"

"Exactly. But no matter the premise, one prerequisite is that there will need to be plenty of zombies." Fang Hui tapped the table with her index finger, like a schoolteacher emphasising an important point. "In the video, the corpses were separated from one another over vast distances, which fundamentally disproves the possibility of a zombie virus."

"Unless," mused Ai Er, "they had cultivated a bacteria that consumed so much oxygen that the humans died from hypoxia or suffocation. After all, most of the sensors were broken when the drone crash-landed, and we were unable to establish the oxygen content on the surface of Planet L."

"Unfortunately, that is also impossible," Fang Hui replied. "Recall what happened when the drone lasered its way into the factory."

Ai Er murmured his assent. In order to enter the factory, the drone had cut a door with a laser, causing a fire …

"Do you remember what materials were ignited?" asked Fang Hui. "Wood, PVC, and something else. I wonder if either of you noticed the other material inside."

Ai Er frowned. "What?"

"Steel wool. Now, humans can survive in an atmosphere with an oxygen content in the range of around 19.5 to 23.5%. And the minimum oxygen content required for steel wool to burn is 19%."

Ai Er nodded in agreement, but Gao Yun remained unconvinced. "There is no way to rule out the possibility of a supervirus," he said. "So long as it has a high enough fatality rate and transmission rate, a long lifespan, and continues to evade immunity, wouldn't that lead to the eventual extinction of Planet L's civilization?"

Fang Hui sighed. "This is a simple calculation problem. Throughout human history, the R0 of any fatal virus, i.e. the average number of people each sick person will infect, has been somewhere around 5. Ebola, for example, has an R0 of 2, AIDS is 4, and smallpox, an ancient virus, ranks between 5 and 7. Measles is highest, with an R0 of 18, but it is rarely fatal. Let's assume that this supervirus has an R0 as high as measles, even a little higher. Say, 20. A simple calculation shows it will still take at least five generations of transmission to infect all three million people living on Planet L.

"During the drone's exploration, the average time taken between locating one corpse and finding another was around 30 minutes. Bear in mind that the drone travels much faster than the spread of the virus through the air. If we assume that it takes three hours for the virus to complete one generation of transmission, then the minimum time required for five generations is 15 hours. But this represents an extremely ideal situation, and the reality is likely to be far more complicated, and much slower. For a crude estimate, we might multiply the figure by 10, that is, 150 hours, or six days. Over such a long period of time, the bodies would have started to rot, turning green or red; but the bodies we saw were at most in rigor mortis, dead no more than three days. Therefore, the situation you proposed can basically be ruled out."

"I've got it!" Gao Yun clapped his hands together. "Nanomachines! If the supervirus was carried by nanomachines, it could spread far more quickly!"

"Remember the image taken immediately before the drone landed." Fang Hui wagged her index finger. "Before the spectrometer failed, we clearly saw that the composition of Planet L's atmosphere was similar to that of the Earth. If nanomachines were present in large numbers, we'd expect to see evidence of excessive levels of certain elements used in semiconductors. Nanomachines, however advanced, are still electronic devices, and as such require semiconductors. Bring me another coffee, will you? All this talk has made my throat dry."

Ai Er smiled wryly, shaking his head.

"So," Fang Hui went on, "as you said in the beginning, it's close to impossible to determine what happened from a purely scientific analysis. We'll need to widen our horizons."

After a moment, Gao Yun brought over three lattes. He stirred the milk, mulling over something. Ai Er took his cup, holding the handle elegantly between his thumb and middle finger as he sipped. "I've been working with instructions for too long, and my thinking has solidified. I'll leave the speculations to you two."

Gao Yun sat down again. "If we can abandon scientific rigour for a moment, I have a few ideas. After all, I've read my share of science fiction. Let's begin with the possibility that many of Planet L's people are hiding underground. The drone was unable to find its way beneath the surface before it broke down. Maybe the bodies we see on the surface are only those who did not wish to retreat underground."

Fang Hui took a sip of her coffee. "If I were from Planet L," she said, "I definitely wouldn't do that."

"Why not?" asked Gao Yun, frowning.

"The usual reason for moving underground is that the surface environment is too harsh. But the whole point of using QGP to wrap the planet inside a black zone is to create a stable living environment; the procedure is almost like moving underground. What's the point of digging down further? Moreover, this hypothesis fails to explain why the people on the planet's surface died at almost the same time. Unless you're proposing that the underground faction unanimously denounced the surface faction as traitors and executed all three million at the same time? Besides," she added ruthlessly, "we might just as well imagine people in the sky and people under the sea."

Gao Yun didn't insist. He pondered for a moment. "The second hypothesis is the Planet L's inhabitants were killed by the planet itself. If the planet is a giant organism, it may regard the humans as foreign objects invading its body. The planet then develops antibodies to eradicate the humans."

"Sure," Fang Hui responded, "it's a common enough premise in science fiction. However, it's rarely human beings that the planet kills, but 'human civilization.' Human beings evolved naturally, while human civilization is an alien, artificial thing. The first thing the planet would do is to destroy the cities, not murder the inhabitants."

"Who knows? Maybe Planet L's antibodies can only recognize living things." Gao Yun was not to be outdone.

"Unfortunately, this is also impossible. In the video, we saw both native flora and fauna, trees and poplars from Earth, even birds and cats. If the human beings are considered invasive objects, the same must be true for the plants and animals imported from Earth. There's no reason for Planet L to kill all the humans while sparing the other organisms."

"A third possibility-" Gao Yun pondered for a moment. "What about quantum entanglement? Those we see on Planet L are actually the entangled backup copies of humans on another distant planet! Sometime before or after the drone landed, there was an accident on the home planet, maybe a meteorite impact, or an interstellar war, and under the action at a distance effect observed in the quantum entanglement state, the backup copies—Ow!" Gao Yun clasped the back of his head, where Fang Hui had slapped him.

"How many times have I told you?" she scolded. "You haven't understood the concept of entanglement. When A is observed, the state of B becomes determined. Until either is observed, both remain in a 'black box' state. So tell me, there were three million people living on Planet L—where was the black box? Quantum mechanics is fine, if we follow the basic principles! The hypothesis won't hold."

Gao Yun slammed the table. He smiled confidently at Fang Hui. "My final move: Cthulhu! Ha! Since you said the sky's the limit, let's imagine some kind of evil, inexorable god exterminated the people on Planet L. Cthulhu might stand for some advanced civilization, or a natural disaster that cannot be explained by our current technology. How about it? You can't deny it this time, right?"

Fang Hui rolled her eyes. *The child is unteachable,* her expression seemed to say. "This kind of *Deus ex Machina,* if developed painstakingly enough, can explain away anything. However, even your evil god must follow basic logic." Seeing her partner's puzzled expression, she went on. "If Planet L's people were wiped out by an evil god, there are only two possibilities: active or passive. In the active case, the inhabitants did something to provoke the god. But then, Planet L is in a black zone. Okay, so maybe your god is so powerful that it can ignore such protections, but then what is the motivation for the people to go seeking the evil god, even through the black zone?

"The passive case begs the question: what is so special about human beings? In the video, we saw only dead humans—the buildings, electronics, and all other life forms remained intact. Refine your answer in response to the above questions, in 200 words or less. Your time is limited to three minutes."

Gao Yun slumped on the table. Ai Er, who had observed the debate in silence, addressed Fang Hui, "Enough. I want to hear your reasoning."

Fang Hui smiled. "Okay," she said, "let's get out from the perspective of scientists and science fiction writers, and analyze this locked room murder puzzle from a detective's point of view." She twirled her empty coffee cup in her hand. "Compared with the standard locked room puzzles, we can simplify the Planet L case further by putting aside questions of *Who* or *How,* and focusing on *When.* When exactly did the people on Planet L die? After the room was unlocked? Or before?

"Let's start with the most extreme case," said Gao Yun, regaining his spirit now that they were back on familiar territory, "which is that Planet L's people are not dead. Since you don't want to consider how they died, there's no harm in making the more audacious hypothesis: *there never were any people on Planet L."*

"Then, how do you explain the corpses we saw in the video?" asked Ai Er. "And, for that matter, the only living person: the boy who appeared at the end."

Gao Yun chuckled. "I once read a story about a monster, a kind of monkfish that disguised its tentacles as beautiful women in order to lure men into its lair, where they perished in the sacrificial bowl of its huge, bloodthirsty mouth. We might just as well imagine that the only living creature on Planet L is the planet itself, and the human bodies are nothing more than tentacles used to lure prey. It's a good thing you sent a drone to investigate, any human would've been devoured immediately!"

Fang Hui laughed uproariously, clutching her stomach. She wiped the tears from her eyes. "Old Gao, you're still stuck in your imagination. Logically speaking, of course, this is yet another theory we can rule out. Tell me, for what purpose does your supposed monkfish monster catch its prey?"

Gao Yun, feeling a little embarrassed, murmured resentfully, "To fill its stomach, of course. Why else?"

"Right. Planet L seeks to capture prey in order to consume mass, heavy elements, energy, information, or whatever—life feeds on negative entropy. But no matter what it needs, why should it shut itself off from outside? It makes no sense. It's as if your monkfish had buried itself behind a wall of reinforced concrete and has to wait for its prey to break through before it can enjoy a good meal."

Gao Yun fell silent, his face sullen. Ai Er took over the conversation. "Let's continue to use the method of elimination. There remain only two possibilities: either Planet L's inhabitants died inside the black zone, that is, before the QGP shield was breached. Or they died afterwards."

"The possibility that they died before the black zone was breached can basically be ruled out." Gao Yun sighed. "It took around five hours for the drone to exit the capsule, enter into low-planetary orbit, and land. This duration conforms with the condition of the corpses discovered. Therefore, it's almost certain that the people on Planet L died after the black zone was breached."

Fang Hui smiled. "Let's discuss the possibility that they died after the locked room was opened. Putting aside the question of *How*, we might imagine a button—press it, and all human beings across the planet immediately go to hell. There is indeed a scenario that corresponds to this hypothesis. For example, if the consciousness of all beings on Planet L was controlled by a single, unified mainframe, then with the destruction of the mainframe, everyone would perish. In this case, however, that is impossible."

Gao Yun and Ai Er both looked at her, questioningly.

"Do you remember when the drone landed? Most of the spectrometry was broken, but the levels below the visible light band were still working."

Ai Er nodded. "But what does that mean?"

"In my debate with Gao, I dismissed the possibility of quantum entanglement technology. If correct, this means that information transmission is limited by the speed of light. Radio waves are the most efficient way to transmit over such a large distance and bypass complex structures. But throughout the video, nothing unusual was observed in the radio wave band. Therefore, this possibility can also be ruled out."

Ai Er was surprised. "Miss Fang Hui," he said, "you have logically ruled out all possibilities, yet the death of Planet L's population remains a definite fact. Does this mean that you too are incapable of explaining their demise?"

Fang Hui smiled again. "The logical possibilities are not exhausted. I ruled out two possibilities: 'died before the locked room was opened' and 'died after the locked room was opened.' Isn't there a third option?" In the face of both men's astonishment, she supplied the answer: "The inhabitants of Planet L died the moment the room was unlocked, the moment the QGP shield was breached.

"We continue to assume that all minds of Planet L are controlled by a single host computer. So, where is this host hidden? We know nothing about the host, save for one feature: that it has been severely damaged, or destroyed. The drone flew all over Planet L and found no sign of destruction other than the dead human beings. But our thinking has been misguided. What was destroyed was right in front of us from the very beginning: the QGP shield. The host we are searching for is not within the locked room; it is the door.

"At the beginning of the video, Mr. Ai explained that Planet L exists in a region similar to our own, with very few people around. In that case, why devote so many resources to the creation of a third-generation black zone? The most reasonable explanation, in my view, is that the black zone served a different function. Planet L's population uploaded their individual minds to the QGP layer, but this host was destroyed the instant the spaceship broke through. Though some part of their consciousness returned to their bodies, too much was destroyed, and almost everyone suffered brain death before the drone landed. Based on the information in the video, this is the most plausible explanation we can deduce. Only, that makes the murderer,"—Fang Hui pointed to Ai Er—"the Yuanyang Starfield Development Group."

Ai Er was taken aback for a moment. He cleared his throat. "Thank you very much, Miss Fang Hui. I will compile your conclusions into a report and submit it to the group's board of directors. To finish, let's discuss your remuneration."

"What's the hurry?" said Fang Hui with a smile. "The Planet L incident may be solved, but I have another story to tell, one I think is worth hearing."

Ai Er raised his eyebrows. "What story?"

"Let's presume that the boy at the end of the video did not die. The minds of his compatriots were destroyed when the QGP shield was breached, yet his own consciousness was preserved intact. When a hard disk is damaged, there is often some data that can be recovered, especially with a base of three million. Perhaps, by some lucky coincidence, the boy had downloaded his mind and was dealing with a real-world problem when the spaceship crashed through the protective shield. Anyway, whatever the reason, the boy dodged a bullet.

"After destroying the drone, he analyzed the equipment inside and learned that it came from the Yuanyang group. Unable to come to terms with the mass deaths of his compatriots, he resolved to infiltrate the Yuanyang Starfield Development Group, in order to discover the truth. His hard work paid off, and a few years later, he successfully joined the company. Over time, he earned the admiration of the company president, Shi Xing.

"Shi Xing has seen the video, of course, but he failed to recognise the little boy—let's call him 'L'—who is now a grown man. Moreover, Shi Xing spends most of his time traveling between the stars at sub-light speed, and the contraction effect has left his perception of time very confused. In short, when Shi Xing first laid eyes on L, he harboured no suspicions.

"While working for Shi Xing, L slowly learned the truth about what happened to his people: this was no accident, but a deliberate assault. Shi Xing had crashed the spaceship through the shield in order to seize the planet. Only fear of reprisals for the mass deaths he inflicted had kept him from selling the planet. The boy gnashed his teeth in hatred. He could hardly wait to murder Shi Xing in revenge. But as the last remnant of his people, he had to protect himself.

"Eventually, L devised a strategy. He located an obscure planet at the junction of the Alpha 23 and Gamma 31 star systems, where there lived a pair of little-known detectives. He took the initiative to mention the planet to Shi Xing, and proposed to investigate the situation with the detectives' help. If they discovered no potentially dangerous elements left behind on Planet L, Shi Xing could sell it at a high price.

"The greedy Shi Xing approved L's proposal. At the same time, he also became interested in the detectives' home planet, and decided to join L on the trip. However, he judged the planet of little development value, and didn't even bother to leave the spaceship. At this point, L's plan had all but succeeded. As he listened to the detectives, he waited for his opportunity to—"

"Sorry to interrupt." Ai Er raised his eyes and looked calmly at Fang Hui. "But there's one thing I don't understand. What can L possibly expect from the detectives?"

"On the day of his visit, their planet will cross the boundary between the two star fields. Relations between their respective governments has always been strained. If Shi Xing was to die in Gamma 31, while L was in Alpha 23, the case would never come to trial. The two star fields will not meddle in each other's affairs, let alone travel to the other's territory in order to arrest someone. Even if Shi Xing's death is discovered, it won't be until much later; by which time L will have already made his retreat. Even if he is suspected, L has a solid alibi, with the detectives as his witnesses. To this end, L rigged the ship early this morning. Shortly after Shi Xing departed, the explosive device aboard his ship will have reduced him to dust."

Ai Er was silent for a long time. Before he spoke, he looked Fang Hui straight in the eyes. "So, Miss Fang Hui, what are you going to do?"

Fang Hui's eyes rested on Ai Er's left hand. Ever since Gao Yun served them coffee, the man's index finger had not moved a muscle. She smiled gently. "You mean, am I going to tell? It's only a story, after all. And besides, I'm tired of the telling." She put her arms behind her head. "The story is finished. Now, let's discuss our fee!"

Copyright © by Fu Qiang. Translation copyright © 2023 by Roy Gilham.

Lezli Robyn is an Australian author, as well as editor and Associate Publisher of Arc Manor, who lives in Myrtle Beach, South Carolina, with her blue-eyed chiweenie, Bindi (which means "little girl" in several indigenous Australian dialects). She's a lover of chocolate and gardening, and is forever drawn by the call of the ocean.

FROM WORKSHOP STORIES TO ROLE-PLAYING YOUR WAY INTO SUCCESS: *GALAXY'S EDGE* INTERVIEWS DANIEL ABRAHAM

by Lezli Robyn

I had the pleasure of sitting down with Daniel in a gorgeous casita in Santa Fe, New Mexico, to discuss his career before we headed out to dinner with friends. Not only was there a lot of laughter and warmth—and fun random side tangents to our conversation that won't make this interview (sorry!)—but I was reminded anew how one seemingly small event can really change a person's life. Daniel's down-to-earth attitude about his own career really gave me a window into someone who seemingly applies himself to everything with an almost casual ease belying his boundless talent and dedication. It makes this a very inspiring conversation for new authors when they realize that many of the early steps needed to create bestselling novels and successful TV shows are both relatable and achievable—if the stars also align the right way.

Galaxy's EdGE: Your first short story publication, "Mixing Rebecca," was in 1996.

Daniel Abraham: It was!

GE: How did your career start? What made you write that story?

DA: I had been getting rejection slips. Everyone collects their rejection slips—I was in that phase of my career. The editor of *The Silver Web* had turned down one of my earlier stories, but with a personalized rejection letter and some commentary, and she had mentioned that she was putting together a music episode specifically of *The Silver Web*. And so I was thinking, "Okay, I'll write a weird music story," and that was "Mixing Rebecca." That story was done to order, with a particular audience in mind, and with the encouragement of Ann Kennedy, who has since become Ann VanderMeer. So Ann VanderMeer is the person who bought my first short story.

GE: That's a wonderful first step in your career.

DA: It was, you know. And the weird thing about "Mixing Rebecca": I got a very strange reaction to it from a particular person. The story is about a sound engineer who overcomes her shyness by sampling somebody and mixing the song of their life. So that's how she's overcoming anxiety. And the woman who she's mixing is named Rebecca. Several months after it got published, I got this email from a guy who was a sound engineer who had just finished an album called *Rebecca Remix*. His name is Daniel Abraham.

GE: Are you serious?

DA: I'm completely serious.

GE: Wow, that is trippy.

DA: He was looking at the story going, "Do I have a stalker?!" and I had to explain [and] assure him that no, this was not anything creepy. Purely coincidental.

GE: Purely coincidental on two fronts.

DA: Several fronts. It was a trip.

GE: You've published stories in *Asimov's* and *The Magazine of Fantasy and Science Fiction*. You also went to Clarion as well.

DA: Clarion West in 1998. I was instructed to go there by Suzy McKee Charnas. I had proctored a fiction writing class for her at the University of New Mexico, and as part of that she let me get in on the critique circle in that class. We talked and knew each other from that. She said, "Okay, your next step is to go to one of the Clarion workshops." And I said, "Well, [since] Suzy said that, I guess I go to one of the Clarion workshops!" And that was as much thought as I put into that decision.

GE: You trusted her.

DA: I was very lucky to have people, very early in my career, who were very supportive and very helpful in guiding me to the right places.

GE: Clarion West has been known to help create the foundation for a career.

DA: It does also break people. I had two semi-pro sales before that. All of the professional sales came after that.

GE: In 2005, you won the international Horror Guild Award for your novelette, "Flat Diane." And you were nominated for a Hugo and World Fantasy Award for "The Cambist and Lord Iron" novelette in 2008. Were they your first "I've got a career!" success moments? What was your first one?

DA: Well, you know … I believe the first time I remember thinking, "Okay, I can make a go of this," was when I sold two short stories to *Asimov's* in the same letter. I received an acceptance letter from Gardner Dozois for two different stories at the same time.

GE: Oh, that is wonderful.

DA: I thought that felt like a magic object.

GE: Editors do not make that decision often.

DA: Well, submitting two stories at the same time was kind of a bold choice too, but it happened. It worked. And that actually came through Clarion West, too. Gardner was one of my teachers there, so he knew me, and he knew the stories from that.

The awards are nice. They're gratifying. It's great that people enjoy what I create. It's just never been the primary driver for me. I was pleased to win. I was pleased to lose to people who were doing high quality work, too. But it was the part where people gave me money and published my works that had a lot more weight than the part where I got the applause. The applause was awesome—I'm not going to say anything bad about that—but it was not the focus.

GE: You have two series that you've written that are fantasy. How did those series come about?

DA: Well, the first fantasy series I did, The Long Price Quartet, again came out of Clarion West. I had to turn in a short story on Tuesday. It was Sunday night and it was Connie Willis's week to teach that weekend, and she said, "Begin with somebody getting hit on the head," and I had no idea what to do, except I had to do it *right now*. So that prompt turned into a short story that came out in *Asimov's* as "The Lesson Half-Learned." And then that turned into the prologue of the first book of The Long Price Quartet.

My first agent—I'm not with her anymore—was Shawna McCarthy from *Realms of Fantasy*. She had published some of my short stories and said, "Hey, I'm also an agent. Do you have any novels?" And I said, "Yes, I have this novel right here," and she read it and said, "Great, this is awesome. Do you have any novels that are *salable*?" *laughs* And I said, "No, I don't, but I do have this short story that I published in *Asimov's* that maybe, could be, expanded into something." And then she said, "That's your next project."

GE: Oh, that's great.

DA: So that's how Daniel Abraham started writing epic fantasy novels.

I had this idea for what I wanted to do with The Long Price Quartet that was a little weird, and people hadn't seen before. It came out pretty well. The next thing I did after that was another epic fantasy, The Dagger and the Coin series. That series was five books—also published under Daniel Abraham—that told a single story. I was pretty happy with them. Now I'm publishing a trilogy of fantasy stories—a new project that's also in that epic fantasy space.

The novel that was not salable was a contemporary literary fantasy—a Jonathan Carroll, Graham Joyce kind of thing. And if that had sold, that would have been what I was known to write.

GE: I find it fascinating that the genre you publish under first can shape or define a career—which isn't completely true in your case now.

DA: Well, it's definitional in a weird way. There's a whole conversation about reader expectation and branding, and the meta story around fiction that's formed by chance a lot of the time, depending on the genre of the first book you sell. And, certainly, that was the case for me.

GE: In 2002, George RR Martin and Gardner Dozois asked you to help finish the *Shadow Twin* novella, that later got expanded into a novel. I have a signed copy of that. Was that your first true collaborative experience?

DA: I had done other collaborations before. There are people who I wrote short stories with. I wrote a short story with Susan Fry. I wrote a short story with Tamela Viglione that never got published. When I was starting off as a little baby writer in high school, I also had a project that I was doing with friends, but *Shadow Twin* was the first one with authors who were really established names.

I think there was a short story, a collaboration, that was published before that, but certainly Shadow Twin was the first time I was playing that far out of my weight class, as far as working with people who were world class. That was amazing.

GE: You were the one tasked with finishing off the novella. Did it feel like extra pressure, or were you just caught up in the euphoria you felt and were excited to do it?

DA: I felt like I was just finishing up for them—the direction was already there. Two-thirds of the novella was done. George had done his part, and then Gardner finished his part, and then there was this space where the third part was. But, you know, the endings are always implicit in the beginnings. I was reading through it and saying, "Okay, well, where is this story going?" And by the two-thirds mark of the story, I *knew* where it was going, so I just wrote the rest of the novella.

Apparently I did a decent job of it. I was not the first person they approached to finish this thing. I was just the guy that signed on to do it. So one of the previous people who had been pitched it, and turned it down, reached out to me later and said that he thought I had done a good structural job pulling it together, and that was flattering. But no, I felt like I was completing a structure that was already implicit.

GE: Then it got expanded into a novel.

DA: Yes, we turned it into a novel called *Hunters Run*. George felt like there was more story to tell. The novella was good—there was just more potential to it than was going to fit into that length. We retold it at a novel length to deepen it and to tell more of the story that was off the edges of the canvas.

GE: How did your collaboration with Ty Franck come about?

DA: Every good thing in my career has come out of shits and giggles. The stuff that I have done where I was trying to game the market, never did as well.

Ty was running a role-playing game at the time, up in Santa Fe [New Mexico]. I had a new baby, so the part where you go off for an evening, do an hour road trip, and spend the night role-playing and then drive back—it's not really easy to do when you've got a new baby. Ty was very kind in running an instance of that game in Albuquerque for me and our wives. It was a universe he'd created that had an incredible depth to it. It had this insane level of detail and richness, and I fell into the universe that he'd built.

There was a point at which I was writing him an email at 3:00 in the morning, talking about my plan for monetizing debt in the Belt and creating a new currency that would then eliminate the necessity to reach for financial institutions on Earth. And I was like, "Okay. I'm into this." If I'm doing emails at 3:00 in the morning, if I'm this excited—something's going on. And I had, I think, six books published at that time, and Ty had done this amazing amount of work already. I thought, you know what, fuck it. I said, "Why don't we write this as a book. You can see what doing a book is like—I know how to do books. You can tell me what the story is, because you know the story. We'll sell it for pizza money. It'll be fun." He thought about it, and he said, "All right!", and that was how we started doing the first novel in *The Expanse* series. He had Wednesdays off; I'd go over and we'd work on it for a while and play Xbox.

GE: How long did it take to write the first novel?

DA: The first novel took about a year and mostly on Wednesdays. It was a very Wednesday-centric novel.

GE: How did that compare to your solo work?

DA: When I was writing with Ty, I was doing The Dagger and the Coin books, and I think they are 130 or 140 [thousand words], and *The Expanse* books are around 150 to 160. So it's pretty close.

I was also writing, for a while there, three books a year.

GE: Were you writing them concurrently?

DA: Yes, because it was just Wednesday that I was busy, and then I had time to write every other day of the week.

GE: How did the collaborative process compare to writing by yourself? Did you find that you could bounce ideas off each other quicker and work out plot points easier?

DA: There's a freedom that comes from knowing at the outset that the book's not going to be what you would have done by yourself. And there's a responsibility to the other guy to get the work done. So between those two, there were some real advantages, and some real loosening of the strings and the uptightness that usually comes as a part of writing. But, for both of us, it was just for fun. We would talk about the coolest idea, then we'd write some cool ideas down …

GE: And it kept expanding.

DA: Yes. The first novel did really well. We got to the end of the first book, and that included all the plot that Ty had developed for the background of his role-playing game. My argument was that we've got a book that's more likely to sell if we can include some ideas and some suggestions so that if the publishers like it, it could become a series. And that was just sales pitch stuff, just to make it more interesting to the publishers. We wrote paragraphs for the next two books, just in case they wanted a trilogy. And they wound up being the descriptions used for the next two books in the series.

GE: What led to the decision to have a joint name as opposed to two names on the byline?

DA: Well, there's a couple of things. One of them we already touched on: Daniel Abraham writes epic fantasy. Do you know that experience when you forget that you ordered iced tea, and you think you ordered coke, and you drink your iced tea and it tastes like this wretchedly horrid Coca-Cola.

GE: Yes, and you say, "This is not what I was expecting."

DA: Something is terribly wrong—you have that moment of rejection. It doesn't matter how good your space opera is if you were expecting epic fantasy. You set expectations for the reader by who the writer is. James S. A. Corey writes space opera. Daniel Abraham writes epic fantasy. So just from the pure expectation level, it makes sense to have a different name. There's also the mistake people make when they see one established author writing with a new name.

GE: They assume the junior author wrote it.

DA: Yes, they assume that the other guy wrote it and we just slapped the first guy's name on the book. That's not what happened. We didn't want to give that impression. It just seemed more graceful—and it avoided a bunch of unnecessary questions—to build a new name for the series.

GE: It was great you had that sense of awareness to create a new name for yourselves before publication. How did the TV series come about?

DA: Well, *laughs*, Ty was still working for George [RR Martin] at the time. We were aware that an adaptation was a possibility, and we decided that we should get a Hollywood agent. So we went out there, and we were talking to Hollywood agents, and we were talking to other people about the series. While we were doing this, we reached out to our book agent—who at that point was Danny Baror—and said, "Hey, Danny, we're in Hollywood. We're trying to find a Hollywood agent who can represent us!" He said, "You have one! We have the guy. He's already been turning down offers for you. You know what—do you want to talk to him?" *laughs* And then we met Brian Lipson, who is our Hollywood guy. He'd been waiting for an offer that seemed like it was real.

GE: Not just renewing an option every year?

DA: Right. Not from people who weren't going to put their backs into it. And we wound up with two offers—two teams of folks who wanted to do the adaptation. And one of them was this really great team who had done scripts on *The Blacklist*. They were known and respected in Hollywood—they were solid guys. And then the other two were Mark Fergus and Hawk Ostby, who had written [the movie scripts for] *Iron Man* and *Children of Men*. I thought that if we would like to get our adaptation made, go with the guys who are known for *Iron Man* and *Children of Men*, because they had a lot of weight. They had name recognition. They also had the status to make the project look serious.

We worked with them from very early on. They wrote a pilot script, and we went out and shopped it around, and found our partners in Alcon Entertainment. Alcon hired on our showrunner, Naren Shankar. In the overall scheme of things, it was incredibly fast. Things continued to move quickly, and you know what? I didn't know any better. I was just showing up, and that worked out really well.

GE: What was it like writing screenplays versus writing the novel?

DA: Screenplays are a completely different object. It took me a long time to really understand what we were doing and how it was different.

GE: It's still your world, it's what you've created, but a completely different process.

DA: Yes—it's a different object. The screenplay is a blueprint that you then hand to a small army of dedicated professionals who then interpret it and bring their expertise to it to create this vision on the screen. Writing a novel is something I do that I hand directly to an audience in the form I created. The part of television and film creation that's the same isn't screen *writing*, it's film *editing*. Film editors are like novelists; they're the ones who are taking that blueprint and putting the story together in the form that will be experienced by the audience. It took me a long time to understand that, and how the tools were different. I had to understand what *doesn't need* to be on the page—what's not supposed to be on the page.

I had a profound *aha!* moment at one point. I always have this urge to write what the person is thinking or feeling for the actor to know. And you don't do that. You write what the camera *sees* and what the microphone *hears*, and that's all you do.

GE: And then the actor tries to *show* what the character is feeling.

DA: Yes. I was talking to Naren and I was saying that I just want him to know what the intent is—what the character's supposed to be feeling in that moment. And if I don't put that on the page, how will he know? And he said, "Well then, you bring it up in the meeting when you're talking to the actor." Oh, right, there's this whole other channel of communication. The screenplay doesn't have to contain the whole context, because you're also going to be talking to people.

That kind of understanding was very foreign—it took me a long time. Ty was much better at that. He actually shifted gears much more gracefully than I did.

GE: Something that is clear from the series is that *The Expanse* has a very diverse cast. Did you and Ty have a lot of say in how much representation of different cultures you wanted in the show, and how they could be shown to have evolved into the future?

DA: It's part of the books even before we did the show. We wanted to have a future in which everybody got there. There are obstacles to that when you're making a project where you have to take into account the acting pool you have to draw from. You have the casting directors you have to work with. There are all these levels you don't control, but from the creative team with Alcon and with Naren—and first with SyFy and then Amazon—there was never any pushback on the idea that diversity was something that was in the DNA of the project and everybody was on board for it. It was important to us to have the future that we've built be as complex and diverse and broad as any teaching hospital in the United States. That was the bar we were aiming for.

GE: That's a fitting example, given my next question. The fact that the off-world colonies have to rely on Earth for their supplements and medical aid to live in the harsher environments of the wider expanse, means that Earth has the ability to exert political and economic control over far flung settlements by controlling the distribution of supplies. How did that concept develop in *The Expanse*?

DA: All of those worldbuilding ideas came from Ty. He had been very open that the kind of well he was drawing from was working class science fiction. It was [Alfred] Bester's *The Stars My Destination*. It was *Alien*. It was a future in which things were gritty and dirty and political. You have people who are arguing about whether they're getting the same share as everybody else. And when you have that level of labor realism or plausibility there are a bunch of issues that just gracefully evolve from that. There's that idea of scarcity, that idea of working in a hostile environment, that adds to the richness.

I have a biology degree. Ty has a lot of background with space exploration. We just tried to find the plausible things you would need in order to make *The Expanse* work.

GE: There are a lot of studies on astronauts—how being in space affects their bone density, and so forth. Did any of those studies or research play a part in plotting out the plights of the various colonies?

DA: It was clear that when you don't stress a bone, it atrophies. That's really all you need to know in order to extrapolate the rest of that out. We know that when you are in 0 gravity, you have heightened blood pressure in your head because you're built to fight against gravity, and you're not doing that. And we extrapolated from that.

There was very little research that we did specifically *for* the project. There was all the research we had done because we thought it was cool *before* we even started the project. We took the bodies of knowledge that we had already gotten as hobby skills and applied those.

GE: You don't often see the medical consequences of living in space. I really appreciated the gritty realism you brought to your series.

DA: What we were trying to do with the whole Expanse project was go from a late *Apollo 13* in the beginning and advance it to an early *Buck Rogers* by the end. And there are some reasons, craft wise, storytelling wise, why you need a very grounded feeling—especially in that first book. Because when the weird comes in, it needs to be shocking. And if it's not really grounded, and understandable, and really plausible in the beginning, then there's no shock because everything has been weird up till now.

GE: You don't have a foundation to expand on.

DA: Right. If you have anti-gravity plating established in Chapter 2, when something strange happens to it in Chapter 30, it's like, "Okay, sure—why not." Anything is possible.

There's a feedback loop in there between what the project wants and how to build what it needs. So, the more inconvenient and the more recognizable the base was, the better the plot worked.

GE: How much control did you have on the "look" they created for the show? The tones, and color saturations and worldbuilding aesthetics?

DA: We were very lucky in that we were very, very, very involved from the beginning. We were there for the interviews when they were hiring writers. We were there looking at casting videos. We had a lot of influence; we had no control. Ultimately, it was Naren Shankar's show and we got to work there.

We were in the Writers Room from the first day. Ty spent more time there than I did. The kind of the thing that Ty did for me with the novels—saying, "Here's what this is. Here's why it's there. Here's how it fits in the world."—he did again with Naren. For example, there was at one point early in Season One where we were talking about how to differentiate Belters from other humans because it's hard to cast actors who look like the Belters from the book. We needed to find some other way to do it, and there was an idea that maybe Belter society has moved towards cybernetics and cyborgs, becoming people who are part machine. Ty was there to say, "That would look really cool but it would undercut the idea of a unified humanity and all of us being the same. It would gut the underlying story that we're telling."

If you have one "race"—note the air quotes—that's actually biologically no longer entirely human …. Yeah, you're getting into a weird territory. That's a strange place to be. And it's much better for the story we're telling if it's a cultural difference that makes you stand out.

GE: Then the people that we *see* struggling—

DA: —are recognizably and absolutely human.

GE: Rather than being Othered and separated out.

DA: That's the kind of detail we were able to affect, the kind of argument we were present in the Writers' Room to make, even if the decision wasn't made by us.

GE: How did you feel when you finally watched the first season?

DA: I have a very different experience watching the show than anybody else does, because I was there when it was made. I can't see it the way that other people can view it. When I watch it, I think, "Oh, yeah—I remember that set. It looks better than I thought it was going to look, but I really wish we hadn't used that table. That table still bugs me" "Man, *I know* we had to cut it together that way, but I wish we were able to stay a little bit longer on this one actor because…" "Oh, wait—what on earth is that that guy doing in the background?"

GE: *laughs*

DA: "What is he even doing? Look at him!"

GE: *laughs even more* It's harder for you to lose yourself in the show as an audience.

DA: I cannot. All I see is the process. All I see is the ways we did it and the choices we made and the things that we tried that didn't work, that we then we shifted into something else so it would work. I can remember the things that we lost, and the things that weren't quite as cool as we had imagined them. It almost feels to me like going back to read one of my books, and saying, "Yeah, I got better since then. Look at that line." There's that constant self-critique.

I'm glad other people like it, and I'm glad that the show they're seeing is more enjoyable than the show I'm seeing, but I don't think I could have had the audience's experience and also have had my hands in the making of it.

GE: Is there a moment where you realized the show was becoming a hit? Is there a specific episode or response you remember that gave you that indication?

DA: There were episodes when I knew we had done good work, but the network system was so good at keeping us on the bubble and keeping us uncertain whether we still had jobs. I feel that when we got the renewal on Amazon—that surprise renewal was impacting.

GE: I was wondering if that was the moment, especially because the fan outcry was amazing.

DA: The fan outcry was huge. The expectation that that it would happen was so low. In public we were positive about it happening, but behind the scenes we all gave up. We were screwed. We knew it.

We were all hugging and promising to work with each other down the road someplace, and getting ready to do other stuff, and then it came back up. I remember very clearly when the renewal actually came through and it was like, Oh my God!" Everybody was relieved and happy and joyful.

GE: And euphoric.

DA: Yes, euphoric. Well, all of us except for Naren who was saying, "We're fucked. We're a month behind where we should be."

GE: Oh, yes, because the schedule was paused! It had stopped.

DA: We'd finished; it was over. Naren said, "We have a problem. We've got to start working right now!" And he was right. *laughs* We had a lot of catching up to do. That was one of those stardust removal realizations.

GE: *laughs* Was the arc or the vision changed at all when you switched to Amazon? Did they have a different season requirement?

DA: No. We picked up where we left off. What we did on Amazon is what we would have done if we had stayed on Syfy, except we had less restrictions.

GE: Less restrictions, how?

DA: Amazon allowed for a lot more flexibility, both in the scriptwriting and the storytelling, and also in the length of the episodes. If an episode needed another 3 minutes to let it breathe, then we could have them.

GE: Because of no advert breaks?

DA: Exactly. That was really nice.

GE: Did it give you increased creative license?

DA: It made the editing process much easier—the part where we took the dailies and formed the final shape of the episode. With that time constraint taken away, we could do what felt right instead of what was possible within a specific count of minutes and seconds. I really appreciated even just a few minutes of leeway.

GE: It means you can include that longer pause moment, originally cut, that adds more tension or weight to dialogue.

DA: Or you can have the scene that just gets the extra time it needs to really land properly. You don't have to rush it. That was very pleasant.

GE: How has *The Expanse* TV show changed your life? Has it fueled your writing career, or has it taken time away from it?

DA: It made me a lot more money.

GE: Yes, that's helpful.

DA: That's huge, actually. Selling books has become easier. The impact and reach of the novels increased, and they still sell really well. And more people are aware of our series in a way they would not have been, otherwise.

It does take up a lot of time—screenwriting and producing television. It's a full-time job, and yet we still had the deadlines for the novels. That meant it changed the workflow between myself and Ty a lot. We missed a couple of deadlines for the books. Some of the novels came out more than a year apart, which was not what we were aiming for, but we still got them all out. We timed it where Season Six of *The Expanse* and book nine came out at the same time, which was perfect timing.

GE: That's wonderful.

DA: I would have more novels of my own published by now if I hadn't spent six years making a TV show, but financially it's given me permission to build projects that I might not have been able to do, otherwise. That's awesome.

GE: What's next for you?

DA: Well, I've got that new epic fantasy series I was telling you about, coming out under my own name.

GE: What's the title of that series?

DA: It's the The Kithamar Trilogy. The first one is out right now. It's called *Age of Ash*. The second one is turned in, and I'm waiting on notes from the editor on that one. It's called *Blade of Dream*. The third one is outlined, and I think it's called *Judge of Worlds*, but the publishing company can make changes—we'll see.

And then James S. A. Corey—me and Ty—have another trilogy, coming out. A space opera in a very different part of the genre.

GE: Is it set in the same universe as *The Expanse*?

DA: No, a different universe. The cool thing about space opera is there's so much space in it. There's so many different ways to do it. In *The Expanse* we were riffing on Niven and Clark and Bester. This new series is riffing on Herbert and LeGuin, and that space in the genre.

GE: Oh, space operas with more of a fantasy vibe!

DA: We're under contract for three of those books. There's also some grumblings and rumors of television work, because, man, union health insurance is great! *laughs* I would absolutely keep that day job, if that were an option.

GE: That's an impressive list of upcoming projects!

DA: Should be enough to keep me off the streets for a couple of years.

GE: Very few writers would disagree. It doesn't sound like Edgar Allan Poe or Ursula K. Le Guin were involved at all.

UV: They were, actually. I read them voraciously. I had one of those leatherbound Poe collections with all the stories of Poe that your well-meaning relatives get you when they know you read a lot of books, but they have no idea what you like. So, they get you the fancy classics.

GE: I think I hear another horror novel being born.

Ursula Vernon: Ironically, one of the creepy things in A House with Good Bones came about because I was digging potatoes with a friend of mine. But that's neither here nor there.

Copyright © 2023 by Lezli Robyn.

Richard Chwedyk sold his first story in 1990, won a Nebula in 2002, and has been active in the field for the past thirty-three years (but who's counting?).

RECOMMENDED BOOKS

by Richard Chwedyk

GOING OUT IN STYLE

Well, the curtain is coming down, the swan is waiting in the wings, the song is sounding. One phase in the history of GALAXY'S EDGE is coming to a close. It's time for me to pack up my bindle and find a new train to hop.

Funny thing: I feel like I never really hopped this train in the first place. I've been running behind it, or alongside it at best, for most of the journey. Which is not to say that it hasn't been informative, educational, and even fun.

I was also fortunate enough to acquire this gig at a time when the field, and the publishing world in general, was undergoing fundamental changes.

Or does it always feel that way?

Perhaps, but for some reason this feels different. "Professional" publishing, for the most part, seems to have become more "corporate" than ever, trying harder than ever to manufacture saleable product, which seems, from a corporate perspective, to necessitate more sharply defining categories and genres. Conversely, our authors are producing work that, where it doesn't defy the old categories, confounds them. Smaller presses and independents are making their own rules, and it's always been from them that the innovations have come.

At one level, it's a fascinating time to be reviewing books. Which makes it a little sad to find myself turning in my last column.

And yet, the less time I spend putting together columns, the more time I have to read.

◆ ◆ ◆

Tasting Light: Ten Science Fiction Stories to Rewire Your Perceptions
edited by A. R. Capetta and Wade Roush
MITeen Press
October 2022
ISBN: 978-1-5362-1938-8

Why hasn't someone thought of this before?

Perhaps they have, and I was just not on the mailing list.

While many of us (looking at the mirror now) have lamented the perceived lack of interest in short science fiction by younger readers, and have also noted that much science fiction in the YA market are variations on dystopic themes or heroic fantasy gussied up with zap guns and warp-drive starships, MITeen Press, through the editorial auspices of A. R. Capetta and Wade Roush, have done something about it with this fine collection of ten stories. The hardcover edition premiered last autumn, so I'm late in including it here, but the trade paperback will be coming out next fall, so I'm not exceedingly remiss (this time).

The goals of this anthology seem to be threefold: 1.) familiarize YA readers with the joys of short science fiction; 2.) with the emphasis on science; and 3.) to do so with as much innovation in style and approach as the authors can provide. One of the stories is written as a sequence of text messages. Another is a graphic story. The others, written in more familiar prose styles, are not slouching in exploring the boundaries of narrative form.

Every story here is of a quality that, if it doesn't command your attention, is worthy of your committed perusal. That being said, the ones I enjoyed most were "The Weight of a Name" by Nasuġraq Rainey Hopson, Capetta's own "Extremophiles," Elizabeth Bear's "Twin Strangers" and "Melanitis" by Junauda Petrus-Nasah. The graphic story, "The Memory of Soil" by Wendy Xu, is also great in its literal approach to its title. Perhaps because it resonates with the attitude to nature I encountered in Nancy Marie Brown's book, of which more later.

Would that more of our "big," i.e. "professional," publishers would think along these lines. Science fiction in many respects has always been at its strongest in its shortest form. And the move to more digital publishing extinguishes many of the arguments against short fiction getting low sales. This may be a good time to re-emphasize the joys and importance of short fiction to a new generation. In fact, there may never be a better time than now.

◆ ◆ ◆

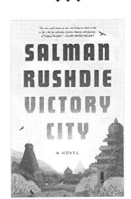

Victory City
by Salman Rushdie
Random House
February 2023
ISBN: 978-0-593-24339-8

Let me say this at the outset: this is a fantasy novel.

The reason I'm saying that is, apparently, critics and Rushdie fans either can't say the word, or can't find the word—fantasy.

There, I've said it again.

When a goddess speaks through the mouth of a little girl who is her namesake, it's fantasy.

When that namesake has a lifespan of 247 years, it's fantasy.

When an entire city is grown from a bag of magic seeds, it's fantasy.

When your protagonist can change humans into other animals, it's fantasy.

And Rushdie, no matter what else he is or what else he does, is a fantasy writer.

Rushdie is a great storyteller, and he first embraced storytelling at a time when the literary currents in which he chose to swim were churning in the opposite direction.

Much of this story is based upon folklore and history—like much fantasy. And, like much contemporary fantasy, he uses folklore and history to explore contemporary themes. It's not so much that he is doing anything different as he is doing some things better.

The tale of Pampa Kampana, and her founding of the city of Bisnaga, a sort of feminist utopia, and the tale itself—and how the tale is told—is very much at the heart of the novel. The prose is presented as a translation from Sanskrit, and as a reflection of that language, so that its cadences and vocabulary seem of another time as much as its content may reflect ours.

In a way, it is South Asian Tolkien.

Did I say that?

I did. And I mean it.

If you've never read Rushdie before, read this one. Just … read it. Forget about the Booker Prizes. Forget about the controversies. Hard as it may be, even try to forget about the fatwa and the more recent horrendous physical attack that nearly took his life. Leave that aside, and just enter the reality, the fabric, of this novel, and allow it to perform its enchantments.

If you're any reader of fantasy, you'll find yourself in familiar territory.

◆◆◆

Wraithbound
by Tim Akers
Baen
April 2023
ISBN: 978-1-9821-9255-6

You can check with my editor: I turned this column in very, very late.

I have an excuse. I've been waiting for a copy of *Wraithbound* to arrive. And I'm pleased to say it was worth the wait.

The premise is simple. Young Rae Kelthannis, the son of a "stormbinder" who is stitched to an elemental wind spirit and can command those forces of nature, wants to follow in his father's footsteps. Hastily, and against his father's wishes, he attempts the procedure—and botches it. Instead of stitching himself to an air elemental, he is bound to a demonic wraith. The world in which father and son live is already dipping into chaos, and the mayhem picks up from there.

I've only recently become familiar with Tim Akers's work, and I'm highly impressed with the economic precision of his prose and his real gift for keeping the action moving throughout his novels. In *Wraithbound* I believe he gets even better. My perception may be a bit blurred because for once I'm actually starting with the first book in a fantasy series, but his storytelling skills are impressive. And on a thematic level, this novel demonstrates the kind of clarity and maturity I wish were more evident in other volumes of this sort. I'm anticipating the release of the next volume in this series, especially since this time I won't have to read it on deadline.

◆◆◆

Looking for the Hidden Folk: How Iceland's Elves Can Save the Earth
by Nancy Marie Brown
Pegasus Books
October 2022
ISBN: 978-1-63936-228-8

I've never reviewed a nonfiction book here, at least not that I recall, but this humble meditation that brings together Iceland, its folklore, climate change, particle physics and … J. R. R. Tolkien(!) is very much worth your attention, no matter where your interests lie.

I've said, I think, in these very pages (if not, I'm saying it now) that fantasy, like science fiction, is not so much a literary category as it is a way of looking at the world (and Damon Knight said something like it before, so there!). In that way, we might find Tolkien the most important of the topics included in this book. Brown quotes from his seminal essay, "On Fairy-stories" extensively. I've always read the essay as a kind of manifesto, not for fantasy itself but for a way of looking at fantasy, and the insights it can provide for how we perceive the world around us. The sentiment is echoed in another book from which Brown quotes, about James M. Barrie. Neuroscientist Rosalind Ridley, in *Peter Pan and the Mind of J. M. Barrie*, points out that fairies, like paper currency, are things that exist and have value only if everyone agrees they do. There are differences between solid objects and socially constructed ones.

Ridley writes: "There are also occasions when art tells us something that science only recognizes at a later time."

That's not news to us. But Brown puts this together with Icelandic beliefs in "hidden folk," like elves and gnomes and such, and how they are held even by hard-edged rationalistic scientists and intellectuals, and how these beliefs inform their attitude towards the environment. Desolate stretches of the countryside, with nothing visible but ice and stone, are seen as having something akin to a sentience, if not a consciousness. They are "alive." We might regard our environment differently if we considered it as connected to ourselves, through the hidden folk, and in turn we connected to it. We might make different choices before digging up rocks to build a highway or an oil well.

And the means by which we can see the world this way is through the fantasy of "fairy-stories"—in the widest sense of this term.

I'm presenting this thesis in only the most elementary fashion. The detail to which Brown gives her thoughts are wonderfully lucid and thought-provoking. In a way, it's what we in the field have always understood, but greatly appreciate its being articulated so beautifully in this book, so that others might see what we're talking about.

◆ ◆ ◆

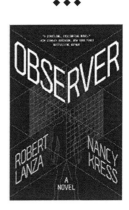

Observer
by Robert Lanza and Nancy Kress
The Story Plant
January 2023
ISBN: 978-1-61188-343-5

And speaking of consciousness …

Robert Lanza is a brilliant scientist and remarkable thinker, but perhaps the smartest decision he ever made was to collaborate with Nancy Kress when he decided to present some of his farthest-out concepts in novel form. Great scientists do not have an outstanding record in the novel-writing sweepstakes. Kress not only is as fine a professional novelist as is working today, but she has explored some similar themes as Lanza presents here with her own work, most notably genetics and the uploading of consciousness—whatever *that* is.

Tolkien once said in an interview that at the heart of all great literature is the inevitability of death. What's at the heart of this novel is to find a way of overriding that certainty. Dr. Caroline Soames-Watkins, whose brilliant career has been derailed by a twitterstorm, is hired by her great-uncle, a Nobel laureate, to work on that very project, with himself as the subject.

The question of surviving natural death often boils down to the question of what actually survives. If you download the memories of a dead person, are you saying a person consists of memories and nothing more? If you can succeed in transferring a neuro-system into some other entity or host, does that mean all that matters is the neuro-system? What is the nature of consciousness, and how much of it is dependent upon the biosystem that houses it? What is the nature of personhood?

Questions like these can be perplexing enough to make a reader want to swear off consciousness forever. And yet Lanza explores them thoroughly in ways that don't make you think you've accidentally dropped LSD. Kress has created characters and settings to house these big ideas in ways that feel perfectly natural and emphasize the tensions and attractions which weave these characters together. This is supposed to be a "novel of ideas," and yet it doesn't feel like one, or not "merely" like one. It is a human (even all-too-human) story with all the depth and breadth one looks for in any good novel, and does so with an enviable simplicity of language and structure.

If anything underscores the mysterious complexity of consciousness (and its scary doppelganger, the unconscious), it's a novel, or any work of art, really.

Which makes, I guess, *Observer*, the novel itself, its own best argument. And a most convincing one at that.

❖ ❖ ❖

High Noon on Proxima B
edited by David Boop
Baen Books
February 2023
ISBN: 978-1-9821-9242-6

Yes, yes, I know. I reviewed David Boop's previous anthology on this theme, *Gunfight on Europa Station*, not very long ago. This time, though, I think he's outdone himself in attracting some fine science fiction with western themes. And I'll emphasize *science fiction*, because very often with "genre-bending" stories, the SF gets a little lost. As Boop makes clear in his Foreword, the authors have done their painstaking homework. And the results are evident.

Especially notable are stories by the always-reliable Brenda Cooper and Walter John Williams, not to mention Ken Scholes and Susan R. Matthews. Thea Hutcheson's "Five Mules for Madame Calypso" took me by surprise; I thought stories about bordello ships were abandoned after Mike Resnick stopped writing them a few decades ago. "Justice and Prosperity" by Milton J. Davis is, frankly, a brilliant evocation of African American themes brought into a new perspective. The story from which the anthology takes its title, "High Noon on Proxima Centauri b," by Cliff Winning, moves its action swiftly and effectively while juggling seemingly impossible loads of astronomical information with grace.

It's all fine work.

Often, when editors return to themes like this for a follow-up collection, the results are not unlike "sequel syndrome" with popular films. In this case, Boop gets better, or his authors do. Personally, I wouldn't tempt the fates with another in this series, but if Boop proves more intrepid than I, and rides the bronco one more time, I'll be more than willing to slap a twenty-dollar gold piece down on the bar and say, "Hit me again."

❖ ❖ ❖

Fort Privilege
by Kit Reed
Doubleday Books
April 1985
ISBN: 978-0385-19405-1

Let us now praise Kit Reed.

I first encountered her work in the pages of *F&SF*. She wrote the kind of short fiction that I considered "experimental" at the time. Kind of a cosmopolitan Carol Emshwiller, with a touch of Margaret St. Clair and even a little Robert Sheckley. Innovative, sophisticated, witty. I still like her short fiction best, but fans also highly value some of her novels, especially *Little Sisters of the Apocalypse*.

Her novel, *Fort Privilege*, has always intrigued me. Critics in the field at the time seemed to pay little attention to it, though it displayed the kind of maturity and stylistic skill they called for. It was like a dish they ordered from the kitchen, then sent back without comment.

Which isn't an inappropriate metaphor, since the novel is about a contingent of New York City's super-wealthy, luxuriously ensconced in the fortress-like Parkhurst apartments (modeled on the famous Dakota) on Central Park West while the metropolis becomes an enormous reenactment of *Escape from New York*. Most of the city's elite have retreated and, in the world of this novel, there isn't much between the super-rich and the super-angry "rabble." Led by the current owner, the Parkhurst residents intend to have at least one more defiant fling—not just interested in fiddling while Rome burns, but adding an entire symphony orchestra doing back flips on roller skates.

I think the novel was not accepted at the time because it didn't engage in the usual class-struggle stereotypes. The wealthy Parkhurst residents, though far from admirable, are not execrable caricatures of all we hate about the super-rich. The mobs outside, justifiably raging against the inequities and filled with criminal intent, are barely depicted at all. Every critic seemed to have a predetermined notion of how this story should be told, and no regard for the story Reed was telling them. She had a distinct take on the growing disparity between the wealthy and everyone else. It wasn't that different from the social justice issues the critics were looking for. In fact, in some ways she had taken those issues for granted to focus on other aspects of human behavior under such severe divisions.

Those aspects? Hard to summarize, if I really have a handle on what they are, but they seem to be expressed or alluded to in this passage early on in the novel, from the point of view of Bart, our closest protagonist and one of those not quite "to the manor born":

> …What if things were as bad as everybody said? The Parkhurst was impregnable. The worse things were outside, the harder you danced. There was a kind of bizarre recklessness about this that pulled him along. They danced before the Battle of Waterloo, he thought; the night before the Sepoy uprising at, he thought it was one of the stations north of Delhi, there was one hell of an officers' ball. Better have fun tonight; no telling what you would be called upon to do the next day.

We don't need to see the rioters in Central Park to understand a common thread may run between "them that got" and "them that don't." To do so might spawn moral questions that are, in this novel, beside the point. And in these times, when the divisions between the "gots" and the "don'ts" have grown further than could have been imagined in 1985 (at least by many of us), it may be worthwhile to rediscover, or reexplore, this novel by an author of speculative fiction who never went for easy answers.

For which we should be ever grateful to her, and always remember her.

Copyright © 2023 by Richard Chwedyk.

Alan Smale is the double Sidewise Award-winning author of the Clash of Eagles trilogy, and his shorter fiction has appeared in Asimov's *and numerous other magazines and original anthologies. His latest novel,* Hot Moon, *came out last year from CAEZIK SF & Fantasy. When he is not busy creating wonderful new stories, he works as an astrophysicist and data archive manager at NASA's Goddard Space Flight Center.*

TURNING POINTS

by Alan Smale

THE MONGOL HORDE

The Mongol steppe of the late twelfth and early thirteenth century was a brutal landscape, rife with violence. The young Temujin could have died in any one of a dozen ways, or a hundred. He was taken prisoner and even enslaved several times in his adolescence and young adulthood, and might well have lived out his life in quiet captivity, assuming he escaped death at the hands of his brothers or other local chieftains. Instead, Temujin grew up to become a cunning and charismatic warlord who conquered and united the disparate tribes of Mongolia, and then—as Chinggis Khan—led a series of brilliant, notorious, and bloody military campaigns abroad, conquering much of what we know today as China and lands west throughout Asia. At the time of his death in 1227 AD the Mongol Khan's empire spanned four and a half million square miles, from the Caspian Sea to the Sea of Japan. His direct descendants continued to conquer and assimilate for the rest of the thirteenth century, doubling the size of this empire and transforming Eurasia forever.

This was surely one of the biggest turning points in Old World history. Or perhaps more accurately, a sheaf of turning points that played out differently in each of the various countries and territories affected, and in multiple ways.

It was also completely unpredictable. No one living at the turn of the thirteenth century could have had the slightest inkling of the calamities and transformations that were on their way.

All set in motion by one man.

How many potential world conquerors have died in infancy? How would our world today be different if they'd lived?

Or: what if some of the great leaders in our own timeline had died young, either from disease or warfare, or from being slain in the crib by an enterprising but morally gray time traveler from the future?

The Alexander we now know as The Great could (easily!) have died in battle even younger than his 32 years in our timeline, or lived on to a ripe old age, having continued to enlarge and consolidate his own empire in his later years. Hitler might well have died during the first World War, and failed to become a leading figure in the Second. In either case, the changes in the timeline would have reverberated in unimaginable ways.

The alternate history literature abounds with examinations of different World Wars, different American Civil Wars ... and the different worlds that resulted. And science fiction in general loves the trope where one person changes a world, a system, a Galactic empire. Whether it's Paul Atriedes in *Dune*, Hari Seldon in *Foundation*, or a thousand other key fictional figures, the works of SF and fantasy often revolve around the One Person—perhaps even a Chosen One—who changes Everything.

But in "the real world", otherwise known as our current timeline: how often does one person really change *everything*?

Temujin was largely raised by his mother Hoelun, growing up among pastoral nomads near the Onon River in Khenteii Province. He was raised amid an atmosphere of almost constant tribal infighting; his father was poisoned by a band of Tatars when Temujin was eight years old. For all that, Temujin's humble beginnings are sometimes overstated. His father Yesugei was a member of the locally aristocratic Borjigid clan and, while not a Khan himself, was a grandson of Qabul Khan and a nephew of Qutula Khan, both significant regional chieftains. But it's certainly true that his family fell on hard times, and Temujin's meteoric rise from this tricky start is nothing short of astonishing.

Temujin was Yesugei's eldest son by his senior wife, although he eventually felt bound to maintain his own seniority by murdering his half-brother. So he was ruthless from an early age, but must also have owned considerable personal charisma, as evidenced by the sheer number of times individuals and groups deserted their former masters to flock to his cause, even after he'd suffered crushing military defeats and been temporarily abandoned. It's the victors who write the histories, and the story of his early life leans heavily upon a single work—*The Secret History of the Mongols*—written soon after his death. Nonetheless, it's clear that Temujin was an extraordinary individual, a military genius commanding highly disciplined troops and introducing innovative tactics to ensure their victories.

By 1197, Temujin had built his power to become one of the preeminent Mongol leaders. He destroyed the Tatars in 1202, then defeated the last major group in his way, a coalition of tribes under Naimans, in a spectacular battle at Chakirmaut in 1204. His rule of all Mongolia was confirmed in 1206 during a quriltai (a council of the Mongol and Turkic chiefs and khans), during which he took that stirring title history knows him by: Chinggis Khan, meaning "firm or fierce ruler."

After which, no respite: off he went again, leading his ever-larger armies on an international rampage.

✧

After Alexander the Great died, his empire was torn apart by his generals in the Wars of the Diadochi. By contrast, after Chinggis Khan's demise his sons and grandsons established a working relationship reasonably peaceably; they divided and continued to conquer, with their new dominions adding to the same Empire. Chinggis's first son Jochi predeceased him by a year, but Jochi's son Batu Khan ruled the Golden Horde, dominating a region that included Kievan Rus, Bulgaria, and the Caucasus. Son *2, Chagatai, inherited large areas of central Asia and built on them, establishing a Khanate that included the Moghal Empire. Despite being "merely" the third son, Ogedei became Chinggis's official successor as Supreme Khan. Tolui, youngest son, served as regent over the home Mongol territories following his father's death; Tolui's sons include Mongke, Great Khan of the Mongol Empire, the well-famous Kublai Khan, founder of the Yuan dynasty of China, and Hulagu Khan, who ruled the Ilkhanate, including Persia, Turkey, Georgia, and Armenia. (Check the books referenced below, or just Google "The Mongol Empire in 1300", to find maps showing just how much territory we're talking about, here.) Chinggis and Sons was quite the successful business, and the women in the family also wielded substantial and decisive power.

And yet Chinggis Khan was much more than "just" an amazing military leader. He also revolutionized the political and bureaucratic structure of Mongolia, introducing a completely new social order. His descendants continued this work.

In *Genghis Khan and the Making of the Modern World*, Jack Weatherford points to the Mongols' command and control of trade routes; the improvements in communications due to their establishment of a system of waystations (an early Asian Pony Express, if you like); the massive increase in printing technology and thus in literacy under their rule; and the religious tolerance that they showed (relatively speaking). Technological innovations from the compass to paper to gunpowder spread far and wide via the Silk Road. Over and above all this, Weatherford credits the Mongols with "creat[ing] the nucleus of a universal culture and world system ... with the emphasis on free commerce, open communication, shared knowledge, secular politics, religious coexistence, international law, and diplomatic immunity." Which is a lot.

Oh, and they certainly revolutionized the art of war. The Romans notwithstanding, Chinggis Khan's was the first really modern army, based on a rational structure with units organized on multiples of ten, and merit-based promotions. They operated with speed and efficiency, and could execute complex maneuvers at will. They also adopted new technologies rapidly: siege warfare, gunpowder, communications and intelligence, even psychological warfare.

They were undoubtedly savage in battle. But it's notable that the warriors of Chinggis Khan did not (generally) torture, mutilate, or maim. And—like the Romans—the Mongols preferred to assimilate enemy troops into their own armies rather than devastating them. Plunder was divided out fairly among the troops of his armies. It might be said that Chinggis earned the loyalty his family and his soldiers gave him.

✡

Opinions of the Mongols have varied dramatically over the centuries. During the apocalyptic years of the conquests, the Mongols understandably spread widespread fear and panic. Swayed by the writings of Marco Polo, Renaissance writers and explorers switched to open admiration of the Mongols, but by the time of the Enlightenment the needle had swung back again, with the Mongols portrayed as illustrating everything that was (to "enlightened" European eyes) barbaric and evil about the Asian continent.

Today, with a little historical distance, we can perhaps see both sides, and for antidotes to Weatherford's rather positive spin, take a look at some of the other books referenced below. But in Chinggis Khan's home country there's little doubt which way the wind blows.

I visited Mongolia in July, 2008, just sixteen years after the end of Soviet rule, and its legacy was still very apparent. Signs in stores were still in three languages: Mongolian, Cyrillic, and English. We still heard Russian being spoken, and a four-meter-tall bronze statue of Lenin stood right outside our Ulaanbaatar hotel. But as the relics of the Soviet era wane in significance, Chinggis Khan is once again on the ascendant. Remembered in the West largely due to his swath of slaughter and destruction across thousands of miles, he's effectively both the father and the patron saint of modern Mongolia. After you land at Chinggis Khaan International Airport and go into Ulaanbaatar to take a selfie with his massive golden statue in Sukhabaatar Square, you can head off for lunch at the Grand Khaan Irish Pub. His image is on the five highest-value banknotes, on buildings, in advertising, and plastered on a bewildering array of products. At least in Ulaanbaatar, he's inescapable. His eyes watch you everywhere you go, and may drive you to sink a chaser of Chinggis Gold premium vodka after you've drained your Chinggis beer.

Whichever spelling you use, Genghis Khan is a hero rather than a villain to modern-day Mongolians, a key figure in their culture and national identity. Which is understandable. By unifying the warring tribes and taking them on tour, Chinggis created Mongolia as a national force and masterminded its emergence onto the world stage. His control of the Silk Road facilitated communications between Asia and Europe, to everyone's benefit. He gets the credit for introducing Mongolian script (*hudum Mongol bichig*) and Mongolia's first written legal code (the *Ikh Zasag*), based on equal protection under the law and ruthless punishments for corruption and bribery. He did a lot for his native lands.

And hey, his proponents say: in terms of genocide and cruelty he wasn't really much worse than other kings and warlords of that era. They're not wrong, though the nations in the path of the Mongol Horde might be forgiven for seeing things rather differently.

✡

The Great Man Theory hails from the nineteenth century, when lots of people were invested in Great Men, especially in Britain and the US. The theory is generally credited to Thomas Carlyle, and in particular to his work *On Heroes*: "Great men should rule, and others should revere them." You've probably got it by now, but the idea is that exceptional individuals shape history; that history itself is largely just the history of great men, as such men are often the deciding factors.

As stated, of course, this is … overly simplistic. We might list any number of pivotal historical developments that were due to broad societal changes, to groundswells in social and economic history, historical materialism, and all the rest of it. There are a multitude of historical changes for which you could remove one significant individual, or even a dozen of them, and that change would still have taken place. If Columbus hadn't "discovered" America, someone else would have been the first European in Tudor times to set eyes on the New World. Without Darwin, we'd still have the Theory of Evolution, and without Einstein we'd still have relativity. Others were working along similar lines at both times. Without Napoleon … well, that one's open to debate.

The point is that the significance of particular individuals in any particular historical narrative is often a massive "It depends, let's talk about that," and future Turning Points columns might have explored many variations on this theme. But I think it's pretty clear that in Chinggis Khan's case, the man himself was key to everything that followed, and without him the history of Europe and Asia would have been *very* different. Would the Mongols have begun a massive and unprecedented feat of unification and empire-building across Asia and Europe without Temujin—Chinggis Khan—himself in a leading role? Hard to imagine.

Like him or loathe him, he's literally one of the most important people in world history.

References:

Thomas J. Craughwell, *The Rise and Fall of the Second Largest Empire in History: How Genghis Khan's Mongols Almost Conquered the World*, 2010.

Timothy May, *The Mongol Empire*, 2018.

Paula L. Sabloff, *Modern Mongolia: Reclaiming Genghis Khan*, 2001.

Stephen Turnbull, *Genghis Khan and the Mongol Conquests 1190-1400*, 2003.

Jack Weatherford, *Genghis Khan and the Making of the Modern World*, 2004.

Jack Weatherford, *The Secret History of the Mongol Queens*, 2010.

Copyright © 2023 by Alan Smale.

L. Penelope is the award-winning author of the Earthsinger Chronicles and The Monsters We Defy. *Her first novel,* Song of Blood & Stone, *was chosen as one of* TIME Magazine's *100 Best Fantasy Books of All Time. Equally left and right brained, she studied filmmaking and computer science in college and sometimes dreams in HTML. She hosts the My Imaginary Friends podcast and lives in Maryland with her husband and furry dependents. Join her newsletter for writers at: https://myimaginaryfriends.net.*

LONGHAND

by L. Pendelope

USING MYTHOLOGY AND CULTURAL STUDIES IN YOUR WORLDBUILDING

Fantasy readers love nothing more than to sink, eyeballs first, into an immersive, well-crafted story world and live there for a while experiencing all the adventures and heartbreaks, the highs and lows of a fictional character. Worldbuilding is critical in bringing these imagined worlds to life. Carefully crafting an immersive setting requires considering the development and impact of everything from art to fashion, language, culture, geography, biology, and economics. Virtually every field of study or inquiry in our lives can be reflected in a fantasy world.

But even as authors allow our creativity to take us into far-flung invented lands, we still need to ensure our readers are grounded with familiar touch points. One tried and true way to do this is to base the imagined and fantastical on elements of the real world. Cultural storytelling practices such as myths and legends are significant fodder for fantasy worldbuilding.

The ability to tell stories is part of what makes us human. As we evolved, we told one another tales of magic and wonder, of gods and monsters and magical creatures, so it's little wonder that we're fascinated with these topics to this day. Myths are generally stories told to explain the world around us. Folklore often helps to acculturate us to our society. Legends purport to be historical accounts of inspiring or noteworthy figures or events, while fairytales make the fanciful come alive close to home. Together, they offer endless raw material for crafting intricate histories, identities, and cultures.

But how do we go about incorporating these kinds of tales from the real world into our invented ones? The first step is to carefully select your source of inspiration. Start with the stories passed down in your own family, or search your own regional folklore, religion, ethnicity, and culture.

When writing my novel *The Monsters We Defy*, I wanted to ground the magic system with roots of Black folk magic such as hoodoo, conjure, and root work. Some of my favorite books growing up by authors like Gloria Naylor and Tina McElroy Ansa, revolved around these topics. But I also pulled from my own family, including stories, superstition, and wisdom handed down by my grandmother. Stories I once considered old wives' tales, I discovered through research, had their roots in West African traditions brought to North America by enslaved people. Others were a result of cultural mixing between Africans, Europeans, and Native Americans.

One of the reasons that when I cut my hair after growing it for nearly ten years I didn't throw it away was because everyone knows the proper way to dispose of hair is to burn it so bad actors don't use it for nefarious purposes. Or at least everyone in my family knows this. Such stories are also why I never sleep with a fan blowing on me, or why my family always cooks black-eyed peas on New Year's Day. I can't say that I know the origins of all the bits of wisdom that hit my ears throughout childhood, but it certainly has fed my ideas about cultural memory and beliefs through many novels.

I chose to have my main character be born with a caul—with the amniotic sac covering her—which gives her the ability to speak with spirits, a belief held in cultures around the world. I also have characters employ a variety of divination techniques, from candles to blue water to chicken bones. Starting with these traditions and then fictionalizing them to create something grounded but new underscores my philosophy of worldbuilding.

Research is also essential throughout this process, both when using stories from one's own identity or culture and especially when moving beyond, using tales from others. When branching out, it's important to ask yourself if this is your story to tell, and if so, why? While I choose to maintain an abundance mindset and don't believe that other writers telling stories from my culture can take anything away from me, whether that be success, bookshelf space, or sales, not every story was meant for every person to tell.

Once you've determined this is the story for you, research can be made difficult when so many folktales and other cultural chronicles are passed down orally. However, when searching for information beyond memory, imagination, or various books and other traditional resources, I've begun to rely on graduate theses and dissertations. Papers on various arcane topics having to do with cultural phenomena can be found on today's internet, written by researchers from across the globe. Over the past few years, while enmeshed in writing historical fiction fantasy, sometimes I feel I've read more dissertations than a PhD advisor. But I always learn something, and since I'm not an academic, these papers give me access to sources and ideas I wouldn't have had before.

After learning everything you can about your inspiration during a predetermined period—you could conceivably research a topic forever, so deadlines are important—it's time to adapt the source material, modifying it to your own character, plot, and themes.

Will your story use the actual tradition,, and simply put your spin on it? Or will you radically shift the idea until it bears no relation to its origination? This depends on your story, but remember that there will be people who hold these practices or beliefs close, and as writers we need to take care not to be disrespectful of traditions that are not our own.

It's also useful to connect your worldbuilding and make it inextricably linked to character and plot. These three should grow together, like plants in a messy garden, vines and branches intertwined until they're woven as one.

For example, in my novel, my main character who can communicate with spirits is forced to use this ability by a bargain she struck with one of these spirits. The focus of the story is how she can free herself from this deal, and also free other characters who are burdened by similar contracts. Creating a magic system where people bargain with spirits for magical abilities called Charms, but are also saddled with a burdensome Trick—a negative counterbalance to their power—was a way to integrate character, plot, and world together.

Basing aspects of your world on real traditions, mythology, folklore, and legends can add real depth and a sense of history and authenticity to your story. But it's also important to avoid stereotypes and clichés. The first and easiest idea on how to approach a given topic is often the most conventional. Would adapting it be better for the story and give you a more unique slant while avoiding potentially harmful pigeon-holing?

By using real traditions as clay and molding them to your own creative specifications, all while weaving them with character and plot, you can create a sound foundation for your story. Your world will feel more immersive and vibrant, and will be a place that readers won't want to leave.

Copyright © 2023 by L. Penelope.

BOOK BALE

A MEMBERSHIP BASED EBOOK ACQUISITION PROGRAM

GET ALL THE EBOOKS YOU LOVE AT A FRACTION OF THE COST

www.BookBale.com

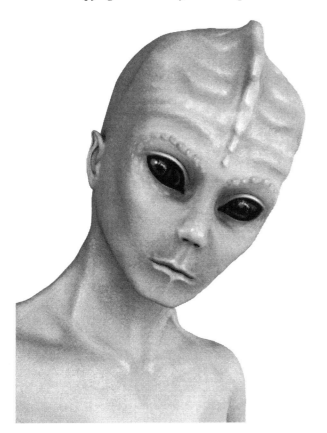

Made in the USA
Columbia, SC
02 May 2023